DARK RECKONING

·RICK DUFFY·

First edition 2024
Published by Greening River

ISBN 978-1-7351954-3-8 (paperback)
ISBN 978-1-7351954-4-5 (ebook)
ISBN 978-1-7351954-5-2 (hardback)

www.rickduffy.com

THE SIGIL MASTERS SERIES

The Sigil Masters

Dark Reckoning

The Last Nowen

*Home is a word stronger than magician ever spoke or
spirit ever answered to in the strongest conjuration*

— *Charles Dickens*

CONTENTS

one league = three miles

PART ONE

SHADOWS

Chapter One

Par tightened his grip on a small brown sack and fled down the cobblestone street. A glance back through the crowds showed a city guard still in pursuit.

"Stop!" shouted the man.

Workers filled the road, carrying loads and leading donkeys. Par ducked and dodged. He lunged under a cart, dropped his bag, spun, grabbed it, scurried out and kept running.

Up ahead, a horse-drawn wagon emerged from between two buildings. Par dove beneath, pitched sideways and scrambled out the rear into the alley. A mound of trash, soggy from earlier rains, had been heaped against a wall. He jumped behind the foul mess and scrunched down.

"You, driver!" the guard called over the bustle. "Did a beggar-brat run past?"

Par quieted his panting breaths. Argent's east quarter was a place of hard work and impatience. His clothes were dirty and worn thin. He looked like a beggar, and beggars weren't welcome here. Worse, if the guard caught him, Par might be questioned by a Confessor. When they discovered Par couldn't invoke, his next stop would be the Mercy House.

Ironically, that's where he'd been headed.

"I ain't seen no beggars," came another voice. The wagon creaked away.

Par felt a small tug. A rat nibbled at his little bag.

"Hey," Par hissed and yanked it away. "That's not for you."

A puddle near the wall caught Par's reflection. His eyes widened, but he couldn't help himself. He looked.

In a moment, he saw it—a shadow forming around his head. It wasn't like the glory of those invoking magic. Or the dun, that dark force that had attacked him in the Urdel woodlands. It appeared as thin, swirling smoke, visible only in his reflection.

Along with the shadow came a chill, deep in his bones, like a finger of death tickling his soul. He stifled a scream. His world darkened.

Par tore away his gaze and shook off his terror. This shadow-thing had begun mere months after he and Enio came here to Argent searching for Lani. It always passed quickly, but he had no idea what it was. Or what to do about it.

He steadied himself and peeked around the reeking garbage.

No sign of the guard.

With a relieved sigh, Par pulled himself out of the trash. He brushed off his clothes and continued past the dirty backs of buildings. After a few wrong turns, he arrived at a high stone wall topped with black spikes. The children's wing of the Mercy House abutted the other side. A long length of twine dangled from a barred window. He tugged it.

A tinkle answered above. A face pushed through the bars.

"Hi, Alba," he said as loudly as he dared. "It's Par."

The girl wasn't much younger than him. She had dirty blond hair, bright eyes and a smile to match. "Hi, Par!"

"Quiet now, Alba. How are you today?" Par kept his voice

cheerful, but whenever he saw this place, his insides twisted like a hard-wrung rag.

"I'm fine," came the reply, less lively.

"I got you cheese-cherry."

Her tone brightened. "Oh, I love cheese-cherry."

He found the woven basket he'd left last time and fastened it to the twine. When he again looked up, a second, younger child peered through the bars.

Par's stomach screwed another turn. "Who's that, Alba?"

"Felix. He's my new roommate. He doesn't talk."

Gods. Another candidate. Par painted on a grin. "Nice to meet you, Felix. Hey, do you like cheese-cherry?"

The boy licked his lips and nodded.

Par removed a pair of day-old pastries from his bag. "Well, here you go. All right, Alba. Pull it up."

She did. As it rose, she said, "Par?"

"Yeah?"

"When I go home, I won't forget you, will I?"

Par's throat choked shut. He swallowed to clear it. "Not so long as there are cheese-cherry pastries in the world."

A lie. Once Alba's examinations were complete—if the Ministry of Reckonings determined she was feeble—they would Reckon her. What memories would remain after that? Or how much of Alba?

The girl drew in the basket. "I'm glad. Thank you, Par."

"You're welcome, Alba. Take care of Felix."

"I will." She waved. The two disappeared.

As Par continued along the alley, frustration stabbed at his heart. He stopped, leaned his forehead on the wall and pinched his eyes closed. "Dammit." He slammed the sides of both fists against the thick stone. "Gods *dammit.*"

But there was nothing he could do to help them—except make their lives a little less bleak.

He pulled himself together and followed the spiked wall to where it opened into a somber lane. A dozen people, clad in black and with matching capes and hats, had gathered before the stark gates of the Mercy House. They walked in an oval, bobbed signs and chanted the painted slogans. "The True Path." "The wise shall rise." "Ortu!"

As Par was about to slip past, a bald man approached the group. It was another city guard.

Crap. Par ducked back. He didn't know if bringing those kids treats was illegal, but hiding the fact that he couldn't invoke—like them—kept him on *this* side of those iron gates. He held his breath and peeked out.

The guard matched the pace of a stout, broad-shouldered woman boasting a necklace of fat white pearls. She held no sign, yet her chants boomed above the rest. The man leaned in and spoke to her quietly.

She stopped and turned. The entire group halted. "Permit?" she thundered, and her bosom heaved like a storm front. "Does a prayer need a permit? Does a *soul?*"

The man stepped back. "But Lady Agatha, your cult—"

"Cult?" Her voice had a deep, spacious echo. Probably from the extra lung space. She spun to her followers. "Cult?"

"No!" they shouted. A man with a long mustache said, "Yes!" Then, "I mean, no!"

Lady Agatha focused again on the guard. Her tone softened as if she were teaching a child. "My dear sir, *we* are the Esoteric *Society* of Ortu, seekers of ultimate truth. *We* believe that only by sigil fasting can one know the deep mysteries of the divine. Ergo, those confined here to be Reckoned, who have never invoked the gods, may be the most enlightened among us."

Par listened with interest. He'd seen these protestors before. And sigil fasting—avoiding any use of sigil magic—was something he excelled at.

The man raised an apologetic hand. "I meant no disrespect, Lady Agatha. But as the wife of an ambassador, you can understand the need for permits."

"Sir, we—"

"Next time?" sighed the exasperated guard.

The lady frowned. "Very well." She turned back to her group. "My friends, such is the persecution of the enlightened."

Shoulders now slumped, the guard ambled off.

Par breathed again, relieved to be overlooked. Ignored. It was the core of his new life.

The protesters from the Society continued their march. They handed a leaflet to a passing man. A few steps later, he grumbled and tossed it to the gutter.

Par stepped into the lane, stuffed the paper in his pocket and hurried on.

CHAPTER TWO

PAR PASSED GRIMY warehouses, foundries of shouting workers and ugly buildings the general public would rather not see. As he entered the central district, the city changed. Shouts of laborers and groans of wagons were replaced by the chatter of pedestrians and the clop-clop of well-groomed horses. The smells of coal smoke and sweat shifted to freshly baked bread and imported spices. This was Par's favorite part of Argent, with its shops and temples and idle crowds. It tolerated the young, even the downtrodden—at least, on certain streets.

He cut through an alleyway that opened near a park of pink-flowering trees and trilling birds. A cobbler's shop cornered the alley; nearby a hunched figure wrapped in soiled blankets sat before a wooden bowl. The black veil of those marked as feeble shrouded the face.

"Coppers?" squeaked a frail voice from beneath the folds.

Par watched from the shadows. He eyed a glint in the bowl.

A tall man in a dark suit and holding the hand of a little black-haired girl approached the beggar. He handed the child a copper coin. "Go ahead, pumpkin. Give it to the poor old woman."

The girl shuffled forward and dropped in her offering. It chinked thinly.

"Thanks be to Saint Toes," croaked the beggar.

The girl skittered behind her father. He patted his daughter's head, and the two walked off.

No one else appeared. Par crept closer.

"Coppers?" repeated the blankets.

"Don't mind if I do." Par snatched up the bowl.

The figure remained an unmoving heap of neglected laundry.

"First, it's Saint *Antose*, not Saint *Toes*." Par dumped the meager donations into his hand.

No response.

"Second, you smell like a dead mud-maggot's armpit."

A snort escaped the blankets.

Par had worked on that one all morning. "And third—"

"Third," the high, scratchy voice dropped an octave. "Someone gave this mud-maggot a mitre."

"A mitre?" That was a *gold* coin.

From behind the veil peeked Enio's broken smile. "Thanks be to Saint Toes."

"Come on." Par yanked up his friend.

They returned to the alley. Par sat on a row of crates while Enio shed his wrappings and stashed them behind a barrel. A shard from a broken mirror leaned against its side.

Par pointed. "Mirror."

With a swipe of his boot, Enio knocked it over. "Is your shadow-thing any worse?"

"I don't think so," Par lied. Their best guess was that it had formed as a side-effect of his encounter with Ridiax and the Immortus. But it had grown, and the chill seemed deeper. He pushed down his worries and held out his little bag. "Lunch."

"Thanks." Enio sat beside him and withdrew its single pastry. "Where's yours?"

"Ate it already."

"You've always been a crappy liar." Enio tore his pastry in two and offered a half.

Sheepishly, Par took it. "There was a new kid at the Mercy House. Small guy. Doesn't talk."

"Doesn't sound too bad," Enio said as he chewed. "A Reckoning could fix that."

"What about the older candidates? The more the Reckoners fix them, the less of *them* is left." Par frowned at his food, then ate it in a single bite.

"You of anyone knows how hard it is to live without invocations."

Par sure did. The wizard Vex had discovered Par's inability to invoke wasn't due to unworthiness before the gods but an unusual thickness to his soul. Yet were it otherwise, if he *could* be fixed, how would he even decide between living as he was or risking the Mercy House treatments?

And how had Alba's family faced that decision?

He picked the last precious crumbs from his palm. "Speaking of liars, do you have to pretend you're an old beggar woman?"

"We saved everyone from Cronus." Enio licked cherry off his fingers. "They owe us."

"Anyway, why don't we use that mitre to get us a decent meal?"

Enio stiffened. His lips drew tight and his eyes narrowed.

It was a look Par knew, and it set his teeth on edge. There almost seemed to be two Enios these days. The first was Par's old friend: carefree, generous; rough, but noble, in his way.

Then there was an unhinged, foaming-at-the-mouth Enio. He mostly kept that part hidden, like his broken teeth. But lately it burst out more. Time to step carefully.

"What's wrong?" Par asked.

"They impounded the *Sea Dog*." Enio clenched his fists. "I

used the mitre to keep it out of auction. But I still owe the back portage fees."

Sadly, their money problems were nothing new. Neither had imagined the cost of keeping a real boat. Par had argued they should move it across the bay to the mainland, where the docking was cheap, but Enio didn't want to be so far from his beloved *Sea Dog*. For someone who'd said you should never get attached to things he'd really flipped his chips. And Par had been ashamed of bugging Enio to get a job when Par couldn't risk getting one himself. To make matters worse, Enio was sliding into the same gambling and drinking habits as his father. At least having to scrounge and beg for their meals minimized those vices.

As a distraction, Par dug out the piece of paper he'd saved from the Mercy House. "Look."

His friend took it and read a few lines. "Ortu again?"

"I've been thinking more about them. They don't invoke the gods at all. They call it sigil fasting."

Enio sat back. His breathing eased. "They're a bunch of rich idiots with nothing better to do."

"Then maybe I can get work keeping their books or writing their leaflets or whatever." With a grin Par added, "And I'll be a master sigil faster."

"That's for sure."

"Plus," Par's smile faded, "they protest at the Mercy House."

"What good does that do?"

In truth? None, from what Par had seen. And what good did his own visits there do? Except to soothe his conscience for his life of lying.

"But you're right. " Enio stood. "We need a decent meal. There's a wedding."

"Yeah?" Par's spirits inched back up. Sometimes the banquets were public.

"Big one, in the ruling quarter."

"That's too fancy. They won't let us in."

Enio tugged him from the crate. "Fancy people, fancy food. Come on. I have a plan."

"What plan?"

"Trust me."

With a glance to the heavens, Par followed. "Saint Toes, be merciful."

CHAPTER THREE

They skirted the park and entered a lane of busy shops and inns.

Par gestured toward the higher part of the island. "The ruling quarter is the other way."

"Like you said, they won't let us in."

"Then what—"

Enio halted. He pointed to the Red Robe Tavern. It was nicer than most, with varnished wooden doors and stained-glass windows that featured feasting saints. Beside it waited a two-horse covered wagon festooned with flowers. A sag-bellied man rolled a barrel up a plank into the back.

"Banquet deliveries," Enio said. "We'll hide aboard."

Leave it to Enio to know the doings around the taverns. As Par was about to object to what seemed a risky scheme, a shorter man with an even larger stomach arrived. He loaded a box that overflowed with plump, glistening sausages.

Par swallowed his objection.

When the men disappeared back into the tavern, he scurried with Enio beneath the wagon.

The first man returned, rolling another barrel. Enio grabbed one of the wagon's dangling garlands. An emerald glory sparkled around his head—Lani's weaving sigil. A vine slid down, snaked across the ground and entangled the man's ankles. On his next step, he stumbled. The barrel rolled. With a fiery shout, he chased it.

"Now!" hissed Enio. They scrambled up and inside the wagon, hiding behind the barrels and crates.

As the man resumed his loading, fortified now with extra curses, Par began to second-guess this idea. His life strategy these days was to keep low, out of trouble. But here they were, crashing a wedding for a meal. Poor and begging were one thing. Had they crossed the line to thievery?

"What's the plan if we get caught?" Par whispered.

"We run," Enio whispered back.

Par nearly choked. "What kind of plan is *that*?"

"The *plan* is not to get caught."

Purple hells. They were broke. They were hungry. And the *Sea Dog* had been impounded. Could this day get any worse?

The wagon jerked forward. A crate shifted and banged Par's head. He stifled a yelp, then gasped as Enio's knee jabbed him in a rib. The ride smoothed out. Par's frustrations didn't.

He kept his voice hushed. "Look at us, Enio. We can't keep doing this stuff."

"What stuff?"

"Sneaking around, living off people. It's been almost a year."

"We're getting by."

"Barely."

"Barely is fairly."

Par shook his head.

"And like I said," Enio added, "they owe us."

"Nobody knows who we are or what we did."

His friend frowned. "Secret histories. Magic portals. They'd never believe us. So we make our own reward."

"Not much of a reward, if you ask me."

Enio was quiet for a moment. When he spoke, his voice was tight. "No one asked you."

Before Par responded, Enio slammed a fist into a crate. "I *built* that boat." He punched it harder. "Damn leeches, all of them. No more!" He drew back for another strike. Blood smeared a knuckle.

Par grabbed his friend's arm. After a brief struggle, Enio eased off.

"I *get* it," Par said. "Just… keep it down."

A few breaths later, Enio mumbled, "Sorry." A brief golden glory blinked around his head as he rubbed his hand. The scrapes on his knuckles healed.

"Don't worry about it." At least whenever Enio's steam broke out, it was a while before the next eruption. "Once we get some money, we can try our luck in another town. Maybe even go home to St. Livius."

"Or sail the Silver Sea," Enio countered, as he always did when Par brought up their future. "After we've found Lani."

That was the best reason they hadn't left Argent. Par's heart told him Lani had survived her fall into the sea. Enio said he felt it too. But despite all their searching, they'd found no sign of her or the *chela élande* or anything else out of the ordinary—except once, when Par swore he saw trees marching beneath the waves, near the cliffs, gone before he could point them out.

With the winter freezes, they'd moved their search along the coasts. Now spring was ending, but they were as stuck as if frozen in ice. Enio still longed to wander the world beyond towns and walls and borders. Par just wanted a place to call home, one that wouldn't judge him because he couldn't invoke. Did such a place exist?

He kept quiet as the wagon stopped for more loads. His legs started to ache. After an agonizing hour of bumps and turns and shifting crates, the road slanted upward. The wagon paused, and a guard questioned the driver. Par crouched lower despite his burning muscles.

When they started again, he needed to unknot. He rose and peeked out the back.

The wagon passed through a gated archway and into the ruling quarter, the highest land of the island, except for the governing sector at the summit. They passed estates surrounded by elegant gardens, statues of noble saints, and ivy-adorned pavilions each the size of a cottage.

At last, they turned off the main road. The driver announced their delivery at another gate and they drove through.

Enio rose from his hiding place. "We're here."

They eased over the crates. The wagon traveled along a gravel lane under sweet-smelling trees.

Suddenly, Enio said, "Hold on to your buttons!" and lunged out the back.

Drawing in a sharp breath, Par followed. They tumbled into the lane and scrambled among the trees.

The wagon continued toward a pillared mansion with a fancy split stairway that reached out like the arms of a giant. Gleaming black carriages lined up before it.

Par hurried with Enio through the rows of trees and past the manor to an expansive trimmed lawn, where a sea of high-dressed people mingled among tall bright tents and linen-draped tables. Plates and goblets clinked and sparkled in the sun. Flute music floated in the air.

"We're not dressed for this." Par dusted off his pants.

"I said I had a plan." Enio pointed toward a tent where another group had gathered, some tying on aprons, others dressed like butlers. A lanky, animated woman strode among them and barked orders.

The plan was that he and Enio would pretend to be servants.

Par wasn't sure what law *this* broke, but at least they'd work for their meal.

They stepped from the trees, restrained the urge to sprint, and walked to the tent like they belonged. No one stopped them.

"Bus their plates," commanded the woman to those in simple white tunics. She adjusted a man's cap. "Warm their food and cool their drinks. If you run out of invocations, don't bumble about like a feeble. Help the scullery."

Par joined Enio at a table stacked with servant uniforms. They found the tunics of the bussers, slipped them over their clothes, and shuffled among the guests with the other staff.

Almost immediately, Par stopped short and gripped Enio's arm. A city guard wandered the crowd.

"Relax," Enio chuckled. "We're invisible now. People don't see servants."

It turned out he was right, though eating food off the tables was out of the question. But as the guests sampled appetizers of buttered snails and smoked fish and other dainties, unfinished plates were abandoned. Par and Enio took these to the washing area, gulping down the untouched morsels.

"What do you think of my plan?" Enio grinned through a full mouth.

Par smiled back. "I haven't eaten this well since the Winter Festival."

"I thought you didn't like snails?"

So did Par. He laughed. Despite their troubles, a full stomach did a lot to boost his spirits.

Their feasting was interrupted when they were handed crystal pitchers bright with wine and told to keep the goblets brimming. The bride and groom arrived to a standing cheer.

While Par continued to tend the drinks—staying close to Enio in case someone requested a cooling or warming invocation—he noticed a familiar broad-shouldered woman in a bulging blue hoop dress standing behind a small, vacant table. She was the same lady he'd seen with the protestors.

"Where is that blasted thing?" She twisted her head, trying to look over her frilly collar at the little chair.

A middle-aged man with perfect posture stood at her side. He had a short, wormy mustache and wore formal black. "Try shifting to the left, milady."

"Rufus, if I shift any more, I'll be in the bay." With a lift of the billowing dress, she found the chair and eased down.

For a long moment, Par eyed her. Regardless of today's progress, he and Enio really couldn't keep living like this. If Enio wasn't going to do anything about changing things, Par had to try.

He nudged his friend. "That's the woman I saw at the Mercy House. Think I could talk to her?"

"Want to get adopted?"

"About a job."

Enio shrugged. "Adopted might be easier."

They moved nearer with their pitchers. Enio served an adjacent table. Par approached the lady.

"Rufus," she said and winkled her nose. "There's bread on my table."

"Sorry, milady." Rufus removed its basket and thrust it at Par. "Get rid of this."

Par took it in his empty hand. "Um," he said as he filled her goblet, "are you the people who protest at the Mercy House?"

Rufus stepped toward him. "Sorry, milady, I'll—"

She waved the man back. "Yes, son, I am. Why do you ask?"

"I, uh," Par hadn't planned his next words. "I hate that place too. Not for the criminals. For the kids."

"Indeed?" she said. Instead of the pearls she'd worn at the protest, a necklace of silver discs flashed across her breast.

Shiny. Polished.

Reflective.

Par's eyes snapped wide. His face stared out from each one of them.

"Son?"

He barely heard her. In each image, a shadowy claw closed around his head.

Recoiling, Par dropped the pitcher. It smashed at his feet.

Enio called from somewhere nearby, "Par!"

"Par?" the lady boomed. "Did he call you *Par?*"

A shout from behind. "Hold him!"

Par spun. A city guard pushed through the confused crowd. Servants scrambled, the guests pressed closer, Enio lost among them.

As Par tried to bolt, the guard was on him. A glory flashed around the man's head. His hand grasped Par's shoulder.

A sudden, irresistible urge to sleep pressed Par into darkness.

Chapter Four

Enio lost sight of his friend through a churning sea of bodies. Shouts rang through the crowd. "What's happening?" "Is there a dog?" "My hat!"

Why was everyone after Par? No one in the city knew he couldn't invoke.

A guard stood on a chair and yelled, "Find the other one!"

With nowhere to run, Enio scrambled beneath a table. He peeked through its linen skirt, trying to see past flashing leather boots and swirling gowns. Still no Par.

Something tapped his side. He whirled, fists up.

Beneath the table, a lady's foot prodded him again. Her hands sank into view. One lifted her large hoop dress to her knees. The other pointed at the ground between her ankles.

Confused, Enio cocked his head.

If a finger could shout, hers did. It motioned urgently. *Here! Now!*

That seemed his only hope. He scurried under the dress. It covered him like a little tent.

The lady pushed back from the table. Enio stayed hidden between her thick stockinged legs.

"Rufus," she said, "fetch the carriage."

"Yes, milady."

A younger woman's voice spoke nearby. "Leaving so soon, Lady Agatha?"

"I'm afraid this excitement has agitated my digestion. Perhaps I overdid the onion sauce."

"Oh, dear. Do you require a healer?"

"I'll be fine, thank you." Lady Agatha waddled across the lawn, Enio struggling to keep beneath the ample dress.

"Try to grunt less loudly," she hissed. "Ill-tempered onion sauce doesn't make sounds like that."

Enio was about to comment it didn't smell the same either when they stepped onto gravel and stopped. A horse whinnied.

"Home, Rufus."

"Yes, milady."

Enio's petticoat cave opened. A step led into a private carriage. He dove on board.

The lady followed and shut the door. "Stay down."

"But Par—"

"Hold your water. At the moment, we can't help him."

Her dress filled most of the foot space, and Enio found himself covered again. But she was right. He'd have to figure out another way to rescue his friend.

The carriage started forward. A minute later it paused and Rufus exchanged words with a gateman. They continued up the road.

At last, the lady pulled aside her dress. "Well, that's one good use for this ridiculous costume. Come on out."

Enio rose and peeked out the window. They had left the mansion property and were rolling past other estates. He settled into the opposite seat. "What's going on? Why are you—"

"Is it true?" She leaned in. "That other boy's name is Par?"

"Who's asking?" Enio narrowed his eyes.

"You may call me Lady Agatha. And you must be his companion—Julio, was it?"

"Enio. How does everyone know our names?"

The lady sat back. "As for the guards, I have no idea. But we of the Society of Ortu dedicate ourselves to probing the deep mysteries of the transcendent realms." She lifted her chin. "Ergo, we have special knowledge—"

"Listen, lady." Enio didn't have time for this drivel. "You rich people don't have any *special* knowledge except how to make money and dodge taxes."

Amusement flickered across her face. "The prophet didn't mention you'd be so precocious. I'm beginning to like you, Julio."

"*Enio.*" He paused. "What prophet?"

"Of course, the true acolytes of Ortu live in caves, perfecting their souls." She chuckled. "Can you see me living in a cave?"

Enio sighed. "Can't you just cut to the cheese?"

"Shut your trap and I will."

He opened his mouth, closed it.

The lady took a breath. "Several weeks ago, a monk of Ortu—a short prune of a man—visited our little group. He told of a new prophecy, that one would come who had sigil-fasted his entire life. He named you both, but spoke mostly of Par. If your friend appeared in our midst, we were to welcome him, draw him into our fold, and send word to the monk."

Enio didn't believe in prophecies—always too fuzzy. But they got the names right. "That's it? They want to recruit Par?"

"Frankly, I'm unsure what they want. And I don't believe in prophecies."

Maybe she wasn't a total twit.

They veered off the main road. "We're here," she said. "Come inside and we'll figure this out."

The carriage stopped before the stairs of an estate house, not as grand as the last but no chicken coop either.

As they stepped to the pavement, Lady Agatha spoke to Rufus. "What became of Par?"

The mustached man descended from the driver's seat. "They took him up the road to the governing sector."

Enio looked toward the island's summit. The triple spires of the High Temple peeked above the highest trees. His stomach sank. "Crap."

"Crap, indeed," the lady said.

She led them up the mansion's marble steps. The inside was no less impressive than the out, with a roomy foyer, colorful tapestries and high-class furniture. Two maids in plain brown tunics chatted at the bottom of a staircase. One jumped to dusting the railing. The other straightened to attention.

Lady Agatha waved Rufus and Enio to a stop and continued to the stairs. "I will change into appropriate attire." She gestured to the idle maid to follow. "Then I'll go to the governing sector and see what I can discover."

"Well, hurry," Enio said. "We don't have time—"

"Not you."

"What do you mean, not me?"

The lady paused halfway up. "As an ambassador's wife, I have certain privileges. You can't—"

"If that guy can get in," Enio flicked his chin at Rufus, "so can I."

"No," Agatha said. "They're looking for you too."

Enio still didn't understand what was going on, but they'd already taken the *Sea Dog* from him—they weren't taking anything more. "Nobody's locking up Par or handing either of us over to some dusty old monk."

"I wasn't going to—"

"I'm coming." He crossed his arms.

She eyed him. "I see you're adamant. Very well, but you'll need a proper disguise. See to it, Rufus."

"Yes, milady." The man slipped out of the room. Lady Agatha disappeared up the stairs. The remaining maid meticulously dusted a bookcase.

Enio shuffled impatiently. Then he wandered the room, dragging his fingers along the polished wooden cabinets, tapping the fancy vases. This was a nice place. A *really* nice place. How did people deserve to live this way when he had to scrape, day after day?

He peeked into a drawer. Silverware. He touched a spoon. A couple of these could bring enough in trade to feed him for weeks. Or pay portage. Get him back into the dice games.

The maid still dusted, her back to him.

And they'd never miss a few pieces. He could slip them into his boot and—

His hand snapped back. Where had *that* thought come from? This Lady Agatha was helping them. Doing her like that wouldn't be right.

He shut the drawer.

Rufus returned with a folded stack of clothes. "Put these on."

Enio took them. He glanced at the maid's back. "Here?"

"If you're shy, use the coat closet." The man gestured to a slim door near the entrance.

"I'm not shy." Enio entered the little room and shut the door.

Several minutes later, Rufus spoke from the other side. "Do you require assistance?"

Clad from head to toe in powder blue and a small cuffed cap with a green feather, Enio emerged scowling. "I feel like a cake decoration."

Lady Agatha strode down the stairs. She now wore a fur cape over a rich green dress. Tiny jewels glinted from her ears. "If you're coming, you're coming like that. You're dressed as a page. It's the *style*."

Rufus reached for an unfastened button. Enio batted him away.

The lady spoke to Rufus. "The carriage, please."

"Yes, milady." He left out the front.

She dismissed the maids. When Enio and Lady Agatha were alone, she said, "I'm as curious as you about what is going on with your friend, and I will do what I can to find out. But I need you to tell me what you know." She held up a finger. "The truth. One does not walk the halls of power in the dark."

Enio hung his head and squeezed his eyes shut. How much should he say? Par seemed to trust her, and his instincts were pretty good. Besides, if the guards used a Confessor on Par, they'd find out all about him anyway.

He looked up. "You can't tell anyone."

There was a sadness in her smile. "The wife of an ambassador learns to keep secrets."

"All right. Par isn't sigil fasting. And he's not feeble, just— sort of thick."

"Thick?"

"It's complicated, but he can't invoke. If the Hierarchy tries to Reckon him, it won't help, but it could make him a feeble after all." That wasn't *everything*, but Enio figured it's what mattered most.

Lady Agatha frowned. "A candidate for a Reckoning is subject to weeks of examination in the Mercy House. Par's removal to the summit instead suggests that the Hierarchy is interested in something else."

Enio thought so too. "And he's got this shadow thing."

"What kind of shadow thing?"

"Who knows? In mirrors. How many kinds are there?"

The lady held his gaze a moment longer. "That is beyond me. But thank you for your trust. Let's see what we can uncover."

They left for the carriage. Lady Agatha boarded. Enio tried to follow inside, but she stopped him. "You must sit in the driver's seat with Rufus."

The carriage had cramped Enio anyway. He climbed up beside the man.

Lady Agatha spoke from the carriage window. "When we reach the governing sector, you must remain with him. I will speak to those with the nosiest ears and hungriest pockets."

"But I—"

"My contacts won't talk around strangers, even servants. Once I learn something, I'll come straight to you. Let's go, Rufus." The lady closed the curtain.

Grumbling, Enio sat back.

Rufus clicked the horses to motion. He now wore a top hat fastened with a strap. As they bumped along, he said, "Will you be able to comport yourself?"

Enio glared at the man, at that wormy mustache flicking in the breeze. "I can comport. Who can't comport?"

The man smirked. "Well, don't make eye contact with anyone. When we arrive, open the door for the lady. And whenever you have an idle hand, keep it behind your back."

"Why?"

The man sighed. "It's the *style*."

Enio supposed he could handle that. "How long have you worked for her, Rufus?"

"A long time."

"Does she—treat you good?"

Rufus kept his eyes ahead. "What's it to you?"

It wasn't much, so Enio shrugged and let it go.

But then Rufus leaned closer. "The idle rich can be as full of themselves as a horse's diaper."

Enio snorted. He began to laugh.

Rufus chuckled too, then cleared his throat. "But they don't *all* come from money, and some *do* care about more than this week's fashions." He snapped the reins.

Had the man answered Enio's question? In any case, he hoped he'd made a good decision by trusting these people. His own freedom was in their hands.

Chapter Five

Par awoke on a velvet couch. He lay there a moment, studying a sparkling chandelier.

At the memory of his arrest, he bolted upright. He wasn't in a jail. Fancy wooden doors stood closed across an elegant room. Portraits of richly dressed men and women looked down from pink marble walls. Even the air smelled expensive.

Nearby, daylight filtered through shimmering drapes. He swung off the couch and peeked out. An airy balcony opened beyond. Past that, below a steep drop-off, stretched the entire island of Argent.

The sweeping view stopped Par's breath. The land terraced down into the walled sections of the city, and finally to the bay. From there, a shining white causeway ran across the water to the mainland town, where surrounding cliffs rose even to Par's own eye level—a thousand feet.

He was in the governing sector—in the palace itself!

Par turned and crept to the door, praying it was unlocked. Before he reached it, the latch clicked. He jumped back.

In stepped an elderly man wearing the royal gold and white of the Hierarchy. Par knew the face, the merry eyes glinting beneath their heavy lids like the sun breaking through clouds.

"Father Abbot!" Par rushed forward and threw his arms around the old man.

The Abbot laughed and patted Par's neck. "It's good to see you too."

Bursting with relief, Par drew back. "What are we doing here? I haven't seen you since—"

"Since you and Enio snuck away from the abbey?"

Shame at the memory of ducking his agreement to go live with Alexander Vex dulled Par's joy. "Is Vex here as well?"

"It's not wise for a sorcerer to wander the capital of Eloria. He's gone to Arcana."

"Arcana?" Par's worries reignited.

"Much has happened since we last spoke. Vex and I spent the past year debating the future of the Vigil. We decided that the hidden histories, and the true reasons behind Eloria's and Arcana's long hostilities, should be told to our respective governments."

Another figure appeared in the doorway. "And told it, he has." Robes similar to the Abbot's wrapped the regal man. White woolly eyebrows and a short, perfect beard decorated the kindly face.

The Father Abbot stepped aside and bowed. "Your Eminence."

"Hello, Cornelius. So, this is Par."

Eminence? Was it—could it be—the Most High Pompeius Maxima Arcalus, Fondiscate of the Divine, ruler of all Eloria himself?

Par glanced at the Abbot, who mouthed, "*Bow.*" Breaking free of his awe, Par did just that.

"Sorry I'm late," said the Eminence. "Temple duties. Three Lusterings today alone." A glow circled his head. He noticed Par's stare. "No, son, I'm not invoking upon you. My glory is almost always there. Comes with the office."

"Our Eminence is humble," said the Abbot. "He is the closest to the gods of any in our country."

The Eminence gave a friendly grin. "Some days more than others. Please, Par, stop bowing. First, let me say I regret the method of your summoning. We instructed the city guards that if they found you, to invite you to the palace. But these days everyone is a bit high-strung."

The chaos at the wedding returned to Par's mind. "I was with Enio. Is he all right?"

"He evaded the guards. I'm sure he's fine. And you're not in trouble. We need your help."

"My help?"

"Let's take a walk."

Along with the Abbot, Par followed into a corridor as splendid as the room. Guards in red and white lined the way. He eyed them nervously, avoiding even their shadows.

As they trailed the Eminence, Par said quietly, "Father Abbot, why am I here? What's going on?"

"Try to relax. It may be nothing."

Considering the situation, Par bet it was, in fact, something.

The Abbot went on, "Alexander and I have continued to study the Immortus. After you and the mage Ridiax closed the rift, you returned with many strange sigils in your head, which you wrote down."

Par nodded; not that he could ever use them—or any other sigils.

"We've noticed," the Abbot continued, "that one of the more complex of the bunch is found on every monolith."

"What does it do?"

"We're not certain, but Vex has found cryptic references to this sigil in the histories he keeps at Xol Tomot."

The man became silent a moment. Then, "Three above, three below, two the balance, then and fro."

"The what?" Par asked.

"Something associated with the text he found. Another thing we're working out."

It meant nothing to Par. "Are the monoliths dangerous?"

"Well, that is the question. They continue to direct their energies upon the center point where once raged the rift. Thanks to you, the rift is long gone, yet the shadows there linger, and deepen."

Shadows? Before Par could mention the ones he'd been seeing in his reflection, the Abbot said, "Therefore, as part of our investigations, we would like to acquire that sigil from you."

Par stopped in his tracks. "But I can't invoke or bestow sigils. If the Eminence finds out—"

The Eminence turned. "That you cannot invoke the gods?"

Every muscle is Par's body tightened.

The man, however, raised a gentle hand. "Don't worry, I won't have you Reckoned. And I won't otherwise invade your mind—though I can't help seeing the truth in what people say."

Until now, the most powerful person Par had met in the Hierarchy was Cronus. *That* experience had not bolstered his trust in the government. He looked at the Father Abbot.

But the Abbot gave a reassuring nod.

Par swallowed and tried to breathe easier.

"A skeptic." The Eminence chuckled. "I like that. There is a procedure called the Rite of Cathexis. If successful, it would provide the lumina you need to invoke a single sigil or to bestow a sigil upon someone else."

"We say *if successful*," the Abbot added, "because your unusual condition brings some risk. But perhaps we are overreacting about the monoliths. They've never proven dangerous—they are over a thousand years old, and over a thousand leagues distant."

Par prayed the Abbot was right. His heart warned otherwise.

They continued through a cavernous foyer and out to a plaza

lined with columned buildings. On its far side, past a central fountain, rose the majestic High Temple, its triple spires winking gold in the late afternoon sun. With no clear idea of what would happen next, Par decided to ask a question that had gnawed at him for months.

"Father Abbot, do you know how my family has been?" The words "my family" seemed awkward. Par hadn't seen them since last year. He'd only managed the money to send a single letter.

"No, Par, I've been in Xol Tomot. But I've kept in touch with the abbey and have heard nothing at which to be alarmed."

Now Par let out a smooth, easy breath. One less worry, at least.

They reached the Temple. Soft chanting drifted through its immense golden doors. Inside, functionaries in gowns sashed with the color of their ranks bowed and made way. The Eminence led onward, to a pillared hall, then up ornate narrow stairs.

He stopped before another guarded door. "Before we discuss these things further, Par, I understand you've done our country a great service—you and your friend, Enio. The Abbot has told me much, and I'd like to hear your story personally. But first, I feel we owe you some reward."

Reward? After the fear of jail and Reckonings and now a Cathexis, that was the last thing he'd expected, and the offer put him at a loss for words. How should he reply to Eloria's highest ruler? Modesty and politeness urged him to decline. *Your gratitude is enough, Eminence. What I did, anyone would do, sir.*

Like preventing Cronus from starting a war.

Or closing the Immortus rift and saving the world.

On the other hand, was a reward so unreasonable? Gods knew he and Enio could use it.

The Fondiscate continued, "Tell me, Parynius Ignatious, what is it you desire?"

Money jumped first to mind. But Par was embarrassed to

admit he'd been a failure at living on his own. Maybe he should ask for passage back to the Borderlands, to Xol Tomot. Or good jobs for himself and Enio, in which Par's inability to invoke wouldn't be an issue.

Another thought drove the others away. Par bowed again and spoke with respect. "Can you help us find our friend Lani?"

The Eminence laughed. "I suspected that might be your answer. That's why we're here." He gestured to the guards. They opened the doors.

This was turning into a day like no other. With a birthday-morning excitement spreading through his chest, Par prepared to at last discover what had become of his half-nymph friend.

Chapter Six

THE ROOM THEY entered was someone's living quarters, though its furnishings had an uncomfortable, stiff appearance, as if they were only for show. Busts of historical figures frowned from marble pedestals. It was all very dignified. And severe.

"This," said the Eminence, "was the chamber of my old High Sigil Master."

"Cronus?" Par's eyes snapped wide.

"Yes. When the Abbot told me of the Vigil outpost, we searched for an ingress, and found one here. I believe that the ledge from which Lani fell is the most favorable spot to invoke a Location sigil."

He guided them into a small, cupped alcove walled with books. Once they were together, the Eminence's glory flashed brighter. The alcove closed around them.

Par grabbed a shelf as the little room began to descend. Pale blue light seeped from the corners of the floor. His last visit to the outpost had not been something he cared to relive, but his crawl along the cliff face, his severed arm floating in a jar, Enio tortured in a cage—Par grimaced as everything rushed back.

The room stopped, and the wall slid aside. A corridor ran ahead; Par recognized it at once.

The Abbot spoke as they walked, "We cleaned the place out, Par."

At least that meant no more jars of floating dead things. Or arms. Par rubbed his restored one.

A passage branched to the left. They followed it through an iron gate to a ledge in the cliff face, where Par had once arrived using a Threshold. The immense Silver Sea spread out to the horizon and thundered far below.

"Tell me," said the Eminence, "do you possess anything that Lani holds dear?"

Par had forgotten that for a Location sigil, they needed an object special to the person being located. These days he had almost nothing to his name. He stood mute, searching his brain for anything that might help.

But the Abbot answered, "From what I understand of their friendship, you might use Par himself as the invocation's locus."

"Me?" Par said.

"That will suffice," said the Eminence, "if Lani's fondness for you is deep."

Par's face warmed.

The Eminence smiled. "Very well. Let us begin." He left the Abbot's side and approached the drop-off. "Stand with me, Par."

With butterflies swarming in his stomach, Par stepped forward. Far beneath his feet, waves spit against ragged rocks. Seabirds dove and screeched along the cliff towering at his back. Par had once scaled that vine-covered precipice to rescue his friends. He'd almost fallen when an angry bird attacked, but a strange green glow had arisen from the water and calmed the creature. When Enio later told of Lani's fate, Par became convinced the light had somehow come from her.

"Is this the spot?" the Eminence asked.

"Yes, sir."

The man took a step back. "Remain still."

A salty breeze cooled Par's face and brushed his hair. It did nothing to settle his nerves. He looked away from the yawning plunge before him, focusing instead on a cloud pinned to the southern sky. "Should I close my eyes?"

"No. This won't take long."

Par jerked as hands rested on his shoulders. He composed himself and waited.

A golden glow caught the bottom of his vision. He glanced down, and gasped. It bubbled from his chest!

He stood rigid, not daring even to blink.

Suddenly the light leapt outward, streaming like liquid fire, bending in a great arc over the ledge and to the sea. It hit the water and shot in every direction. At the same instant, its color changed from bright gold to a dazzling emerald green.

Par stared, breathless, as the remarkable display faded. With his heart pounding against his ribs, he turned to the Eminence, waiting for an explanation.

The man peered downwards. "Odd," he said and frowned. "It's never done *that* before."

"It *what*? But Lani! Is she—?"

"I believe she's alive, though I am unclear where. Perhaps this sigil is incompatible with matters of the élan…"

Lani had survived! Par didn't hear the rest. Months of worry fled like the gloom at daybreak. Even the cawing sea birds seemed to cheer.

"I suspect," the Eminence went on, "after you've told me more of your journeys, I'll have a better idea what to try next."

An additional concern inched from the back of Par's mind.

He'd forgotten to tell of the shadow in his reflection. Had that interfered?

He took a breath. "I, um, have a shadow."

The creases in the Abbot's brow deepened. "You speak of the thickness of your soul?"

"No, in my reflections. I've seen it the past few months."

"Indeed?" The Abbot's voice took on a shadow of its own.

Par looked at both men. "I should have said something. Did I weaken the invocation?"

Neither the Fondiscate nor the Abbot replied, but Par sensed a brooding weight settle between them.

The Eminence knelt. He brushed his hand in a circle over the stony ground. After a brief glow of his fingers, a small area became as reflective as a mirror. "Show me."

The three gathered around. The Fondiscate's natural glory still twinkled through his snow-white hair. They waited in silence.

Right on cue, Par's shadow formed in his reflection, spreading around his head. He grimaced as a familiar chill gripped his bones.

"My word," whispered the Abbot.

The Eminence shook his head. "Cornelius, does this remind you of the shadows you've seen at the Immortus?"

"Perhaps, Eminence. Though a shadow is a shadow."

"True. Many mysterious things fill the Higher Realms. Upon Par's return, one may have hitched a ride."

Par couldn't explain, even to himself, half of what he'd seen in those realms of spectral light. He'd hoped his extra shadow was just that: a shadow, an aftereffect. Now he cringed at the thought of something hanging to him like a leech.

"How do I get rid of it?" he said, more loudly than he'd planned.

"Would you allow me to try?" asked the Eminence.

"Please, yes!"

"Very well. Father Abbot, stand away."

The Fondiscate's glory expanded. Rather than reflect, it penetrated the makeshift mirror. Par's shadow shrank and retreated. But as he began to feel some relief from the coldness in his chest, the shadow pulsed back larger.

A soundless battle began, a tempest, a push and pull between the light and the dark. Two opposites grappled within the mirror, spinning like a cyclone, deepening like a whirlpool.

Par couldn't look away. The vortex beckoned. It whispered. It clawed…

It seized him.

He plummeted into a bottomless void. Invisible icy jaws pulled him down and down as if to devour him in darkness. He couldn't scream. He could only fall.

Then a brilliant flash broke the deadly grasp. Par tumbled backwards.

The Abbot was at his side. "Are you injured, son?"

Steadying himself, Par sat up. His head cleared. "I don't think so."

The Fondiscate remained over the mirror, staring at its now tranquil surface.

"Eminence?" the Abbot said.

The Eminence held up a hand. "Stay." His ever-shining glory had disappeared. His gaze found Par and seemed to brim with surprise. A grin touched the man's lips. When he glimpsed the Father Abbot, his amusement flickered.

He rose to his feet. "I—" He rubbed his throat. "May I speak to you alone, Abbot? Parynius will remain here."

"Of course, Eminence."

"Father Abbot…?" Par began.

The Abbot patted Par's shoulder. "We won't be long."

Par nodded.

The two returned to the cliffside passage. Par waited. He ran his fingers over the mirror's smooth surface, not sure what he'd seen, or felt, in that tangle of light and darkness. Though shadows no longer formed around his reflection, his anxiety remained. What had the Fondiscate learned that he wouldn't discuss in Par's presence?

As the minutes crawled by, he again checked the waves below. No strange lights reappeared. At the sound of footsteps, he turned. It wasn't the Abbot. A guard stood in the passage, his shoulders stiff, his hand on his sword hilt.

Something wasn't right.

The Eminence returned with a second guard in tow and pointed at Par. "Take him to the cells."

The guards gripped Par by the arms.

"Hey!" Par struggled, though with nowhere to run. "What's going on? Where's the Father Abbot?"

The Eminence only spoke to the guards. "You need not worry about invocations. The boy is a feeble—unworthy before the gods."

Feeble? Unworthy? The words struck Par like a blow.

The guards dragged Par to the same cell where he'd once tried to rescue Enio. They threw him into a hanging cage and locked it. A high, deep-slotted window glowed with the late sunlight. Near the wall, a nearly naked old man, bound hand and foot, dangled five feet off the ground from a black chain wrapped around his chest. A hood covered his face.

"Par?" he croaked.

Par scrambled to the bars. "Father Abbot?"

The cell door clanged shut. The Eminence staggered, then turned down the hall. "I... must rest. Lucius will never be far."

A scruffy guard smiled, then left with the others.

"Are they gone?" breathed the Abbot.

"Yes. What's—"

"Quick." The words came urgent. "Tell me what you saw."

"A guard—"

"No, in the mirror. What did you see?"

"I don't—nothing. Black. Cold. Smothering."

"Think, Par. Did you *sense* anything? Anything familiar?"

As Par closed his eyes, he shuddered at his plummet into that abyss. Yet there *was* something familiar about it. Last year, when he'd fallen through the Immortus rift, he'd been attacked. The feeling was the same. It was—

Par's eyes snapped open. "Cronus?"

The Abbot sighed. "Yes. I felt his presence too."

"But he was lost in the purple hells!"

"I have no answers. Except that Cronus has… overshadowed our Eminence."

His palms now slick with sweat, Par squeezed the bars of his cage. "You mean, taken over?"

"And I fear that's not the worst of it. No mortal has the means to accomplish such a return from the Lower Realms. Whatever his plans, Cronus does not act alone."

"What do we do?"

Even through labored breathing, the Abbot spoke with a courage Par envied. "My bonds prevent me from doing much of anything. Yet Cronus seems weakened by his crossing. Let us take this time to rest and gather our strength. We'll need all our resources when we face him next."

Par's hands slipped from the bars. He slumped back in his cage, the hopes of the day gone to ash.

And as for resting, he wondered how he would ever sleep again.

CHAPTER SEVEN

"P SST."

The sudden sound startled Par from his dozing.

Enio peeked in from the deep-slotted window. His chest pumped like a worn-out hound's and he dripped with sweat.

The cage swayed with a rusty squeal as Par leapt up. "Enio!"

A shout echoed from the corridor. "Shut it, you maggots!"

Par waved his friend back into the window's narrow tunnel.

The guard Lucius arrived before the cell. "What's goin' on in—"

"I can't move, I can't see," barked the Abbot through his hood. "Is chatting with my cellmate such a peril?"

Lucius kicked the stout cell bars. "Save your air. You'll need it for screamin'." He chuckled and strode away.

"Horrid person," mumbled the Abbot. "One of Cronus's old guards."

When the footsteps had faded, the Abbot whispered, "Enio, can you lower me?"

"Hold on." Enio dropped the end of a ropey vine from his high perch and descended to the floor.

Par couldn't fathom how his friend had gotten to that window. Its stone shaft opened to a sheer cliff, five hundred feet above the sea, and another five hundred to the summit.

"How—" He cut himself short at seeing Enio's filthy blue clothing and green-feather cap.

Enio raised his chin. "It's the *style*." He crossed to where the Abbot's chain ran to a lever in the wall. "And the plan was not to get caught, remember?"

"Cronus is back," Par hissed.

His friend froze.

"My shadow, in the mirror," Par added. "It was Cronus."

Enio's eyes grew as round as hens' eggs. A tremor moved across his face. "No, Par. You said he died. He's gone. Dead and gone."

Par should have eased into the news. Cronus had tortured Enio with memories of his mother's death. "We don't understand it either, but he's taken over the Eminence."

"Dead and gone." Enio's voice rose. "No. He's gone. He's—"

"*Enio*," Par snapped. "Help the Abbot."

"Right, right." Enio shook himself. He examined the chain where it ended in the lever. "This looks heavy. I don't—"

"*Hurry*," the Abbot said. "Before the guard returns."

Enio grabbed the chain, dug in his heels, and threw the lever. Pulleys screeched as the Abbot dropped and the chain yanked Enio off the floor. He let go and landed on his feet. The Abbot fell prone with a heavy grunt.

Boots stomped down the hall. "I warned you maggots!"

The Abbot rolled onto his side. "Quickly, remove my hood."

Enio did.

Lucius appeared, sword drawn.

The Abbot's glory blazed. The guard stumbled back. His eyes rolled up and his mouth fell slack. He slumped against the passage wall.

Par turned to the Abbot. "Are you hurt?"

"No worse for wear." He struggled to his feet, hands still bound. "For the next hour, Lucius will be in a prayerful ecstasy."

The guard gibbered contentedly.

"A temple sigil," the Abbot added, "meant to evoke a sense of awe. I'm not a fan, but it might do him good."

Par doubted that. "Enio, how did you find us?"

Enio worked to untie a shiny black cord binding the Abbot's wrists. "Lady Agatha hid me from the guards at the wedding. We followed them to the summit. She heard someone mention an outpost, so I knew where to look. But I had to tell her about your invocation problem."

"You *what?*" Did the entire country have to know?

"What was I supposed to do?" Enio countered. "I needed her help. She'd already been looking for you."

This was news to Par. "Why?"

"Some cave-monk told her society you were in a prophecy."

The Abbot rubbed his wrists. "What society is this?"

"The Esoteric Society of Ortu," Par said. "They protest at the Mercy House and—"

"Ortu?" The Abbot's expression turned grim.

Par pushed his face between his cage bars. "You've heard of it?"

"Yes, from Vex's library at Xol Tomot, and it may explain something of Cronus." He stood slowly with Enio's aid. "The emanations from the Higher Realms create the mortal worlds and empower our sigils. But some emanations also fall into an endless outer void: the domain of the Lower Realms."

"The purple hells." Par had once glimpsed the shadowy places that were like vast festering wounds in the very heart of night.

The Abbot went on. "In the beginning, only darkness ruled there. But eons before man invoked his first sigils, those fallen emanations birthed deep, strange glimmers. One such region has been called the Ortum."

"Hey." Enio jiggled the lock on Par's cage. "Do we really have time for a history lesson?"

"Life is an education, son." The Abbot pointed a finger at the cage door. It clicked open. "Now, as Elorians enlighten their sigils with the lumina from the gods, and Arcanans use the numena of the cosmos—"

"And nymphs, the élan," Par said as Enio helped him to the floor.

"—others, such as the cultists of Ortu, have learned to harness the obscure, darker powers of the Lower Realms."

"Lady Agatha uses evil magic?" Even as Par said it, he didn't believe it.

The Abbot scanned the drooling guard. "Is it the magic that is good or evil, or how it is used?"

"But her society sigil-fasts," Par added, "so they don't use magic at all. And the Ortu stuff is like their hobby. They're not cultists."

"In any case," the Abbot said, turning back, "Cronus disappearing into the purple hells, a monk of Ortu searching for Par, Par's shadow allowing Cronus to possess the Fondiscate—something doesn't quite add up."

But it did for Par. "Now Cronus can rule the country."

"Yes, but why did he not go after the Eminence directly? Why did he involve you? He could not have ever hoped you would bring his shadow to the Eminence as you did."

Par worried about where this was going. "Then what—

"I believe the Eminence's interference was unplanned. Cronus was after you alone, Par."

"Me? But the rift is closed. I'm no use to him anymore."

"Perhaps he wants the sigils the mage Ridiax gave you."

"Cronus was gone before I ever met Ridiax, so he couldn't know about that." At least, Par hoped not. A worse thought occurred to him. "Or revenge for…" He couldn't finish.

Enio didn't seem to mind. "For you killing him?"

"Whatever the reason," said the Abbot, "Cronus may have access to powers beyond our understanding. But with the insights Alexander gained from his time in the Vigil, and your access to the Citadel and the knowledge it protects, we may have a chance to discover and defeat his plans."

Par couldn't think of any better help than that of the wizard Alexander Vex. "Can we get out through the Threshold?" That chamber was just down the hall.

"I no longer have the keystone." Like a deep thinker working out his philosophies, the Abbot started to pace.

His last time here, Par had fled through that magic portal. But he'd had a keystone to make it work. "Cronus took it from you?"

"No, thank the gods. When I returned from Xol Tomot, Vex kept it. We worried that, if my ongoing revelations of the Vigil were not well received, the Eminence might arrest me and gain usage of the Threshold, which would tip the balance of power between Eloria and Arcana. A fortuitous foresight, as it turns out, since Cronus now can't use it either."

The Abbot stopped in his tracks. "Vex is in Aurix, the capital of Arcana. In one week, he'll leave there through another Threshold and arrive in Jod. A week later, he'll use Jod's Threshold to return to Xol Tomot and open a portal for my return." The Abbot's eye twitched. "At midnight, atop the cliffs, under the full moon. He may be brilliant, but he's annoyingly dramatic."

"Two *weeks*?" Par said along with Enio.

"As things are," the Abbot continued, "I seem unable to keep that appointment, and I fear the damage Cronus can do in the meantime. Before you defeated him at the Immortus, he thought to bring war and remake the lands under his rule. And there is still the worry of the shadows among the monoliths."

"Maybe that was Cronus," Par said, "hunting me there because that's where we fell together into the rift."

"The timing does suggest it, though we can't be sure."

Enio waved his hand before the unseeing Lucius. "Can you get this guy to take us out the front door?"

"No, Enio. The *front door*, as you call it, is through the entire High Temple above us, and past dozens of guards, which Cronus now commands in the guise of the Eminence. But you've already shown us the exit." The Abbot looked toward the high, slotted window.

Enio followed his gaze. "Are you kidding? I used everything I had to get down that cliff. I can't sigil any more vines until tomorrow."

The Abbot seemed unruffled. "With your permission, I will invoke a common sigil often used to refresh soldiers in battle. It allows me to rejuvenate your capacities so you can ascend the cliff with Par."

"Wait," Par said. "Me and Enio? What about you?"

"The window isn't large enough. Besides, Enio could never bring us both up. I will buy you time to escape." A glory blinked around the Abbot's head. "Look behind you."

Par did. A shadowy figure hunched in his cage.

It was Par!

"A mirage," the Abbot said as it winked out. "I'll project that to fool the guards."

Gesturing Enio closer, The Abbot placed his hands over the feathered cap. The Abbot's glory pulsed, brightening their cell like a lightning flash. Enio's eyes flashed with a light of their own.

When the Abbot's glory dimmed, Enio all but vibrated.

The Abbot's brows knitted. "As this strengthens you now, it will weaken you later. And considering your youth, there may be… side effects. There's no help for it."

Enio hopped in place. "I feel *great*."

"To catch Alexander before he travels on to Xol Tomot, you

two must reach Jod within seven days. That cuts off half the time to secure his help. I wish it could be more."

"How do we find him in Jod?" Par said.

"The Threshold and Vigil outpost are hidden beneath the city in a cave off the Crescent River. Wait for him there. Everything now depends on you."

With another glance at Lucius, who mumbled something regarding rainbows, Par said, "Father Abbot, we can't just leave you."

"You must. But if Cronus wanted me dead, I'd be dead already. Perhaps I can learn what his true goals are."

Par hated to leave the Abbot, but he saw no alternative.

The Abbot described further how to enter the outpost, then said, "Now, rebind my hands and replace my hood—but break the threads across my eyes, so I may see to produce your mirage."

After they had done this and raised the Abbot again on his chain, Enio climbed to the window, almost running up the wall.

Par followed and pulled up the vine. But his worry for the Abbot made him pause and turn back.

"Father Abbot, how did they capture you?" He'd seen the power the Abbot could wield.

"Once Cronus had me alone, he threatened your wellbeing. I saw no choice but to cooperate."

"I'm sorry." Par's shoulders slumped.

"Nonsense, Par. You've done nothing to warrant his actions. It's not your fault."

Par nodded, struggling to accept the Abbot's words. "You're sure it's wise to stay?"

The black hood muffled the Abbot's words, yet there was a smile in his voice. "Wisdom is knowing on which side of the bars we do the most good. Go now, Par. And godspeed to you both."

Chapter Eight

Enio waited at the far end of the window shaft. "Par. Par. Par."

"I'm coming." They'd have to scale the soaring cliff where Par had once hung, terrified, to sneak inside. As he crawled through the tight tunnel, his palms left sweaty smudges on the cool stone.

He reached the opening to the cliff face. At least the winds were calm. Enio had moved onto a thin ledge and was wrapping himself in vines. He held out his hand. "Over here."

Par drew in a shaky breath. With his gaze anywhere but on the fearful plunge to the sea, he grasped his friend's hand and took the step. The rock wall seemed to climb to the clouds. He steadied himself again and said, "I've never seen ropes sigiled that far."

Enio draped leafy vines and creepers over Par's shoulders. "And I bet going up is harder than coming down."

"Then how—"

"Vines aren't ropes. They're alive. And I'm using Lani's weaving sigil. It's the élan, Par. The plants know what to do."

At mention of the élan, Par remembered. "Enio, Lani survived."

Enio stopped what he was doing. His eyes grew as wide as they had at the news of Cronus. "You've seen her?"

"The Eminence used a Location sigil. He says she's alive but doesn't know where."

Enio's broken smile stretched across his face. "She's alive?" It wasn't really a question.

Par's heart swelled with the same joy. But it changed to alarm when a bright green glory burst around Enio's head—brighter than Par had ever seen him invoke.

"She's alive!" Enio shouted.

At that instant, the vines squeezed and yanked them both upwards. Par's feet left the ledge. He opened his mouth to shout, but his words, like his heart, seemed stuck in his stomach. Then he made the mistake of glancing at the dizzying drop. He swallowed his panic and looked away.

The vines dragged them up the rough cliff face. Debris rained on Par's head. Into his mouth. He gagged and spit and faced the rock wall. Weeds and roots and rocks encrusted with bird crap crumbled past his eyes.

But Enio was right; the vines knew their job. As one ended, another took over. Yet, like a crude bucket brigade, the plants occasionally missed their timing. Par yelped at every slip. Each time, before they fell, Enio coaxed help from a new direction. When Par could no longer stand these episodes of terror, he closed his eyes to shut it all out. And at last, when Par thought he must scream, their movement stopped.

He opened his eyes, ready to kiss the sweet flat ground.

Gods, no. Fifty feet still stretched to the summit.

There they hung, swaying in mid-air, high above the water. Peaceful sea birds glided along the cliff. Par found Enio's soiled face in the tangles, panting through a serene grin. His glory sputtered and went out.

"Well?" hissed Par.

"Tired," Enio breathed, his pupils wide. The last time Par had seen that look was when Enio had gotten into a cask of festival ale.

The vines began to loosen.

"Enio!" Par scrabbled for the rock wall.

But the vines tightened once more, snugged like a protective cocoon, and resumed the ascent. High above, Lady Agatha and her servant Rufus extended their arms over a low stone wall. Golden glories shone around their heads as they invoked, looking for all the world like merciful angels.

Par no longer cared about dirt in his mouth. He laughed. They would make it.

When they reached the summit, Rufus helped them onto a paved patio. Trimmed trees and flowerbeds set with humble stone benches bounded the little overlook. Par dropped to his hands and knees. What better place to thank the gods than in the shadow of the High Temple? Breathlessly, he did.

"Hey," Enio said and helped him up. "You all right?"

Not quite ready to speak, Par nodded.

Wiping sweat from her brow on a fur cape, Lady Agatha staggered away from the wall. "Oh dear, my vertigo."

Rufus hurried to her side. "Milady—"

She waved him off. "Have you ever seen such an invocation, Rufus?"

"Never. I swear the boy gloried green."

Enio still grinned like an idiot. He was a mess, dirty and scratched and smudged with gods knew what. Sadly, the feathered cap had survived the ordeal.

Just as filthy, Par brushed himself off. He turned to the people who had saved them. "I—"

"Five hundred feet!" Enio suddenly shouted. Without warning, he grabbed the sides of Par's head and, quick as a hiccup, kissed him right between the eyes.

"Gah!" Par jerked back. "Enio!"

Enio did a little spin. "We did it, we did it, we—"

"Quiet," Lady Agatha said, and corralled him. "These are the meditation gardens."

"Oh, right." Enio put a finger to his lips. "Shh."

Rufus leaned in and sniffed. "Has he been drinking?"

Shuffling again to Par, Enio draped an arm around his shoulder. "Hey, Ags—this is my best friend, Par."

"So I gathered." She narrowed her eyes. "Ags?"

Par ducked Enio's arm. "The Abbot used a sigil on him so we could make it up the cliff, but said there'd be side effects." He eyed her a moment, and realized he had to trust, for now, that she was on their side. "Sigil Master Cronus died a while back, but he's back and has taken over the Fondiscate."

She gasped. "Died? Possessed?"

"And it involves the Lower Realms, the purple hells, the home of the Ortu."

"No Par, you have misunderstood. The Ortu is a philosophy whereby we use sigil-fasting—"

"No, *you* don't understand. I'll explain later, but we have to get out of here."

She peered hard, then nodded.

They crept through the gardens. Long-robed priests, and others who appeared to be tourists, silently wandered the pebbled paths. The garden ended at the edge of the central plaza. A black carriage waited.

Enio, with bits of debris dropping from his clothes, tried to follow Rufus to the driver's seat. But his foot kept missing the step.

Lady Agatha pulled him back. "Sit with us. You look like you just robbed the place." She ushered him inside.

He sat next to Par and chuckled.

Par sighed. "What's so funny?"

"I did rob the place." Enio leaned closer, his eyes mere slits. "I stole *you*."

Par scooted away to avoid any more sigil-lit behaviors. The carriage bumped forward. They drove around the central fountain.

"Hunch low," Lady Agatha said, "until we've left the capitol grounds."

Par did. Enio dozed.

The lady watched through the window. "That's odd."

"What is?" Par said.

"The monk that told of your coming. He's at the gate, waiting for entry."

Lunging at the curtain, Par snapped it shut.

Lady Agatha started. "Par, what—"

"Cronus might have summoned him."

They passed through the gates. Lady Agatha focused again on Par. "Now, considering I just helped break you out of custody, I think I deserve to know what's going on."

Par was grateful for her help, but how much more should he say? At least she didn't admit a connection between her society and the dark magic of the Ortu.

"What has Enio told you?" he asked.

"He was brief. You can't invoke the gods and you have a shadow in your reflection. Otherwise, he said it's complicated."

Enio snorted, but his eyes stayed closed.

"It's true," Par said. "I can't invoke, and not because I'm sick or unworthy. My soul has a thickness that prevents me from collecting enough lumina. Last year, I failed my Lustering and fled my home. Cronus chased me." Par frowned, not sure he should trust her with knowledge of the Immortus, much less the entire Vigil history. "He wanted to experiment—use me to increase his powers and rule both Eloria and Arcana. Then… he died."

Lady Agatha's face grew tight. "His extended absence… then it's true? Our High Sigil Master is dead?"

"Dead, but not gone. He was the shadow Enio told you about. When the Eminence tried to remove it, Cronus possessed him."

She shook her head. "I'm not a Confessor, but that story has more holes than a beggar's boot."

"There *is* more. But right now, I need to leave Argent. There's someone who can help me in Jod."

"This is all astounding." Lady Agatha peeked again through the curtains. "As for my society, I assure you we have no interest in the Lower Realms. And I admit, I've had an uneasy feeling ever since that monk showed up."

"Enio said the monk had a prophecy about me?"

"Yes—you, the foretold sigil faster." Her brow crinkled. "Perhaps the monk's prophecy was only a ruse to motivate my membership—whom he'd impressed with his arrival—to help find you."

"So he's working with Cronus?"

She shrugged. "Assuming I believe any of this."

Par caught a glimpse out the window. They were passing trim green lawns and mansions. "Where are we going?"

"My estate," the lady said. "I still have many questions."

"There's no time!" Par's words shot out of his mouth. "We don't know how long until Cronus notices I've escaped. Plus, with that monk at the gates—I have to leave the city right now. We have a boat—" He winced. "But it's impounded."

The furrows in her forehead deepened. Then she slapped the carriage roof. "Rufus," she called, "take us to the impound."

"But we can't afford—" Par began.

"I'll handle the fees. If you're lying,"—her expression darkened—"I'll deal with you appropriately. If not, then the monk was lying. Either way, I abhor being used."

No one talked much after that, which suited Par. As long as Lady Agatha helped them get to the impound, he didn't need to explain more.

They left the switchbacks below the ruling quarter and drove through the center of Argent. The day neared sunset, and the traffic was thin. As Par finally caught his breath from all that had happened, a piercing horn blast echoed over the island.

He sat bolt upright. Horns were often blown at the start of festivals. But there were no festivals today.

"It's the Horn to Attend," Lady Agatha said. "It directs the city guards to return to their district stations. Perhaps to take new orders."

Par's throat tightened. "To search for me."

The lady banged on the roof. "Faster, Rufus."

The carriage leapt forward. They veered off the road of late-filling taverns onto a narrow lane, making the ride more perilous for its handful of pedestrians. But Agatha said Rufus was avoiding the main gate, a central guard station.

High walls soon rose ahead. They passed through a small, unattended archway out of the city, onto a road along the shipyards and civilian docks. The few city guards huddled together in conference.

The carriage slowed. Before long, a stout wooden building blocked the entrance to one of the piers. Its sign read, *Impound.*

They stopped there. A man with a bushy red beard to his chest watched them from a barred window.

"Wait here," the lady said. She left the carriage and strode toward the impound window.

Enio roused and rubbed his face. "What's going on?"

"Lady Agatha's paying the fees for the *Sea Dog*."

"Oh, that's nice." He blinked several times. "She is?"

"Yeah, we're leaving."

"Now? What about Lani?"

It hit Par too. They still had no idea where she was and had to leave without finding out more. He shook his head and sighed. "We need to get away from Cronus and find Vex. When this is over, we'll—"

"Absolutely not, milady!" Rufus said. Lady Agatha said something in reply that Par couldn't quite make out. Then she waved a large key at where Par watched from the carriage. "Are you boys waiting for a warrant? Move it."

They left behind a grumbling Rufus and followed her into the impound building. She led them down a straight hallway of busy offices and out the back. Vessels of all sizes were tied at slips between the piers.

"There!" Enio took off running.

Several berths ahead floated the *Sea Dog*.

Par ran after him. The boat looked no worse. The sails were furled, and the hull was still rough, but stout and intact.

Mooring ropes tied its stern and bow. A rusty chain ran to the helm. Enio jumped from the pier, caught the chain, and scrambled hand-over-hand on board.

"Send down the gangplank," Par shouted.

As Enio did, Lady Agatha caught up.

"Thank you again for your help." Par spoke to her with a deep relief. He held his hand out for the key. "I promise one day to tell you the entire story."

"We'll have time," she said, pushing past him.

Par turned with her. "Time?"

She stepped onto the plank. "I'm coming with you."

Chapter Nine

Pain ripped through the Father Abbot's side.

"Do *me* like a fool?" snarled Lucius. "See how I do *you*."

Another kick from the guard knocked the air from the Abbot's lungs. He gasped and rolled across the floor.

A new voice approached. "That's enough, Lucius."

"Yes, Master Cronus. Just showin' him his place, is all."

"So I see. Remove the Father Abbot's hood."

Lucius yanked it off.

Cronus, in the body of the Eminence, entered the cell.

A short, grey-robed figure followed. The man's black hair curled like sheep's wool, and the lines in his face seemed carved by hard living and harsh weather. His voice, however, had a civilized lilt. "You say he used an illusion, Master Cronus?"

"A weak one."

The Abbot caught his breath enough to speak. "Weak, but it did the trick."

The short man stepped closer. "Father Abbot Cornelius, I presume."

"Retired." The Abbot grimaced and strained to sit up. "I'm afraid you have me at a disadvantage."

"Quite literally," chuckled the man. "I am Legate, a humble monk of Ortu."

So the Ortu was indeed at work here. But to what end?

The monk continued, "I don't suppose you'd care to make things easy and tell us where Par has gone?"

"Life isn't meant to be easy, Legate. Struggle is growth."

"Yet struggle beyond one's means brings growth to a swift end."

As the Abbot tried to reply, he fell into a coughing fit. He groaned and cleared his throat. "While I enjoy a rousing discussion of existential philosophy, I'm afraid I'm a bit indisposed. What is it you want, Legate?"

"The same as you, Abbot."

"And that is?"

The monk smiled through tight, pale lips. "Freedom."

A cryptic answer—though, in this cell, the Abbot found some value in it. "Then tell me—"

"I'll tell you nothing. And unless you would speak of Par, be silent." The monk turned to Cronus. "What news, brother?"

"I've notified the city to search."

"Nothing more?" The patronizing cheer left his voice.

"I—" Cronus paused. "The gods, my sigils, are dark to me. We might use a temple Confessor to probe the Abbot's mind."

"Unnecessary," Legate said, "and unwise. Par will not get far. And the Abbot also knows you control their Eminence. We cannot risk that being discovered by a Confessor."

With growing curiosity, the Abbot studied the two men. Cronus didn't have a brother, so the title used by Legate perhaps implied equality within their cult. But why would Cronus not demand the same deference from Legate as he did from others? Moreover, Cronus was an accomplished Confessor; he could rip the knowledge from any mind he chose. Yet despite the Abbot's weakened state, Cronus had not even tried.

The monk went on, "Did I detect regret over your new Reckoning, Cronus?"

"Of course not."

"Very good. It brings new strengths. You made the right choice."

Reckoning? A Reckoning altered a person's inmost self or healed an illness of mind or soul. But Cronus seemed as loathsome as ever. The Abbot steadied himself and spoke over the throbbing ache in his side. "Tell me, Cronus, why do you still seek Par? You now control the Fondiscate's body, and through it, the country. With the Immortus rift healed, Par is of no more use for your experiments. Your efforts there did not end well, anyway—for you, I mean."

Legate glared at the Abbot. A shroud of shadow with strange streaks of bruised light rippled around the monk's head. A rawness, as of Death's own breath, chilled the air. The Abbot had never seen an Ortu conjuration, but he had little doubt that such was the sigil the monk used.

Suddenly, the Abbot's eyes felt as if they'd been pierced by needles. He shouted and fell back, writhing, unable to reach with his bound hands.

Legate spoke. "Let us leave the Abbot to embrace his *growth*. If we do not acquire Par soon, I trust the Abbot will be more forthcoming during my next visit."

"Very well, Legate," Cronus said.

The agony faded, the pain dulled. The Abbot opened his eyes. For a moment, Lucius stood before him in a white fog. Then the world darkened.

The Abbot blinked. He squeezed his eyes shut. Opened them. He was blind.

"Lucius," said the monk, "don't bother with the hood."

"Yes, your Legate… ness."

The cell clanged shut. Footsteps receded.

The Abbot had not the strength to heal his side, much less his eyes. Yet even with these tortures, Legate could not see into his mind—a blessed limitation of the monk's powers.

But why couldn't Cronus?

There seemed to be only one answer. The Reckoning spoken of by the monk rendered Cronus's normal invocations unusable. His very soul was now aligned with the purple hells and the Ortu. He'd undergone a Dark Reckoning.

Slowly, the Abbot again sat upright, stunned that such an extreme change was even possible. But why, now that Cronus controlled the Eminence, was he still after Par? Did he know Par had a sigil that was duplicated upon the Immortus monoliths? Was Cronus's endgame to once again tap the power of the Higher Realms?

Or, this time, the Lower?

Too many questions. The Abbot swiveled toward where he thought the window was. The day was too far spent to bring any warmth. But it was comforting to imagine the sun still shining bright on its path across the Silver Sea.

A path, he prayed, Enio and Par now followed.

Chapter Ten

Lady Agatha marched up the *Sea Dog's* gangplank. The wood gave a painful groan.

Par stared from the dock. "You're what?"

"I'm coming with you."

At the plank's deepening sag, Par decided to wait where he stood. "Lady Agatha, we're very grateful for your help. But Jod is a long way and—"

"I've been to Jod," she said, ignoring both Par's and the plank's complaints. "I'm familiar with the merchant routes and regulations, as well as the customs of the Borderlands."

That knowledge would be helpful—a wrong word to an official might bring disaster. But how could Par involve anyone else in his troubles? When Lani helped last time, she'd almost died. Enio too.

He shook his head. "It's too dangerous. Enio, tell her."

His friend watched from the deck rail. "Um, maybe she *should* come."

Par's jaw dropped. "Are you serious?"

"Thing is,"—Enio rubbed his temple—"after the cliff, I can't invoke much more than a candle. So I can't work the rigging by myself. Might take all three of us."

Par wouldn't deny they could use help to sail the *Sea Dog*, yet for a different reason. Enio had only known the Greening River when he'd built the boat. But once on the open sea, they'd struggled to keep from foundering. The keel wasn't stout enough for strong wind and chop.

Lady Agatha reached the deck. Par scurried up the plank.

She faced them. "You need me. Besides, do you suppose it's any safer for me to stay? I broke you out of custody. That makes me an accessory to a crime."

An Ambassador's wife must have ways around such allegations; Par didn't buy it. "You're just trying to manipulate me."

She smiled. "Is it working?"

"But," Par tried again, not ready to give in, "you're, you know…" He groped for a tactful word that meant wealthy but idle. Accustomed to good meals and feather beds.

Her smile fled. "Soft?" She loomed closer. "Heavy?"

Par shrank back. "Comfortable?"

The lady grunted and turned away. "I haven't always been rich. But I'll never be useless." She grabbed the plank, and with a mighty grunt hauled it back onto the deck.

If anyone doubted the competence of the wealthy, it was Enio. Par glanced at him.

"You're outnumbered," his friend said. "Right, mates, release the moorings and stand by the braces." He disappeared into the small cabin.

Par accepted defeat. He sighed to the lady. "That means—"

"I know what it means." Lady Agatha climbed the stairs to the helm. Using the key she'd gotten from the attendant, she released an iron lock that secured the captain's wheel and tossed the lock and its chain back to the pier. While she untied the stern's mooring rope, Par took care of the bowline.

Enio returned from the cabin. He'd changed out of his grimy page's clothes and into a simple tunic and trousers—though he still donned the green-feathered cap. He strode up to the helm. "Ready the mainsail!"

Par unfurled the large square sail. With more commands, Enio maneuvered them out of the impound. By rounding the island's east side before turning west toward Jod, they'd avoid waiting for passage under the great causeway that connected the island to the mainland. And if Cronus had alerted the city to their escape, they'd also avoid the navy shipyards.

The sail fluttered and snapped. "Trim those sheets!" Enio shouted.

Par helped Agatha adjust the patched, billowing canvas to catch the full bounty of the wind. Argent's shoreline rose higher, the city walls ending where the cliffs began. Favorable breezes ushered the boat along. For once, the gods seemed on their side.

When at last the *Sea Dog* reached the open sea, Enio turned them along the cliffs into the setting sun. White birds screeched and glided through the sharp, salty air.

Agatha stood with Par near the mast. "We're sailing to Jod in *this* thing?"

He kept his voice low. "Enio will never give up the *Sea Dog*. We'll stay near the shore—that got us to Argent. When we had problems, at least we were close to dry land."

They approached the rocky waters below the Vigil outpost, where the Eminence's Location sigil had landed. The breezes strengthened and shifted impishly. Par climbed the steps to the upper deck rail and pointed out the spot.

"Lady Agatha," Enio called, "can you take the wheel?"

She hurried to the helm. "Aye, Captain Enio."

Enio's chest swelled at the title. He joined Par at the rail. "She's not bad at this."

Par shrugged. "Not as good as your first mate."

His friend chuckled.

As they gazed at the area where Lani had disappeared, Par's spirits turned as solemn as if he visited a shrine. But there was no stopping now; they had to leave, abandoning not only their search for Lani, but Par's own search for a place to call home. Considering the threat of Cronus to everyone, it seemed a selfish complaint.

Movement beneath the waters, dark outlines like the leafless branches of small trees, caught his eye. He thrust his arm and pointed. "They're back."

"Who?" said Enio.

"The trees or—whatever. Remember? I saw them once before."

This time, his friend saw them too. "What *are* those things?"

The murky silhouettes drifted like a roaming forest beneath the waves. Some shimmered with a dim green luminosity—perhaps a trick of the late sun through the seaweed.

One shape broke from the group. It circled a pillar of rock and returned.

Enio pointed. "On that rock. It looks like—is that Lani's weaving sigil?"

Par peered over the rail. A curvy design had been carved where the waves licked the stone.

Lady Agatha shouted, "We've got company!"

Far ahead, a navy ship rounded the cliffs, the towering masts clothed with sails upon sails, all bulging with muscles of air.

"And to aft," Agatha called.

Another vessel followed in the *Sea Dog's* distant wake.

Enio ran to the wheel. "We need to get out to sea." He barked orders. Par and Lady Agatha pulled on the rigging lines, tilting the sail.

Another ship joined the one in front, another behind. In each pair, one vessel remained on a straight course toward the *Sea Dog*, while the other hooked farther out.

A silent flash blinked on the ship ahead. A small object shot through the air. It whistled over the mast and crashed into the waves.

"Purple hells, they're *rockshooting* us." Enio spun the wheel.

"That's a warning," Agatha said. "If they want to strike us, they will."

But the shot scored a direct hit on Par's hopes of escape. How could they outrun four full-masted warships?

It dawned on him: did the navy want only Par, not the others? The Abbot said wisdom was knowing on which side of the bars we do the most good. Was that a subtle suggestion that Par should remain while Enio fled? Was Par putting his friends in danger by running off with them?

Enio called out, "Par, heave!"

As the old terror of Cronus shot through him, Par yanked the ropes. No, they had to escape together. They had to find Vex. And Par was the only one who could enter the Citadel. Plus, once the members of the High Council realized Cronus controlled the Eminence, they'd intervene, help the Abbot, stop Cronus from whatever he was planning.

Like capturing Par for gods knew what.

Par pulled the ropes harder. Yes, they *had* to get away. Not because he was afraid, he repeated to himself.

At least, not *only* because of that.

Enio shouted, "They're surrounding us."

"Run us along the cliffs," Par called back. "It's too shallow for them."

"It's too shallow for us too!" Then Enio's serious expression broke, and he laughed.

Par hoped his friend hadn't lost it. "Enio, what—"

"Listen." Enio shook his head and sobered. "Ever since you said Cronus was back, a hot coal's been burning through my guts."

"He terrifies me too. He—"

"No. I *want* to see the bastard again." Enio spit the words. "I want to use a flame sigil and burn his brains out—like he burned through my memories. He needs to *die*, Par. Die and *stay* dead."

This only made matters worse. If captured, Enio might do anything to defy, to hurt Cronus. If he tried, Cronus would kill him.

The navy ships had sailed into a net formation. The cliffs blocked any retreat.

"Hey," Enio waved down at the water. "Get away from my hull!"

Beneath the waves, the strange shifting branches again circled the rock. The low sun created shadows in its etched design. Why was the only nymph sigil Enio knew—the one Lani had given him—carved where she'd fallen?

There must be a reason. It had to be for them.

Par spun to his friend. "Enio, you said you could invoke enough to light a candle. Can you do Lani's weaving sigil?"

"Maybe to lace a boot. Why?"

"Can you do it on that rock?"

"You can't weave rocks, Par."

"We have to try *something*. Can we get closer?"

"To the rocks? Are you crazy?"

"It's where Lani fell. It's where the Fondiscate's invocation landed. What have we got to lose? And if Cronus captures us,"—Par picked the best argument he could think of—"we'll never seen her again."

Enio closed his eyes and worked his jaw as if chewing steel. The *Sea Dog* rolled with the waves. The shadowy shapes drifted beneath the water.

The navy ships continued their approach.

Enio's face snapped up. "Ags, take the wheel. Par, man these lines."

Working under Enio's direction, they maneuvered the *Sea Dog* toward the cliffs. But the shifting winds and waves kept them back.

The Navy vessels tightened their net. The *Sea Dog* was still twenty feet from the rock.

Par shouted to Agatha. "We have to get closer."

"We can't!" she yelled, struggling with the wheel.

Enio studied the water and shook his head. He spun on Par. "I hope you're right about this." Without another word, he tossed his cap onto the deck, jumped the rail and plunged into the sea.

"Enio!" Par called.

His friend thrashed to the rock.

The ship ahead was close enough for Par to hear the captain's commanding voice. "Heave to and prepare to be boarded, by order of the Eminence!"

Enio made it to the stone. He gripped the side and slipped off. He found footing underneath the water on a ledge, and grasping the rock, he invoked. Unlike the bright emerald glory he'd emitted climbing the cliff, barely a spark ran through his hair.

But Enio touched the design, and the stone erupted with green fire. He yelped and pushed away.

The fire flowed through the sigil's grooves like molten metal filling a mold. Then it flashed out, bright as a beacon, but beneath the water.

Enio made it back to the hull. Par threw him a line.

A new shout from the closing vessels, "Ready grapples!"

"For that?" another called. "Break out the fishing tackle."

Laughter.

Par pulled a dripping Enio aboard. The stone's light extinguished. The ship ahead would be upon them at any moment.

All at once, the *Sea Dog* lurched. Par gripped the rail. Had they hit the rocks? But as he peered at the water, he gasped with wonder.

The branching trees had broken through the surface.

And they weren't branches. They were antlers.

Elk-like beasts with glistening greyish coats swarmed the *Sea Dog*. Water shot from their nostrils, and their chests bulged with the power of the sea. Instead of legs, each body ended in a hefty fishlike tail.

The boat heaved again. Par stumbled to his knees. The *Sea Dog* careened toward open waters.

Enio scrambled to the wheel. "They're pushing us!"

The waves around them surged up and up, into the gigantic mounds of a storm-swollen sea. So high did they reach that they shoved aside the navy vessels as if they were bath toys.

But the *Sea Dog* sped on, propelled by the creatures, their antlers flaring with bright green glories. Par had never seen an animal invoke, but he dared not question the miracle. They might escape with the help of these strange beasts.

The mountains of water to each side peaked into crests, threatening to crash down on the *Sea Dog*. Their vessel sailed through a deepening trough.

Lady Agatha staggered to the deck rail. "They're taking us down. We have to jump!"

Enio hugged the wheel, giving no sign of letting go.

High overhead, the crests pinched together and touched, squeezing out the sky and sealing the boat in a dizzying tunnel. Par held on to the railing for his life. Had he guessed wrong? Was the glyph not a sign, a charm, from Lani? Had they instead violated some sea memorial and now paid the price?

Their boat listed left, right, left. Enio shouted as he wrestled the wheel. The mast dug into the roaring walls of water and foam. An echoing groan, a thunderous *crack*! The mast splintered and exploded as if struck by a thunderbolt. Broken tie lines twisted and snapped like enraged snakes. The vessel convulsed. Par cried out as he flew off the deck, weightless in a chaos of spray and debris. Below him, the *Sea Dog* plummeted away into a watery abyss. Enio was still at the helm, body wrapped around the wheel, eyes wide, mouth in a silent scream.

Something grabbed Par and yanked him through the cataclysm. He thought he must drown, yet the sea did not choke his lungs. Faster he went, battered and tossed, helpless in the maelstrom. Darkness and light.

Darkness and light…

PART TWO

DARKNESS AND LIGHT

Chapter Eleven

WITH HIS HANDS still bound, the Abbot bumped aside his dinner bowl and inched slug-like across the cold stone floor. Porridge dribbled down his chin.

His sight had not improved. Cronus had provided him with food, but not enough to build strength for a powerful invocation. The Abbot might still manage enough lumina to cure this evil blindness. He didn't know—he'd chosen not to try. Instead, he now settled in the spot where he remembered the sun reaching through the cell's high window. He discreetly invoked, counting that the guard outside would not see the Abbot's weak glory in the morning light, if morning it was.

Pressure grew inside his ears, then a rising ring, until *pop!* His hearing became crystal clear, as if he'd dislodged a wad of wax.

There was a sigil the Abbot didn't happen to have, one used by scouts and sailors that gave them views of distant objects, the horizon, the stars. Long Eye. The sigil he now invoked was similar. Long Ear. It wasn't the most ethical of invocations, but still handy in an abbey of whispering monks and mischievous students.

Lucius breathed outside the cell. A cockroach cleaned its shell in a far corner.

The Abbot focused his hearing past all this, down the hall.

"Perhaps another visit by Lucius?" That was Legate.

"Torture will not work on the Abbot." The voice was that of the Eminence, his body now controlled by Cronus. "He's as stubborn as he is old."

"Not so doting that he didn't once defeat your Confessor sigil."

The Abbot smiled at the memory. Last year at the abbey, Cronus had rummaged through the Abbot's head for Par's location, and the Abbot had outfoxed the fox.

"That was long ago," Cronus said. "And you are not one to talk. Sigils of Ortu cannot see into a mind at all."

"Careful, Cronus." The voice rose, and the Abbot winced at the volume. "You shall not—"

"Have your *own* care, Legate."

"How *dare*—"

"I tell you how I dare." Cronus's voice dropped. "You received your Reckoning after a lifetime of service in your cult. Well and good. But don't presume any privilege over me. I was chosen."

"A loose word, Cronus. None ever fell as you into the realm of the Ortu. Maybe you were a low apple on a convenient tree."

"A loose analogy, Legate. Low apples are devoured. I found rapport with the Ortu and seized the moment as an apple of my own."

The Abbot frowned. *Plenty of bad apples to go around.* But one outcome of Cronus's plunge into the purple hells became clear: when Cronus had embraced the Ortu and had the very windows of his soul turned to the Lower Realms, he'd lost the ability to gather the lumina of the gods to enlighten Elorian sigils.

"And how," Legate said, "has your possession of the Eminence brought either of us closer to our grand designs? Leave that man's body. Kill him and resume your hunt for Par."

"I think not."

"Your old ambitions will be your undoing, brother."

"My ambition is peace throughout all the lands under just rule, *brother*, and my possession of the Eminence is a useful accident toward that end. Further, we now command the resources of an entire country to find the boy."

That confirmed the Abbot's worst fears: Cronus had been after Par, not the Eminence. Still, it did not explain why.

"This bickering gets us nowhere," Legate said with a sigh. "Once we have the boy, I will have all I need for the ritual. Then the Ortu's might will be ours and you will have your rule. Let us see to the Father Abbot."

Footsteps.

The Abbot ended his invocation, chilled at that last revelation. Was that their plan? Releasing the full power of the Ortu, tapping it through some ritual for their own uses? And Par was the key?

"Lucius," Legate said. "Any change with our guest?"

"Smells worse."

A sudden wind hit the Abbot's face. He stiffened against it. In a moment, it ceased.

"There," Legate said. "I've given you a brief spring cleaning. I trust it will last while we talk."

The Abbot struggled to a sitting position. "I make no promises."

Legate chuckled. "Fair enough. I'd like to apologize for our first visit. The escape of the boy had me rather upset."

"Is Cronus with you?"

"I am."

The Abbot angled his face toward the voice. "I recall that Par also defeated your security here last year. Have you considered barring the windows?"

Cronus grunted.

Legate spoke again. "The navy reported his vessel taken by strange sea beasts. There is indeed a trend around here to underestimate the resourcefulness of Par and his friends. We will not make that mistake again."

Strange sea beasts? Those boys got themselves into the most extraordinary situations. But at least they'd escaped Argent. Hope renewed in the Abbot's heart that they would continue to elude Cronus and Legate, and find Alexander Vex.

"However," Legate added, "it was not merely Par's disappearance that caused my ire. Our possession of your Eminence was unintentional. We had meant that for Par. This has thrown certain plans into disarray."

The Abbot did not even try to feign surprise. "And why Par?"

"Communication is a two-way street, Abbot. I imagine you have not changed your mind about cooperating."

Certainly he had not. The Abbot tried a different question. "Then the freedom you spoke of earlier. What did you mean?"

"That I shall answer, as perhaps it will make you more sympathetic to our cause. Our cult, as you call it, exists in the shadows. We do not kneel to your gods, so your country rejects us. We do not call upon the moon and stars, and so we are outcast from Arcana. Like you in this cell, we are confined to the world's malodorous corners. We wish to walk free in our beliefs."

"There are the Borderlands, Legate."

"Populated by whom? Elorians and Arcanans. They may no longer hold allegiance to their countries of origin, but they hold to their beliefs. We are as persecuted there as anywhere."

The Abbot had to admit, fringe beliefs such as Legate described often brought persecution, deserved or not. "I don't see how enslaving the body of the Eminence, or of Par, bolsters the claims of your value for freedom."

"I shall explain it this way: many of our petitioners come from what you would call the lowest rungs of society—the beggars, the broken, the castoffs. Others have climbed the golden ladders of the world. But whether from gutters or from gilt, we are all equal in the darkness. The ways of Ortu offer the cool and peace of the shadows; freedom from the world's glaring vulgarity."

"I don't argue the fundamental value of every soul," the Abbot said. "Yet one can stumble without the light. How is sitting alone in your caves a better way?"

"You think we sit alone?"

"What then?"

"We are a family. Together we wait for freedom."

"But Par—"

"I weary of this," Legate said. "Brother Cronus, see if you can talk some sense into our guest."

One set of footsteps receded.

The Abbot lay back, considering not so much the meat of the conversation, but how it had been served. Cronus and Legate seemed unclear which of them was, in fact, in charge.

"A private audience with the Eminence?" the Abbot said. "I'm honored."

A wooden chair squeaked outside the cell. "You realize your stubbornness is useless."

"Our definition of the word *useless* may differ."

"Then let me be clear," Cronus said. "I assume that given the choice between betraying Par or dying, you would choose death."

"A fair assumption."

"And with my new Reckoning, I cannot enter your thoughts to discover his plans."

It was as the Abbot had suspected: Cronus could not use Elorian sigils, and illumination of another's mind was apparently incompatible with the sigils of the dark. "Then we are at an impasse. Yet I suspect you do not keep me around for the conversation."

Cronus sighed. "We have more in common with each other, Cornelius, than with Legate. We both hail from Eloria. We're both respected men of the cloth."

"Same cloth perhaps, but different tailors."

"Further," Cronus said, ignoring the jab, "you and I are old enough to understand that Eloria's and Arcana's ignorance and superstition fuel their hatred of one another. You and I are of the same stock and forge. From an enlightened perspective, you and I are family."

"Yet it is Legate you now call brother."

"Let us not fence words. You remain alive because Legate agrees that once we locate Par, you may be a useful negotiation chip."

"When you have accomplished your goals, both my life and Par's are expendable. Again, an impasse."

"Except your lives are not the only ones on the table."

Now we get to it. "You'll have to be clearer still, Cronus."

"There is little chance I can locate a Confessor with the skills to ransack the mind of such a talented abbot. Even if a Confessor discovered from you Par's plans, my past would also be gleaned from your mind."

"Such as your murder of the Vigil, and your victims of the Immortus, and your original plot to bring paradise by throwing the lands into war?"

"And now my possession of the Eminence. The point is, when that Confessor discovers these things and resists further cooperation, Legate would not hesitate to kill them. Even if they appeared cooperative, we could never be sure that you hadn't silently persuaded them to lie."

"This all sounds quite inconvenient for you."

"Quite. Of course, we might continue to apply Confessors, one after another, killing each afterwards. Perhaps among the pile of dead, some truth might be found."

"There is little truth among dead bodies."

"You know what I mean, Abbot."

Tragically, the Abbot did. "Regardless of Legate's desires, I can't accept that you'd kill off the most accomplished invokers in the capital for such a slight hope. As the Eminence of Eloria, you can impose your rule, conduct your war, promote your lies, anything you wish. You'd be wasting your best assets."

"Legate need not kill many before your morals forced you to reveal Par's location and prevent more men from dying before your eyes. Pardon me—before your ears."

Much as the Abbot might prefer death to betraying Par, how could he allow others to join him? "Perhaps," the Abbot said, hiding the bluff in his voice, "you overestimate my morals. As you noted, we are both old men, and with age comes perspective. They'd die for a noble cause. What higher value in any life than saving a young one such as Par?"

"Your stubbornness never fails to impress, Cornelius. Yet I see the design behind your argument—you hope to buy him time. Once you deem he is far enough on his journey, you would tell us everything, preventing other deaths. Not a bad plan, I admit."

That was exactly what the Abbot was hoping.

"And so," Cronus said with a long exhale, "at dawn, Legate will order my guards to bring guests. Children, I believe. One by one, they will die until you talk."

The Abbot's eyes widened in blind horror. "Even you, Cronus—"

"I wish no such thing, of course. But bear in mind, should you choose to cooperate after those children have been brought to this secret outpost, they will still be Reckoned to remove the memory. At least Legate has agreed to that. But between you and me, I can't help wondering if they might meet with some accident before ever rejoining their families."

The chair squeaked again. "As to our definitions of *useless*, we do indeed allow different shades of meaning. If you tell me of Par's plans, Legate will have no need to apply his regrettable strategy."

The Abbot could lie, send them looking for Par in the wrong direction. But when that lie was discovered, it would bring a worse demonstration of Legate's displeasure—and not upon the Abbot alone. Cronus had him cornered.

Out of cards, the Abbot said glumly, "Par has gone to Jod."

"Why Jod?"

"To seek aid from the one member of the Vigil you failed to kill."

"Vex survives?" Cronus's tone held a smile. "I see. What of the sea creatures that took Par's boat?"

"I'm as much in the dark as you."

"I am inclined to believe that, Cornelius. My ship's captains said the boys seemed entirely surprised by the affair."

"Cronus, what is it you want with Par?"

"Legate told you. Their cult desires the freedom to—"

"No!" The Abbot slammed a palm against the stone floor. "I know you better than that. Not what *he* wants. What do *you* want?"

Cronus was silent for a moment. "I have been given a second chance at the life which Par stole, and to at last bring peace and paradise to the lands."

"You believe Legate can, or will, fulfill that promise?"

"It is not from Legate I seek it."

"Who, then? Someone else who wields the Ortu?"

"The Ortu is more than a weapon. Much more. Sleep well, Cornelius."

Footsteps receded.

Cronus's puzzling comment on the Ortu left the Abbot deeper in the dark than even his blindness. He had hoped to discover more of Legate's and Cronus's plans while giving Par time to escape. All he'd accomplished so far was to betray Par's destination. Perhaps Cronus's definition of *useless* was closer to the mark than his own.

Chapter Twelve

Something pinched Par's thumb.

"Ow!" He jerked and opened his eyes.

A small lobster-like thing retreated across a beach. Gulls screeched and wheeled through the clear midday sky. Stunted trees stood back from a bright sea.

Par groaned to his feet. His muscles ached and his forehead stung. Weeds and driftwood dotted the sand.

One clump coughed.

"Lady Agatha?" He hurried over. "Are you hurt?"

She shook her head. As Par helped her sit up, her eyes locked on something in the water. He followed her gaze. An antlered beast, like an elk, watched from the shoals.

"That's what took the *Sea Dog*," he said. "A whole herd."

The beast's branching tines sparkled in the sunshine. Then abruptly they bent and melted, sloughing like foam over the creature's face and shoulders. The animal likeness washed away, replaced by a dark muscular man, chest deep in the water.

For a moment, Par couldn't speak through his amazement. He found his voice and shouted, "Hello! You brought us here?"

But the figure turned and plunged beneath the surf.

Agatha cleared her throat. "What was *that?*"

Rather than try to explain the transformation they'd just seen, something more alarming jumped to Par's mind. "I saw Enio go down with the *Sea Dog.* Gods, you don't think—"

"We survived," she said reassuringly, heading off his panic. "That bodes well for him."

Par hoped so, but *they* hadn't been dragged down with the boat.

Or been too crazy to let it go.

Agatha focused on Par's forehead. "You've got a nasty bruise. You told me you can't invoke."

"But Enio—"

"First things first." She reached out. "May I?"

Par scanned the water and the beach. A few gulls pecked at the scattered driftwood. At least the debris didn't look fresh.

He took a breath and nodded.

Agatha invoked and brushed a finger above his eyes. The pain faded.

"Thanks," he said, rubbing the spot. As he did, he remembered Lady Agatha's society didn't use invocations.

But she just had. Par eyed her. "What about your sigil fasting?"

"I had a six-week streak going before I helped you up that cliff." She poured water out of a shoe. "Right down the pipes."

Par appreciated the healing and didn't push the issue. Soggy grit oozed inside his boots and he sat to empty them. "Any idea where we are?"

"None. But I could use some food. What about you?"

"Now that you mention it." He lay a hand on his stomach.

She glanced around. "Though provisions might be a problem."

Rubbing his pinched finger, Par gave a wry grin. "Maybe not."

Back on the Greening River, Enio had shown him how to trap crawtads—which resembled tiny lobsters—by lowering a jug behind the creatures and snatching at them from the front. The crawtads shot straight backwards into captivity. Par left Lady Agatha and waded into the shallows to try his boot on the little lobster things he'd seen when he awoke. It worked. At one success, he had a vision of Enio's approving face, though it faded into his friend's terrified expression as he sank.

Lady Agatha had gathered wood and fashioned a spit. They dispatched their meals and speared them through. The lady invoked again and lit a fire. As Par turned the spit over the flames, she filled a curved piece of driftwood with sea water and invoked it into fresh.

They settled in the broken shade to eat. Par's objection to Agatha joining his journey had flipped. How would he have managed, washed up here alone? He couldn't make a flame, or even clean water.

Lady Agatha interrupted his pang of self-pity. "It's been a long time since I've eaten plain lobster. A dab of butter would be nice."

Par's spirits inched up at memories of the river festivals back home. He handed her a stick with a cooked critter and took one himself. "Or a boil."

The lady gasped and rolled her eyes. "*Yes.* Fresh corn and sausages."

"Spicy sauces from Choga." Saliva ran in his mouth. "Beer from the abbey. Fresh bread and—"

"Keep the bread."

"You don't like bread?"

Agatha turned the stick in her fingers. "We ate it a lot when I was a child. I was seven before I discovered it could be soft without being wetted. Or that raw meat wasn't always grey."

Par peeled back a shell and took a nibble at the sweet goodness inside. "Where was this?"

She cracked off a claw. "In the Borderlands. I was born there."

Agatha was born a foreigner? "But you use Elorian magic."

"Even within the Borderlands, there are borders. Elorian culture here, Arcanan there. The lines shift with each war. My upbringing was Elorian, but my great grandmother immigrated from Arcana. I'm named after her."

That explained why the name Agatha had never sounded quite Elorian. "How did you wind up in Argent?"

She spit out a piece of shell. "I used barter and trade to help my family. Turns out, I had a knack. My circle of connections grew, and I traveled farther, sending money back to my parents— though that ended with the Grey Wars."

"Why?"

"My village was sacked. They died."

"I'm sorry," Par said softly.

She stopped chewing. Par thought it best not to pry further.

But after a drawing a deep breath, she tossed aside an empty claw and went on. "I met my husband in Jod, on one of his trips for the never-ending trade disputes. He's from money and always looking to make it grow. I had begun to focus on jewelry. He knew that market did well, and I damn didn't want to be poor again. So, after a brief courtship, we married."

"The Ambassador?" He recalled her mentioning the title at the Mercy House gates.

"Ambassador Blandus. Heard of him?"

"Blandus? Maybe," Par said. He hadn't. "Any kids? If you don't mind me asking."

She filled a shell with a little water and sipped it with her pinkie out. "It's not that kind of marriage."

"Oh." Par sensed an iciness in her voice. He shifted uncomfortably.

"I'm not lonely," she said, "if that's what you're thinking. I have my social clubs. And the servants. And my pets…"

She trailed off. Her brief grin seemed forced. "It's been a good life. Before Blandus, I'd never worn clothes made to fit. Or had new undergarments for each day."

"Each day?"

Her sudden laughter broke the tension. "It's not as luxurious as it sounds. Not like comfortable, well-worn ones."

Unsure when he'd last replaced his own, Par could only chuckle.

"Sometimes," she said, sobering, "I miss those indulgences."

"I'd think with your wealth, you'd wear whatever you wanted."

"Not in the ruling quarter. How people see you is everything. It's funny," she added. "When I was poor, dreams of the future seemed a luxury. Now it's dreams of the past."

Par had landed on the poor end of the luxury scale. She seemed to hint the other end wasn't always an improvement.

"Anyway," she continued, "early on, when Blandus was around more, he'd tell me the juicy gossip of the Hierarchy. For instance, did you know Cronus was once married?"

"He was?" Par couldn't imagine who would marry that monster. But Agatha's next words surprised him even more.

"Yes, and he had a daughter."

"Wow. Where are they now?"

"They disappeared. The talk was he'd exiled them to better his career."

Before Par expressed his horror, she said, "But that was just a rumor."

They finished their lunch. Agatha brushed off her dress. "I think it's time we found out where we are."

Par doused the fire, and they started down the coast. When rugged hills crowded out the beach, he suggested he scout the higher inland ground—alone. He worried how well the lady could handle the climbing landscapes. But she insisted on coming along.

Valleys of stunted trees stretched among the rocky rises. Up one of the gorges, a gentler slope came into view. They tried that way. Agatha needed several rests on the steeper parts, but at last they reached the breezy summit.

She took a quick look around, gasped, and sat on a wide, flat rock. "This is higher than it looked. Tell me what you see."

Remembering her vertigo, Par nodded.

The sun had dropped halfway down the western sky, and the sea spread vast and glittering to the horizon. Par could almost believe he was looking out from his own country's shores, except that in Argent, the sea's horizon was south. Here, it circled everywhere.

"Looks like we're on an island," he said. "The hills go overland another league before they meet the water again."

"Any roads? Cottages?"

"I don't see any. No boats either." He sighed—and no *Sea Dog*. He joined her on the rock.

After a moment, Agatha asked, "Why not tell me what's really going on with you and Cronus?"

Par realized he'd told her very little. Now he saw no reason to hold back. So as they sat on their high overlook, he told her his story, from his Lustering in St. Livius, through meeting Lani in the Urdel; of the Vigil and the Citadel and his thick soul; and of Cronus and the Immortus. Until now, she'd seemed a pretty pushy person. It turned out she was also a good listener.

But when he spoke of Alexander Vex, she interrupted. "Of Vex Imports and Exports?"

"You know him?"

"By reputation. The name is quite respected in trading circles."

"That's who we need to find." But how, trapped on this island? He resumed his tale.

When at last he finished, Agatha stood and took a deep breath. "All this because of one man's twisted ambitions."

Par couldn't have said it better.

They headed down the hill, careful to avoid slips and stumbles. The shadows were long when they reached the beach.

"The day's almost gone," Agatha said. "Let's settle in for the evening."

They found a pocket of low trees close to where they'd landed. Par gathered additional wood, and they made a fire and got comfortable. Stars began to peek through overhanging branches, but before he could sleep, a question still nagged at him.

"Lady Agatha?" he said.

"Hmm?" She lay opposite the fire, visible through wisps of smoke.

"Why did you join that society, anyway?"

"The Esoteric Society of Ortu? I started it."

"You?"

"Yes, me. Argent is full of clubs and societies. I can't count the number I've supported, but that's expected of the ruling class. Before Ortu, I was second chair of the Hummingbird Benevolence League."

"Huh," was the best Par could manage.

"Try to hide your enthusiasm."

"Sorry."

The lady continued, "Blandus brings me literature from his travels. One was a short discourse on Ortu. I became interested in its philosophy. It surprised me how well one can manage without invocations."

"Then it's nothing, uh, *dark*?" Par said.

"As far as I knew. The basic philosophy is that by sigil fasting, one becomes more sensitive to the Higher Realms and the lumina which enlightens our sigils."

"Then why do you protest at the Mercy House?"

The fire crackled. She was silent, then spoke almost sadly. "Living without invocations made me see that place in a different light. We all want unfortunate people to get the help they need. Yet when their problem is invocation, and the solution is a Reckoning, I wondered why they couldn't live as they were—with more support from society."

"You're preaching to the choir."

"So I gather. It's strange how we say those who can't invoke must be unworthy before the gods, yet criminals invoke just fine. Why would the gods judge thieves and murderers worthy of their lumina, but not innocents?"

Par didn't answer. He had no idea how the gods worked.

She went on. "I've heard answers that involve faith and free will and the unknowable. Yet it's also said the most scenic route to madness is through theology." She rolled over. "Get some rest, Par."

The night was quiet except for the soft surf and an occasional lonely bird. In Eloria, questioning the gods got you in trouble.

But they seemed a long way from Eloria.

And from Vex and Jod and…

Par squeezed his eyes shut and sent up a quick prayer for Enio, in case the gods were listening.

Chapter Thirteen

Dawn reached through the trees into the little camp. Par stretched and sat up. Lady Agatha lay on the other side of the burned-down campfire. She grunted a half snore.

Like the firewood, Par's spirits had fizzled to mere embers. Regardless of the peaceful setting, he was lost in the vast Silver Sea.

So was Enio.

His attention snapped to movement. Something crept up Lady Agatha's leg: a swollen, mottled-brown spider. Wispy hairs on its back swayed in a light breeze. Its ghastly head twinkled with a constellation of black eyes.

Par stopped breathing. What should he do? He didn't want to startle the fiend. Such a big spider might be dangerous—or deadly.

A cluster of the creatures approached across the sand.

"Crap!" He leapt to his feet.

Lady Agatha jerked awake. "What? What is it?"

"Spiders!" Par pointed to… to…

Not a single one was in sight.

"Spiders?" She stood. "Where?"

"Your leg?"

The lady slapped at her thick, pale calves. She twisted, straining to see. "Are they gone?"

"Um, maybe."

Her lips tightened. "What does *maybe* mean?"

"We were surrounded." He peered at the brush, at the sand. Nothing.

Before he relaxed, narrow dotted lines drew themselves across the loose ground.

Par jumped back. "There!"

As he landed, a shrill squeal erupted at his heel.

He spun. A small, cream-colored spider chittered and scurried away.

All at once, spiders were everywhere. They covered the ground, hung motionless in the bushes, stared with glistening eyes from the tree branches.

The one he'd almost squashed limped back to the others and held out its spindly leg. It seemed bent the wrong way.

A large purple spider brushed its appendage over the head of the smaller one and lifted its own frightful head toward Par and hissed through a mouth of dripping fangs.

Par dove to the fire and yanked out a stick. One end still glowed red. He jabbed it before him. "Stay back or—"

"Don't you *dare!*"

The words hadn't come from the spider, or from Lady Agatha. He turned.

A slender woman watched through an opening in the trees. Long amber hair fell over her shoulders, draping a gown that gleamed like young seaweed. She wore a shell necklace and…

The stick slipped from Par's hand. He barely breathed the name. "Lani?"

She beamed the bright smile that had always seemed too wide for her face. "Hi, Par."

For a moment, he couldn't move. Then his muscles exploded with energy. "Lani!" He rushed forward.

She spread her arms. Par plunged into them and pulled her close. The long winter that had chilled his soul, melted.

"I knew you'd survived," he sniffled as they eased apart.

It was the same Lani—but also different. Her hair, her skin, glowed with life and health. Her eyes sparkled like the sun on the waves.

He had so many questions that he wasn't sure how to start. "We searched for months and—"

"Enio told me everything."

Par gasped. "Where is he?"

She cocked her head toward the water. "See for yourself."

Just beyond the shoals floated the *Sea Dog*, its shattered mast restored. A figure at the bow lowered the anchor.

If Par's heart leapt any further, it would fly from his chest.

Lani laughed. "Go on."

"I'll be *right* back." Par ran to the beach. "Enio!" he shouted.

His friend waved and dove off the deck toward shore.

Par waited for him at the edge of the sand, waving, glancing at Lani and laughing.

Enio sloshed and panted from the water. "I see she found you too."

"I—oh hells." Par clutched his friend and whispered, "I was afraid, when you went down—"

"They took me away," Enio whispered back. "Me and the *Sea Dog*."

Par stood back. "Took you where?"

Enio hesitated. He started across the beach. "Come on. Lani can explain it."

They returned to the campsite where Lady Agatha was watching. Enio no longer wore his feathered cap. Par didn't even joke about its demise.

"Lani," Par said, "this is Lady Agatha. She helped us escape Cronus."

Lady Agatha stepped forward. "Par's told me about you."

Lani smiled. "A friend of his is a friend of mine."

The spiders had mostly disappeared, except for a few that lingered at the edges.

"Excuse me one moment," Lani said. She approached the little spider with the bent leg and held out her hand.

"Are they dangerous?" Par asked, wincing as she got closer.

"Families protect their own." An emerald glow winked around her head. She touched the spider's leg. The creature chittered in a way Par took as happy. So did the bigger one. Then both melted into the air.

Par jolted. "They're magic?"

"They're chameleon spiders," she said. "You can still see them if you look sharp. But everything in nature is magic to me."

Her connection to nature had always awed Par. "Are you a full-fledged nymph now?"

"Let's sit down and I'll tell you what happened."

They chose a spot under the trees. Par brushed the sand first for invisible spiders. Enio poked at the fire.

"I found the *chela élande,*" she began. "The heart of the élan. Or it found me."

Par nodded. "Didn't you tell me wherever that happened, you had to stay there, like your mother at her lake?"

"This is where things get muddy. The élan decides a nymph's destiny—whatever's best for the balance. But perhaps because I was born half-human, I am as yet unbound to a place. That's normal for males, but not females."

"Males?" Par said, a little too loudly. "There are male nymphs?"

Enio snorted. Lani laughed, then stopped herself. But it burst out again.

"What?" Par said, wondering if he should laugh along.

"Sorry." Her eyes danced with amusement. "Yes, there are. There'd be no new nymphs otherwise."

Par's face warmed. He was sure he was blushing.

"Don't be embarrassed," she said. "How could you know? But you've already seen some."

And Par realized. "The sea elks!"

"The sea *stags*, yes. Male nymphs find the *chela élande* in a creature, not a place. After that, the males can adopt that creature's form, even live and travel with them. Some meet a female nymph and decide to settle down."

She took a deep breath, as if relishing a pleasant odor. "Though I'm not bound to the sea, I feel a strong connection to it. Even now, I sense birds skimming the surface, fish darting among the reefs, the scuttle of rock crabs and the dance of sea grass in the waves. It seems to ebb and flow in my veins."

"Remarkable," Agatha said from across the fire.

Par thought so too. "Did you carve that sigil on the rocks?"

"I had help. I trusted that no one in your country would recognize it, except Enio. The stags volunteered to keep watch. When Enio triggered the beacon, they brought you to me. Well," she glanced at Enio, "they tried."

"I steered us right out of the vortex." Enio raised his chin. "They said that took special skill."

It seemed Enio had missed a back-handed compliment. Par spoke again to Lani. "I'm sorry we didn't look harder for you. But the winter—"

"No, Par. You wouldn't have found me."

"Why not?"

"Well, for a while, I was within the élan's embrace, beyond your reach. Then..."

She trailed off and gave Enio a quick wink.

He returned it.

"A story for another time," she said.

Par opened his mouth to ask something but stopped. What was this winking stuff?

She continued, "Enio tells me you need to get to Jod."

Par put away his last question, also for another time. "Do you know where we are?"

"I think your people call it the Boundary Islands."

Lady Agatha joined the conversation. "Halfway to Arcana? That far?"

"Traveling enchantments speed the stags through the sea," Lani said. "They landed you here after you fell overboard, but they've agreed to take you on to Jod."

That was fantastic news since Par now worried they'd miss Vex. As he mused, he got another idea. "Can the stags take us to Arcana instead?"

"Arcana?" Enio said, his voice full of disbelief.

"Hear me out. If we go straight to Jod, we won't meet Vex for almost a week. While we're waiting, the Abbot's stuck in that cell, and Cronus is doing gods know what. But right now, Vex is in Aurix, the capital of Arcana. What if we can find him sooner?"

"You're off your rudder, Par. In case you forgot, Arcana is the enemy."

"Excuse me," Agatha put in, "but if anyone's going to Arcana, it should be me alone. I have some familiarity with their customs. I have a better chance to blend."

Enio crossed his arms. "Do you even know what Vex looks like?"

"Well…" She frowned. "No. Perhaps you and I should go together. Par can wait for us in Jod."

"I'm not sitting useless in Jod," Par said. "Besides, if Cronus finds out from the Abbot I'm there, he'll send the whole navy after me."

No one disagreed.

"Then it's settled," Par added. "We go to Arcana. And Cronus can't get to us there, even if he looks like the Eminence. Neither can the navy without starting a war."

Agatha's face darkened. "There's another issue. As Par stated, if we go to Jod, we'd have a week to wait. If we go to Aurix and can't locate Vex, we'd have to backtrack to Jod. Any delay and we'd miss him in both places."

"Maybe I can help," Lani said. "I'll give Enio another nymph enchantment, a Sea Call. If he stands in the sea and calls to me, I'll hear and bring the stags. If you don't find Vex in Aurix, or you need to flee the country, they'll get you to Jod within a day."

Enio nodded enthusiastically.

Par's spirits shot up. "Could they take us farther? Like up the Crescent to Xol Tomot?" The Abbot had mentioned Vex would return there after Jod, and it might give them more time to search Aurix.

"No, that river is freshwater. The stags are sea creatures. Ready, Enio?"

Lani and Enio leaned their foreheads together, and after a brief green spark, pulled back.

"Got it!" Enio said.

But as Par watched the bestowal, the rest of what she'd said hit him. "Lani, you're not coming?"

Her tone became somber. "I must stay near the sea while my changes work themselves out. But I'll accompany you to the shores of Arcana and remain close as long as possible."

"But we just found you again," Par said, joy leaking from his heart.

"Oh Par, how I wish I *could* stay. But it has to be this way. At least for now."

For *now*. Hopefully, *now* wouldn't last very long.

Lani looked around. "But we can't part again until we've at least had a short reunion celebration, don't you think?"

Even in their predicament, Par wouldn't miss at least a brief time with Lani. She excused herself to the sea to collect edibles. As Lady Agatha refreshed the fire, and Enio explored a little up the beach, Par watched the waters. Lani returned with a basket of woven weeds full of sea greens and funny rainbow-colored vegetables.

Together they prepared the bounty, roasted some, feasted on it all. Par's relief at the survival of his friends returned full force, and he could finally laugh and joke. A few times he squeezed a sea fruit and sent a stream of juice onto Enio's black mop of hair, who then shook his head and yelled at the trees. Everyone laughed. Enio never figured it out.

CHAPTER FOURTEEN

For one short hour, Par buried his worries and feasted with his friends. He'd almost forgotten the profound sense of comfort Lani's presence brought him, like shade in the summer. Her emerald eyes seemed different somehow—deeper maybe—but her bright, sudden laughs were the same.

At last, Enio broke the serenity. "Well, when do we leave?"

It took an effort for Par to muster the words. "As soon as we can."

"The stags aren't far." Lani stood. "I'll call them."

"One moment," Agatha said. "Where in Arcana will we arrive?"

"There's a large bay, busier than any other on the coastline. The stags don't know the land geography, but they assume that's Aurix."

"It's a good assumption," Agatha replied. "However, we don't want to arrive anywhere near it."

"But Vex—" Par began.

Lady Agatha raised a hand. "What I know of their customs doesn't include local sailing regulations, or the proper colors to fly, or the normal rigging of an Arcanan vessel. We can't risk look-ing suspicious."

Enio nodded. "She's right."

"Instead," Agatha continued, "have the stags leave us a dozen leagues down the coast. The walk will give us a chance to adjust, so we don't show up looking like Elorian tourists."

That meant losing another day. Maybe two. But Par agreed it was better than being noticed and captured.

They smothered the ashes and strode across the beach.

Lady Agatha gestured to the *Sea Dog*. "Does that thing have a shore boat?"

"Who needs one?" Enio hurried ahead.

"We sold it," Par muttered, "a couple months ago. We needed the money."

They joined Enio on the shoreline. Lani had already dived in.

Par glanced at Agatha. "Can you, um, swim?"

"It's been a while." Still dressed, she splashed in, rolled over like an otter, and began to backstroke.

The *Sea Dog* wasn't far, just off the shoals. Par swam with Enio, passing Agatha. They reached the anchor line, shimmied on board, and dropped a rope ladder over the side. Agatha pulled herself up. When they were all on deck, they weighed the anchor. The sail was furled on the stout mast—the one that had shattered.

"Hey, Enio," Par asked. "How did that get fixed?"

His friend looked away. Then he pointed. "I think they're ready."

Lani rode one of the nymph-beasts like a horse. A forest of antlers surrounded the vessel.

"Hold on!" she called above the surf.

Enio reached under his shirt and drew out his feathered cap. He wrung it out and planted it on his head.

Par rolled his eyes. The hat was back.

Lani called once more, "And no fiddling with the rudder."

"Got it." Enio's face remained serious. He stood at the helm. Par and Agatha crouched near the rail.

With muscles bulging under glistening coats, the stags crowded against the hull. One by one, their antlers gloried green. The *Sea Dog* began to move, and as before, walls of water rose and met overhead, creating a tunnel. Then, with a sudden jolt, the vessel exploded forward like a rockshot pebble. The sun became a streak, a bright river of green and white through the watery roof. Par hugged the rail tightly; his breath raced with his heart. They were traveling the very veins of the sea.

Their speed increased. The hull trembled and groaned. But this trip was smoother than the last, and Par's alarm turned to thrill. Enio remained a pillar of concentration, gripping the wheel, eyes hard ahead, his expression one of triumph. Agatha, however, was white as a ghost. She'd closed her eyes. Her lips seemed to move in prayer.

On and on they flew, for how long Par couldn't say. But finally their movement slowed. Sunlight cut through from above as the wet sky cracked open and the blue heavens reappeared.

The briny walls fell. The *Sea Dog* slowed and stopped. They rested once more on the lap of the sea. A hilly shore loomed ahead: if that was Arcana, they had covered roughly a hundred leagues.

Par helped Agatha to her feet. "Are you—?"

"I'll be fine," she said, rubbing the color back into her face.

The stags ushered them toward the shoreline. The land was not unlike Eloria's southern coast, with valleys and beaches breaking between the lofty hills. Enio directed them toward a tree-wrapped cove. There were no signs of civilization.

It seemed a perfect place to leave the boat, so they found a spot near the banks and anchored, close enough to where they could hop almost onto shore. Enio brought dry rations and water skins from the hold.

Lani joined them on the beach. She waved to the stags. With a plunk and a splash, the beasts disappeared.

"Did you thank them for us?" Par had wanted to, but didn't know how.

"I will," she said. "You're about ten leagues west of Aurix."

"I wish we didn't have to leave you." Par's spirits sagged again. "Are you all right in the sea? Are you… alone?" Par wasn't sure how to put what he was feeling. "I mean, other than the sea stags. They're full nymphs, and you're…"

"I'm more worried for you than you should be for me. And no, I'm not alone. There's more life in the sea than you imagine." She glanced at Enio. "Right?"

"Right," he said with a grin.

Before Par could ask more, she added, "Enio, can I talk with Par a moment?"

"Sure." Enio joined Agatha in organizing their provisions.

When he was out of earshot, Lani said, "Enio had a rough time of it before we rescued him. The stags tried to heal his bruises, but he fought them off—viciously. He cut one of them with a shard from the mast."

"Maybe he was just shaken up?" Par had never seen Enio that bad.

"Maybe. Once he recognized me, he became my old Enio again. But for a minute… Well, you're probably right that he was just shaken."

Par wished he believed that. Yet he found himself wondering what else had happened when Enio was with Lani, off in the sea.

"Anyway," she said, "keep an eye on him."

"Always." Par forced a smile.

She stepped closer and took his hand. Hers was soft and warm, like the sun on the sand. "You have a long walk to Aurix. You should get started."

At the touch, Par caught his breath. Warmth rushed down his cheeks into his chest.

She squeezed and let go. "We'll meet again soon."

Enio returned. "Right. You can't get rid of us *that* easy."

Par nodded dumbly to his friend.

Lani stepped into the water. "By the way, don't think of me as half-human anymore. Or half-nymph."

"Then what?" Par said, not finding any other words.

As she dove beneath the waves, she called back, "From now on, whatever I am, I'm a full Lani."

Chapter Fifteen

Par gazed at the gentle waves where Lani had disappeared. Enio stood beside him. The surf whispered at their feet, muttering the secrets of the sea. Secrets no human knew.

But maybe Lani did.

"I'd always thought," Lady Agatha said behind them, "that the tales of nymphs were just stories. But your friend seems a lovely, uh, person."

"She is," Par said, together with Enio.

"Before we go," Agatha added, "we must deal with a few things. Par is short for Parynius, yes?"

After a last glance at the shimmering water, Par turned to face their journey's next stage. "Parynius Ignatious, with the enlightened part."

"Both are blatantly Elorian. You need something different."

"A new name?" Par liked the one he had.

She rubbed her chin. "If we change them too much and one of us forgets, we would draw suspicion. So drop the Ignatious, and if anyone asks, Par is short for Paracelsus."

Enio snorted. "Sounds like a fancy name for the runs."

At least Par got to keep the main piece. He shrugged. "I'll take it."

"And Enio is short for…?"

"Enius Marius," Enio said, puffing out his chest.

"All right. Enio is now a nickname for Asenio."

"Asenio." Enio rolled the word around his mouth. "Works for me."

"Not bad," Par said. "How many s's in that?"

"Yeah, how many—" Enio stopped short and narrowed his eyes at Par.

Par smiled smugly.

"Next," Agatha went on, "if we're asked our business, we need a backstory. You two have completed your Ascension—the Arcanan version of a Lustering. You've just left your homes near Dado in the Borderlands to seek your fortunes in Aurix. None of us have ever been there. Your parents have entrusted me to be your patron."

"Patron?" Par asked.

"A sponsor. It's my responsibility to guide your transition and vouch for your work ethic. I'll say I managed my husband's silversmith shop, handled the books and helped with the plating. Which reminds me: your Lustering medals—you'll need to leave them here."

Par touched the chain around his neck, another sure giveaway he was from Eloria. His heart made a quiet complaint. His pendant had come with long struggles and pain. So had Enio's.

"We have no tokens of Ascendancy to replace them," Agatha said. "Rings and crystals and such. But they aren't mandatory, like your pendants are in Eloria. Still, we must assign you to celestial houses."

"What's a celestial house?" Par removed his pendant from his neck.

"It's like your enlightened names. There are dozens of houses. The date, or the season and circumstances of your birth often dictate the choices. Families pick among those or let an officiant do it. In our case, we're limited by the ones I remember. You, Par, will be of the House of the Traveling Mage."

Par grinned. "Mage? Nice."

"What's mine?" Enio asked.

Agatha seemed to consider. "House of the Temperate Spheres."

"The what?"

"The Temperate Spheres. Think of the vast night sky, its peace and balance of—"

"I want a different one."

"Why? Celestial houses don't confer any special status."

"Well, what temperature is it?"

"What temperature is what?"

"The temperature sphere."

"No, it's the *Temperate*—"

Enio spun to Par. "Trade me."

"Nope."

"You're anything but a mage."

"And I never will be. But I like the sound of it."

"I broke you out of prison. You owe me." Enio's voice tightened. His eyes became hard, unblinking.

Par could argue he'd done plenty for Enio too. But he'd seen this reaction before, and it often led to another outburst.

"Fine. Take it." They couldn't afford that *other* Enio around right now. Besides, living with the name Asenio was bad enough.

"Enio, the traveling mage." Enio smiled.

"Now you owe *me*," Par said.

Agatha sighed. "Now that you've gotten that settled, our clothing."

"I'm keeping this." Enio put a hand on his green-feathered cap.

But Par saw a chance to get rid of the ridiculous thing. "Sorry. Not if—"

"The cap is not a problem," Agatha cut in. "One thing you learn with travel—every place has its odd characters. It might just help him blend."

For a moment, Par imagined robes and funny hats, like Vex sometimes wore. All they had now were plain tunics and trousers. "Where do we get different clothes?"

"You're both fine. The poor look the same everywhere. It's the rich whose dress differs. Stash your pendants. I have alterations to make." She hiked the hem of her dress.

Par nudged Enio, and they climbed aboard the *Sea Dog*. Enio tucked the pendants into a nook in the hold. Before looking back to the beach, Par called, "Are you decent?"

"Yes," Agatha said. Her dress had been transformed. The fancy pleats and tucks were gone—just a simple, dull olive tunic. "In my early trading days, I spruced up used clothing. Never had to spruce down before. But this is also more functional."

She removed her earrings and pocketed them. "I suppose that's everything. Let's get moving."

Enio patted the mast. "Wait here, *Sea Dog*." He hopped from the boat. Par followed. They left the beach with Lady Agatha, following the trickle of a creek through the trees and up a vale until they crested higher ground. A dirt road ran above the sea. They followed that east.

No one else was in sight. The road rose and fell along the coast, or nudged inland before bending seaward once more. Snow-crowned mountains peeked above the southern horizon under a steel-blue sky. At first, Par and his companions chatted over their backstory or recent events. But the conversation dropped off—quiet seemed safer. They were behind enemy lines.

When the sun reached its summit, they stopped for a short midday meal, then dusted themselves off and continued up the road. The raw countryside flattened into tended fields. In the distance, homesteads appeared, some with workers at their labors. Par watched them suspiciously. *Arcanans.* His insecurity grew.

Late in the afternoon, an open-bed wagon pulled by a stout chestnut horse rumbled toward them.

"I'll do the talking," Agatha said. She waved to the driver.

"Whoa, Moonshine!" The grey-bearded man wore a wide, flat hat like a plate, and a heavy black coat. Wool, and in this sun? Par itched just looking at it.

The horse whinnied and stopped.

"Lovely day," Agatha said.

The man spit a thick brown liquid onto the roadside. A thin streak of it painted his beard. "No finer."

"We're bound for Aurix. Is it far?"

He looked them up and down. "You're goin' ta Aurix?

"These two are newly Ascended. We're—"

"Didn't mean ta pry. On foot? Another day."

"Any towns between?"

"I just come from Wishbone. About a league back."

He leaned forward, his eyes catching the sun with a sharp glimmer. His chapped lips grinned over yellow teeth. "Looking ta buy some quartz?"

"Quartz?" Agatha said.

He tossed his chin toward the back of his wagon. "Finest between here and the crystal road. Got most houses. What I don't got, I can get."

"Thank you. We just need a place for tonight."

The man's grin evaporated. "Well, Wishbone's got a inn."

They thanked him again. He snapped his horse and continued past.

Par let out a relieved breath. Their first encounter with an actual Arcanan had gone without a problem.

Soon the spaces between scattered homesteads shortened. A

plump man on horseback overtook them but rode past without a word. A larger, cloth-hooded wagon approached from ahead and passed with the laughter of children.

"We must be getting close to something," Par said.

The road crested a gentle hill. He was right. A village lay below, at the water's edge, near a modest harbor dotted with boats with hanging nets and unfurled sails.

"Think it's safe?" Par asked as they walked down.

"Well," Agatha answered, "we wanted to accustom ourselves to the culture before we reached Aurix. This place looks as good as any."

Par was still eager to get to Aurix and search for Vex. But Lady Agatha was right. And they needed to rest. Better a village than a strange road or wilderness. "What if there's trouble?" he asked.

Without hesitation, Enio said, "I'll handle it."

Unsure how serious his friend was, Par eyed him.

Enio wasn't smiling.

Chapter Sixteen

They followed the road to where it met the harbor. The town stretched inland, beyond a wooden arch that read *Wishbone.* There were no gates or guards. Par and his group entered beneath the arch into the town square.

It looked like every coastal or river village he'd ever seen. Crowds wandered the tented booths and the tables of fishmongers. There were shops and simple rustic buildings, troughs and chicken cages, and people laughing or arguing or hurrying along with their bags and baskets. Even the pungent smells of the fish and horses were familiar.

Yet this was a village of Arcana. Par looked harder for differences and found them. Many doorframes were decorated with colorful pieces of crystal. No temple spires rose into the sky, and no stained-glass windows or statues of the saints glistened under the low sun: things Par had taken for granted back home.

He tried to ooze innocence, as if he were another Arcanan out for a stroll. But despite the anxiety he hid, the villagers barely gave him a glance.

As he passed a break between the shops, shouts of laughter

caught his ear. A large dirt field spread behind the buildings. Several youths, about his age or younger, gathered near a long wooden rail that ran down the middle of the plot. Two wore grassy hats and held tall, stiff reed stalks.

Enio paused beside him. "Jousting?"

Agatha stopped too. "Before we find the inn, I need to trade my earrings for local money. You two mingle. Much can be learned about a people from their children."

Par nodded. It seemed safe enough. Plus, that game looked interesting.

"But remember." She lowered her voice. "Don't do anything to stand out."

Agatha continued into town. Par and Enio walked up the sidelines.

A short scrawny boy sat alone on a set of bleachers, scratching in the ground with a twig. The others chatted near the center wooden rail. Their clothes were dusty with dirt and straw. Another boy with his arm in a crude sling squatted over a smoldering campfire.

Par settled with Enio near the younger kid on the bleachers. His clothes weren't dirty like the others.

"Hello," Par said.

"Hi." The boy did a double-take at Enio's feathered cap.

"I'm Par. I mean Paracelsus. I mean Par." Par grimaced—he should have practiced that. "This is Enio."

"I'm Leo," said the boy. He focused on Enio's green feather.

Enio tipped his head toward the field. "What are they playing?"

Leo dropped his gaze back to the dirt. "Fire joust."

The jousting setup was familiar. Par had seen something similar in his hometown. But *fire* joust?

Enio pointed to Leo's dirt drawing. "That's a fire-fly sigil."

"What's a sigil?" Leo looked back up.

Par's heart skipped a beat. Enio had used the Elorian term. "It's, um… it's a glyph or a rune. We say it in the Borderlands sometimes." He knocked Enio's ankle with his boot. "Because that's where we're from."

Enio grunted, but Leo turned instead to the field. The voices had risen.

"Who's my next victim?" barked a tall redheaded boy. He held up his stalk, thick at the grip but tapered toward the top.

"You just went, Galen," said a scraggly-haired girl.

"You're not in charge, Ophelia. How about Joran?"

Joran rubbed his chest beneath a green cape. He was a bit more stocky than the rest. "My numena is dubious. And you hit too hard."

Galen laughed and jabbed the stalk at the boy's stomach. "Through all that? Elek, then."

Par had been stuck on the sidelines of enough sigil games to understand that Leo wasn't seen as a valued player. He leaned toward the boy. "What are the rules?"

Leo pointed his twig at the jousters. "Two captains face off, riding up on someone's shoulders. They charge, and the first captain that gets knocked off loses."

"Isn't that dangerous?" Par's asked in disbelief.

"The lances are bendy at the tip. It's mainly the grabs and punches that get you."

That didn't much improve Par's opinion of the game.

But Leo hadn't finished. "They also light the tips on fire."

"They what?" Par nearly choked.

"And," Leo continued, "each captain wears a hat, called the *tower*. If one captain can swipe the flame from the enemy lance onto that other captain's hat, he's taken the tower and is general for the day. His word is law."

Enio nodded. "Using a fire-fly. Nice."

"But that hardly ever happens," Leo added. "Mostly, one side wins when the other captain falls."

"What if," Enio said, "a captain holds their lance away, so the other team can't reach his flame?"

Par eyed his friend, hoping he wasn't getting any ideas.

"There are lots of strategies," Leo said with a shrug. "That one leaves him open, and he gets knocked off hard. Watch—Stefan's starting a joust."

Ophelia had persuaded Joran to be her steed by promising him a cinnamon muffin. The boy with the arm sling returned from the fire, carrying a burning stick. He lit the clumps of straw on the tips of the stalks. Ophelia wore a cloth around her head tied like a bonnet. Galen wore a dirty, frayed cap. Each had a fist-sized tuft of straw rising from the top—their towers—which remained unlit.

Stefan positioned the opponents twenty paces apart. Joran squatted to help Ophelia get on his shoulders. Across the rail, Galen hiked onto the pony-tailed Elek. The steeds wrapped their arms around their riders' legs and took a moment to find their balance and stand straight.

When everything was set, Stefan held up his good arm. "Lances ready!"

Ophelia and Galen pointed their stalks more or less toward each other.

"Charge!"

The steeds stumbled forward beneath their riders, picking up speed. The others cheered them on. As the jousters reached the rail's midpoint, the silver sparkle of an Arcanan incantation twinkled around each rider's head.

Galen swiped and missed the oncoming flame. His own stalk had tilted high, toward Ophelia's face. She slapped at Galen's flame as she ducked and twisted. The flame arced away and fizzled.

Everyone booed.

But Par shook his head, less amazed at the fire-fly than at the fact that no one had gotten hurt.

"They're ham-fisting it," Enio said. "like trying to punch smoke."

Leo turned to him. "You know how to do it better?"

"I know how not to do it wrong."

"Do you think…" Leo hesitated. "Could you show me?"

Par stifled a chuckle. Enio might be a gifted sigil user, Elorian and otherwise, but he'd never gotten the hang of any teacher-student relationship.

"What's so funny?" Enio peered at Par.

"That wasn't me. That was your past instructors choking on their tongues."

"Please?" Leo said.

Enio pursed his lips. "You've got the fire-fly, uh, glyph, right?"

Leo nodded enthusiastically.

"All right." Enio glanced around. "Behind the bleachers."

Leo's face brightened. He hopped to his feet and dashed that way.

Par gripped Enio's arm and whispered, "They're *Arcanans*."

"I know." Enio pulled loose.

"But Agatha said—"

"—to mingle."

"Yeah, mingle, not stand out."

"We stand out by just sitting."

Before Par could work his way through that logic, Enio disappeared around the bleachers. Par hurried after.

The ground there was littered with broken, brittle straw. Enio found two short pieces and handed one to Par. "Hold this up."

Other than Leo, no one else could see them. Maybe this would be all right.

Enio backed away. He invoked to light his own straw. As he did, his glory flashed gold. Par gasped. It was such a basic sigil that Enio hadn't thought twice. But a golden glory was a dead giveaway that they were from Eloria.

Luckily, Leo's gaze never left the straw. Par chewed his lip. He'd yell at Enio later.

With the smooth gesture of a monk conducting morning chants, Enio invoked again—this time, with the silver glory of his Arcanan fire-fly. He finger-brushed the flame. It leapt from the straw and traced an easy arc through the air, landing on the very point of Par's.

"Wow." Leo hurried to the lit straw. "That was perfect."

"Thanks," Enio said. "Some people don't appreciate *how* perfect." He glanced at Par.

At least to himself, Par had to admit it had been flawless.

"See," Enio continued, "instead of clobbering the flame, you need to guide it, help it go. It *wants* to fly. It *wants* to land on something. That's like its purpose in life." He handed Leo the burning straw. "Now you do it."

Par had never heard a sigil explained so well. He'd mention that to Enio later—after yelling at him.

Enio found a fresh piece. "Remember, easy. Don't force it."

Leo's head twinkled with a faint silver glory. He brushed at his flame, but missed. Tried again. Missed.

"Focus," Enio said.

Leo took a breath, narrowed his eyes, then brushed once more.

The flame shot from the straw—straight at Enio's face.

Enio jerked and dodged. The flame missed his face by a hair and snuffed out.

"Sorry!" Leo yelped. "Are you hurt?"

"I'm fine." Enio rubbed his nose. "You did it too hard, like *they* do. But it took a good fly. You can do it. Just keep practicing."

A voice drifted from the field. "No one else?"

Leo's nostrils flared. His lips tightened. "Me!" He took off running around the bleachers.

"You think he's ready?" Par said, frowning.

Enio opened his mouth to say something, stopped, and bolted after Leo.

"Crap." Par hurried behind them.

Leo was already with the group. "I can do one."

"You?" Galen laughed.

Joran shook his head. "Dubious."

Ophelia rested a gentle hand on Leo's shoulder. "You shouldn't—"

"No one's going to be your mount, anyway," Galen said.

Leo slumped and began to turn away.

But Enio stepped beside him. "I will."

Chapter Seventeen

Par reached the jousting rail just after Enio had opened his big mouth.

"Who are you guys?" asked the red-haired Galen.

"I'm Par. He's Enio. We're passing through from Dado. We should get going."

Enio ignored him. "How about it?"

"With Leo?" Galen rolled his eyes. "You're kidding."

"Afraid you'll lose?" Enio said.

Galen studied Enio, sizing him up. Enio was on the skinny side, like Leo, though taller. Galen's gaze fell on Enio's feathered cap and a grin grew across his face. "It's your funeral. Who's my mount?"

The others crowded around Leo. Whispers of "You're sure?" "You got the numena?" and "Dubious" floated among them.

Par pulled Enio aside. He kept his voice low. "*Now* who's off their rudder?"

A smile flickered across Enio's lips. "I'll be the first Elorian to battle on Arcanan soil since the Grey Wars."

"Don't even make jokes like that."

"All right, but listen: Galen is fat-headed and clumsy. Leo's got the stuff. He only needs a chance to show it."

There was an unspoken remark in Enio's expression. *You know what it's like.*

Par did. How many years had he struggled with his own self-worth because he couldn't invoke? He glanced at the kids surrounding Leo—and at Leo himself: full of fear, full of hope.

"Fine," Par said, not quite feeling it. "But promise. No showing off. No more Elorian sigils."

"Don't worry. I'm just the mount." He handed Par his feathered hat and turned to Leo. "Let's do this."

Joran agreed to be Galen's mount to even out the height differences. Ophelia strapped a straw-topped bonnet onto Leo's head. Once their lance-tips were lit, both teams separated twenty paces. Enio helped Leo onto his shoulders. The rest of the kids backed away. Stefan moved near the middle and raised his arm. "Lances ready!"

Galen and Leo raised their stalks.

Par clenched his teeth.

"Charge!"

To a thunder of shouts, Joran and Enio stumbled forward carrying their riders. Leo's lance pointed along the rail, level with Galen's chest. Several dusty strides later, Galen's lance whacked Leo's lance sideways. As Leo's grip fumbled, Galen swiped with a fist. It struck the side of Leo's head.

Leo cried out, dropped his lance, and grabbed his ear.

Enio held tightly to Leo's legs and kept him from toppling off. Both sides turned and stopped.

Leo's face was red. He seemed to hold back tears.

"Hey!" Ophelia yelled, "not the head!"

"I wasn't," Galen called. "That new kid weaved."

"He didn't!"

"He did!"

"Very dubious," Joran said.

Stefan hurried back to the middle. "Nobody fell. It's a tie."

Leo straightened up. "No. Someone hand me my lance."

Par brought it over. "Leo, are you sure?"

"I'm going again." He wiped his nose.

"You tell 'em," Enio said.

Par lowered his voice. "Enio, Galen seems pretty rough—"

"Galen is an ass. We can do this." He spoke to Leo. "Focus on where you want the flame to land, not where it is. Once it flies, your job's done. Duck then if you have to."

Stefan checked each rider, adjusted their hats and relit the stalks. He paced them off and returned to the midpoint.

"Ready!" he called.

Par took a deep breath and held it.

"Charge!"

Leo shouted, "Gah! Gah!" Dirt and straw flew from Enio's heels. Galen's lance jiggled and bobbed. He was laughing.

Again the riders met. Galen raised his fist for another blow, and his stalk took an upward bounce. Leo's hair sparkled with a silver glory as he reached for the flame, but before he could dodge, Galen's lance hit his neck—and splintered. Leo's shouts broke off; he flew from Enio's shoulders. Galen's fist slammed into Enio's face. Enio twisted and tumbled into the dirt.

Everyone cried out.

Enio seemed shaken but recovering. But Leo lay flat on his back. Par got to him first. He wasn't moving. Blood pooled in the dirt beside his neck.

"He's hurt!" Par shouted.

The others arrived. Elek leaned closer. "Anyone have enough numena for healing?"

Ophelia dropped to her knees beside Leo. A faint silver light blinked around her head and she touched his neck.

Blood continued to pulse from a gash.

She drew back. "It's not enough. Someone get help."

Elek ran off.

Then, his face contorted like a rabid dog, Enio pushed into the group. He went straight at Galen. "You son of a—"

Par leapt between them. "Don't—"

Enio backhanded a fist at Par and caught his chin.

Par staggered to the side.

Enio strode on.

Galen stumbled back. "Wait, I didn't—"

Enio tackled Galen hard to the ground.

"Enio!" Par yelled, shaking off the punch.

"No *more*, Cronus." Enio wrapped his hands around Galen's throat.

Cronus?

Galen squirmed and gagged.

"Enio," Par yelled. "Stop! Leo's hurt!"

With a toothy snarl, Enio glanced up. When he saw Leo, his grip loosened. "Oh, crap."

He left Galen and hurried to Leo. After a quick examination of the wound, he looked at Par. "It's bad. I have to."

There was no choice. Par nodded. "Do it."

A golden glory shone around Enio's head. He kept it going longer than Par had ever seen. The others gasped and backed away.

As Leo opened his eyes, Enio's glory flickered out. The bleeding had stopped, and the wound had healed.

Galen joined them, panting. "Did you see? That kid's aura was gold! He conjured like an Elorian!"

Par turned to the remaining kids. They watched wide-eyed, confused.

He shook his head. "I can't explain it. But if you tell, we'll be in terrible trouble." He didn't know what else to say.

Leo was sitting up. "What happened?"

"You got knocked. Are you all right?" Par helped him stand.

The boy winced and rubbed his neck. "I think so."

"That wasn't my fault," Galen said. "And we warned him—"

"Wait." Stefan pointed to Galen's hat, now on the ground.

The top was smoldering.

The others seemed as stunned by the sight as by Enio's invocation. They glanced wordlessly at each other.

Ophelia broke the silence. "Leo won."

"I did?" Leo said.

"You did!" cheered Joran.

Par hadn't yet seen Leo smile. The grin he gave now looked like an entire day's worth.

"But that new kid's aura—" Galen began.

Leo cut him off and asked Stefan, "That means I'm general, right?"

"Your word is law."

"Then I order no one says anything about Enio's aura being gold." He looked around.

One after another, they nodded. Some even chuckled.

"But—" Galen tried again.

Ophelia jabbed a finger at him. "If you do, we'll tell *everyone* you've been aiming high."

"I didn't—"

"You'll be banned from the fire jousts," Stefan said.

Joran crossed his arms. "Nothing dubious about *that*."

Galen's shoulders slumped. With a sigh and a nod, he held his hand to Leo. "You took a solid hit. You're pretty tough, General Leo."

Leo shook it. "Thanks."

Enio murmured to Par, "I still want to hammer him."

"Yeah," Par said and passed him back his feathered cap. "But he's shutting up about your invocation. Leave it alone."

Elek returned with several adults. Lady Agatha was among them.

A short, middle-aged woman with curly brown hair and a surprising amount of freckles ran forward. "Leo?"

Leo met her, brushing off his pants. "I got knocked, Mom. I'm fine now."

She checked him over. "Your clothes—the blood—"

"I got cut, but he healed me." Leo gestured to Enio.

Lady Agatha advanced. Par could almost feel the heat in her stare. But she took a breath and spoke to Leo's mother. "I'm sorry if there's been any trouble. We're passing through from Dado. Come, Paracelsus and Asenio. I've found the inn."

Leo's mother traced the run of blood on Leo's shirt to his neck, then hugged him tightly.

"*Mom.*" Leo rolled his eyes.

She turned to Enio. "You healed my son?"

Enio shrugged. "It wasn't that bad."

The mother stood and faced Agatha. "The innkeeper is a crook. You'll stay with us."

"That's very kind," Lady Agatha said. "But—"

"We've got the space. I won't take no for an answer."

"Great!" Leo grabbed Enio's arm. "They can sleep in my room."

Agatha hesitated. "Then we gratefully accept. I promise we won't be a burden."

As they walked off the field, she leaned to Par.

"Especially," she whispered, "after I strangle you both."

Chapter Eighteen

THEY LEFT THE field of battle. The other kids waved from behind and shouted, "General Leo! General Leo!"

Leo waved back, his head high.

His mother introduced herself as Nell. She asked them to wait outside a fish shop where she'd been buying supper.

Once Nell went in, Par expected Lady Agatha to let loose. But she didn't. She only stood before him, arms crossed, her face granite. He decided he'd explain everything later, though he wasn't sure he could justify any of it.

Nell returned with a covered basket and they continued on. Leo walked beside her, answering questions about his injury and telling of his victory.

Still Agatha said nothing.

Soon they came to a lane near a creek lined with cozy cottages and apple trees, the low sun's rays falling pink through the branches. They turned into Nell's small home. A man with a thick black mustache and bushy ear tufts stood inside, undoing his full leather apron.

Nell and he shared a quick kiss. "We have guests, Cyrus."

"Well, then," he said and grinned, "come in and let your sleeves down."

As they entered, Nell ushered Leo aside. "Put on a clean shirt. Agatha, you and your boys can wash up out back."

"Thank you, Nell." Agatha gave Par an icy stare.

He gulped and followed her through the little home.

Leo called after them, "Smoky doesn't bite."

"Your dog?" Par asked.

"My crow."

Outside waited a lidded water barrel. Old but clean wash-cloths hung on pegs. A large crow rested on top. It cawed and flew over the roof.

They each took a cloth. Par dusted himself and splashed his face.

After a minute of silent cleaning, Lady Agatha said abruptly, "Exactly what were you *thinking*?"

Par sighed. "It just sort of happened. Leo—"

"Leo got hurt," Enio said, fingering out an ear. "What were we supposed to do?"

Agatha grunted. "He wouldn't have needed healing if you hadn't taken sides."

"There weren't really *sides*."

"There are always sides. And it's critical *ours* remain secret." Her tone softened. "However, once that boy was wounded, I suppose I'd have done the same."

"Speaking of staying secret," Par said, "you accepted Nell's invitation awfully quick."

Agatha twisted out her cloth and hung it back on a peg. "Too much protesting also draws attention. Besides, we'll need money in Aurix and I'll get more for my earrings there than here."

She smoothed out her dress. "Let's go inside. Watch what you say."

They returned to the cottage. As the odor of sizzling fish filled his nose, Par got his first chance to really examine the inside of an Arcanan home. It was tidy and clean, not unlike the cottage in which he was born. The main room had a central table, a stone fireplace and hearth. Small nooks decorated the walls, as in his parents' cottage, and it gave his heart a stab of homesickness. In Elorian homes, these nooks might be filled with statues of saints or gods. But here they held colorful crystals that glistened in the firelight. Some were beautiful, like glass flowers.

Par paused at a pink, fist-sized orb with fingerlike spikes.

Agatha whispered in his ear. "Also, don't touch anything." Then she eyed a nook with an orange crystal and her voice rose. "Is that citrine?"

Nell filled cups from a pitcher. "You know your quartz. We had a milky one for our house crystal, but this type promised success in business." She glanced at Leo, who chatted with his father, then lowered her voice. "And they say citrine helps with self-esteem."

Agatha followed her gaze. "I'd say it's working."

"Perhaps, thanks to your two young charges."

Agatha glanced at Par.

He gave his most angelic smile.

Once everyone had helped lay plates and spread out the food, they settled into chairs. Leo's crow landed on a windowsill and pecked at crumbs. Agatha snatched off Enio's hat and handed it back to him.

"Sun is setting," Cyrus said. He raised his cup. "High the Umbriarch."

"High the Umbriarch," repeated Leo and Nell.

Agatha nodded to Par and Enio. They echoed the words, though Par didn't know what they meant.

"So," Cyrus added as they began their meal, "what brings you to Wishbone?"

Agatha answered with the simple details of their backstory,

then nudged the topic back to Nell and her family. They learned Cyrus was a leather worker, and Nell a teacher about salt and other herbs, though not dealing with food. Par didn't quite understand that either.

Nell passed Enio a loaf. "With your healing skill, you'll have no trouble finding work in Aurix."

When neither Enio nor Agatha responded, Par said, "He's been practicing. But Leo just got a bad scratch."

"That scratch—" Nell began.

"I'm *fine*, Mom," Leo said. "And I won. So… can we do Happy the Table?"

Leo's father lowered a cup from his lips. "Perhaps we shouldn't inflict that upon our guests."

"Happy the Table?" Agatha asked enthusiastically, apparently encouraging the shift of topic.

"A tradition for celebrations and happy times." Cyrus frowned. "It involves singing."

"Come on," Leo urged.

"We'd love to hear it," Agatha said.

Nell eyed her husband. "Then you *shall*."

Cyrus sighed.

Leo tapped out a steady rhythm on his mug with a spoon. Nell followed the beat with her hand on the table. Par glanced at Enio, and they did the same.

Cyrus held up his cup, cleared his throat, and sang:

> *Happy the Table when family's together*
> *Sharing our supper or telling a tale.*
> *But happier still if I'd sold all my leather.*
> *To hells with a flagon, I'd drink from a pail.*

He took a hearty swallow.

Par laughed. Enio snorted.

"Dear," Nell said, "I don't think that one is appropriate."

Cyrus winked and wiped his mouth.

Leo continued his tapping. "Now you, Mom."

She stood and clasped her hands. A few practice notes suggested she couldn't quite hit the tune.

Happy the Table with new friends around it.
We'll miss their dear faces when they must depart.
But happier still, since here or in spirit,
They'll always be welcome in home and in heart.

"Lovely," Agatha said with a broad smile.

Cyrus held up his mug. "Better than mine."

"Now me." Leo stood. Everyone's tapping continued as he worked something out in his head.

"Any day now," his father prompted.

"All right, all right." Leo filled his lungs and bellowed,

Happy the Table where sits General Leo.
He fought and he conquered. His word is the law!
But happier still 'cuz his friends Par and Enio
Helped him to… um… helped him to…

Just then, the crow cawed.

Par gestured at it with his cup. "Helped him to caw!"

"Caw!" Everyone laughed and drank. Full of cheer, they returned to their meal.

The conversation stayed light and, thankfully, away from Leo's healing. Soon, the adults were talking among themselves, and Par and Enio listened while Leo told them about his town.

It was dark outside as they finished. Nell asked, "When will you leave for Aurix?"

Lady Agatha patted a napkin to her lips. "First thing tomorrow."

"It's fine timing," Cyrus said. "Our astromancer predicts good weather."

Nell chuckled. "And sometimes, he even gets it right."

"Are you on foot?" Cyrus asked.

Lady Agatha nodded. "We are."

"I'm sorry we don't have horses to lend."

"That's very kind, but we enjoy the walk."

Par didn't agree, but he kept quiet.

They cleared the table and cleaned the plates. By this time, Leo was nodding off. Nell jostled him awake and led them all to his little bedroom with its simple cot and single window.

"Make your friends comfortable," she said. "Agatha, I'll show you the spare. It's small, but the bed is soft."

"That will be wonderful." Lady Agatha followed her out.

Leo cleared clothes and other small items from his bedroom floor. He pointed at a closed wooden box. "Put that someplace. I'll get blankets."

Enio took the box. The contents rattled. "What's in it?"

"My collections. Shells, buttons, beaks…" Leo was out the door.

"Beaks?" Enio peeked inside. "Kids here are weird."

"You collected bootlaces," Par said.

"That's apples and onions. I sold three for a copper, cleaned up."

Leo made two trips for bedding. They laid out comfortable heaps that filled most of the narrow floor space. Everyone said their goodnights.

Par lay beside Enio, back-to-back. Soon Leo was gently snoring. A waxing moon glowed outside the window. It felt strange to Par that the moon should look so similar to the one that had risen past his bedroom in St. Livius. Of course, it was the same.

But even with the differences—the crystals, fire joust, Leo's beaks—Arcana didn't seem as alien as Par had expected. The farms and towns, the kids and stores and families, were close cousins, if not brothers, to those in Eloria.

"Looks like we're getting some luck," he whispered.

Enio muttered back, "Wishbone is living up to its name."

Thoughts of the fight with Galen returned to Par's mind. Had he heard right? Had Enio called Galen *Cronus*? But thank the gods, Enio had focused on healing Leo instead of fighting. Otherwise, how far might things have gone?

Par decided not to bring it up and risk an outburst. Besides, there was another big question still drifting around in his head.

He rolled over and propped himself on an elbow. "You haven't told me what happened with you and Lani." The last time Par had asked, he'd gotten no answer. He wouldn't bring up Enio's attack on the stags, but that wink Lani and Enio had shared…

When Enio didn't answer, Par tried again. "I said, you haven't—"

"It's… kind of private."

"Private?" One thing his friend had never had much use for was boundaries. A funny feeling raked through Par's stomach, like butterflies with cold wings. "What's going on, Enio?"

Another dark pause floated between them. "I'm not supposed to say."

"Why not?"

"They made me promise."

"Who? The stags?"

"No, not the stags."

"Was it Lani?" Par spirits slumped more.

"Well, not exactly, but she—"

Par took the opening. "You think she wouldn't tell *me*? Your best friend? After everything we've been through, you and me and Lani?"

Enio was silent for another moment. He flopped over and faced Par. His eyes glittered with the barest sheen. "You can't tell *anyone*."

"Seriously, who would I tell?"

The words spilled out, hushed and urgent. "The stags took me, Par, me and the *Sea Dog*, a long way. Out beyond Eloria and Arcana. Past the Eastern Barriers, I think."

Par could barely believe his ears. Those monstrous reefs and jagged islands were as far as any sane ship dared to sail toward the rising sun. Beyond that was endless sea.

"We went faster," Enio continued, "and deeper, until it was pitch dark except for the élan around the stags. Then, I saw the lights."

"Lights? Under the sea?"

"Not only lights. Mountains! And things swimming around them. Amazing things, Par. Gigantic, awful, crazy things. Some only shadows, some bright with glories."

On his cot, Leo yawned and stirred.

Par waited a moment. "Think he heard?"

"If he's listening," Enio said a tad louder, "we'll have to kill him."

Par smirked. Leo's breathing steadied again.

Enio went on. "Below the mountains was this huge trench cut into the sea floor. The stags took me in there. We seemed to go down forever. But finally, everything opened big and bright and… into another world."

Par stared, wide-eyed.

The moonlight caught one of Enio's broken side teeth with a weird glitter. "The lands were lit by shining clouds above burning horizons, as if dawn came from all directions but never broke. We flew—or swam, I don't know—over forests and meadows and hills so alive, Par, they seemed to breathe the élan like we breathe air. And then I saw towers, and palaces, I think made of coral and crystal."

This was so fantastic that Par wondered if his friend had imagined it; he must have been pretty knocked around in the *Sea Dog*. But the look in his eyes pushed away any doubts.

Enio licked his lips. "The stags took me to one of those palaces. Lani found me there."

"That's where she's been?"

Enio nodded. "She called it the Deep World. And there was a lady with green hair—their queen, I think. Lani told me these people helped lay the charm on the rock at Argent. They even fixed my mast and keel."

"Why is this all so secret?"

"They don't want the land nations to know they're down there. I'm not sure why."

All this must be the reason for Lani's wink at Enio. The guilty jealousy that had been simmering in Par's liver fizzled a bit. "Maybe, after we've found Vex, she can show me the Deep World too."

"Lani said they don't let anyone in who can't commune with the élan."

"Oh," Par said, a little disappointed. "Well, as long as she doesn't spend too much time away, right?"

Enio seemed about to say something before changing his mind. He lay back. "Yeah. But you haven't seen the Deep World. It's hard to get it out of my head."

They were quiet after that. Par didn't fall right to sleep. It wasn't images of the Deep World that kept him awake. It was the other thing Enio had said. Or hadn't said.

However long Lani stayed in the Deep World, Enio could join her.

But not Par.

Chapter Nineteen

A FTER A BREAKFAST of griddle cakes, Par and his friends prepared to leave. Leo's father had a quick errand to run and said to wait for his return. They lingered beneath an apple tree as Leo showed them the things he'd taught Smoky, like how to eat from his hand.

Cyrus returned down the shady lane carrying a small bundle. A woman in a grey traveling cloak walked beside him. Straight black hair framed her ruddy cheeks, and she wore long leather gloves and boots that stretched to her knees. A mud-brown donkey with swollen saddlebags trailed the pair.

"Food for the road," Cyrus said and tossed his bundle to Par, who scrambled with Enio to catch it. "And this is Kaj. She's a courier on her way to Aurix and has agreed to escort you."

She lifted a pendant that hung from her neck, shaped like a half sun against a half moon. "Pleased to meet you."

Nell pointed it out to Leo. "See? That's a medallion of trust from the capital."

"Can I touch it?" Leo said.

Kaj smiled and bent forward. "Go ahead."

Her words were dusty, like her clothes. She didn't seem much older than Lani, but something in her voice and her weathered eyes held additional years.

When Leo finished examining the pendant, Kaj straightened and patted her donkey. "My stoic friend here is called Lightning."

"Lightning?" Par said. The animal sure didn't look like lightning.

Kaj gave an easy laugh. "You'd be surprised. We make good time."

"Thank you for the offer," Agatha said. "But I'm told if we keep to the sea road, it will take us to Aurix." She grinned politely, but Par had known her long enough to tell it was forced.

"Nonsense," Leo's mother said. "You can't just go all niddle-noodle down roads you've never traveled."

"And it's no trouble," Kaj added. "Plus, there's always more safety in numbers."

Agatha seemed to consider, then broke into a nod. "Perhaps you're right. We're grateful to have you along."

They made introductions all around, followed by thanks and farewells. Enio gave Leo a few last pointers on his fire-fly as Kaj packed their food bundle on her donkey. They left Leo and his family with waves and well wishes and hopes to meet again. While Par was eager to get on with their journey, his heart softly complained at leaving a place that felt like a home.

As Kaj led them back to the sea road, Agatha spoke out of her earshot. "I know this wasn't the plan, but if she's already heading to Aurix, there's no avoiding her on the road. Just remember our backstories, and for Oä's sake, don't invoke any Elorian sigils in her presence."

"What if she finds out—" Par began.

"If she's a problem," Agatha said, "there's three of us, and one of her."

Enio strode boldly on. "And one of *us* is from the House of the Traveling Mage."

A last glance back showed the village waking to the day. Fishing boats threw off their lines and let out their sails. Ahead, the road rose once more along the shining sea.

Kaj seemed a cheerful companion, often making comments to Lightning, or whistling a tune. Best of all, she never asked questions. Agatha told her their false backstory. Kaj shared tales of her own travels through Arcana and the Borderlands. Par listened with interest, but whenever a glimmer out on the sea caught his attention, he wondered again about the Deep World Enio had seen beneath the waves.

By noon, the road had risen to its highest point so far, running close along the drop-off above the sea and through a stand of trees. Just ahead, two roughly dressed men leaned against a fat oak. One man was thin, with a cap and a grizzled face, the other short and bald.

The thin one tipped his cap. "Good day to you, noble travelers."

Kaj halted her donkey several paces back. "Good day, friends."

"Friends? Friends and more," the same man replied. "Think of us as business associates."

"Business associates," echoed the bald man with a chuckle.

Par was getting a bad feeling about this. Enio stiffened beside him.

"I see," Kaj said. "Can we help you with anything?"

"Lay down your wallets and jewels, and we'll help ourselves." From beneath his cloak, the thin man raised a pipe of glass or crystal, a forearm long and a finger thick. Par had seen similar metal ones in Eloria—weapons of fighting and of war: rockshooters.

Enio didn't have a wallet, but he reached for the ground. What he had, Par realized, was the Elorian rockshoot sigil. Was he going to grab a stone?

The thin man's glory flashed silver. A spray of dirt puffed from his pipe's barrel, and a pellet shot out. It ricocheted off a rock near Enio's fingers.

Enio fell back.

Lightning bucked. Kaj lost the reins.

"Hold your beast!" barked the man.

The donkey backtracked toward the cliff. Its rear legs kicked rocks over the edge. Par was closest. He grabbed the reins and pulled with all his might, stopping the animal.

"That's better," said the robber. "Now, if you don't want a trip off the edge yourselves—"

He never spoke another word. His head snapped back and his eyes rolled upward, straining toward the knife in his forehead. He slumped to the ground like a sack of grain.

The bald man gaped at his friend. Then raised his hands. "Don't kill me!"

Kaj stepped forward, holding knives in each of hers.

"Please!" He dropped to his knees.

She raised a knife to his throat. With the other, she sliced a string that held a purse to his belt. It dropped to the ground with a heavy chink. "Well, we don't want to keep you."

The man stumbled to his feet and ran gibbering through the trees.

Kaj took the corpse's purse too.

Agatha came to Kaj's side. "Bandits?"

"Or worse," she said.

Enio prodded the dead man with his boot.

Par had pulled the donkey's reins so hard they cut into his palm. "Enio, don't—"

"Just checking." Enio picked up the rockshooter and eyed it along its length.

"May I?" Kaj asked.

Enio gave it to her.

She tossed it off the cliff.

"But—"

"We can't risk carrying a stolen rockshooter into Aurix," she said.

Enio sighed and nodded.

The dead man's mouth hung open, as if he were about to speak. A thin line of blood from the knife trickled over his nose. Kaj yanked her blade out of the man's brain, and at that, Par's stomach heaved. He leapt behind a tree and lost what remained of his breakfast.

As he crouched there, catching his breath and rubbing the burn in his palm, Enio came beside him. "You all right?"

"She killed him," Par gasped.

"They threatened us. They rockshot me. What else could she do?"

"I don't know. Just given them her money?"

"Lady Agatha might. But Kaj isn't her, and she knows the road. Let me see your hand."

Par held it out. It stung even worse than it looked, but after a quick glance back, Enio healed it, out of sight of Kaj.

They returned to the group, Par still a little shaky and trying not to show it.

Kaj packed away the two purses. "I hope you don't mind if I keep these."

"We owe you at least that," Agatha said. "And… the body?"

Enio pointed to the sea. "Toss it."

"We'll leave him be," Kaj said. "The other may come back for him. Perhaps they were family."

Par eyed the man one last time before turning away. They continued along the road. Lady Agatha fell back with Par. Enio stayed near Kaj. They seemed to be discussing her fighting style.

"What do you think of her?" Par asked Agatha.

"I think she may be a blessing after all."

Kaj had spoken the truth in saying she made good time. The pace was brisk, except for rests, mostly when Agatha's breathing became too heavy to hide. Off to their right, the country greened as it spread toward the snow-crusted southern mountains. An occasional wagon or rider appeared on the road. Otherwise, the day turned uneventful.

The road dipped again near sunset, and they camped among trees near a creek and low hills. Par's legs were tired and sore. He could tell so were Enio's and Agatha's. Kaj seemed fine.

"I'll find us some firewood." She shuffled into the brush.

Agatha waited until she had disappeared. "Quick," she said, "heal 'em if you got 'em." Her golden glory twinkled in the dusk. She rubbed her ankles. The strain on her face melted like ice in the sun.

Enio did the same to his calfs.

Par just sat and massaged his muscles as best he could.

Agatha reached over. "Let me." She invoked her sigil once more.

Waves of warmth flowed through Par's legs, up his spine, down to his toes. "Oh, gods…" He sagged blissfully onto his side.

A few minutes later, Kaj's whistling floated from the trees.

"Quick, sit up," Agatha said.

Kaj arrived with an armful of kindling. Par chewed his lip, hoping she didn't expect any of them to invoke and light it.

Their new companion dropped the wood. As Enio helped arrange it with dry grass, she drew a flint from her belt and struck it with a knife blade. After a few tries, sparks ignited the tinder.

Par tried to hide his surprise. Why hadn't she used a flame sigil? In Eloria, those were the most basic ones around. But he knew not to ask Kaj about her methods. The very question might arouse some suspicion, either of their ignorance of normal Arcanan life, or their own avoidance of sigil use or—

"Why don't you use a flame, um, glyph," Enio blurted.

Par almost bit his tongue.

Kaj blew on the embers and coaxed the flames higher. "I've learned to save my numena for emergencies. In the wilds, numena can be the difference between life and death. In the towns and cities too."

"That's fine advice," Agatha said. "We will do the same." She eyed Enio.

But his eyes remained only on Kaj.

They unpacked the food Leo's father had provided—goat cheese and cooked chicken—and shared it around. Kaj's donkey grazed nearby, and as stars speckled the skies, everyone settled in for the night. Except for the robbers, their plan to accustom themselves to the enemy lands of Arcana had gone well enough that Par almost believed, if it came to it, he could live here. But tomorrow he would again focus his all on finding Vex, rescuing the Abbot, and stopping Cronus.

CHAPTER TWENTY

ENIO PLUNGED AGAIN into a black vortex. He spun the wheel of the *Sea Dog* and shouted for help, but the water's roar drowned his words. Down he went into the crushing deep…

He gasped and snapped awake. Par and Agatha slumbered across the ashen remains of the campfire. Kaj sat nearby, in the predawn gloom, cleaning a knife.

"You all right?" she whispered.

Enio caught his breath and nodded.

She rose to her feet and motioned him to follow. He slipped into his boots, his heart still pounding. Careful not to disturb the others, he followed her around a hillock.

He'd shaken off most of the dream as they reached a grove of saplings. "You're up early," he said.

Kneeling, Kaj spread a small, square cloth on the ground. "This is my favorite time of day. Everything's easy and peaceful. You can almost hear the grass yawn."

Enio smiled at the notion.

She met his eyes. Hers twinkled like the last fading stars.

"Even time still seems asleep," she added. "No yesterdays. No tomorrows. Nothing to push us forward or hold us back. Just a precious moment of freedom."

Enio sensed it too. His troubles, his past, seemed muffled and distant.

One by one, Kaj removed knives from within her cloak and laid them on the cloth. "It's also a great time to get a jump on the day." She rose, turning the last knife in her hand, eyeing the blade and handle, testing the weight. Then with a snap of her arm the knife shot through the air like an arrow. It stuck into a tree, in the very center of the bark.

"Nice," Enio said, impressed.

She picked up another and nodded to the one she'd thrown. "Would you mind?"

He hurried over and tugged the blade from the trunk. As he did, she said, "What were you dreaming?"

"I was sailing someplace, I think." He brought the knife to her, trying to remember. "Then I was sinking. Falling."

She took the knife and wiped off the blade. "People say a falling dream means we don't feel in control of our lives."

"Well, I—" Enio caught himself, careful not to give away their mission. But Kaj had hit his frustrations dead center. Last year, when he was at last free to sail the Silver Sea, he'd instead gone to Argent with Par to find Lani. Now, Lani had found him and showed him the Deep World. He longed to make a life out there, away from everything, above the sea, or below.

But freedom had cheated him again. He had to help Par get to Vex because that bastard Cronus was back.

Kaj continued, "Now that you're Ascended, leaving your home must be hard."

Enio figured he could answer *that* much. He grunted. "Wasn't much for me there, anyway."

"No family?"

"None I'll miss."

She offered him the knife. "Want to try?"

Taking it, Enio faced the tree. He was a fire-fly expert, and this would be a chance to show off his perfect aim. He pinched the blade confidently between his fingers and flung the knife forward.

It bounced off the bark.

"At least you hit the tree," Kaj said.

"Hold on." He retrieved the knife. Then he steadied himself, took a breath and threw it again, harder.

It bounced off harder.

"Dammit." Anger and embarrassment flared in his chest.

"Knife throwing takes practice," Kaj said. "If you—"

"I can do it." He prepared for another throw, ignoring the blood pounding in his ears. Ignoring her watchful eyes.

He threw the knife. With a dismal ping, it glanced off the bark.

"Gods dammit!" He kicked the dirt and dropped to his knees, trying to hide a sudden anguish, as if he'd failed some important contest. The world had rigged it like always, snatched away his victory.

Even awake, he was still falling.

"I understand what you're feeling," Kai said. She touched his shoulder.

He looked into those dark eyes with the deep twinkles, and believed she did.

With a soft sigh, she settled beside him. "Sometimes, when we feel out of control, it's because other things have their hooks in us. Things from the past we've tried to ignore. To be truly free, we have to dig them out, get rid of them. Like a bad tooth."

He wiped his nose. Images of his father, of his miserable life in St. Livius—and a life not much better in Argent—marched through his mind. And of everything he'd lost—beginning with his mother. And of Cronus, fouling even her memories.

Enio wasn't being torn up inside because Cronus had returned. The bastard had never really left. Cronus might have been a shadow haunting Par's soul, but he'd infected Enio's soul too.

"How do you do that?" Enio asked as softly. "Get rid of them."

She nudged him playfully and stood. "You're throwing the knife like it's a rock. Come on, let's try again."

He joined her. She handed him a knife. "This time, examine it closely. Get a sense for the balance."

Enio focused on the feel as it rested in his palm.

"It's difficult to get loose from the past," she said, near to his ear. "Something in us never really wants to let go."

Before Enio could stop himself, he blurted, "Par thinks I'm turning into my dad." He couldn't remember Par actually saying it. But Enio was sure that's what his friend was thinking.

"I understand only your frustration, Enio. Your story is your own."

"Yeah," Enio said. "That's what I have. Frustration." And anger.

"Because you're not in control?"

He nodded. The warmth of her breath brushed his cheek.

She pointed to his knife and stood back. "A lot of this is in the make of the weapon. You might do better with one that's more balanced. Mine are blade heavy. This time, grip it by the hilt, not the point."

Enio wrapped his palm around the worn, discolored leather.

"Forget about rocks," she said, "or how you threw things before. Let that all go."

He steadied his breathing. The anger twisting behind his eyes, unwound.

"Remember," she added, "you're more in control when you don't hold tight. Let the knife slip away."

He shifted his weight, bent back his arm and brought the knife near his ear. One deep breath, and he imitated her throwing style. The knife flew. It flipped handle over blade one time and stuck into the tree, drooped, fell out.

"Well done," Kaj said. "With more practice, you'll be as good as me."

Enio smiled. The morning sun was touching the tree-tops.

Kaj collected her knives. "A boat sinks when it's overloaded. To reach your goals, Enio, get rid of the things that weigh you down. No matter how tight you want to hold on to them."

He nodded.

She headed back to the campsite. "Remember, you can't steer your boat by someone else's star."

CHAPTER TWENTY-ONE

PAR SEEMED TO have just closed his eyes when he awoke to morning sun.

Agatha still slept. Kaj sat on a log beside the campfire, whispering with Enio. They were cleaning knives.

Enio giggled at something she said.

Giggled?

Enio's outbursts had occurred less frequently since they'd arrived in Arcana. There was the fight with Galen, but Leo's injury had turned Enio from his rage. Par couldn't remember the last time he'd heard his friend giggle, so having Kaj around must be good for him.

Kaj whispered something else. Enio smiled.

She also appeared to like Enio the best of their group. Suddenly, Par experienced the same gnawing uncertainty he'd felt at the wink Enio and Lani shared. Why did Kaj like Enio better than him, anyway? Was it Enio's independence, his confidence? Or was it the whole bad-boy thing? The dark eyes? The broken side teeth?

Par licked his own teeth. Not perfect, but better than Enio's.

Kaj looked over. "Good morning."

Agatha sat up and yawned. "Good morning, Kaj."

As Agatha discussed with her more details of what lay ahead, Enio joined Par and showed him a knife.

Par touched its dry leather handle. He kept his voice low. "How long have you been up?"

"Not long," Enio balanced the knife across his palm. "She showed me how to throw. Not too different from aiming a fire-fly. Easy does it, you know?"

Par didn't, but he nodded. "What do you think of her?"

Enio's face brightened. "She's smart. She knows the wilderness and the mountains. And you saw how she handled the robbers. We're lucky we found her."

"She found us."

Enio shrugged.

Par hesitated. "You like her?"

"Don't you?"

"No, I mean *like* like."

"What in the purple hells does that mean?"

Par's ears began to warm.

A grin grew across his friend's face. "Wait—you think I'm tight for her?"

"Well…"

"Like you are for Lani?"

"Enio!" Par pushed him.

Enio fell back, laughing.

Agatha and Kaj looked up.

"Um," Par stammered, now feeling like an idiot. "Guy stuff."

Agatha rolled her eyes.

Kaj stood and attended to Lightning. "If all goes well, we'll be in Aurix before sunset."

Enio left Par and offered the knife back to Kaj.

She didn't take it. "Why don't you hold on to that?"

"Can I?"

She nodded and handed him a cloth to wrap it. "You wanted the robber's rockshooter, but this is better. No numena needed."

Par's jaw tightened. Now his friend with the temper had a knife.

Soon they were back on the road. When Agatha wasn't walking beside Kaj, discussing more of Aurix—Kaj knew of a place they could stay on the cheap—Enio pumped Kaj for more details on fighting and her life as a courier. Par was the only one who hadn't spoken with Kaj one-on-one. He began to feel like *he* was the outsider.

Then, when everyone except Par was up front laughing about something, Kaj handed Lightning's reins to Enio and dropped back.

Par took a breath and brought to mind their backstories. He wouldn't be the one to give them away.

"I haven't thanked you," she said, joining him, "for saving Lightning."

"He seems a nice companion." Par kept his eyes down.

"He's like family." She paused. "Why all alone?"

"No reason."

"You three seem a close family, yourselves."

"Oh, we're not—"

"Family is more than blood, Par."

Par pushed away the memories of his own family, now far across the sea. And he didn't want to dwell on Leo and his happy home in Wishbone. He turned the topic back to her. "Do you have any other family?"

"No one close. It's just me and Lightning. Enio is a bit of bagged lightning too, isn't he?"

"He can be." Par chuckled.

"I hope you don't mind me giving him some throwing pointers."

"Why would I?" It was too late to object, anyway.

She lowered her voice. "Because I sense he's somewhat… troubled."

Par glanced up in surprise. How much had Enio told her? What had they talked about? But as Par took his eyes off the road, he stumbled.

Kaj caught his arm. "Careful."

"Um, thanks."

She continued. "I can tell, of the two, you're the thoughtful one. It must be hard sometimes, being his friend."

It sure was. Par didn't know what to say.

"Now that you've completed your Ascendance and are heading for new lives, how long do you plan to stay together?"

That simple question set off a flood of thoughts. Par had never considered his time with Enio might have its limit. But Par's inability to invoke had always hung over them, like a heavy, unsettled cloud. Enio never seemed to judge him for it, yet Par knew it held Enio back from things he might otherwise want to do. How long could Par be a burden to his friend?

He took a breath. For now, Par needed to worry about the present, and finding Vex. He focused on the road before their feet. "We just want to get to Aurix. After that, we'll see what the stars decide."

Par impressed even himself with his answer. A perfect Arcanan response.

Chapter Twenty-Two

The road climbed higher through the morning with sweeping views along the coast. Livestock wandered the inland fields, and horse and wagon traffic increased. The people seemed friendly—or at least not hostile. Par could almost convince himself he was a native, living his backstory for real.

Sometimes, a lane ran off to a village or a small port. Fishing boats dotted the waters, once joined by a majestic, multi-masted ship.

Par pointed it out to Enio.

"That has to be a navy vessel," Enio said, his words hot with excitement. "I hope we see them up close in Aurix."

But Par had no desire to get near an Arcanan warship. Having docked the *Sea Dog* several leagues away now seemed an even better decision.

Later in the day, massive rust-colored cliffs jutted farther up the shore. The sea traffic became more organized, as if following great curving tracks that converged somewhere ahead. When Par and his group topped the highest rise yet, Kaj stopped and pointed.

"Holy sticks…" Enio muttered.

Par couldn't have said it better.

Below, in a deep, wide valley, sparkled a city. *Sparkled* was the right word: towers and domes glittered and gleamed as if they were jewels in a monstrous treasure chest. A magnificent waterfall tumbled down the valley's rear cliffs, as lofty as the highest point in Argent. Its waters flowed through the city, at last passing beneath a colossal wall guarding the valley from the sea. Busy piers and tall ships adorned the outer bay.

"I'd heard it was a sight," Agatha breathed with wonder. "But I'd never imagined."

"You should come in winter," Kaj said, "when the moonlight spreads blue diamonds across the snowy rooftops. There's nothing to match it."

As Par gazed over the spectacle, something flashed high above the city. He tried to focus and find it again. The cliffs bounding the valley's far side were dotted with structures up and down the rock face. Lone towers, some round and open on top, others capped with steeples, still others in the shapes of strange monuments and statues, gleamed pink and orange in the late sun. They didn't seem arranged in any kind of pattern, but were all niddle-noodle, as Leo's mother might say.

The flash again caught his eye, in the air between himself and the cliffs.

Enio noticed it too. "Birds?"

"Too big." Par squinted until he made out a group of silver creatures gliding toward the bay. "I think… people?"

"City guards. Shieldriders." Kaj tugged on Lightning's reins. "Let's not lose the daylight."

The donkey brayed and shuffled forward. Par marveled a moment longer at the guards riding their shields through the very air, high above the rooftops. If it wasn't enough avoiding the authorities on the ground, now they'd have to worry about the skies. He took a breath and followed the others.

The road wound downward to the outside of the fortified bay walls. Banners of silver and blue snapped and fluttered along the battlements. Each displayed the symbol of Arcana, the same as on Kaj's medallion—a half sun against a half moon. She led them to the grand main gates. They were wide open, with hinges like tree trunks. Par and his group joined the traffic passing in and out. He held his breath, worried about being stopped and challenged.

But Kaj seemed unconcerned, and they passed inside without issue. A wide plaza opened beyond. Many shops in Wishbone had been decorated with colorful bits of crystal, but the adornments here were in a different class. Glimmering mosaic chips formed elegant designs like the stained-glass windows of Eloria.

Dead ahead stood a large, ball-shaped sculpture, with lesser orbs set on extended rods. A fountain burbled around the base.

"Is that a sundial?" Par asked as they wove through the crowds.

"Not quite," Kaj said. "It's an orrery. It's powered by water and keeps position with important stars."

Par needed to focus on their mission, on finding Vex, on blending in, but with all the new curiosities, it wasn't easy.

Kaj led them deeper into the city, to a two-story inn with an attached stable. "Will you watch Lightning while I speak with the innkeeper?"

"Of course," Agatha said. If Par had any sugar, he'd offer it to the donkey in thanks for its company. He patted it instead.

While they waited, a young man with hair spiked like an orange sunrise passed by.

"Must be the style." Par pointed.

"I wonder if I could get mine to do that?" Enio removed his cap and brushed his bushy black hair.

"You do," Agatha said, "and I'll cut it off."

Enio replaced his cap. "I'd like to see you try."

"You have to sleep sometime," she added.

Par chuckled.

Kaj returned from the inn. "Your room's at the end of the hall. I've paid the innkeeper." She offered a key.

Agatha took it. "You're being too kind."

"It's my pleasure." Kaj jiggled the coin purse she'd taken from the robbers. "My room is next to yours, but Lightning and I have deliveries to make. Is there anything else you need?"

Par touched Agatha's arm. When she looked, he mouthed *Vex*.

She nodded. "Kaj, do you know of Vex Imports and Exports? We were told the owner, Alexander Vex, might employ these two young Ascendants."

"I'll ask during my rounds. Come along, Lightning."

As she led her donkey back down the lane, Par and his group entered the inn. The innkeeper directed them to their room, but not before they noticed an archway to an area with tables and chairs. Chatter drifted from that direction, as did a rich, meaty odor.

Their room was clean, with a single bed and two stuffed chairs that bordered a latticed window on the ground floor. A table with candles, a wash basin, and a pitcher sat against the wall.

When they'd closed the door, Par asked, "What now?"

"We wait for Kaj." Agatha peeked out the window.

"How long?"

Enio stood by the door. "That food smelled pretty good."

Agatha turned back. "I was thinking the same."

Par had been too. He sighed. "Hot meals."

"Cold drinks." Enio licked his lips.

Agatha dug into the folds of her peasant dress and pulled out a dumpling of cloth. "I'll go ask the innkeeper where I can sell my earrings. Latch the door."

"I wonder," Par said, "if we should have left an earring at Leo's house."

Lady Agatha spoke as she slipped out. "I offered, but Nell refused. They did us a kindness, and I think paying would have cheapened it."

Par closed the door. Enio flopped onto the bed and laced his fingers behind his head. "Hey Par, we're in Aurix."

"Yeah, but not for sightseeing. We need to find Vex. Do you think—" Par hesitated. "Do you think they do Reckonings here?"

"Kaj said they didn't."

"Why were you talking to her about Reckonings?" Par watched his friend suspiciously. "What did you tell her?"

"Nothing I wasn't supposed to. We talked about the big ships in the bay. Then the wars, and those *dumb* Elorians." Enio snickered, "See? I'm subtle."

"Like a poke in the eye."

"Anyway, we got to how Eloria treated prisoners. I said I heard how they used Reckonings to change their personalities or something, and she said they didn't do that here." He sat up. "Good thing we've got her along. Did you see how she killed that robber?" He made an arm throw.

"I'll never forget."

Enio slid to the edge of the bed and sat facing Par. "Maybe Arcana isn't as bad as the Hierarchy says."

While Enio seemed fairly comfortable with the whole situation, Par wasn't ready to let his guard down. Still, his experiences so far had thrown a different light on at least some of the citizens.

"You know," Enio continued, "Kaj said if Aurix didn't work out, I—uh, we, could go off with her."

"Go off? Where?"

"Travel around Arcana. Be couriers."

"Never go back home?" Par cut that objection short: Enio had all but disowned any family he had left.

"We still need to save the Abbot," Par added instead.

Enio turned away. "I know. Why can't Cronus just die and stay dead?"

"Vex will figure it out."

"How long until he's supposed to leave for Jod?"

Par had kept careful track. "Three days. Too bad we don't know where the Threshold here is. We might find him there."

A knock came at the door. "It's me."

Par opened it. "That was quick. Anything wrong?"

Lady Agatha stood in the hall. "Quite the opposite. The inn-keeper knows Kaj well, and he himself paid me a fair price for my jewelry." She gave a bow and a formal, sweeping gesture. "Shall we retire to the banquet hall, gentlemen?"

The rich odor came from today's special: a seafood stew. They ordered three hot, wonderful bowls. After a few spoonfuls, Enio suggested they deserved the inn's best ales after their long journey. Agatha agreed and stepped away to ask.

Par leaned closer to Enio. "Is that a good idea?"

"Why?"

"Once you get going—well, it's not good for your health."

Enio stirred his stew. "I knew this one guy, lived to be ninety."

"He drank a lot?"

"What he did was, he minded his own business." Enio ate another spoonful, dribbling a little down his chin.

Maybe he meant that as a joke. Par wasn't certain.

Agatha returned with three full mugs. Enio raised his. "Let's have a toast."

Par could at least agree on that. With all their problems, they had a lot to be thankful for. Like finding Lani. And, in fact, for Kaj's help. And making it to Aurix, and—

"Here's to Arcana." Enio took a deep draw.

To Arcana? Par's mug paused before his mouth. Regardless of

his uncertainties about this country, he was still Elorian, Arcana's enemy.

A burly man at another table bellowed, "Hear that? Kid's toasting Arcana. That's what I like from our youth. To Arcana!"

Others at his table lifted their mugs. "Arcana!"

The entire room joined in and everybody drank.

"Get that boy another ale!" laughed the burly man.

Enio wiped a sleeve across his mouth and gave his broken smile.

CHAPTER TWENTY-THREE

After they'd filled their stomachs, Par and his group returned to their room. Night had fallen, but Kaj hadn't returned.

Lady Agatha tucked herself into the bed. Enio stumbled to one of the stuffed chairs and was out before he hit the cushions. Par curled up in the other. They'd resume their search for Vex in the morning, hopefully with news from Kaj.

Par woke to soft sunlight and the creaks of passing wagons. With a quiet stretch, he peered out the window. A few pedestrians wandered the lane, and a man swept a pottery store's steps.

Enio stirred. His face puckered like he'd bitten a lemon. "Shut the damn curtain."

Grinning, Par let it close. "It's not the sun, it's the suds."

"Good morning," Agatha said, and eased herself from the bed. Her dress was horribly creased, but after a quick invocation, the wrinkles faded.

Enio watched her through one cracked eyelid. "Can you spare some of that lumina?"

"Can't invoke?" she said.

"Can't focus. Got a headache in my eyes."

Agatha obliged and touched his forehead.

He took a deep breath and rubbed his face. "Thanks."

Before Par made another wisecrack over his friend's drinking, Enio jabbed a finger at him. "Don't."

Par didn't need to say more. He smoothed out his own clothes and washed his face in the water basin. Enio did the same.

"Let's check on Kaj," Agatha said.

They slipped into their boots and locked the door behind them. No one answered at Kaj's door. The innkeeper hadn't seen her since yesterday, and her donkey wasn't in the stable. So they found a table where they could watch the inn's entrance. But as they lingered over breakfast, Kaj still didn't show.

"She wouldn't just leave, would she?" Par couldn't remember her saying one way or the other.

Enio poked at a piece of fried potato. "Kaj goes where she wants, when she wants."

Par wasn't sure if he heard frustration, or if Enio was still hungover. Maybe both. "Are you saying—"

"I'm just saying we're not really her problem."

Agatha pushed away from the table. "Perhaps she came in through another door."

Par let Enio's comment go. His friend was right: Kaj owed them no explanations.

Again, no one answered at her room. They returned to their own.

When they opened the door, they froze. A blue-robed man, his head bent, sat by the window.

Enio drew his knife.

The man looked up. White hair framed a shaven face, and bright eyes flashed under black brows. "It's good to see you too, Enio."

"Vex!" Par shouted. They pushed into the room. "Thank the *gods*."

Vex stood. "Your friend Kaj passed word that you were here. But what in blue blazes are you doing in Arcana?"

Par's joy thinned. "Cronus is alive."

The wizard's eyes widened. "Did you just say—"

"And he's taken over the Eminence. They've imprisoned the Abbot in the outpost at Argent and—"

Vex raised a silencing hand and turned to Agatha. "My dear woman, could you excuse us?"

"This is Lady Agatha," Par said. "We've told her everything."

The wizard frowned. "What do you mean, *everything?*"

"The Vigil, the Immortus. All of it. She helped us escape."

For a moment, Vex studied them. "It appears I have some catching up to do. Everyone, take a seat."

They did. Vex listened intently as Par spoke of the shadow that had haunted his reflection, and of Cronus and the Eminence, and of Par and the Abbot's capture. Enio added the parts about their escape from Argent, and about Lady Agatha and the sea stags.

When they'd finished, Vex addressed the lady. "We owe you a great debt, madam. Their trust in you is well placed."

"From what I gather," she said, "in you, as well."

"Let's hope so." The wizard rubbed his chin. "I agree with Cornelius that Cronus does not act alone. However, not all the Abbot's speculations on the Ortu are correct."

"He told us he read about the Ortu at Xol Tomot," Par said.

"My library there is not complete. The ancient Vigil scholars studied the Outer Realms. It was they who named that region of the purple hells the *Ortum,* meaning to *reach,* or to *rise.* They speculated that was its primary instinct."

"Instinct?" Par jolted at the implication. "You mean, it's alive?"

"Not as we understand life. Perhaps as some mindless beast, surviving off the pure energies of the Higher Realms—and of ours." Vex seemed to ponder. "How many days since Cronus possessed your Fondiscate?"

Par counted back. "Five."

The wizard's face darkened. "Two days ago, I used the Threshold to check again on the Immortus. The shadows the Abbot and I saw remain, and deepen."

"The Abbot thought they might be from Cronus hunting me. But if Cronus is in the Eminence now…"

"Then," Vex continued, "I fear the Ortu is trying to enter our world through the Immortus. If Cronus acts in league with it, that explains what he wants with you."

Par's throat was almost too dry for him to ask: "To help it… rise?"

"Indeed. Did the Abbot mention the special sigil I found on the monoliths? The sigil that matches one you received from the mage Ridiax?"

"He did. Is that what Cronus is after?"

"In fact, I suspect Cronus knows nothing of that sigil. Even if he did, it would be useless to him. The monoliths are creating the conditions allowing the Ortu's rise, and the sigil might disrupt that. But I think I know what he wants."

Par waited, almost not wanting to hear the rest.

Vex went on. "Our world's emanations feed the Ortu, but those very pressures hold it back, as a current turns a fish. And so it only consumes what falls within its reach. With the rift closed, the monoliths now interfere with those natural pressures, yet we remain safe, unless the Ortu were to grow much stronger—or unless it were to gain a shield."

A shield! The mage Ridiax had once used that term to describe the thickness in Par's soul.

"The Abbot was right about one thing," Vex said, turning to the window. "We need to get to the Citadel. It's still sealed, so Cronus can't capture you there, and the tomes you discovered in the vault will, I trust, reveal more about the monoliths and that sigil. My hope now is we can use it to stop the Ortu."

"Would the Blink stones help?" Par asked. They had used one against the monoliths last year to disrupt their power.

"Those provide only the briefest interruption—a blink, as they're named. No, we require something much more permanent." Vex searched the view outside. "But returning to the Aurix Threshold may be difficult. While I have not revealed its existence to the Majesties, I am being watched."

"By whom?" Agatha asked.

"The Arcanan version of Eloria's High Council. It calls itself the Orbit, made up of twelve Prevgrades. My revelations of the Vigil's history to the Majesties have been well received. But the Prevgrades haven't been included, and some grow suspicious of my motives."

He sighed and turned back. "I'd prefer to wait until nightfall to make a dash for the outpost. But we can't waste a moment. Gather your things."

They did, and left through the inn's back door, hurrying between buildings.

"Hey," Enio asked as they turned a corner. "What about Kaj?"

Panting now, Agatha replied, "She believes we came to Aurix to find you employment. How would we explain your sudden exit? It may be best simply to disappear."

Par didn't care for the idea, and Enio's expression suggested he liked it even less. Yet Agatha was right. This seemed the best way.

After another extended scurry, Agatha wheezed from behind, "Wait—I need a moment."

They stopped. Par admired her strength, but she was no sprinter.

"Where are we heading?" Enio asked Vex as the lady caught her breath.

"The Vigil outpost is upon the Astrologer's Aerie, one of the Oracularies in the cliffside. I normally fly to it under the cover of darkness. In your case, we'll have to take the stairs. Fortunately, most of the public ignores those old shrines."

Their journey continued to the city's far side, past the last buildings where the land became rough and unpopulated. The bounding cliffs soared before them. Vex led them along stony paths near the base, passing little pavilions and monuments set against the looming rock walls. Then he turned up a brief run of shallow steps ending near a statue of a man gazing skyward. A wooden sign read *Astrologer's Aerie*.

Lady Agatha stopped before it, examining the area. "Well, that wasn't so bad. I had worried..."

She trailed off. The blood left her face.

Par followed her gaze.

Narrow steps, like the fossilized spine of a monster, twisted up the cliff wall higher than he could see.

He swallowed. "We have to climb those?"

"I'm afraid so." Vex took the first step.

Par didn't even see any landings. But if that was what it took—

"I'm sorry," Agatha said. "I can't."

Vex turned back. "There's no other way up, madam."

"We'll help you," Par tried, though he wasn't sure how.

She gave a gentle smile. "I'm afraid I've gotten a bit soft over the years. And the height would make me quite dizzy. I'd endanger everyone."

Par still wasn't willing to leave her. "What if we went to the bay instead? Enio can call the stags. They can take us to Jod and we can use the Threshold there." Then Par grimaced. "Oh, but Cronus might know about Jod by now."

Agatha laid a hand on Par's shoulder. "My goal was to get you to Alexander Vex. That's done. I'll be fine on my own. Remember, no one is looking for me. I'll return to Wishbone—we have friends there, thanks to you. Then I'll make my way to the Borderlands."

"Find my import-export office near the bay," Vex said to her. "Tell a man named Clive that *Tomot* calls. He will help you travel where you need."

Par was out of ideas. Sadness nearly choked his words as he wrapped his arms around her ample frame. "We'll miss you."

She hugged him back. "It's quite mutual. But you're in better hands now than mine."

He didn't think he could make that judgment.

As Enio stood nearby, looking awkward, Agatha grabbed his arm and pulled him into the embrace.

"Hey!" Enio yelped but didn't much resist.

Agatha released them, and with a last smile beneath misty eyes, hurried back down the path. Par watched her disappear, a familiar emptiness widened inside him, as if another family were going to pieces.

"But she's right," Vex said. "The risks of your climb are not to be underestimated."

Enio, blushing slightly, eyed the heights. "Can you fly us up?"

"I can't carry that much weight. But that gives me an idea. For safety's sake, I will bestow upon you the Arcanan flying sigil."

Enio's eyes snapped wide. "Really?"

Vex motioned him close and bent down. They touched foreheads. After a brief flash between them, they stood apart.

"Now," Vex said, "don't use it unless—"

A bright silver glory erupted around Enio's head. Air blasted Par's face and tossed Vex's robes. Enio flew from his feet, arced through the air, and landed hard on his backside.

"Son?" Vex said.

Enio sat up, seeming unharmed, but scowling. "Ow."

"As I started to say," Vex continued, "don't use it unless you have no other choice. It will take practice to get the balance correct. And next time, give yourself more room. I'm afraid I have nothing to help you, Par. If you fall—well, don't."

Par nodded, taking the advice to heart.

The steps were as steep as they were narrow. An old, frayed rope followed through rusty iron rings. Par gripped it tightly, focused on Vex's back, and began the climb. Up and up they went, until after so many steps Par had lost count, he dared a look out over the city.

They were much higher now than when he'd beheld it from the valley's opposite side. A flock of geese streamed through the great open air. The fact that they flew below him twisted his stomach, as if he were already higher than the clouds.

Vex continued their ascent. By now, Par's legs felt weighted with sandbags. But at last the steps ended in a wide lip of rock. Several tall, oddly thin statues of robed figures guarded the edges, their arms reaching up to clasp the hands of their neighbors, forming high arches. These continued around the shelf, until finally bounding a tunnel disappearing into the back wall.

A figure stepped from its throat.

Vex halted. Par froze beside Enio.

The man wore purple robes edged with silver. Black, curling designs covered his bald head. A handful of caped guards emerged behind him.

"Prograde Juris?" Vex said. "What is the meaning—"

"Alexander Vex," the man cut in, "you and your two Elorian spies are under arrest."

CHAPTER TWENTY-FOUR

Par didn't dare move.

"Arrest?" barked Vex.

Prograde Juris stood before the guards. "By decree of the Orbit."

"Outrageous. I am a guest of the Majesties."

"And to the Aubade you may appeal." Juris spoke over his shoulder. "Captain, summon the chariot."

A red-caped woman stepped forward. Her sleek silver helmet angled over her raven-black hair like an eagle's beak. She gestured to a short, thin guard. Holding his shield before him, he ran to the edge and leapt.

Par gasped.

But the man didn't fall. He sailed through the air and up the cliffside, keeping the shield beneath his feet as if riding a kite.

"Shieldrider," Enio whispered with the same awe Par felt.

Vex interrupted their astonishment. "You think you can arrest me?" His silver glory flashed. Lightning crackled between his fingers.

The other guards conjured their own glories. Some aimed

rockshooters. Others brandished swords and knives. Flames ignited over the blades.

But the Prograde seemed unimpressed. "I am aware of your skills, Alexander. You may well escape us—in the end. But your young companions would not survive the fight."

Par had seen Vex summon lightning. The wizard could blast the Aerie to dust. But they were hundreds of feet above the valley floor. As if things weren't bad enough, Enio's hand was inching toward his knife. Par grabbed his friend's arm.

Enio tried to pull away. Par held tight.

For what seemed a lifetime of seconds, no one moved. Then Vex doused his glory and lowered his hands. "Very well. We'll accompany you to the Majesties."

"Your wisdom matches your powers." Juris made a gesture. The guards stood down.

Enio's arm also relaxed. Par let out the breath he'd been holding.

"Prograde Juris," Vex said. "Would you mind telling me who accuses us?"

"That is the business of the Aubade. But may I ask, why are you visiting the Astrologer's Aerie?"

"I like the view."

A sudden wind from above tossed Par's hair. A white chariot floated downwards. Six shieldriders hovered around it, each holding a pole protruding from the sides. It landed in their midst like a feather.

Juris motioned toward it. "If you would, Alexander."

Vex ushered Par and Enio into the seats. "Whatever happens," he muttered, "stay close."

Par had planned nothing less.

As the shieldriders lifted the chariot into the air, Par yelped and again gripped Enio's arm. Enio didn't seem to notice this time. His own hands gripped the chariot's rails.

They soared up and along the cliff face, toward the thundering waterfall at the valley's tail. Then they curved back, down toward the shining city. Their circle tightened as they approached a central rise topped by an enormous dome-shaped structure, its smooth sides dotted with windows and balconies. A less massive but similar dome rose from that, and a third with skyward windows topped them all. The chariot continued to the hill beneath and to a blocky building dug into the slope.

The shieldriders brought them to rest. More guards awaited.

"Search them," said the captain in the eagle helmet. They left Vex's necklaces and baubles alone but took Enio's knife.

"Follow me, please," she said.

Considering the swords, Par didn't see how *please* meant anything.

A corridor led through the gated building into the hillside. A strange bittersweet odor hung in the air, as if of flowers thrown on a fire. They came to a passage lined with cells.

"But we are to see the Aubade," Vex said to the captain.

She ignored him. The guards locked up Par and his companions and left. Two cots lined the narrow room. Light seeped through the door's barred porthole.

Enio stood on his toes and tried to see out. "What's that smell?"

"Incense." Vex sat on a cot. "It fogs the mind so prisoners can't use their sigils."

"Now what?" Par said.

"We wait. If Prograde Juris was being truthful, we'll be brought before the Aubade, and then, I trust, released."

"The Aubade?"

"He's one of the Majesties—the Song of the Morning."

"Will we tell him about Cronus and the Eminence?"

"Good question. I'll do the talking." Vex leaned back and closed his eyes. "I'm getting too old for this sort of thing."

Par joined Enio at the door. "Did they get Lady Agatha too?"

Enio tried to rise higher. "I can't see."

"Help me up."

Now Enio dropped to his hands and knees. Par stepped onto his back. He whispered out the portal. "Lady Agatha?"

The words echoed into silence.

"Hello?" Par said louder.

"My spine," Enio grunted.

"Sorry." Par stepped off his friend and helped him up. At least Lady Agatha had gotten away.

Enio rubbed his back and lay on the other cot. "What do you think they'll do with us?"

"At least they don't do Reckonings in Arcana." Par sat next to him.

"No," Vex mumbled, his eyes still closed. "But there's the crystal road."

Par had heard that term before, from the quartz merchant. "What is that, anyway?"

"A gentle way of referring to a life sentence in the quartz mines. But they dumb your mind first. Permanently. Can't even conjure after that."

Dumb your mind? If that wasn't a type of Reckoning, Par didn't know what was. He eyed Enio, who'd said Arcana didn't do Reckonings. But his friend looked wiped out. After the climb and the capture, Par could relate, so left him alone. Plus, that bittersweet incense was clouding his senses. He slumped back, and drifted off.

The jangle of keys woke him. Their door was pushed open. "Let's go," said the guard.

Par rose from his cot, stiff and a little muddled. They followed the man through more gates and up many grueling levels, at last climbing a grand spiral staircase. The view out the windows showed they had reached the highest dome. It was nearly sunset.

The guard ushered them into a large round chamber. A handful of aged men and women occupied tall chairs around the walls, which rose to looming windows of late orange sunlight. Ahead rested two thrones. A severe-faced man in white robes and a spiked gold crown sat in one. The other was empty.

The guard led Par and his group to the room's center, stopping on a tiled design of the sun and moon. "Alexander Vex, my Aubade."

"Vex!" thundered the man on the throne. "Was I not clear that our consultations remain private?"

Vex bowed. "This is not my doing, Majesty."

Prograde Juris rose from one of the surrounding chairs. "Majesty, the Orbit does not wish to interfere in your private matters, but—"

The Aubade gave a derisive snort.

Juris continued. "But Vex has been caught consorting with the enemy. These two children—his companions—are in fact spies from Eloria."

"I warn you, Juris…" The Aubade leaned forward, his face reddening. "Your animosity toward Vex has not gone unnoticed. If this is some maneuvering—"

"There is more, Majesty." The Prograde approached the thrones. "He hides an ancient bewitched doorway through which he can travel to and from Eloria."

Crap, Par thought. How did Juris know about the Threshold?

The other members of the Orbit began to murmur.

"You can prove these claims?" the Aubade said.

"I can." He turned. "Captain."

The captain of the guard strode in. Lady Agatha followed.

Par's spirits sagged; they'd nabbed her too.

The captain brought her forward. Agatha never once glanced at Par or his friends.

"Lady Agatha is my witness," Juris said. "She is also one of my agents."

"Agent?" Par blurted along with Enio. "But—"

"Hush," Vex said.

The Aubade glared. "In order to verify her testimony, the law requires we obtain truth warrants."

"She has waived that right," Juris said.

"Is this the case, madam?" asked the Aubade.

"Yes, Majesty."

One by one, each of the Progrades lit their glories.

So did the Aubade. "Speak," he said.

Agatha's eyes remained fixed forward. "The Eminence of Eloria delivered these children to me and asked that I take them to Arcana."

"That's a lie!" Par shouted. It *had* to be.

"Quiet!" barked Juris.

Par couldn't believe his ears. Agatha had been lying the whole time? Had his desperation blinded him to her deceit?

"And to what end?" the Aubade said, his glory bright.

She spoke in a flat, emotionless tone. "The Eminence offers you the hand of friendship. As a token of goodwill he manipulated these boys, known contacts of Vex, into seeking him out. I guided them here, forcing Vex, in his duplicity, to flee with them to the hidden doorway and so reveal to you its existence."

The Aubade doused his glory and looked around the room. "What say you, Orbit?"

As one, the circle of Progrades answered, "Truth."

The Aubade turned his dark countenance on the wizard.

Vex sighed. "The Vigil called it a Threshold. It is upon the Astrologer's Aerie."

The Orbit broke into urgent side whispers.

The Aubade raised a hand.

All became silent.

The Majesty went on. "I have listened to your tales for weeks, Alexander Vex. We've given you our ear because of your past diplomacies in the Borderlands and your trade acumen. Yet you hold back such a momentous revelation?"

"There was still much to tell. These two boys are at the crux."

The Aubade lunged to his feet. "I will get to the bottom of this. Prepare warrants for all!"

"Hear me, Majesty," Vex said. "A force from the Lower Realms has taken control of the Eminence of Eloria."

The Aubade's face showed genuine surprise. "Your stories continue to strain belief, wizard. Perhaps while I prepare my warrants, a stay in our deepest dungeons—"

Just then, a thunderous *Gong Gong* filled the air. Par winced at its volume. It must echo throughout the city.

The Progrades rose from their seats. Two runners dressed in red entered the room. They invoked the wall sconces to bright, steady flames. All eyes turned toward the entrance.

A tall, elegant woman strode in. A shimmering silver gown trailed behind her, flowing across the tiled floor like water in moonlight. Like the Aubade, she wore a crown, though hers was silver with points thinner and longer than his.

The guards nudged Par and his group to make way.

She stopped before the thrones and bowed. "My Aubade."

"My Umbriarch," the majesty replied with an obvious effort to calm himself.

Umbriarch. Par remembered that word. The family at Wishbone had used it for a toast.

The Aubade and the Umbriarch raised their hands and touched palm to palm. Their glories reached out, mingling almost with intimacy. Then their glories withdrew, and the woman moved to the throne beside the Aubade. She sat down. He remained standing.

"So," she said through a smile Par found somehow tricky, "we see before us our friend Alexander Vex, denounced as a traitor. We've just been told of a secret Threshold capable of opening a doorway to Eloria. A force from the Lower Realms controls the very ruler of that country, and we have two boys accused of being spies. Did I get that right?"

"It is so," said the Aubade.

Her bright eyes settled on Par. "Busy day."

Chapter Twenty-Five

Par's eyes darted between the Umbriarch and the Aubade, lost at what was happening. One moment, he and his companions were to be cast into a dungeon. The next, this elegant woman arrives and takes over.

"The queen?" he whispered to Vex.

"Not exactly."

The woman nodded to Agatha. "Is there more?"

"Yes, Majesty. The Eminence of Eloria requests a conference through the Threshold."

"When?"

"He waits for your appearance each midnight. He said Vex can open it with a keystone."

"I see." The Umbriarch turned to Vex. "Instead of a dungeon, our guests will accompany us to this meeting."

The Aubade grumbled but said nothing.

"My Umbriarch," Vex said, "it may be a trick. We—"

"We will be careful. Until then, I have duties, and you must be hungry. We will meet again at midnight. But I ask that you surrender the aforementioned keystone."

Vex hesitated, but then slowly removed the black stone from around his neck. A guard brought it to the Umbriarch.

She examined it. "I trust, Alexander, you will not try to escape."

"No, Majesty."

A Prograde spoke from his chair. "Majesty, the Orbit is still kept in the dark—"

"Apparently," the Umbriarch said, "so are the Majesties. I will brief the Orbit once we have verified these claims."

The guards escorted Par and his friends away. "Lady Agatha…?" Par tried as they passed her.

She ignored him.

Enio spit at her boots. The guard yanked him on.

They were led through the domed palace to a small chamber with a table, couch, and deep chairs. A writing desk sat near a window, empty except for pen and ink near a stack of parchment. An arch opened to an outside balcony.

Enio peeked through the archway. Vex settled at the table.

Par sat near him. "Agatha, an agent of Arcana? I don't believe it."

"I didn't know her long," Vex said. "But, just now, did she seem different to you?"

Par knew exactly what he meant. "Quiet? Distant?"

Enio watched but said nothing.

With a slight nod, Vex went on. "It's possible she has been altered."

"To lie?"

"To speak as she has been told, believing it is her will. Without a deeper examination, the Progrades would not detect that."

A guard returned with food and drink. Enio joined the table and picked through the grapes.

Par nibbled on a pungent yellow cheese, pondering more of what had happened. "If the Umbriarch isn't their queen, who is she?"

"A king and his queen do not govern Arcana," Vex said. "The Umbriarch rules by night. The Aubade rules by day."

"They're not married?"

"No—not that the Aubade hasn't tried." Vex chuckled. "Romantic intrigue knows no rank or border."

Par raised an eyebrow.

Vex cleared his throat. "Arcanan Majesties are often unrelated. Sometimes they're brothers, sisters, anything."

"Then it's lucky for us that night came," Enio mumbled over his food. "That other guy was ready to toss us out a window."

"Well," Par said, "I'm not sure being dragged before Cronus counts as luck."

At the mention of Cronus, Par caught a tremor flashing across Enio's face. He didn't like its look, but another thought interrupted his concern. "Instead of opening the Threshold to Eloria, why don't you open it to the Citadel?"

"Too risky," Vex said. "We will be under the close eye of the guards and the Umbriarch. Besides, speaking directly to Cronus may be our best chance to learn more of his plans, convince the Majesties that he controls your Eminence, and help the Abbot. But you're right, it's imperative we get to the Citadel as soon as possible."

Vex selected a smoked sardine from a plate he'd been examining. "Which reminds me: since you were there last year, I've wondered if it's possible, once inside, for you to open a Threshold and bring me and Enio in, circumventing the seals. Then I can search the vault myself."

Par had never considered that, but it brightened his spirits. This time, he might not have to travel those corpse-strewn corridors, that tomb of the long dead Vigil, alone. And it would be a lot easier to get past the skarix.

The wizard must have noticed his relief. "But the seals may still prevent it. If so, we'll wait outside and return home together."

After more discussions of potential strategies—each vague and dependent on the meeting with Cronus—Vex lay on the couch. Par joined Enio on the tight balcony and looked from the domed high palace over the darkening city. Enio pointed to tall masts in the bay that he said were navy vessels. But Par thought mostly about Cronus, the Citadel, and the Abbot. At last he came inside, dropped into a chair and dozed.

Later that evening, a guard returned. "The Umbriarch awaits," he said.

With tense glances at one another, Par and his friends followed. They were brought to a wide terrace where a chariot waited. Shieldriders ushered them on board and, as before, lifted the craft into the air. Below rushed the sleeping city of Aurix, and soon the flicker of firelight appeared high up the granite cliffs, marking the Astrologer's Aerie. The chariot came to rest there, and everyone entered the circle of tall, thin statues through ancient arched and grasping hands.

Prograde Juris waited with more guards. The Umbriarch stood beside him, examining a statue. "It's been a long time since I was up here." She brushed it gently. "This is one of the city's oldest shrines. Pity it's not better cared for."

"It's held up well," Vex said. "The Vigil made it to last."

"Unlike your loyalty," Juris added. "Or the morals of these young spies."

Par couldn't help himself. "We're not spies."

Juris chuckled. "The facts betray you."

"Prograde Juris," said the Umbriarch, "as your witness Agatha testified, these children were sent in a scheme to expose Alexander. This hardly makes them spies. My judgment will reflect that."

"Of course, Majesty." Juris bowed.

"Yet," she faced Vex, "a mystical doorway would seem something to have revealed early in our meetings, Alexander."

"Forgive me. I'll correct that now." Vex stepped before two

statues, their archway looking out high over the city. "This is the Threshold. It can only be utilized with the keystone."

For the first time, Par noticed that the dusty ground there hid black stone, just like the Thresholds he'd seen before.

The Umbriarch handed Vex the keystone. "Not until I say."

"Yes, Majesty."

They waited in silence. There was no wind, but a chill ran up Par's neck. He couldn't help but envy the boldness of those around him. The lovely Umbriarch stood tall and proud, a majesty indeed. Vex peered at the Threshold's empty arch, his brows bent, his face an image of concentration and vigilance. Juris loomed still and stoic, only the glint of torchlight in his eyes revealing he wasn't another stone statue.

Even Enio seemed undaunted. His stance, his taut, thin muscles, the flare of his nostrils, said he was ready for a fight.

But Par saw none of his own feelings reflected in the others. He'd fled Cronus for days, and was about to stand before him again. While he seemed safe enough among this company, he also felt the least prepared or capable for the encounter.

The stars twinkled in their deep abysses. A moon shy of full watched over all. "It is time," the Umbriarch said.

Vex held forth the keystone. The archway flickered. Through it appeared the rock lip of the faraway Argent outpost, lit by blue-white globes in bowls.

The Eminence of Eloria stood beside a shorter man with black woolly hair. Before them knelt the Abbot, bound and hooded. He seemed bent with weariness, but Par breathed in relief that the old man lived. Then a longing tugged at his soul. He was looking upon his own country, his real home.

Or it used to be. Unless Vex found a way to stop Cronus, would that ever be Par's home again? Would anywhere?

"Which one is Cronus?" whispered Enio.

Par focused on the present. "He's inside the Eminence. The tall one."

Vex stepped aside. "My Umbriarch, you may speak through the Threshold. But have a care: people, weapons, even magics may pass. We must keep our distance, and our wits."

The Umbriarch addressed the portal. "Good evening, Your Eminence. It's been some time since we last met."

Cronus, the imposter, bowed. "It is unfortunate we amend that under these circumstances."

"The method by which we do so," she added, "is extraordinary."

"Indeed. And by your discovery of the Threshold, I gather you've received our gift of the boys, and of Vex's deceits."

"We have yet to confirm these accusations."

"Of course," Cronus said. "But as an act of reciprocity for our good faith, we ask you to return our dear children. Are they there?"

Enio pushed in from the edge of the group, his snarl dreadful in the firelight. "Someone give me a knife."

Before Par could say anything, two guards pulled Enio back.

The Umbriarch went on. "These children must face Arcanan justice. I cannot release them."

"A quaint policy for domestic affairs. But I must demand deportation under the Treaty of Banes."

"For what crime?" she asked.

Cronus frowned. "Vex uses his export business as a front to smuggle information. He himself is wanted for crimes against Eloria. These children are his accomplices, though perhaps unwittingly. Beyond that, it is a private matter, and the Treaty does not require we speak of it."

"But the Treaty does not prevent it," the Umbriarch replied.

"That is true. You are quite wise, Umbriarch. We are willing to negotiate. Is Par there?"

She motioned him over.

"Par," Cronus said with a grin.

"That's not the Eminence," Par stated. "He's got no glory. It's Cronus."

Cronus raised a hand. "To start, we are willing to accept a single boy. And Par, we will release the Abbot in exchange for you."

Par stiffened at the offer, at falling again into Cronus's hands. Yet he ached to help the Abbot. Would Cronus make good on the exchange? Par rather doubted it.

Just then, the Abbot made a violent lurch toward his ledge's drop-off. "Don't, Par!"

"Father Abbot!" Par shouted.

The short, woolly-haired man, quiet until now, gestured. With a gasp, the Abbot was yanked away from the drop-off as if by an invisible net. He fell back panting, but seemed unharmed.

Once peace had again settled, the short man stepped forward. "I am Legate, Majesty. I can best negotiate this matter."

Even in the pale light, Cronus's face seemed to darken.

Legate continued, "To be honest, these children have done nothing wrong."

"Is that so?" said the Umbriarch.

"It is. Let us dispatch with the political arts. We speak for the Ortu. You know of us?"

"The cult?"

"It is little understood in the circles of the elite. As you in Arcana draw your magics from the celestial spheres, and Elorians from their gods, we of Ortu draw our powers from other realms. It is the Ortu that demands you deliver Par. If you refuse, I'm afraid we must take him by force."

The Umbriarch replied with no warmth. "Then you threaten war?"

"If it comes to that, you would have no hope of victory. And to convince you this is more than boast and bluster, we shall now provide a demonstration of the power of the Ortu."

A dark aura polluted with sickly purple formed around Legate's head. A similar glory grew around the head of Cronus.

"Have a care," Vex hissed to those around him.

Legate's arms rose high. "You embrace the power of the Higher Realms. See, now, the power of the Lower!"

A guard shouted.

Par spun. The man pointed to the western sky.

A long, dagger-like shadow stretched across the stars, cleaving the constellations in two. When it reached the moon, it stabbed into that orb's pale heart. Darkness oozed from the wound.

The other guards yelled and made superstitious gestures. One dropped to the ground. In their terror and confusion, they released Enio.

Without missing a beat, Enio yanked a knife from a guard's scabbard and rushed at the Threshold.

Taking no time to think, Par leapt to block his friend.

But Enio was lost in a spitting rage. "Cronus!" He barreled into Par like a bull.

Par cried out and crashed backwards through the Threshold. He landed hard, knocking even the shout from his lungs. Enio tumbled over him.

"Stop!" yelled Juris. He ran toward the portal. A glory wrapped his head, dark and purple like Legate's.

"The tomes!" shouted Vex. He threw something. A small object sped past Juris and through the Threshold.

The doorway vanished, ahead of Juris, along with Par's view of the Aerie. He lay on his back, trying to breathe through a searing pain in his shoulder. They were no longer with the Umbriarch— yet neither were they with Cronus. The panorama before him showed only the distant silhouettes of jagged black mountains.

PART THREE

THE RISE

Chapter Twenty-Six

THE ABBOT'S ATTEMPT to leap blindly from the cliff and remove himself from the negotiations had failed, defeated by what felt like cold, grasping claws. Cronus and Legate kept him just where they wanted: vulnerable and on display.

Then, in the middle of the discussions with the Umbriarch, chaos broke. Cries and shouts filled the air. A body crashed into the Abbot, knocking him back. His hood twisted off.

In that instant, he summoned his meager strength and invoked to clear his blindness, if only for a moment.

Alexander Vex stood beyond a shimmering doorway that hovered in the air beyond the cliff's edge. The Abbot managed one last invocation just as the portal disappeared. The icy chill of another conjuration slammed into his head, sending his vision again into darkness.

"Juris?" Cronus said. "But what's happened to Par?"

The man who'd landed on the Abbot pulled off him. "He's not here?"

"Par and Enio fell into the portal, but only you arrived."

Thank the gods, thought the Abbot, struggling back to his knees.

"Unacceptable!" Legate shouted. "We must—"

"Did you not sense it?" interrupted Cronus.

"Sense what?"

Cronus's words came wrapped in a smile. "As the boys leapt forward, the portal closed. But like us, Juris was in communion with the Ortu. Its power sustained the Threshold a moment longer and brought him here."

"Indeed?" Legate paused. "Can we now open the Threshold that sits useless in this very outpost, that we might search for Par?"

That was precisely what the Abbot wondered. And feared.

"Not at this time," Cronus said.

"Would you mind explaining what that means, brother Cronus?"

Cronus cleared his throat and spoke with his old authority. "After tonight's demonstration, the Ortu must regain its strength. However, by the time we have Par, we will be able to use our Threshold and deliver him to the Immortus."

"If you'd told me about the keystone earlier," Juris said, "I could have taken it from Vex and brought Par—"

"—to the Immortus, yourself?" said Legate. "You do not know the ritual of rising. And the blessings of the Ortu are not for you alone."

"Your distrust in anyone but yourself hinders our goals, Legate. I've spent half my life as your eyes and ears among the Majesties. I captured the boy. I deserve those blessings."

"And you lost him. What does that deserve, Juris?"

"That wasn't my doing."

Cronus cut in with the voice of reason. "We each had a part in tracking down Par, and we each shall share the blessings—if we might bicker less."

"Quite right," Legate said. "And it's rude to argue in front of company. Our Abbot here seems to have been hoarding his invocations for an escape. Perhaps we've overfed him."

The Abbot forced a chuckle from his weak lungs. "I must get the recipe for your gruel."

"Our next steps, then?" asked Juris.

Legate replied coolly, "Brother Cronus will launch the Elorian navy and take us to war."

"War?" Juris said. "Do not underestimate the strength of Arcana. War will not bring us the boy."

"The war is not to gain Par."

"Then why?"

"Tell him, Cronus."

Cronus's voice remained steady, though the Abbot detected a hint of disapproval. "Even with Par's aid, the Ortu must exert great effort to rise. Since it draws its strength by consuming the lost energies of our world and the Higher Realms, Legate believes that any lives lost in war may provide additional… nourishment."

"And you approve of this?" Juris asked.

Legate answered instead. "We waste no advantage. If nothing else, the conflict will ripple through the lands, frustrating the privileged and elite, as wars do, and creating other such distractions while we search for Par. I will acquaint you with more of our plans while Cronus returns the Abbot to his cell."

"Come along, Cornelius." Cronus helped the Abbot to stand and guided him into the tunnel.

Once they'd parted from Juris and Legate, the Abbot said, "At last, Cronus, after all this time, you get your war."

"War has never been my goal."

"No? Just a scenic stop on the way to your paradise?"

"Glibness is beneath you, Cornelius." The cell bars groaned aside. Cronus passed the Abbot to Lucius, who brought him in and reattached his chains.

"One more question, Master Cronus."

"Yes, Cornelius?"

"I'm gratified that Legate still values my company. But why, with Par gone?"

"The risk of your demise remains a motivator for Par."

"As long as I last, that is."

"As long as Par believes you do. Therefore, make no further trouble. Legate is not as forgiving as I."

"Or as generous. I gather he doesn't work, as you, for a shared paradise."

Cronus didn't answer. The cell clanged shut.

The Abbot settled back. He couldn't do much more in his captivity, except perhaps deepen the cracks between Cronus and Legate.

Other thoughts darkened the moment. Failing his lunge toward the drop-off, he had, in fact, not used his next invocation—after a brief cure of his blindness—to attempt escape, as Legate had surmised. But had his true aim succeeded? Had Vex received what the Abbot had sent, mind to mind, of all he'd learned of Legate and Cronus?

And what had become of Par and Enio?

CHAPTER TWENTY-SEVEN

ENIO SCRAMBLED TO his feet. Spit still flew from his lips. "Cronus! Bastard!"

Par tried to sit up. The knife in his shoulder tore a shout from his throat.

As Enio's eyes fell on Par, his rage drained into a grimace. "Par, you're bleeding."

"Really?" Par gasped. "I hadn't noticed, what with your *dagger* in the way."

"Oh… purple hells." Enio dropped to Par's side and with a quick motion slid out the knife.

Par bit back another scream.

"Sorry!" A golden glory from Enio pushed back the night. He lay both hands on the wound.

The pain faded. Par's breathing eased. He rubbed his shoulder and glared. "You *stabbed* me!"

Enio wiped off the knife—it was the same one the guard had taken from him earlier, the one from Kaj. "I *said* sorry. And you jumped in the way. Dammit, Par. I could've—"

"What? Gotten captured? Killed?"

"Killed Cronus."

Par eyed his friend and for an instant wondered who was the more dangerous.

Enio scanned the area. "Where'd everybody go?"

The moon shone bright again, and the black gashes through the constellations had healed. A squat stone building sat nearby, its opened doorway veiled by a curtain of blue fire. Par recognized the place immediately. "We're on the Citadel's high tower." He found the object Vex had tossed. It was the keystone. "Vex must have shifted the Threshold as we fell through."

Enio now stared in one direction.

Par followed his gaze to the desolate plains of the Devastation. They were as awful as he remembered. Luminous yellow mists, sickly and pale, swept across the lifeless terrain. Farther off rose columns of spinning sand with green internal fires. Somewhere, countless leagues away in those deep, dead lands, waited the circle of the Immortus monoliths.

The spinning columns stilled a moment, then moved like a herd in the tower's direction.

"Hide!" Par crunched behind the parapets.

Enio joined him. "What are those things?"

"Dust demons. They attacked me and Vex before. I escaped into the Citadel and Vex flew to another Threshold."

"We can do the same. I've got the flying sigil."

"Yeah, but—" Par didn't want to discourage his friend, but the last time Enio had used that sigil, he'd crashed like a sick seagull. Steps descended the outside of the tower, but they were steep and treacherous and the monsters might arrive before Enio was halfway down.

And there was another problem: whether Enio fled by air or by stair to a Threshold—wherever one might be—it meant giving him the keystone. Par squeezed it in his palm. That would mean Par not having a way home himself. If that was what it took, he'd hand it over. But Enio needed to escape those demons and find a Threshold in this maze of buildings and towers—all in the dark.

It was Par's call, either way.

A sudden wind began to strengthen.

"Listen," Par said, "there are Thresholds inside the Citadel. Only I can get through the blue seals, but if Vex is right, I can use a Threshold to bring you in. So stay here, as long as you can." Par prayed the wizard was correct. It seemed Enio's best chance.

Enio nodded and held on to his cap. His feather flailed sideways.

With a last worried glance at his friend, Par ran to the tower doorway and through the blue veil. Tight spiral steps disappeared into the floor. He raced down and down until he reached a landing. The skeletal figure he'd seen on his last visit lay before an archway. He leapt the body and charged into the hallway beyond. More robed skeletons surrounded a dry fountain. He shot past like an arrow in flight. The pale light from familiar blue orbs lit his way, his speeding shadow barely brushing the dead Vigil members.

At last he came to the open doors of the Council Chamber. He bolted inside. The clothed remains of the Vigil still filled the amphitheater. Sand blowing outside the tall windows showed the dust demons were close.

Off to one side stood the Threshold, a door-sized dent in a wall. Par dashed to its single black step and grasped the keystone. "Hold on, Enio," he panted, and brought to mind the last spot where he'd seen his friend.

A murky view of the night atop the tower replaced the wall. The winds howled and sand swirled like a freakish blizzard. Par didn't see his friend.

"Enio!" he shouted.

Nothing.

His heart beat faster. The demons of dust, their green fires crackling with fury, had crossed the landscape and were nearly upon the tower. Had his idiot friend tried to fly off?

On the wind came a faint response. "…here!"

Par turned the view.

Enio curled on his knees near a parapet, one hand keeping his cap in place.

"Enio!" Par thrust his arm through the Threshold.

A gust knocked Enio back as he tried to rise.

"Come on!" Par called.

His friend shielded his eyes and plowed against the gale.

Green fires, like the eyes of devils, rose above the parapets. A lash of flame whipped over the top.

"Watch out!" Par yelled.

Enio zagged to the side. The flame missed.

Par reached half his body through the Threshold, nearly blinded by the sand and wind. Enio grabbed his arm.

With all his strength, Par yanked. They tumbled to the floor inside the Citadel.

Chapter Twenty-Eight

The Threshold blinked closed. Par lay beside Enio on the marble floor, their chests heaving.

As they caught their breath, Enio glanced around the skeleton-filled amphitheater. "So this is your famous Citadel."

"And the Vigil's tomb." Par got to his feet and helped Enio up. "Vex wants books from the vault. Since I could bring you through the Threshold, I can bring him here too."

"Then do it."

"I can't, not yet. Passage through these things is once a day. I could open it to the Aerie, just to look." Par rubbed the keystone and hesitated.

"Well?" Enio said.

"Did you see that thing? Cutting across the sky?"

"The shadow?"

"Or the Ortu. Who knows what it can do. We better wait a while."

Enio shrugged. "Your call." He removed his cap and shook his head. Sand flew from his hair.

"Hey, watch it." Par ducked the splatter. They needed to

figure their next move, but he'd put something off too long. Now, more than ever, he needed to know he could rely on his friend.

Par narrowed his eyes. "Enio, are you all right?"

Enio motioned toward a blue-robed, bony corpse. "Better than him."

"No, I mean, your temper. It scares me."

"I'm not my father, Par."

"I never said you were. But your problem with Cronus—"

"*My* problem?" Enio threw up his arms. "He's Cronus! He's—"

"Yes, *your* problem. When you choked that kid in Wishbone, you called him Cronus."

"What?" Enio showed genuine surprise. "No, I didn't."

"Yes, you did. And you went wild on the Aerie. You almost killed me."

"We settled that. It was an accident."

"Even so, you've been getting worse for months. I'm afraid you're losing it."

"Losing it? My sainted foot." He kicked a skeleton. It rattled over.

"Don't." Par grabbed his arm.

With a sudden jerk, Enio pulled back, tripped over the skeleton, and fell. Bony arms flopped around his chest. "Crap!" He scrambled away from them.

This was getting as ugly as Par had feared, but he was determined to see it through.

Enio stood and brushed himself off. He eyed the bones before him. When he spoke again, his voice was oddly soft. "You can't understand what it was like. What he did in my head."

"You said Cronus messed with your mother's memories."

Eyes closed, Enio rubbed his temples with his fists. "Yeah, and now, he's *in* them."

"In them?" That sent a shudder through Par's own bones. "Gods, Enio."

"I can't see her anymore without seeing him." His voice dropped to a whisper, as if they spoke in a temple. "She's at the table, he's there. She's by my bed, he's there. She's dying by that wagon—"

His eyes snapped open. They glistened with restrained tears. Before Par said anything, Enio turned away. He filled his lungs and screamed. The sound was raw with pain and anger. It echoed through the lofty chamber and among the unmoving dead.

Par wasn't sure what to say. What to do. Finally, he laid his hand on his friend's shoulder and squeezed.

Though Enio trembled and muffled a sob, he didn't resist. He gasped and steadied his breathing.

"I didn't realize," Par said gently. "But… do you think killing Cronus will help?"

Enio took another deep breath and sighed. "I can't *think* anything. I just want him gone."

"We'll ask Vex and the Abbot to fix your memories."

"No one messes with my head," Enio said with disgust. "Ever again."

All this time, Par had thought Enio was mad at life, at the world's unfairness. Now Par understood better his friend's struggles. Even so, it didn't ease his worries. "You're not all right."

Enio looked Par straight in the eyes. He gave a meek smile. "I know. I'm going nuts."

Par smiled back. "Well, you've never been all there. But you're still half there. That's like half all right. Maybe together we make an all, all right."

With a chuckle, Enio shook his head. "And maybe you're just talking out your butt."

"Wouldn't be the first time. Anyway, another Threshold is near the vault. Let's get out of here."

"Yeah." Enio scanned the chamber again. "I might have my problems, but hanging around with dead people isn't one of them."

"You took the words right out of my butt."

CHAPTER TWENTY-NINE

PAR SNAKED AROUND the skeletons and out the chamber doors. He stopped and looked both ways.

Enio came beside him, knife in hand. "Where now?"

"I haven't been here since last year, when Vex put a map in my head. But it's faded." Par made his best guess as to the vault's direction. "That way… I think." They took a single step and pulled up short. Wrapped in a skeleton's arms were the small-boned remains of a child.

"Think he knew?" Par said.

"Who?"

"Cronus. When he released the skarix and killed the Vigil. Think he knew there were children?"

Enio grunted. "Think he cared?"

They continued, and soon reached a grand staircase, then a modest hall lined with plain stone doors. More dead Vigil dotted the passage. A few turns later, a hum drifted from another corridor.

They ducked back and stopped.

"Skarix?" Enio whispered.

"Not sure." The sound was coarse, but musical, not the high monotone of those flying scorpions.

As they listened, the humming became lyrics.

Someone burnt a workshop wall
Playin' with a fireball.
Scrubbed away the sooty scrawl
With water, soap and alkeehaul.

Enio whispered, "You said everyone was dead."

"I'd never seen anyone else." Par peeked around again.

An older man in brown work clothes and a tight cap moved among the bony figures. His face was shaven and gaunt. There was something in his hand. A rockshooter, or a stick or—

It was feather duster.

He was dusting the dead.

Par chewed his lip, unsure what to make of this. But if he and Enio ran the other way, they'd get more lost than they already were.

And the man, casually dusting a leg bone, didn't look dangerous.

"Enio," Par whispered, "put away your knife."

"You sure?"

Par nodded. He stepped into the hall, Enio close behind him. The man looked up. "Well?"

When no one answered, he turned away. "Suit yourself." He shuffled to another robed skeleton.

"Who are you?" Par managed.

"Augle."

"You're one of the Vigil?"

"Them lot? Not me." Augle bent and brushed a skull.

As the feathers poked into an eye socket, Par winced. He tried again. "Are you alone?"

"Apparently not."

"I mean, other than us."

"None I've seen. At least, not on my route."

"How did you get in?"

"Where else would I be?" The man continued his cleaning.

Rugs to beat and floors to swab.
Wash the winders, buff the hobs.
Just don't ask I use my nob.
Sorry, but that's not my job.

This wasn't getting them anywhere. Par focused on what seemed most important. "Do you know where the vault is?"

"Course I do."

"Great!" Par said, nudging Enio. "Where?"

"Do I know where the vault is," grunted the man, dusting a jawbone. "I know every blessed fork needs polished and plant needs watered and shoe needs shined and—"

"Can you show us?"

"I'm a caretaker, not a tour guide. Cut the cobwebs, clean the smut, 'cept behind the doors that's shut." Augle paused his work and scanned Par from head to foot. "You're besoilin' my floors."

A few sand grains dropped from the creases of Pars's shirt. His eyes snapped back up and he froze—the man had somehow advanced to within inches, faster than Par had guessed he could move.

Augle's eyes blazed with an odd inner light. "And sweepin' day's not till tomorrow. But let's catch it now before it gets worse. Hold still." He raised his duster.

Par steeled himself. The caretaker appeared harmless. And if this was the price of finding the vault, Par would pay it. Still, the idea of being dusted like one of the dead made his skin crawl.

Thankfully, Augle made quick work of it. "There, now. Clean as a bean." He turned to Enio. "All righty, you next."

Enio shrugged and held out his arms. Par waited for the man to finish.

When he had, he eyed the sand on the floor and sighed. Suddenly, like a comet, he disappeared down the hallway in a blur of light.

Par yelped and jumped back. Before he blinked twice, Augle returned in the same fashion, now with a broom and a dust pan. He began to sweep.

"How did you do that?" Par asked through his awe.

"Just a quick trip to the broom closet."

"Can you take us to the vault that fast?" Enio said.

"Break your necks, it would."

"Then please," Par tried again, "just show us the way."

The man finished his work and seemed to consider. "Fine, if it'll keep you from trailin' a mess through my halls." He pointed with his broom.

Relieved this strange individual had gotten them back on track, Par nodded encouragingly to Enio. And the Citadel, Par had long since learned, was a strange place in general. They resumed their journey. Augle followed, pausing at times to brush up a bit of something.

They continued through elegant halls, down wide stairways, past closed doors and high-domed galleries. The going was steady but slow. Augle didn't sing anymore, and all but ignored them, except to guide them in a choice of directions. At one point, the man cut through a room with a long table and empty wooden chairs. A bowl of shriveled, mold-encrusted fruit sat on the table. Augle grabbed the bowl and shot away like lightning. A moment later, he was back with fresh produce.

"Can we..." Enio reached for an apple.

"That's what it's for."

Enio bit into it. Par left the fruit alone, a little too suspicious of where Augle had gotten it.

As they continued, Par recognized a turn ahead. The vault room was close. So would be another Threshold. A monotone buzzing drifted through the air.

The skarix.

Par stopped. "Augle, can you get rid of those bugs?"

The caretaker glanced at the ceiling. "Bugs?"

"In the vault."

"Oh. I don't go in there. Not my route."

That ruled out his help with the vault. But when they found Vex with the Threshold, he could handle the deadly insects.

"Anythin' else?" Augle asked, impatience obvious in his voice.

Par had begun to like this mysterious man. He was surly but helpful, in his way. What if he were trapped in this place? Did he need help too?

"Why are you still here?" Par asked.

Augle sighed. "Waitin' to see what else you need."

"No, I mean, still in the Citadel. Since the Vigil's dead—" Par cut himself off. Pointing that out felt awkward. He tried again. "We'll be leaving soon. Do you want to come with us?"

For the first time, Augle laughed. "Who'd do the cleanin'?"

Something about the laugh made Par chuckle as well. He shook it off and said, "I guess we don't need anything else. Thanks for your help."

"Whatever you say." Augle left the way they'd come. Lyrics floated in his wake:

> *Got no trouble pushin' brooms*
> *up the stairs and round the rooms.*
> *Sand and mud and stain and fumes,*
> *Cleanin' is this phantom's doom.*

Enio nudged Par. "Phantom? Is he…"

"Is he what?"

Enio rolled his eyes and hung his tongue to the side.

"Dead?" Par didn't believe in ghosts. But whatever Augle's origin, he was the first moving thing here that hadn't tried to kill them.

As Augle disappeared around the corner, he called back, "No, not dead. Only the livin' get dead."

The statement was about as useful as the rest of Augle's answers. But he'd gotten them to the vault, and for that Par was grateful.

"Now what?" Enio said.

"The other Threshold is past the Vault room. Let's try to find Vex."

Par peeked through the high-arched entrance of the chamber containing the vault. The skarix darted and buzzed within. He crept instead to a pillared gallery. The black step of a Threshold waited in an alcove.

He stopped before it. "Before you stabbed me, Juris had a shadow-glory around his head, just like Cronus and Legate. Juris must be part of the Ortu cult."

Enio drew his knife again. He came to Par's side. "If he tries to come through…"

Par said nothing—he didn't need to. He grasped the keystone and brought to mind the Astrologer's Aerie. Since their spying might be noticed by hostile bystanders, he had to do this quickly.

Bright lanterns lit the area within the statues. Two guards leaned against the wall near the tunnel. One dozed. The other picked his fingernail with a knife. No one else was in sight.

He snapped the Threshold closed. "No Vex. I'll try the palace." He opened the Threshold into the great domed throne room, far back from the center. Prograde occupied a few chairs. A man with wild hair read a scroll before the Umbriarch. It seemed to concern Borderland tariffs.

He closed the Threshold again. "Not there either."

"Try the prison," Enio suggested.

Par did. The room was dim. A man lay on a cot.

"Vex?" Par whispered.

The man stirred. A shaft of light through the cell's portal caught his black-bearded face. He gasped and his eyes widened. "What in the purple—"

Not Vex. Again Par shut the Threshold. He tried the small chamber where they'd been taken from the cell to wait, but it was empty.

"The Aubade mentioned deeper dungeons," Enio said. "Try there."

"I can't. Only places I've seen." Par couldn't think of anywhere else Vex might be. "We'll try in the morning. Let's find someplace to sleep."

A room nearby looked promising. It had stark wooden tables, chairs, and not much else. But it was clean and dusted, so apparently on Augle's route. Par closed the solid oak door, feeling, for now, safe from the skarix. And with Enio beside him, safe enough to sleep.

CHAPTER THIRTY

"Wake up, wake up."

Par cracked open an eye.

Before him stood Enio, grinning like he'd done something clever.

Par was almost afraid to ask. "What's going on?"

"Been poking around." Enio dropped a bag. "Found more fruit."

"Oh. Thanks." As Par snagged a pear, Enio held out a small black object.

Par nearly choked. "That's a keystone! Where did you find it?"

"Not found. Borrowed."

"Borrowed?" Par checked his pocket. No keystone.

Never losing the grin, his friend gave it back. "I went looking for Vex."

"And?"

"Come see." Enio raced out the door.

Par bolted after him, to the gallery. A cloaked figure bent before the Threshold examining its single step.

With a flood of relief, Par skidded to a halt. "Vex!"

The figured turned. It wasn't Vex. It was Kaj.

His relief popped like a soap bubble.

"Hello, Par," she said, but beamed at Enio. "You're right. This is all incredible. I knew there was more to your stories."

Par stared, speechless. Then he focused hot eyes on Enio.

"I hope I can help," she added.

"I know you can," Enio said.

Instead of the pat on the back Enio seemed to expect, Par wanted to twist his neck. But he kept his voice steady. "Kaj, I need to talk to Enio a second."

She nodded and returned to examining the Threshold.

Par took his friend's arm and yanked him down the hall. When they were out of earshot, he stopped and spun. "What did you *do*? She doesn't know anything about Cronus, or the Vigil, or—"

"Yeah, so I told her."

"You told her—?"

"Yep. I couldn't find Vex, but I found *her*. At the inn."

"Why didn't you *wake* me first?"

"Wasn't time, she was leaving." Enio glanced back toward the gallery. "What's your problem? She's like one of us. I trust her. Why don't you?"

"I never said I didn't. But she's Arcanan." As Par said it, he realized it wasn't much of an argument, considering the good people he'd met in Wishbone. Then again, after Agatha's betrayal he wasn't sure who to trust.

And besides, how was Kaj "one of us"?

Enio snorted. "She's Arcanan, you're Elorian, we're spies, Vex is—or was—a secret Vigil agent. Who cares? We're not even in anyone's country anymore."

He had a point. The Citadel was hundreds of leagues from anywhere.

Enio continued, "Now we've got more help. Show some gratitude for once."

"Gratitude?" That was going too far. "Did you forget that Thresholds only allow passage once a day? Now we can't bring Vex until *tomorrow*."

"Isn't it a new day for the one upstairs?"

"What's a new day? Twenty-four hours? After midnight? After sunrise?"

"Well, maybe *you* should've asked Vex about that."

Par took a deep breath. There was no point in arguing further. Kaj was here. He'd have to make the best of it.

He strode back to the Threshold, Enio at his heels. "Um, Kaj, Enio shouldn't have brought you. It's dangerous."

"The skarix?" she asked.

"That's part of it."

She brushed off her hands. "Why don't I take a look?"

"I don't—"

"It's this way." Enio waved her on. The two left together.

Sighing, Par followed. He caught up at the entrance to the grand chamber that surrounded the vault. "Careful," he whispered as they peeked inside.

All remained as he'd left it last year. Columns like marble trees supported the high ceiling. Solemn statues lined the walls. In the room's center stood an inner chamber, domed like a private crypt, its entrance covered by a curtain of blue flame. That was the vault. On its roof rested the massive, bulbous hive of the skarix. The deadly insects buzzed around it.

Par pulled back with the others. He kept his voice low. "I could run to the vault. But even if I made it inside, the skarix might swarm and attack you."

"A fire-fly could burn up their hive," Enio said.

"Wouldn't get half of them. And you'd just piss off the rest. Besides, what would Lani think of that?"

Enio nodded. "You're right."

"I have a sigil," Kaj said, "that helps me in the wilds. It fogs an animal's mind—or a group of little ones. Should keep them confused and passive."

Despite his disapproval of Enio bringing her here, Par brightened. "That's worth a try."

"Just don't watch me when I use it," she added. "You'll get fogged too."

They agreed. Kaj moved into the doorway.

"See?" Enio said. "Helping already."

Par hoped so. They turned their faces away.

The buzzing increased, loud and angry.

Par gasped and jerked back toward the door.

Enio grabbed him. "She said don't look."

The buzzing dropped almost to silence.

"We're good," Kaj called.

Par leaned around the entrance. The air was empty of skarix. A couple traced drunken paths across the marble floor. "How long do we have?" he asked.

"For most bugs, quite a while."

"Then let's hope they're like most bugs." Par peered up at the now peaceful hive; Kaj might be more helpful than he'd thought.

"Can you bestow me that sigil sometime?" Enio asked.

Kaj didn't seem to hear. "What's next, Par?"

He considered. "Vex never said which books he wanted. I guess we grab all we can. I'll hand them from the vault to Kaj, and she can take them past the skarix. Enio, you bring them to the room where we slept. That seems safest. Then we'll figure out our next steps."

Everyone agreed. As Par and Kaj approached the domed vault, the stunned skarix left them alone. Par continued through the vault's blue curtain of fire. Kaj poked at the rippling flames once. But like the Citadel seals, it only allowed Par to enter.

The inside also appeared as he'd left it. Bare stone shelves covered the walls, lit by tiny star-like orbs in the ceiling. A low-walled well opened in the center of the floor, its brim covered with geometric designs. Far below would lie the vault's treasures, hidden layer after layer in the deep shadows.

The Luminary's ring still sat beside the well. Par searched through the designs until he found a circle wreathed by eight tiny rectangles. That marked the level where he'd seen the tomes.

He touched the ring there.

A flash of light, a rush of air, and the shelves filled with murky jars, ancient iron boxes, and rows of books and scrolls. Par ignored everything but the written materials. Some tomes were huge, as large as a stout man's chest. The first he pulled had a rotten binding. Pages fell out and scattered at his feet.

"Crap." He gathered them up again.

"Something wrong?" Kaj said from outside.

"I'm all right." He stuffed the brittle pages back between the covers—probably out of order—and promised himself to be more careful. Then he tested a corner of the tome in the doorway's blue fire. It passed undamaged, so he held through the entire book. Kaj carried it to Enio, waiting near the entrance of the main chamber.

The next he took was thicker than Eloria's Rule, with strange silver words etched in charred and blackened leather. It was more intact than the last. He passed it out to Kaj and continued the process, delivering as many books and scrolls at once as he could manage. His progress slowed when he reached the higher shelves and had to climb. But row by row, the shelves emptied.

He came to the last row of books. Among them was a set of a dozen smaller volumes. He gathered them in his arms, but a few slipped out and hit the floor. The ones he'd managed to hang on to, he brought to the waiting Kaj. A skarix flew across the room behind her.

"Watch out!" he shouted.

She glanced around. "They're beginning to rouse, but we've still got time. Leave them to me."

Par took a breath, nodded, and returned to the books he'd dropped. He snatched them up and figured he'd send them out the door before finishing the shelf.

Kaj stood with her hands raised, conjuring at the skarix.

Par remembered she had said to turn away. Before he could, her head bloomed with purple shadow, the same glory as that of Cronus and Legate and Juris.

She was in league with the Ortu!

Her dark eyes fell on him. Her shadowy glory faded. She stepped toward the blue curtain.

In complete shock, Par dropped his books and staggered back. "You're—"

"Yes." She stopped, her face unreadable. "And if you tell Enio, I'll kill you both."

Chapter Thirty-One

"How many more?" Enio shouted from the hallway.

Too shocked to speak, Par couldn't answer. Kaj was one of the Ortu. She'd kill them if he told.

She leaned closer to the vault's blue veil. "We'll talk later." She called back to Enio. "Almost done."

Par turned away. He glanced at the jars, at the chests, pondering what powerful magics he might use against her. But even if he knew what he was looking for, or how to use what he found, Kaj might grab anything he brought from the vault to use herself. A simple weapon wouldn't help either: he was no match against her in a knife fight.

Was there anything he could do? He was safe in here. But what about Enio? If she attacked his friend, he wouldn't know what hit him.

As Par teetered on the edge of disaster, he realized that whatever Kaj's plans, she was still the key to getting past the skarix with the tomes. He had to play along until they'd found Vex. He'd have to trust that the wizard's magic was stronger than hers.

So he held his tongue and gathered the final few books.

When he'd removed the last, he used the Luminary's ring to send the untouched jars and boxes from the shelves back into the well. He considered bringing the ring to Vex. But again, Kaj might steal the magic for Cronus. He set the ring on the low wall and left the vault.

Kaj followed him across the chamber.

Enio waited outside. "You look tired, Par. You all right?"

Before Par figured out an answer, Kaj said, "He had to climb a lot of shelves. Let's go rest."

"Yeah." Enio rubbed his shoulders. "Good idea."

They returned to their sleeping room, where Enio had piled a small mountain of books and scrolls on the table. Kaj thumbed through a tome.

"Don't," Par said, not wanting her to learn anything more. "They're not for us."

Enio plopped into a chair. "Once we find Vex, it's his problem, anyway. We're done."

"And if we don't find him," Par said darkly, "what about the Abbot?"

His friend's eyes flashed. "Can the Threshold get us to the Argent outpost, to Cronus?"

"Only to the ledge, not inside. It's protected. And by now, Cronus has blocked the windows." He half expected Kaj to react to his mention of Cronus. But she remained composed.

"Like I said, we're done." Enio sat back.

"We're not done," Par said. "Unless you want us to just stay here and hide."

"Or go someplace else."

"Like where?"

"Like with Kaj."

She smiled.

Par's stomach chilled.

"But," Enio added, "maybe you're right. Maybe you're safer staying here."

Par took a moment to digest that. "You mean, you want us to split up?"

"Well, you've got food. You've got the vault to explore; the entire Citadel. You'll have the keystone so you can leave when Cronus isn't after you anymore. And," Enio shrugged, "hiding is kind of what you do."

"I… sorry?"

"You know what I mean. Your invocation problem."

Par's chilled insides began to steam. "I don't hide because I want to. I have to. Like you have to run."

"Run?"

"Away from St. Livius. Away from Argent. Away from everything. It's what *you* do."

Enio grinned a fierce, broken smile. "Like I run from Cronus?"

Par couldn't argue with that. His friend was obsessed with killing Cronus, even though it was crazy.

"Hells," Enio added, "I'd join the Arcanan navy if they'd get me within a league of the bastard."

"Join Arcana's side? How could you just—"

"Guys," interrupted Kaj, closing a book.

Par snapped around. For a moment, he'd forgotten Kaj and her threat. Enio's statement about Par *hiding* had hit just that deep. Was that really how Enio saw him?

She went on. "It's natural for friends to see things differently as they mature. Remember, no one can sail their boat—"

"—by someone else's star," Enio said, finishing for her.

That fancy language didn't sound like Enio.

"Anyway," Kaj continued, "from what Enio's told me, hiding from Cronus isn't a bad thing."

Par didn't believe for a minute she meant that. "Then what should we do, Kaj?" He tried to keep the sneer from his voice.

"Is there a hurry to decide? We seem safe for the moment."

If she was working for Cronus, she'd want to deliver Par straight away. What was she up to now?

"Fine," he said. "We'll find Vex together."

"After that," Enio began, "I'll show Kaj the *Sea Dog* and—"

"Do what you *want*, Enio!" Par was on the verge of letting Enio fend for himself with Kaj. He took a breath. "The next time we open a Threshold to Aurix, Vex or not, we send the books through. If you and Kaj want to leave after that, whatever." Hopefully, this would give Par a chance to tell Enio about her threats. Enio would never go off with Kaj once he knew she was part of the Ortu cult.

At least, Par hoped not.

"All right?" Par added, glancing from one to the other.

Enio shrugged again. Kaj said nothing.

"It's settled," Par stated. "But I hate waiting another whole day for this Threshold to work. And hauling these piles of books up to the Council Chamber would take almost that long, assuming we can find it again."

"Can Augle help?" Enio asked.

Par hesitated. "Come look with me. Kaj can guard the books and—"

"Let's stay together," she said.

Before Par objected, Enio agreed.

With a frown, Par followed both. He wondered again how Enio would react when he learned Kaj was with the Ortu. Would it break him, send him forever over the edge?

Or would he even care?

Chapter Thirty-Two

"Hey, Augle!" Enio's words echoed down the corridor. Par winced at the shout, but at least *inside* the Citadel, only the skarix had presented any danger. That is, until Kaj.

After several more intersections, Augle's sing-song hum drifted from ahead. He stood at the bottom of an elegant banister, shaking the hem of a prone skeleton's robe. A swirl of dust floated between the rails.

"That's Augle," Enio mumbled to Kaj. "He's a phantom."

"Goodness," she said, "you're a fountain of knowledge, aren't you?"

Enio grinned.

Par shook his head at Kaj's obvious guile. He stepped forward. "Hi, Augle."

The man frowned. "Now what?"

"Sorry to bother you again. Do you know where a Threshold is?"

Augle's frown sagged into a scowl. "A what now?"

"It's like an archway, with a step."

The caretaker returned to his job. "Lots of archways. Lots of steps."

Enio stretched his arms wide. "A big black one with sigils."

"Oh, them." Augle ran his finger along the banister, eyed it, then brushed the rails with his duster. "One by the vault."

"Any others?" Par said.

"Council Chambers."

"Besides—"

Augle glared.

"Sorry, Augle. Are there any closer?"

"There's one in the gardens." The caretaker heaved a sigh. "S'pose you want me to show you?"

"Please?"

The man dusted off his hands. "Guess I got time. Been years since the latrines needed a scrub."

He led them through the maze-like halls. Kaj whispered to Enio about the size of the place. Enio tried to explain more of the Vigil. When he glanced at Par for help, Par turned away, not wanting to add anything to Kaj's knowledge. But it was agonizing that he couldn't tell Enio why.

At last, a gentle ramp rose to a wide doorway. Beyond and to either hand stretched an immense chamber of well-ordered planters, trimmed trees and leafy bushes, many budded or fruiting. Carts and wheelbarrows dotted the area—plus a few crumpled and aproned skeletons. The ceiling was all latticed glass.

"Out there." Augle pointed across the room toward a set of closed doors.

The air hung sweet and musky. They arrived at the doors. "Help me push," Par said.

Enio came to his side. Kaj stood back.

The doors opened slowly, pushing through a familiar blue shimmer—another Citadel seal. Trees, vines, and overgrown vegetation crowded the sun-speckled courtyard outside.

Par turned to Augle. "Where—"

Too late. In a streak of light, the man shot off.

"Hey," Enio said, "look at this." He pushed his arm through the seal.

"Don't—" Par began.

Enio stepped out into the courtyard.

"Enio!"

His friend turned, grinning. "See? I'm fine."

"That's not…" Par sighed. "Can you come back in?"

When Enio reached out a hand, it sparked as it touched the blue glow.

"Ouch!" He yanked it away.

"Dammit, Enio." Par considered telling Enio, right then, the truth about Kaj. His friend couldn't get back near her.

But she could still get out.

So Par stepped through the seal to the courtyard. Kaj kept on his heels.

Enio pushed aside a clump of foliage. "Where's the Threshold?"

Kaj peered through a thicket. "Is that it?"

Several paces away, a vine-shrouded gazebo stood in patchy sunlight.

"Must be." Par glanced back at the greenhouse. "Wait here. I'll go get the tomes."

"I'll come too," Kaj said.

"You can't. Only I can get back inside."

They locked eyes, tension hanging thick between them. Despite Par's exasperation with Enio, Par hated leaving him alone with her. But there seemed no other option.

Enio was already easing through the vegetation. "We'll check out the Threshold."

Par watched them a moment longer, then passed back through the blue veil. Inside, an empty wheelbarrow caught his attention. He rolled it down the ramp, through the long halls to the room where they'd stacked the books, and filled it up. With many grunts and groans, he pushed it again through the Citadel and back up the ramp. Augle was nowhere in sight.

He paused outside the exit to catch his breath. Kaj stood beside Enio. He was invoking with a green glory—Lani's weaving sigil. Vines and tangles dropped away from the gazebo. A stone arch stood in its center, with a single black step.

The Threshold.

"The élan?" Kaj was saying. "I've heard of it, but I've never known anyone who could use it."

Enio rubbed the back of his neck. "It's not so hard."

"Is it common in Eloria?"

"Hells, no. Anything other than lumina is forbidden. They'll arrest you."

"I suppose we've all got secrets to keep." Par grimaced and pushed his burden over to them.

Just then, Kaj grabbed Enio and yanked him to the side.

His glory blinked out. "What—"

Par dropped the handles of his wheelbarrow. Before he dove to help his friend, she pointed above them. "Careful. It's venomous."

What had seemed like another hanging vine writhed and curled. It was more grey than green and glimmered with a noxious sheen. Then, with unnatural speed, it snapped away and disappeared.

"Snake?" Enio said.

Kaj studied the overhead tangles. "Shadow vine."

Enio shrugged. "I can handle vines."

"These aren't normal. They keep to the gloom, hunt in the shadows. So stay in the light. Needless to say, we don't want to be out here after sundown."

There was no way of telling whether this was true. Par eyed the other vines. None moved. In any case, sunset was still hours away. "I'll get another load," he said. "Stack these near the Threshold."

"I got it." Enio took over the wheelbarrow.

Kaj came beside Par and lowered her voice. "Listen—"

Uninterested in more threats, Par left her there and reentered the greenhouse.

The next wheelbarrow he came across was heaped with parched soil. But he found a flat-topped pushcart and took that instead. Once he'd stacked it with books, trying to make the fewest trips possible, he returned to the courtyard. The tomes he'd brought last time rested in piles near the Threshold. Enio and Kaj sat next to them, eating something.

She licked her blue-stained fingers. "When I was young, we called these berries 'fairy eyes'."

Enio chuckled.

As Par approached, they looked up. "It that all?" Enio asked.

"One more trip." Par picked a few berries and popped one in his mouth. The tart sweetness barely registered. He returned inside with the emptied wheelbarrow for the remaining books. This might be his last chance to do something about Kaj. But what?

As he loaded the rest, he worked through his options. Attacking her wasn't one of them—she was more than capable of killing him, just as she'd threatened. He had a darker thought: even if Par tried to knock her out, would Enio help him? Or protect her?

Maybe he could strand Kaj here when they left through the Threshold. It seemed like a long shot, but he'd watch for the opportunity.

But if not…

Par selected a book that was in pretty bad shape. He removed a page, and using the juice from the berries, scratched out a note.

Kaj is Ortu!!

He blew it dry and slipped it back. Then he returned to the greenhouse and out through the seal.

"That's it." He pushed it to the gazebo. Everyone began carrying the books to stack near the rest. Again, he watched Kaj from the corner of his eyes, where she moved, how she turned, looking for any chance to catch her off guard. He found none.

When they'd moved all the books to the Threshold, Par lifted his keystone. "First, I'll search for Vex. Don't put anything through yet."

Enio stood back, Kaj beside him.

One by one, he opened the portal to the same places as before. Still no Vex.

"Now what?" Enio asked.

"Let's bring the books to the inn," Par said. "That should keep us out of sight of the Arcanan authorities long enough to work out our next steps."

"The innkeeper respects my privacy," Kaj said. "He won't bother our rooms."

Par suddenly wondered if the innkeeper was a follower of Ortu as well. But anywhere would be a risk, and there was no place that seemed as safe. He opened the doorway to their old room. No one had disturbed it since they'd left.

"All right," Par said. "Put the books across the Threshold, but don't step through."

They began moving the tomes and scrolls into the room. Par divided his concentration between holding the portal open and Kaj. He kept the book containing Enio's note to the side.

When they'd transferred the stacks, Par passed the tattered book to Enio. "Be careful with this one. I think it's extra important." He winked.

Enio didn't seem to get the hint, but just reached the book through the doorway.

With his every ounce of strength, Par shoved him.

Enio yelped and tumbled forward.

Par tried to follow. Kaj grabbed him from behind.

Par fell back. He wouldn't make it. He tossed the keystone. "Enio, find Vex!"

The room, along with Enio, flashed and disappeared.

"No!" Kaj shouted. She leapt through the arch. But only the jungle now showed beyond.

Par bolted full speed back to the greenhouse.

"Wait!" she shouted.

He reached the doors, dove inside and scrambled to his feet. Kaj pulled up short before the seal.

"Kill us?" Par said. "Who's dead now?" Before Kaj responded, he strode away.

Yet he felt no triumph at his escape. No joy.

Sure, Enio was safe with the tomes, and with any luck would soon find Vex.

But Par had tossed him the keystone, and now had no way home himself.

Chapter Thirty-Three

KAJ CALLED FROM outside the greenhouse. "Wait, Par! Listen!"

Par shook her words from his ears and continued deeper into the Citadel. She was one of the Ortu cult, like Cronus, Legate and Juris. Enio would bring Vex the tomes. Par's goal now was to find a way home.

He hurried back to the vault, hoping it might hide another keystone. As he got closer, the air filled with the buzzing whine of the skarix. He slowed and peeked into the vault's outer chamber. The skarix had roused.

Later, when they became less active or Par found a torch to drive them back, he'd try to get past them. He returned to the room where he'd last slept. Enio's bag of fruit still sat on the floor, but Par had no appetite. He tied the bag to his belt and left.

The quiet halls stretched away like the streets of an abandoned city. For the first time since the alleys of Argent, Par walked alone, with only his thoughts for company. The further he wandered, the less comforting those thoughts became.

He checked each skeleton he came across for a keystone. A

shiver climbed his neck whenever a bony hand slipped from a sleeve, or a vacant eye socket seemed to ask a silent question—the question he'd begun asking himself.

After leaving Wishbone, Kaj had saved them from the bandits with the accuracy and quickness of her knife-throwing. Outside the greenhouse, even if she needed Par alive, she could have nailed him in the leg, dropping him before he'd gotten away.

Why hadn't she?

He had stranded her outside the Citadel seals. She might be skilled in wilderness survival, but how would she handle the shadow vines after dark? Or the dust demons haunting the nearby Devastation? What other monstrosities roamed these lands?

But she'd threatened to kill him. She'd brought this on herself.

As he searched, he entered a balcony above a chamber lined with somber portraits and statues. Augle stood below, buffing a sculpture.

Par watched him for a moment. The man appeared satisfied with his life, barren of company. Par called down. "Hello, Augle."

The custodian peered up.

"Hey," Par said, "any idea where I can find a keystone?"

"What's that?"

"It's a fat black key, but more like a stone."

"No idea."

"Oh. Well, thanks anyway."

"Where's the rest of you?"

Without giving a lot of background, Par couldn't explain the circumstances around Enio and Kaj. And there seemed no point. "They're—they left."

"Good. Less work for me." The man returned to his labors.

Par leaned over the stone banister. Perhaps Enio was right. They'd retrieved the tomes; they were finished with this fight. Par had everything here he needed. In time, he'd dare the vault again. But what was the rush? Cronus couldn't get at him.

Besides, hadn't Par wanted a home with no one to judge or persecute him? The Citadel might be the answer to his prayers.

He sighed; his prayers hadn't included being alone.

Augle hummed some rhythmic tune and moved to another statue.

Then again, Par had this so-called phantom for company. And Par had become accustomed to a small social circle. For years, his closest companion had been Enio.

Yet that thought brought no cheer, only a heavier heart. Were his journeys with Enio over? Each had grown. Maybe apart.

He spoke through a tightness in his chest. "I might be here a while, Augle. I can help you with your work." The man was odd, but Par might someday call him a friend.

"Don't need no help."

"Well, I'll need to keep busy."

"Why's that?"

Par shrugged. Getting a job was another out-of-reach thing he'd wanted. "I want to make a living."

"Not much livin' in here."

A pair of skeletons near Augle lay in a crumpled heap. Par would have to get used to that kind of grim sight. A fitting task might be to bury them. Not in the Devastation, of course. In the outer gardens? But there were those shadow vines…

With sick horror, Par realized the Citadel would seem even lonelier without the dead.

A moan broke from his throat. He choked it back.

Augle stopped his work. "Sumptin' wrong up there?"

Par rubbed his face. "Everyone's gone, Augle. What good is anything you're doing? Can't you just leave?"

"I don't go beyond the lights." He nodded to the ever-present blue-white orbs along the ceiling.

"Why not?"

"They make me."

It was as Par had feared but refused to accept. The Vigil might be gone, but their magic remained. Augle wasn't real.

"Besides," the man added. "Who'd do the cleanin'?"

For a moment, Par's grief hardened into anger. "Who cares! What does it matter?"

"It's my job. I'm the caretaker." Augle continued his chores.

As Par stared, his useless anger dissipated like Augle's dust. The caretaker had his job, and his place, with no concern for anything else. Wasn't that all Par wanted himself?

He realized that, in fact, it wasn't.

Cronus had once hunted Par across Eloria and the Borderlands. Even defeated, the man had chased him across life and death. Par could create a peaceful, solitary life here, safe from Cronus and Legate. But the Abbot was still imprisoned. Enio and Vex weren't out of the Ortu's reach. Neither was anyone else.

Enio had been wrong. The Citadel didn't have everything Par needed.

He watched the caretaker. Augle was hollow. This place was hollow. Par would become hollow too, if he abandoned the people he cared for.

The Abbot's words returned.

Wisdom is knowing on which side of the bars we do the most good.

Now Par was certain. This was the wrong side.

Without a word, he left the balcony. Whatever he did next, he had to make sure of something before leaving Kaj outside, alone, to die.

He strode the halls back to the Greenhouse. Kaj sat on the steps of the gazebo, sharpening a knife.

Par took a breath, ready to jump aside if she managed some dark magic through the seal. "You're one of the Ortu," he called.

She looked over. "I'm Dark Reckoned, yes. When I was younger."

"Why?"

"It wasn't my choice." She paused. "Juris is my father."

"Juris?" Par said sharply. He'd never imagined. "So you both work for Cronus?"

"All I know about Cronus is what Enio told me." She approached the door.

Par backed up.

She stopped and leaned against the outside wall, looking away. "Months ago, the Ortu chapters were told to watch for you. Last week in Wishbone, I heard someone mention your names. I helped you to Aurix to turn you in. I'm sorry."

Though Par grappled with these new revelations, he said nothing.

"I realize my apology doesn't mean much," she added. "Even though I'm stuck with this Reckoning, I don't follow the ways of Ortu. Years ago, when I told my father I wanted to be normal again, he sent me away, said he didn't want to see me anymore until I understood the gift, the power, he'd given me. He made me a courier for the capital."

This brought up a worse possibility. "Do the Majesties know Juris is Dark Reckoned?" Did Arcana support Ortu magic?

She shook her head. "My father hides it. He doesn't even conjure in public. He has servants for that, so no one sees his dark aura."

Par realized Kaj had hidden hers as well. He'd never seen her conjure until the vault.

"I don't expect your forgiveness," she said.

"I wasn't giving it. You threatened to kill me."

"Yeah, well, that was a bluff. I didn't want Enio to find out about me. I like him and… I keep running out of people I like."

Her head sagged. "It's been lonely, never settling in one place long enough to make friends. Then I saw a chance to reunite with my father, make him proud. I told him you were at the inn looking for Vex. He'd already suspected Vex of keeping secrets from the Progrades, so he followed you all to the Aerie."

The story cleared Lady Agatha as the one who'd betrayed them. Still, how much of this tale should Par believe? He was angry with Kaj, no doubt about it. But if she spoke the truth, she'd struggled with a problem not of her making, only to be cast out to live a life of lies. Par understood from personal experience how that kind of life could twist you up.

Yes, he was angry, but not enough to hate her.

Much less let her die.

"If it's any consolation," she said, "I know now I'll never follow my father's dark philosophies. And if I can, I'll make things up to you."

Par frowned. "How?"

"I know the ways of Ortu. Maybe there's something you can use against Cronus."

That might be true. They were silent as Par's brain wrestled with his heart over everything she'd told him. Finally, he said, "I went looking for another keystone, but haven't found one."

"This is a big place. You weren't gone very long."

"I wasn't?" It had felt like hours.

Her voice came soft. "When you're not used to being alone, time seems to go on forever."

Par chewed his lip, then took a fortifying breath. "Kaj, put away your knife. I'm coming out."

She turned to him. "Why? And how can you trust me?"

"I guess I can't. But I can't let you die more than I can't trust you."

"Even without a knife, I'm a better fighter than you."

"I know. But I'll feel better anyway. And you need me to get back home."

Kaj nodded and tucked it away.

Par stepped through the seal. "If I have to, I'll search the Citadel top to bottom for a keystone. But there might be a faster way back to Aurix."

Chapter Thirty-Four

PAR STUDIED THE overgrown trees and thickets.

Kaj stepped beside him. "What's the plan?"

"If Enio tries to use the Threshold at Aurix to bring us home, my guess is it won't work until midnight. That marks a full day after we last used it. Even then, it's probably guarded."

"You can't be in these gardens after dark."

"I know, but—"

"Look," she said, "it's my fault you're still here. Go inside for now. I'll take care of myself."

Though Par was still unsure of how much he trusted her, he'd committed to not letting her die. "As long as Enio brings the tomes and keystone to Vex, I'll—we'll be rescued. But you're right, we can't wait here. There's another place they'll search. I need to get us there."

"Where's that?"

Par decided not to be too specific: if she were still lying, at least she'd need his help to get home. "Nearer to the Devastation and the dust demons."

"The *what,* now?"

"I'll explain later." It would be easier once she saw for herself. "I can duck into the Citadel then, if I have to. But you—"

"The Ortu sigils are handy for creating shadows and gloom and confusion. I'd likely remain unnoticed."

Was she reassuring him just to get him moving? To appear open and honest and regain his trust? If she were manipulating him again, the risks were on her.

Except, of course, this was his idea.

Crap. Why was dealing with this person always so complicated?

He scanned the winks of sunlight through the branches to get his bearings, then pointed along the wall. "The Devastation's that way."

Staying as much in the spotty sunlight as possible, they pushed through the brush. The going wasn't easy. Trees and bushes, untended for years, slowed their progress. He stumbled into a muddy puddle; water sloshed into his boot. After a swampy stretch forced their path deeper among the trees, Par spotted a wooden cottage.

"What do you think?" Kaj said.

Par wiped his forehead. "I think I need a breather. Let's check it out."

Another cottage lay nearby, and more beyond that. Small fenced areas spread between them, all long claimed by the forest. Par recognized a crumbling chicken coop.

They crept to the broken window of the closest cottage. Nothing moved inside.

Kaj disappeared around the corner.

A moment later, she yelped. Par hurried after her. "Kaj?"

The trees thinned beyond. The cottages rested on a hill high above the sands of the Devastation. Kaj stared from the front porch toward the grim barren landscape. Though dirty clouds blew across the distant horizon, the rest seemed dead and undisturbed.

"Dust demons," Par said. "But still far off."

"I hope they stay that way."

"You and me both."

Beyond the cottages, the Citadel continued along the rocky hilltops, its buildings and elegant towers yellow with age and wind and sand.

"We're going to that tower." Par pointed to where he and Enio had arrived. This time, he'd have to climb the soaring outer steps. The mere thought weakened his knees.

"Is that a road?" Kaj asked.

Par saw it, running below the walls in full view of the Devastation. "We should wait until sunset. Maybe then we'll be less visible to the dust demons."

"Good idea." She stepped into the cottage.

At the doorway, Par paused. The place looked long abandoned. A table, chairs, stone hearth, cupboard, the floor now a carpet of soggy leaves. The walls were grey with unpleasant blotches, and the sagging roof was cracked along one side. Even the air was dank and moldy. Partway back, a door hung open to another room.

Kaj stooped to examine the hearth. "We could light a fire, but it's a bit clogged."

Par came closer, careful not to touch anything. "Even if we tried, the smoke might attract something."

She straightened and brushed off her hands. "I can dry the place, at least. Watch out."

Before Par asked what Kaj had in mind, she invoked. The shadowy glory of Ortu surrounded her head.

He backed again toward the entrance.

She held her hands over a damp blanket that draped a chair. The material twisted and shriveled, like it was catching fire, yet it didn't smolder or flame. As she moved around the cottage, the leaves dried and rustled. The chairs creaked. Whatever spores and mold filled the stuffy air fell away, and the atmosphere freshened.

Kaj ended her conjuration. "An Ortu sigil called a Withering."

Par frowned at the word.

"You're right," she said. "Dark sigils aren't generally life giving, but this one's helpful in the wilds. I can do your boots if you want. You'll have to remove them first if you don't want tinder toes."

After watching the writhing blanket, Par didn't need to ask what she meant. And his feet were indeed marshy. He took off his boots. She dried them too. Then he helped straighten the furniture and shake the blankets outside.

The second room held a bed and cradle—both, thank the gods, empty of bones. Par settled at the table. Kaj had found a tattered doll with ratty brown hair and sat across from him, tidying it.

She seemed more and more a contradiction. A follower of Ortu, but in other ways as normal as anyone. All he could do was watch and wonder.

Kai glanced up. "Go ahead."

"Go ahead and what?"

"Get down to the salt. Ask your questions."

In fact, Par had several. One pushed to the front. "Did you do something to Enio?"

"Sort of."

Par narrowed his eyes. "What's that mean, sort of?"

"That morning you awoke in camp and found us talking, I'd sent a gloom into his mind while he slept. He turned it into an anxiety dream. That made him more... suggestible."

"So he's under some witchery?" It explained a lot.

She shook her head. "Ortu is in many ways weaker than other types of magic, but it can influence emotions, *dark* them. That's what I did to Enio as he dreamt. But that's long worn off. He's his own person again."

Somehow, this wasn't the answer Par had wanted. His friend's moods, his distance, his growing attachment to Kaj, would have been easier to explain with magic. But it didn't seem to be the case.

"What did you want from him?" Par asked.

"To be honest, I wanted to split you two up."

"Why?"

"I thought he'd try to keep you safe."

She was probably right. But Par wasn't the only one Enio might want to keep safe. "He likes you, you know."

"I like him too."

"When he finds out you're with the Ortu…"

She nodded. "I owe it to him to tell."

"I wrote him a note." Par wasn't sure why he should feel guilty about that. But at the moment, he did.

"Oh." She paused. "You're a good friend to him, Par."

Par wondered if that friendship still went both ways.

She focused again on the doll, untangling its hair. "Someone tried to make a home here."

"Yeah," Par said, welcoming the change of topic. "I guess it didn't last."

"Not much does."

That touched something inside him.

Suddenly, tiny insect legs poked from the doll's hair.

Par lunged forward and slapped the doll from her hands. It skated across the table.

Kaj yanked back. "What's wrong?"

A grey spider crawled from the doll.

"Is it dangerous?" Par asked. The smaller a skarix, the deadlier it was.

Amusement flickered across her face. "The doll or the spider?" She reached a finger toward the crawling creature.

As it inched onto her knuckle, Par gasped. In a land of deadly insects and demons of the Devastation and shadow vines, the little grey spider just sat there, innocent and oblivious.

Kaj nodded at the doll. "But you can never tell with strange women in the wilderness, can you?"

Par warmed with embarrassment. He'd had the same overreaction with the chameleon spiders when Lani appeared after her long absence.

For some reason, he laughed.

Kaj laughed too.

"Sorry." Par caught himself.

"No worries. It's just a harmless house spider." She set it down. It wandered slowly off, exploring the table.

"Maybe someone lived here while the Vigil was alive," Par said.

"I'm sure it was a pleasant spot, once."

Par remembered the bag of fruit on his belt. He lifted out two pears. "This might be the strangest picnic I've ever had. Except once with Enio, we were eating berries, got attacked by bats, and fell into a swamp." That was how he'd first met Lani back in the Urdel woodlands.

Kaj accepted the fruit. As they ate, he added, "But I wonder why people wanted to live outside the Citadel walls?"

"Stone walls and iron gates aren't for everyone. Some of us would rather sit beneath the trees."

In certain ways, she reminded him of Lani too.

"By the way, Par, thanks for saving me from the spider."

He forced a smile. "I get it. I panicked. Don't rub it in."

"I'm serious."

"You said the spider wasn't dangerous."

"Yes." She picked the doll back up and brushed a smudge off its face. "But you didn't know that."

CHAPTER THIRTY-FIVE

ENIO LED LIGHTNING up the late morning streets of Aurix. Passersby ignored him. They had no clue about the things he knew that threatened all their lives—such as Cronus, who now controlled the Eminence of Eloria. Or this whole Ortu thing. Those who had seen that shadow stab the moon probably thought it was a cloud.

In fact, he and Par had saved everyone from Cronus just last year, and here Enio was, doing it again. At the Citadel, he'd tried to convince Par they were done with this fight. That was a lie; Enio hadn't finished with Cronus. Not by a long throw.

The donkey gave a frustrated bray. Without money for a cart, Enio had overloaded the animal with book-stuffed sacks. "Sorry, boy. Let's rest a minute."

As they stopped, someone bumped into Enio from behind. He stumbled. "Hey—"

"You're blocking the road," grumbled a square-jawed man in a floppy hat. He pushed past, carrying a large reed basket.

Enio narrowed his eyes. After a quick glance around, he invoked.

The basket's corner unraveled. An apple dropped out, followed by several more.

The man pulled up short. "Crap crackin' crust buckets…"

"Let me help," Enio said sweetly. While the man repaired his basket, Enio gathered the apples for him—hiding two down his shirt.

"Watch yourself next time," grunted the man. He trudged on.

Tipping his cap, Enio offered Lightning an apple. "With all we've done, they owe us."

The donkey crunched it, seeming to agree.

Enio ate the other, but his thoughts were far away. He still didn't understand what had happened at the Citadel. When Par shoved him through the Threshold, it seemed like a joke at first, or payback for Enio stabbing him. Had Par taken his advice to stay hidden in the Citadel?

Maybe. But Kaj too?

And as Enio fell through the Threshold, Par had shouted, "Find Vex!" He had sounded panicked. When Enio turned, the Threshold had closed.

He shook his head. It didn't make sense. Too much didn't these days. Except getting these books to Vex.

And killing Cronus.

As they continued through the city, Enio caught sight of the dome-shaped palace on its high hill. He guided the donkey that way. The streets weaved in frustrating directions, like the paths of crazy birds, but he kept a bead on the palace. At noon, they reached the base of the hill. A gated wall blocked the road. Two hulking guards stood before it, one in a red cape. Both held crystal-tipped spears.

"What's your business?" the caped one asked.

"I'm here to see the Umbriarch."

"Papers?"

"She's expecting me."

The other said, "Verily, Captain, for tea." They both laughed.

Enio rubbed Lightning's nose. "Hey, you guys heard the rumors of Elorian spies?"

"What of them?" The captain lost his amused smile.

"I happen to know where they are."

"Do you, now?"

It was then Enio made his gamble. He invoked a simple healing sigil, though not to heal anything. Just to twinkle the golden glory of Elorian lumina around his head.

Both men's eyes widened like saucers.

"Verily," Enio said, "you're looking at one."

"Hold!" barked the captain, pointing his spear. A silver glory burst from his head, and a dagger of light sprouted from the spear tip. It reached out and stopped at Enio's throat with a hot, unsettling prick. He had no plans to resist.

"Bind him," the captain said.

The other tied Enio's hands and hooded his head. They searched him, but he'd hidden his dagger, along with the keystone, among the tomes.

Then they muscled him forward. Close behind, Lightning brayed a few times, but soon seemed resigned to his new masters.

The guards delivered Enio, bound and hooded, back into the bittersweet air of the palace jail. A door thudded shut, and he was alone. If all went as planned, the guards would tell the Majesties of their prisoner, the Majesties would summon him, along with Vex, and Vex would get the tomes.

But then what? How could Enio get to Cronus?

Sitting in the heavy silence of his cell, he wondered if that was even possible.

He lay back. Par might be right. Enio should let it go. He could live in Arcana, find Kaj again and become a courier. Or sail the *Sea Dog* back to the Deep World. Par had accused him of running. None of these things were running. They were fresh starts, following his own star, like Kaj had said. And he had a flying sigil. Maybe even the stars weren't beyond his reach.

Yet none of these thoughts were quite convincing. As long as Cronus was out there—and in his head—Enio would never be free.

An hour later, his cell door opened and someone escorted him blindly out. After many stairs and jangling keys and creaking doors, they halted.

"Release him," boomed a voice.

A guard removed Enio's hood and untied his hands. He stood again in the throne room. The Progrades sat as before in their gilded chairs around the perimeter, minus one member—Juris. From the throne, the Aubade watched with a frown. Vex stood before the Umbriarch's empty seat.

"Enio," Vex said, "where's Par?"

"He's still at the Citadel, but I—"

The Aubade interrupted. "When were you last in Argent?"

"Argent? We left there last week and—"

"You've seen their navy, firsthand?"

Enio nodded.

"Very well. You will record what you know of their numbers, their sigils, everything."

"Majesty," Vex said. "We should focus on the Ortu. Last night—"

"Yes, yes, the Umbriarch has so informed me. Others will debate the significance of that demonstration."

"I brought the tomes," Enio said, raising his hand.

Vex spoke again, excitement obvious in his voice. "Majesty, let me examine them. They may be the key—"

"I will prepare my defenses against Eloria, not speculate over some obscure cult."

"Eloria is not the danger, Majesty. The Abbot confirmed

these things to me through the Threshold. A force hostile to all controls their Eminence. The Ortu is rising. We saw—"

"You saw a show of shadow. For a copper, you'll see another in a theater."

"Yet the guards could not use their sigils during that time."

"The guards were afraid." The Majesty's voice rose. "Panic is the best destroyer of one's mind, and one's magic."

"But—"

The Aubade slammed a fist on his throne. "Eloria has threatened Arcana. Arcana will respond." The words echoed through the lofty chamber. No one dared speak.

Finally, the Aubade took a deep breath. "For the moment, you are not needed in that regard. Examine your tomes and tell me what use they may be. Guard, bring their books to Vex's chambers."

Vex bowed. "Thank you, Majesty."

When the guard had led them into the palace halls, Enio tried to tell Vex more of what had happened at the Citadel. But Vex quickly hushed him. Enio got the hint: Vex didn't want to speak of it in public.

They were taken to the stables. Lightning seemed well cared for. With the help of two servants, they brought the sacks of books and scrolls to Vex's room and were left to themselves. The sun slanted in from the balcony onto the table. A serving tray waited with goblets and wine.

"Put this someplace, would you?" Vex handed Enio the tray.

As Enio moved it to the writing desk, Vex began rummaging through the sacks. "Wonderful work, Enio. But Par—"

"He pushed me through the Threshold. He didn't follow."

Vex turned. "Why?"

"Who knows? Kaj is with him."

"Your companion, the courier?"

Enio didn't need another lecture about bringing her through

the Threshold, and so he skipped the details. "We tried to find you, but we found her instead."

"Well, there's nothing we can do about it now. Hopefully, Par will return when he is safe."

"He can't, not without the keystone." Enio retrieved it and his dagger, wrapped in cloth, from a sack.

Vex's face darkened. "Then he'll need our help. Give it to me."

Enio did, but kept the dagger.

"Our Threshold will allow passage again at midnight." Vex tucked the keystone away. "Until then, my best use of the time is to dig through these books." He placed an armful on the table, sat, and opened a tome bound in blue cloth.

Enio lifted one as well. "What are we looking for?"

"Anything regarding the Immortus. But the Aubade gave you your own task."

"Why does he care about Eloria's navy?"

Vex turned a page as if it were precious silk. "The Aubade has interpreted the threats by Legate as a declaration of war."

"War?" The Aubade had mentioned preparations, but Enio hadn't imagined that war was so close. The last one had ended before he was born.

"The Aubade gathers his forces and makes his strategies. Now let me focus."

Enio sat at the writing desk, pushed aside the tray and lifted a pen. Thoughts of the navy brought images of mighty ships with hardy crews launching spells and missiles. But other than the brief sea chase from Argent, he'd only ever seen that kind of display during high holidays. In a war, the missiles would aim at actual people. Whether Eloria or Arcana, some of those people, like the Abbot, and Leo, and Kaj, had been decent to him.

His pen paused over the parchment. "What if I tell the Aubade I don't remember?"

"He will force you to remember. And we need his permission to get to the Threshold and rescue Par. We can't afford to anger him."

"I think he's always angry."

Vex grumped and continued his studies.

While Enio sketched details of what he recalled of the ships, Vex went through book after book, page after page, dividing the tomes into different stacks.

"Indecipherable," he'd mumble and push a book aside.

"Waste of time." He'd abandon another.

"Blue blazes, I'd never imagine…" He'd pace the room with those.

Enio tried to ignore him, though one comment carried unusual weight.

"Three above. Three below. Two the balance, then and fro."

"The what?" Enio said.

Vex made no response.

Enio shrugged and continued his writing. When at last he'd finished, he showed it to Vex.

The wizard nodded. "That should satisfy the Aubade. Now, a couple of books there are falling apart. Would you mind putting them in order for me?"

"Sure." Enio straightened their pages and set them aside. One with a rotten binding he recognized—hadn't Par said it was important? He opened it. A note written in purple ink slid out. He read the blurry letters. They were in Par's hand.

Kaj is Ortu!!

Enio blinked at the words.

Kaj is Ortu!!

The meaning took form in his head.

No.

He read them again.

And again.

Images of Kaj marched before his eyes: her laughing face as they traveled the road, her skill with knives, her stories of life as a courier, her patient voice as she helped him see the things holding him back.

"Something wrong, son?" Vex was staring at him.

Enio squeezed the note in his palm. "Tired."

"Rest, then."

"I need some air." He looked toward the balcony. Kaj was with the Ortu? But she had helped him! Shown him how to fix his life.

Was Par wrong? Lying?

Was she?

Or was Enio going mad?

He rubbed his temples. Crazy was possible, with everything Cronus had done to him. And whether it was Kaj or Par deceiving him, Vex had been right. Enio could do nothing about it. At least, not from here. He felt worse than useless. Caged without a cage. Tortured by his own soul.

He wanted to shout, scream. He couldn't take this anymore. Had Par been right, and Enio was running? Was he running toward Cronus, or away from his life, from himself? Enio wasn't sure anymore. But he needed to get loose, like Kaj had said.

Vex had his nose buried in a book. Enio left his feathered cap on the writing table, emptied the metal serving tray and brought it out to the balcony. Across the city, the sea sparkled silver in the sunlight. Ship masts in the bay reached toward the wide blue sky.

He peered over the rail, where the walls of the domed palace curved downward like a massive half-buried apple toward the ground. If he messed up this next part, he figured the curves would catch him, slide him down.

Way, way down.

He gripped the tray and invoked the flying sigil.

A blast of air threw him back against the balcony wall.

He gasped and caught his breath. Not enough room for the invocation.

So he concentrated his numena, and with a grip so tight that he dented the tray, leapt over the rail.

Chapter Thirty-Six

Enio's only other attempt with Vex's flying sigil occurred at the base of the Astrologer's Aerie, and it was a disaster: he'd crashed. Still, he'd gotten the feel, and since then watched the shieldriders. The way they handled their shields seemed the key. He tried to hold the serving tray the same.

As he leapt from the balcony, he shot upwards. But his movement slowed like a stone tossed high. He reached the top of an arc and began to fall. His stomach slid into his throat. He panicked. The sigil blinked out.

"Crap!" Enio invoked again. His plummet paused, and he tumbled forwards through the air, head over heels like a drunken monk. He wrestled the tray tight under his feet—all but gripping it with his toes through his boots—and steadied his mind. For a moment, the tumbling changed to a nosedive. But instead of cutting back, he boosted the power, like he'd seen the shieldriders do on a fast descent. He focused less on the tray and more on his hips and belly, the way he'd ridden his canoe through the rapids.

A fresh blast of wind, and his downward plunge became an unsteady forward flight. It demanded more finesse than steering the old *Sea Dog*, but as he adjusted his stance, he found he could go slower, slower, until he floated in the eye of a tempest, the wind whistling around him. Except for an occasional wobble, he hung motionless high above the ground.

Vex's flying sigil took less numena than Enio had expected, though he wasn't sure how long he could maintain it. He leaned forward again. The tray obeyed and moved. Gliding turned out to be easier than holding still.

Faster, he willed. Faster he went. Soon he was soaring above the city like a hawk. The wind whipped his hair and stung his eyes. Tears streaked his temples. He was laughing.

The bay lay to the north. He headed that way. Though he had no delusions about flying across the sea to Eloria, his new freedom brought a clarity. The knots in his brain loosened.

Fishing vessels and high-masted ships dotted the water beyond the city walls. Buildings lined the docks and shipyards. He swooped lower.

Without warning, the very air seemed to evaporate. He shouted, dropping like a rock. He landed near the docks on a heap of old sails.

A wide-shouldered man in a white and blue uniform rushed over, his own glory just dousing. "You, there. This is a no-fly zone!"

Enio brushed himself off. "I've come to join the navy." The words leapt from his mouth, surprising even him. Was that what had driven him here?

"There's an office for that." The man pointed to a stone building.

"Thanks. Sorry."

"Next time it's a fine."

Enio started there, but his eyes wouldn't leave the piers. Great stout ships stood shoulder to shoulder, a forest of masts and rigging. Their sails were furled, but if a single one were spread out, it would cover the entire *Sea Dog* with canvas to spare. Sailors shouted, hammered, wove nets, some using Arcanan magic to help with their jobs.

In Eloria, they would assign someone his age as a dockworker or an errand boy. That wasn't for Enio. He needed to sail.

So he turned down a pier, toward the mighty vessels. He'd talk his way to something better. Good sailors knew their own.

Enio stroked one of the magnificent hulls as he reached its gangplank. "Ahoy!" he shouted up.

A chubby figure with a red woolen cap leaned over the rail. "Ahoy."

"Can I come on board?"

"What's your business, lad?"

"I'm a sailor. I want to enlist."

The man laughed. "Sure, come aboard!"

Enio ran up the plank as if his boots were on fire.

"Wait here." The man strode to the rear cabins.

Enio wished he had more eyes to take everything in. Tall masts and wide sails reached up and up over his head. The sun kindled the crow's nest as if with a glory. Sailors focused on their tasks, unbothered by anything else.

The red-capped man returned. He pointed Enio toward the cabins. "The captain will see you."

Weaving through the busy crew to the door, Enio knocked.

"Come," said a voice.

He peeked inside.

Two white-haired men in blue uniforms sat at a table spread with parchments. Windows in the back lit the room.

Enio waited a minute and coughed.

The men turned. One had a ponytail. An impressive beard decorated the other's face. How that one saw anything through his bushy eyebrows was a mystery.

"Yes?" the pony-tailed man said.

Enio pushed out his chest. "I want to enlist."

"There's an office—"

The bearded man raised a hand. "I've always got time for an ambitious youth. Eager for adventure, boy?"

"Or free rum," said the other.

"Now, now, Lieutenant."

"Admit it, Captain. He looks as useful as a drunkard on night watch."

Enio slumped a little, though the free rum *did* sound appealing. "I want to sail. And I want to fight the enemy."

Cronus.

The captain nodded. "Runaway or Ascended?"

"What?"

"He's a dim one," the lieutenant said. "Your *house*, boy."

Enio stared until it hit him. "The Traveling Mage." Was that a good house for sailors? With any luck, it was better than the one he'd traded Par.

The lieutenant frowned. "And what do you offer the Majesty's navy?"

"Uh, I don't have money."

The captain chortled beneath his whiskers. The lieutenant did not seem amused. "Blast it boy, skills! What skills?"

The parchments before them were line drawings of hulls and parts of vessels. "I built a boat. Not like those, but—"

"No, son," said the captain. "The sea builds ships. Each sail, board and beam, timber to tackle. A shipwright merely takes notes."

Enio understood what the man was saying. He pointed toward a drawing. "That keel is beautiful."

"It is, isn't it? Good eye." The captain motioned Enio to a chair.

Enio took the seat. "Have you been in many battles?"

The lieutenant snorted. "Captain Morten commanded during the Grey Wars."

"You did?"

The captain's eyes glinted beneath his thick brows. "The sea is a strange battlefield. Ships are great noble beasts, reined by the waves and lashed by the winds. The world slides and heaves. Death comes from the arrow, fire and storm—or your own hand, if you're unlucky in the rigging."

Enio's heart beat faster.

The captain took a deep breath, let it out. "I tell you, nothing can compare to sailing a warship. Not everyone's cut out for it, mind you. Yet when the dark masts become as musical notes upon the parchment of the skies… There's no better way for the strong to live."

"Or for the weak to die," the lieutenant added.

"Or a more patriotic one," said Morten.

Enio could almost see it, taste it. He nodded enthusiastically.

"Very well." The captain returned to his papers. "He's all yours, Lieutenant."

"But Captain—"

"If he wants to work, he can work. Find him a job."

The lieutenant sighed. "We might tie him to the bowsprit. Face like that, he'd scare away the sea hags."

"Tie me—?"

Morten cleared his throat.

"A little humor, sir. Weigh anchor, boy. Let's go."

The lieutenant ushered him out of the cabin. "How are you with your incantations?"

Enio opened his mouth and closed it. He didn't dare mention he knew Elorian sigils. Or élan. "Uh, I can fly."

"Fly? We're seamen, not seagulls. Wave? Wind? Wound? What?"

"I can learn what I need."

"Then you'll learn—from the bottom up."

The lieutenant led him past the workers and down steps to a lower deck open at both ends. An odor of sawdust hung in the air. Enio sneezed and wiped his nose. "Will I need special incantations?"

"You'll manage. And the bilge isn't so bad when it's not been used for a chamber pot."

Though Enio had never been on a warship, he knew a few sailing terms. The bilge was the lowest part, farthest from the sails and mast—and the action. He scowled. How could he follow his star if he couldn't see it?

"But I can fight," he said. "I forgot to mention I've got fire-fly."

"It takes many jobs to run a ship. We're brothers in arms and we do what we're told."

Enio tried to find a light in this darkening situation. "How do I get promoted?"

For the first time, the lieutenant laughed.

They continued down a ladder, through a cavernous hold, and to a deeper level lit by lanterns. The smell of oil and tar, and a heavy wave of heat, made it difficult to breathe. Two men, one tall, the other short and round, but both filthy with grease and grime, stirred barrels.

"Jake," the lieutenant barked. "How's this one?"

The tall man stopped stirring. "He'll do, sir."

Enio grimaced. "Isn't there something else? I want to be top-side, casting spells and—"

"There's a keel hauling if you don't clam up and get to it," the lieutenant said, and left.

"About our tea time, isn't it, Piles?" Jake wiped his forehead, smudging the dirt.

"I expect so." The other man smiled through a round, toothless face.

Jake pointed to a gap between the deck planks. "Grab a brush, swabby. There's places we can't reach."

There seemed to be no choice for the moment. And Enio had pitched his own boat, though not into a bilge. He rolled up his sleeves.

They handed him a brush dripping with hot tar. He lay on

his stomach next to the gap and reached in. He squeezed his arm farther, took a breath, and caught full-force the fumes from the brush mixed with the odors from the bilge. Tar, soap, pee and—

He gagged, lost the brush, and yanked back, sick and dizzy.

"Useless cur!"

Enio's head spun. His vision blurred. Beyond the fog loomed a tall, dark man. Enio had stood before him, long ago.

Cronus!

Enio tried to invoke, to send a lantern's fire at the man. But he couldn't focus. And if he hit the barrels, he'd blow them all to the Higher Realms.

In that instant, he didn't care.

A fist hammered his ear. He yelped and fell to the side.

"Think we're made of brushes?"

Enio gripped his throbbing ear. His head cleared. It was Jake standing there, not Cronus.

"What you waiting for?" the man said. "Go find a new brush. Shove off!" He sent a kick Enio's way. Enio dodged and stumbled, coughing, up the steps.

Would he have done it? Killed everyone to be rid of Cronus?

No, he told himself. That had been the fumes talking. Anyway, he'd never get to Cronus from the bilge.

Enio slipped onto the main deck. Men still scurried about. The lieutenant was nowhere in sight.

He timed his movements to avoid the workers, then ran across the deck and down the gangplank. He hurried back to where he'd left his tray, near the pile of sails. With no one watching, he invoked the flying sigil, rose into the air, and sped back over the rooftops toward the palace.

Chapter Thirty-Seven

Enio crouched on his tray and flew a wobbly arc back over the city wall. When he'd nearly exhausted his numena, he landed and walked. By sundown, he spied the palace's lower gates. With a few stiff breaths, he invoked the flying sigil once more. Two unplanned dips and he made it to Vex's balcony.

The wizard still had his nose in the tomes. Enio had used every last drop of his numena, plus muscles he didn't know he had. He grabbed his cap from the writing table and collapsed on the couch. Earlier he'd been confused, desperate. Now he didn't know what he felt, except too tired to think. That felt good in itself.

"Do you smell tar?" Vex sniffed a few times.

"Find anything?" Enio mumbled.

"Enough, I hope. It's time we reported to the Majesties. Bring your notes."

Enio groaned and pushed himself up.

Vex carried two old, black volumes. The guard outside led them to the throne room. Like last night, the Aubade had withdrawn and the Umbriarch presided. A few Progrades sat in the surrounding chairs; most were empty.

"Majesty." Vex bowed. Enio did too, barely straightening up again.

She came right to the point. "You have the details of the Elorian navy?"

Enio held out his notes. The guard brought them to the Umbriarch.

She examined the papers. "I will present these to the Aubade at his dawn transition."

"Majesty," Vex said, "I believe I have found a solution that avoids war."

"That was my next question. Most of the city slept through the Ortu's demonstration, yet rumors have spread that magic throughout the capital weakened during that time. We must act before rumors turn to panic, and panic to violence or revolt."

"Yes, Majesty." The wizard opened a tome and read the words that had earlier caught Enio's attention. "Three above. Three below. Two the balance, then and fro."

He closed the book, handed it to Enio, and opened the other. "During our private sessions, Majesty, I've related to you and the Aubade the events of last year. With the rift healed, the monoliths—which these books call Sentinels, and whose sole purpose was to confine the rift—now have nothing to counter their magics. This creates a void or shadow in the energetic chaos of the Outer Realms."

Vex turned the book around so Enio and the Umbriarch could see. Strange drawings of spheres within spheres, intersecting lines and spiraling sigils filled the page. Enio had no idea what any of it meant.

But the Umbriarch leaned forward, her eyes locked on the diagrams. "Continue."

"The Ortu, a region of the Lower Realms, now spreads upwards through this shadow." Vex traced a line. "The higher it reaches, the more energy it consumes from the realms above. This also strengthens the magic of its cultists."

"Then thank the stars," she said, "those cultists are few."

"Which means its power is concentrated in those few. During our confrontation with Cronus and Legate, the Abbot mentally sent me all he'd learned of their plans. This offshoot of the Ortu can approach only so close to our world. But I believe if Par and his natural shield were placed at the focus of the Sentinels, it could… allow a passage."

The Umbriarch's voice darkened. "What does that mean, Alexander?"

"Cronus believes he has a rapport with the Ortu. How that's possible, I can't say. But such unimaginable power may allow Cronus to force his own brand of peace upon the lands, with Legate and his cult ruling at his side."

"I see." She sat back. "Then we must center our arrows on Cronus."

Enio's weary mind perked up.

But Vex paused and scratched an ear. "Killing Cronus means killing the Eminence—a good man, from all I've heard. Even this may not stop their plans, since Cronus may transfer to yet another body. And there's still Legate and his followers to worry about."

"Such as Juris." Her tone sharpened. "Your solution, Alexander?"

"I am now convinced that a sigil, common among the Sentinels, controls their power. Par possesses that sigil—though he cannot use it or any other."

"He's thick," Enio said, now wide awake.

The Umbriarch nodded. "Then you plan a thaumaturgic innervation on Par?"

Enio turned to Vex. "A what?"

"A Cathexis, in the parlance of Eloria."

"Oh. Why didn't you say so."

"Sorry, son. The procedure allows one person to empower a sigil within another."

That sounded familiar. "Like the Abbot did to me so I could use Lani's weaving sigil to climb the cliffs at Argent."

"Not quite. The Abbot can't invoke élan. Rather, he rejuvenated you, and you collected it on your own. In contrast, a Cathexis transfers the élan, or lumina or numena, itself."

Enio had only seen Par manage a sigil once, with the power of the rift backing him up. "But Par's thick, remember?"

"Yes, so you enjoy reminding us. The Cathexis may need to be quite strong. However, I do not intend for Par to invoke the sigil, but to bestow it upon me. That should reduce the effort required. And once I have the sigil, I will then bestow it on others."

"Why others?" the Umbriarch asked. "And upon whom?"

"From these tomes, I have learned that each Sentinel is attuned to a different magic. This sigil must be given to those capable of using each type."

"The same sigil, empowered by different magics?" She frowned.

"It is a strange one, Majesty, with many roots."

Though Enio had been keeping up—more or less—this part lost him. "Wait. There are eight Sentinels."

"Quite so," Vex said.

"But there aren't *eight* types of magic. Lumina, numena, and the élan. Isn't that it?"

"Those are the Three Above, the magics of the Higher Realms. The Ortu is one of the Three Below."

Enio sighed. He had hoped he was done using his brain for today.

Fortunately, Vex waved off the rest. "There's no point in discussing the others. We know no one capable of those."

"If not," the Umbriach said, "how can you disable all eight Sentinels?"

"It's true that the more Sentinels we disable, the better our chances of pushing back the Ortu. But I believe if we disable at least half, we might prevent its passage into our world."

"Might?"

Enio was asking himself the same thing.

Vex closed the book with the drawings. "The Abbot also learned of a ritual to be performed by Legate and Cronus. If we wait until that moment, as they call forth the Ortu, our chances are excellent. Yet they need Par for that ritual, and, of course, we cannot turn him over. Our chances with half the Sentinels, and without the ritual underway…" He shook his head. "To be honest, Majesty, I can't say. But it's the best plan we have."

Enio didn't much like those odds. He guessed by the Umbriarch's face she didn't either.

"I will, of course, be the one to disable the Sentinel that requires numena," Vex continued. "Lady Agatha will handle lumina: now that she has been abandoned by Juris, she will have no choice if she wishes to avoid imprisonment. There is a nymph named Lani who I trust will control the Sentinel of the élan." He looked at Enio. "You can call her, can you not?"

Enio hesitated. "I think so. But that's still only three."

"Yes. Juris uses Ortu magic. Majesty, did you ever find him?"

"We did not."

"There must be others of his cult. We need your help to locate some. You may have to force them to cooperate."

Kaj is Ortu. Enio remembered the note. That couldn't be true. He pushed it from his head. "You still need Par's sigil. He's stuck at the Citadel."

"You brought us the keystone," Vex said. "We can—"

"Alexander," interrupted the Umbriarch. "The Aubade plans to use your Threshold for a secret attack on Eloria's seat of government."

"What? When?"

"When he deems it most advantageous. I expect that will be soon."

"I'll go with him!" Enio's heart leapt. This could be his doorway to Cronus.

Vex laid a hand on his shoulder. "Hush."

"Yet while the night rules," the Umbriarch added, "the Aubade's plan is not my will. If Legate makes good on his threat and has launched the Elorian fleet, it will require three, perhaps four days to reach our shores. As you've explained, we can only use the Threshold once per day, but we will not overly disrupt the Aubade's timing if you use it first to retrieve Par and delay the Aubade's attack a single day."

"Um," Vex said, "two."

"Two?"

"Once we've rescued Par, we must use the Threshold again to travel to the Sentinels."

"A second day would certainly strain the Aubade's patience, Alexander."

"Yes, Majesty. But depending on our success, the Aubade's attack may not be necessary. Tonight, I beg you allow me to recover Par."

Enio looked from Vex to the Umbriarch, torn between the plans. Par was probably safe where he was.

He shook his head. "The Thresholds can't open past the Citadel seals. If we can't get to Par anyway, we should help the Aubade."

"Par is a smart young man," Vex said. "I trust he will help us help him. Then you and he can hide until this is over. But now you must go to the harbor and contact your nymph friend."

Enio clenched his fists as another door to Cronus slammed in his face.

The Umbriarch stood. "Very well. You may attempt to retrieve Par. I am trusting you not to betray us, Alexander. The Aubade would not give you this opportunity."

"Thank you, Majesty."

A guard escorted Enio and Vex back to their chamber. Pale moonlight spilled in from the balcony. Vex lit a lamp and lay his two tomes on the table. "I'll search for Par at midnight. You don't need to wait. Go call Lani."

"Yeah," Enio said, though his doubts about this entire plan continued to grow. "Make sure you ask the Aubade to bring me with him when he attacks."

"What? I certainly will not. Besides, I hope to prevent the Aubade from using the Threshold at all."

Enio had worried he might say that. "Even without the Threshold, he can still reach Argent with the navy. Tell him to let me help—and not as some stinking bilge swabby. You know, on the decks, using the big sigils."

"You would go to war against your own country?"

"Against Cronus."

Vex turned to his books. "Fighting the ruler of your country to save your country. It's an ethical dilemma, to be sure."

"I'd be great on a navy ship. Have you seen them?" Enio paced the room, tracing shapes in the air with his arms. "The *huge* sails, hulls like sea monsters, the missiles and spells and—"

"What could you know of war?"

Enio stopped near the wizard. "I know plenty. Back at the abbey, John and Buckets told us—"

"Old soldiers are within their rights to tell of their battles and glories. You're young. Your friends at the abbey spared you the… other parts."

"I bet the other parts are even better."

Peering at Enio, Vex said, "I caution you, son, do not rush to war. I don't think you'd like it."

Enio snorted. "How do you know?"

The wizard's eyes flashed. "Would you see that of which you speak?" A glory shone around his head. He raised his hands.

Enio's eyes widened. He couldn't resist. He swallowed and nodded.

Vex reached out and touched Enio's head. The room seemed to explode with light. Enio winced, but the glare faded and he found himself standing on a castle wall high above a stormy sea. Flashes of lightning sent bright cracks through dark, angry clouds. Shapes moved upon the waters—warships. Their massive sails billowed and flapped.

Never had Enio seen such a sight, such a throng of power. With new surprise, he realized he was singing. Others along the parapets sang as well. They wore armor, metal and leather, new and old. They beat spears and bows on their shields in rhythm with their music.

As he formed words he'd never heard, his heart swelled. The warships heaved closer upon the waves, their chins high and proud. Flags and banners fluttered from the masts like tongues.

Suddenly, their decks were lit with flashes, but not of lightning. The scream of missiles tore through the air.

The singing of his brethren ended with a crash behind him.

He spun. A wall exploded in a hail of stone and mortar. Men shouted and screamed, some plummeting with the rubble toward the rocky waters.

Towers nearby sent their own flash of missiles rushing through the grey air.

Enio tracked their paths to the ships. The beautiful masts, like the musical notes Captain Morten had described, shattered in splinters and fire. Another boat split in two. The harsh winds carried distant screams.

The ships flashed again. A black cloud as of swarming insects flew toward his position.

Frantically, Enio searched for cover. Before he took a step, an archway to his left blew apart. A barrage of gravel hit him. He shielded his face as he fell onto his back.

Someone landed beside him—a man who had sung at his side. But this brother-in-arms would sing no longer. His head was nearly ripped away.

For a moment, Enio's terror consumed his thoughts as if he, too, had lost his head. Then another ear-splitting crash shook the parapets. He scrambled up, choking on dust, started to run, collided with another soldier. The man's chest had a hole, a red pit of blood and bone, but for that instant, life still shone in his terrified eyes. He slumped onto Enio, crushing him again to the ground.

Enio struggled and shouted. "Help! Help me!"

Another explosion, and his world blew apart. He was falling, his screams wasted in the blast and roar. And when he was certain all hope was lost, he landed in soft silence.

His heartbeat thundered in his ears and his lungs still drew breath, but he squeezed his eyes tight, lest he open them and discover he was, in fact, dead.

Vex's gentle voice touched the silence. "That was but a memory, Enio. I was young. I survived." He paused. "I was lucky."

Enio opened his eyes. He was back in Vex's chamber, curled on the floor like an infant. He'd never imagined the horror of what he'd just seen. One moment, the singing. The next…

Vex helped him up. "There are times when we must fight. But as a last resort. Only a fool rushes to war."

Enio nodded, unable to speak. The wizard ushered him to the couch and let him be.

As Enio recovered, he remembered Lady Agatha saying there are always sides. But Enio didn't care about sides anymore. War seemed like two sides of the same coin. It didn't matter to him now who flipped it, Cronus or the Majesties, Eloria or Arcana. Enio wouldn't play along. He wasn't interested in killing anyone—except Cronus.

He just had to figure out how.

Chapter Thirty-Eight

PAR RESTED HIS head on the cottage's weathered table. He didn't dream, but he must have dozed, because Kaj shook him awake.

"What's wrong?" he said.

"Quiet as a moonbeam. But you slept a long time. It's dark."

"Sorry. We better go."

"One minute." Kaj stepped into the back room and tucked the doll she'd cleaned into the crib. Par found the sight touching: it reminded him of his mother tending to his baby brother.

When she finished, they left the cottage. The moon shone bright, though its light changed the dull yellow of the Devastation into an eerie green. The Citadel walls weren't far, and like the cottages, stretched along the hilltop—in Par's opinion, not high enough above those dead sands.

Bending low, they crept through the night to the weedy road that ran along the stronghold. The luminous dust demons never rested, but came no closer. After a few juts and corners, Par found an open archway through the fortification's walls, unblocked by the blue fire of the seals. He stopped and peered through. It didn't open directly into a building, but into murky courtyards and columned lanes cloaked in shadows of lunar light. Other doorways within glinted with the seals, preventing anyone but Par from entering further.

"It may be safer," he said, "if we leave the road and move to the inside of the wall. We'll be out of sight of the Devastation."

This new course turned out to be trial and error, often ending in dead alleys or looping around a maze of courtyards. Then Par spied the tower where he'd arrived with Enio, so tall it seemed to lean against the moon.

He led Kaj closer. The tower sat in the center of a plaza, surrounded by statues of simple, everyday people, even dancing children—a stark change from the noble portraits and sculptures he'd seen inside.

The tower had no entrance, sealed or otherwise. Par pointed at the stairs that enwrapped it. "If Vex got the keystone from Enio, that's where he'll try to find me. On top."

Kaj tapped the lower step with her boot. "Seems stable enough. Mind if I go first?"

He forced a smile, not looking forward to the climb. "If you insist."

With one hand on the curving stone wall, she strode up. Par followed. Just scanning the winding stairs made him dizzy. He concentrated instead on putting one careful foot before the other. At least the night hid the drop below—mostly. But the constant turn of the stairway became worse than the zigzag steps of the Aerie. There was no banister. Not even a rope. What did the ancient mages who'd built these things have against railings? Maybe it didn't matter to them, since they could probably fly anyway.

"You all right down there?" Kaj said from the darkness.

"No talk. Too high."

"Oh. Well, take your time."

"If you insist," Par mumbled.

The fearsome dust funnels across the Devastation continued their dances. Par kept climbing, up and up, not giving in to any other distractions, watching only the winding wall, or his knees, rising and falling. At last the stairs ended at an opening in the crowning parapets. Before him sat the small tower house with its blue glowing entrance. A brief run of stairs continued up that building's side to the ancient altar on top. He motioned Kaj to hunker with him beneath those steps.

"How long do we wait?" she asked.

"Midnight, at the earliest."

She scanned the night sky. "Another hour."

He prayed he was right about Vex finding him on this tower. If not, and the dust demons attacked, he'd escape through the seal and into the tower house. But not Kaj. And this time, he didn't have the keystone to save her like he'd saved Enio. Still, it was the best plan for rescue he had.

The spinning storms on the horizon weaved back and forth in their puzzling patterns. Not much time had passed when a sudden flash of light cut through the darkness.

"Crap," he hissed, fearing they'd been noticed.

"What is it?" Kaj asked.

"Pull in."

Yet the flash hadn't come from the Devastation.

Then a man's voice. "Par?" The ghostly rectangle of a Threshold glowed nearby. Vex stood within it.

"It's Vex!" Par said to Kaj. "Wait here." He leapt from their hiding place.

The wizard reached through the portal. "Excellent. Come on."

Par stopped. "Is Enio there?"

"He's on an errand. Hurry, now."

At least that made this next part easier. He called over his shoulder. "Kaj."

She joined him.

Par took her hand. "You said another hour."

"Well you said midnight."

With his other hand, he took Vex's and led Kaj through the Threshold and onto the Astrologer's Aerie. Guards with lanterns lit the high ledge.

Vex closed the portal. "As for midnight, you were hundreds of leagues from here, beyond the Ults. The Immortus is over a thousand. All under different skies. Not worth explaining now."

Par nodded. "Did Enio get you the tomes?" He assumed so, since Vex also had the keystone again—but he had to make sure. Enio had been too unpredictable of late.

"Yes, and they have given me much hope."

"What did you find?"

"I'll tell you as we travel."

A chariot waited. They mounted between shieldriders and were soon soaring through the night.

Vex leaned in. "I explained to the Umbriarch that I redirected you and Enio to the Citadel to prevent you from falling into the hands of Cronus. Juris tried to follow—he is a member of the Ortu."

"Where is he now?" Par asked, avoiding a discussion of Kaj's relationship to Juris.

"Perhaps with Cronus and Legate. We don't know for sure."

Kaj said nothing, her head lowered.

They circled down toward the city, its lights aglow in the darkness. Vex told of what he'd learned from the tomes, and of his plans to retrieve the sigil from Par's head. He also told of the looming possibility of war. The night appeared to darken more with the wizard's every word.

"Enio has gone to the bay to call Lani," Vex finished as they landed.

That news brought a little light into the gloom. "When can I see them?"

"I promised the Umbriarch I'd bring you straight to her. Enio will join us when he completes his task."

Guards escorted them back to the throne room. The Umbriarch presided. Enio sat on the floor near her throne, thumbing through a tome. Lady Agatha stood nearby. Lani was nowhere in sight.

"Enio!" Par called as they approached.

Enio flashed a brief, obviously fake smile to both Kaj and him, but stayed where he was.

Before Par asked what was going on, Vex squeezed his shoulder. "Your Majesty," the man said, bowing. Kaj bowed too.

Par did the same. As he rose, he noticed Lady Agatha seemed different from when he'd seen her last—when she'd accused him of being a spy: smaller somehow, and sad.

He started forward. "Lady Agatha?"

She burst into tears.

Par stopped in his tracks.

"I'm sorry." She steadied herself. "I didn't mean to accuse you."

"It was Juris," Vex said. "The Umbriarch has determined that Juris captured her after we parted at the Aerie and put her under his control."

"I guessed as much." Par glanced at Kaj. Her face was tight. How was he going to tell everyone that Juris was her father?

Agatha dabbed her eyes with a kerchief. "You guessed?"

"About you not being yourself. You said the Eminence delivered us to you, but we met because I decided to approach you at the banquet. And on the *Sea Dog*, you didn't lead us to Arcana. That was my idea. You've only ever helped us."

She lifted her chin and brightened. "As long as it's in my power, I always will."

Kaj remained silent. Par couldn't avoid that part any longer. He turned to Enio. "Did you get my note?"

His friend hesitated. "What note?"

"I wrote a note and stuck it in the last book I handed you. You didn't get it?"

Enio shook his head.

"The boy lies," said the Umbriarch. A slight glory twinkled around her head.

"Oh, *that* note." Enio shrugged. "Well, it wasn't signed."

"What note is this?" Vex asked.

"I…" Par trailed off and looked at Kaj, unable to finish.

"Majesty," she said, not meeting his eyes. "I was Dark Reckoned when I was younger. Juris is my father."

The guards drew their swords.

Par stepped in front of Kaj, trying to decide what to say in her defense.

But Enio jumped to his feet and drew his knife. "Leave her alone! She's only ever helped us, same as Ags."

Half the guards whirled their weapons toward Enio.

"Wait." The Umbriarch raised a hand. The guards advanced no farther, but kept their swords out.

Enio stayed as he was, knife ready.

"Enio," Kaj said, "it's all right. I use Ortu magic, but I'm on your side, not my father's."

Vex hadn't moved. "Umbriarch, does she speak the truth?"

"I sense no deception. Though if Juris hid his treachery for this long, perhaps she can as well."

"She already told me about her past," Par said. "And without her, we'd have never gotten the tomes. She's on our side now, like she said."

The Umbriarch gazed at Par. Then she smiled. "You, however, have one of the most trustworthy auras I've ever seen. And if there's one thing that sways me, it's honesty. For now, I will give Kaj the benefit of the doubt."

The guards lowered their swords.

Par took a deep breath, relieved at how much more reasonable the Umbriarch seemed compared to the Aubade. He doubted things would have gone so smoothly with *that* man. "Thank you, Majesty." He turned to Vex. "Isn't Lani supposed to be here?"

"I wondered that myself. Enio, what did she say to our request?"

Enio glanced at Par, at Agatha, finally at the Umbriarch. Her silver glory twinkled again.

He sighed and tucked away his knife. "I never called Lani."

"You never—?" Vex began.

"We can't make her do this."

"She is *critical* to our plans." The wizard's voice rose.

But Enio ignored him. He met Par's eyes straight on. "If Lani leaves the sea, she can't go back."

Par started. "She what?"

"She didn't want you to know. Remember how she said she couldn't come with us because her changes were still working themselves out? She has to choose between life in the sea or on land. It's part of those changes. If she comes with us, it forces the choice. We can't do that."

Stunned, Par stood like a statue. First, Enio had hidden his trip with Lani to the Deep World. But friends trusted each other, so it hadn't been hard to get it out of him.

But *this*? Why hadn't he told Par *this*?

An ugly suspicion, perhaps the same one that had begun back on the island at their shared winks, rose again in Par's chest. "Are you sure that's the reason you didn't call her?"

"What are you talking about?"

"You told me the Deep World only let people enter who used the élan. So you could go live there with… with Lani. Without me in the way."

There. He'd said it, the thing that had been quietly eating at him since the island.

For a moment, Enio's face showed only confusion. Then he barked out a laugh. "For Oä's sake. Don't be thick, Par. Yeah, I can use the élan. That means I can use it on the Sentinel myself. We don't *need* Lani."

Before Par digested that, the Umbriarch interrupted. "The élan? This child is a creature of nature magics?"

"Majesty," Vex said. "Enio is one of those rare individuals who can use magics beyond his inherited traits. However,"—he focused again on Enio—"not only is the sigil we plan to use quite strange, the élan is not his native orientation. Enio, the strain may be more than you can bear."

"I can do it," Enio repeated firmly.

Vex paused a moment. The wrinkles deepened in his forehead. "Or is this just your latest plan to confront Cronus?" His voice came harsh. "Listen to me, son. Your obsession with him is going to get you killed."

By Enio's expression, Vex had hit a nerve. Par feared an outburst was seconds away.

But the Umbriarch's glory reached out, covering the room like moonlight over a secret glade. "My friends."

Peace filled the air. Everyone calmed, even Enio.

Her glory receded, and her words came soft. "Generations of distrust have divided our lands, our peoples. Let us not add to it here. If we are to defeat this evil, we must have faith in one another."

A gentle quiet followed. Though Par had been running and chasing and hiding for what seemed a lifetime, this small welcome peace, magic or not, settled his frazzled wits. Enio, regardless of his anger and obsession with Cronus, was still Enio, Par's friend, and not so selfish as to run off alone with Lani. Par should have known that all along. Enio was protecting her. And Lani's secrets were to spare Par more worries. Par might have done the same for either of them.

He held his hand out to Enio. "Sorry."

But Enio narrowed his eyes. "You ditched me."

"You stabbed me," Par said. "But we can't get rid of each other *that* easy."

Enio snorted. "All right." He took the hand.

"Kaj's arrival is timely," Vex said, also more composed. "We need someone who can invoke the sigil using Ortu magic."

"Whatever you need," Kaj replied, "I'll do it."

Enio nudged Par. "Told you."

Chapter Thirty-Nine

"Now," Vex said to Enio, "if there are no further surprises…"

Enio remained silent.

"Fine." The wizard faced the Umbriarch. "To retrieve the sigil we need, we must perform a Cathexis on Par. Do you possess that ability, Majesty?"

"Its Arcanan form, yes. Come before me, Par."

Par glanced at Vex.

The wizard's lips tightened, but he nodded.

Par stepped before her throne. The Umbriarch rose. "Alexander has described the sigil you possess. With your permission, I will innervate you with the numena needed for bestowal."

The only time Par had successfully used a sigil was at the Immortus, when he'd burnt through a rope holding both him and Cronus above the rift. The rift itself had powered that flame sigil; Par didn't think he'd ever use such magic again. And while his plunge into the Higher Realms had been excruciating, invoking the sigil itself had been painless. Maybe this wouldn't hurt either.

The expressions of Vex and the Umbriarch suggested otherwise.

"I can't use lumina," Par said, as much in curiosity as hoping for a way out of this. "So how can I use numena?"

Vex answered. "The people in your country can't use numena because they weren't born or raised to recognize and collect it. As those in Arcana can't use lumina."

"But for different reasons than me. My soul—"

"Is thick," Enio finished for him.

"In this case," Vex said, "the Umbriarch will channel it into you."

Par cringed at the idea of numena being pumped into him—especially by this powerful person from Arcana he didn't really know, or completely trust. But everything depended on him bestowing that sigil.

As he stewed, Vex cleared his throat. The guards, the few Progrades in their fancy chairs, the Majesty, Kaj, Agatha, Enio, all watched and waited. Par realized he hadn't answered the Umbriarch's request for his permission.

And, of course, right then Enio made things worse.

"Don't tell me you forgot how to bestow," he said. "All that time we practiced at the abbey?"

For an instant, Par's mind blanked. But he hadn't forgotten. Bring the sigil to mind. Let it soak up the lumina, enough to trace its form. And as Enio described it, cast the sigil out, like a fishing line, and wait for a bite.

There was more, but he'd never gotten past the soaking-up part.

Par steadied his nerves, took a deep breath. No matter what, he had to try. "All right. Who do I give it to?"

"Me." Vex joined him.

The Umbriarch stepped forward. "Very well. I will try to be

careful, Par, since I don't know how a Cathexis will affect someone with your… condition. Sit and bring your foreheads together."

Par and Vex settled to the floor. They leaned in.

"Ready?" the Umbriarch asked.

"Yes," they replied. Par braced himself.

She rested her hands on his head. They were soft, and smelled a little like rain. He closed his eyes and tried to relax.

Before he even envisioned the sigil, a distant star sparked to life in his mind's darkness. As the light grew, it pulsed with bright silver rays.

The pulse became a knock.

The knock, a hammer against his skull.

Par grit his teeth and endured. It spread, beating hot down his spine, into his arms and legs. He couldn't concentrate. He became dizzy and nauseous.

The pressure doubled, tripled. The heat became fire. An inferno. Par screamed. Then, as if lightning had struck and stayed, blinding white pain blasted him backwards.

He writhed on the floor, barely noticing as someone touched his arm. A healing coolness washed through his body.

"Par?" Vex said.

The room lurched as Par opened his eyes. He turned to his side, and on his hands and knees, vomited. At least his head hadn't split open, though for a second, he thought it must have. He remained bent over, ashamed at getting sick in the throne room—and at his weakness in front of everyone. In front of his friends.

"Don't be embarrassed," said the Umbriarch, standing above him. "I've never attempted such a strong innervation, or met such resistance to one."

"I didn't mean to resist," Par said, looking up.

She gave a gentle smile. "I know."

Feeling a bit more himself, he turned to Vex. "Did you get the sigil?"

The wizard's tone was as grave as Par had ever heard. "I did not."

After all that, it didn't work? Par nearly vomited again.

"I was afraid of this outcome," the Umbriarch said. "Par's astral opacity is quite substantial."

"I could've told you that," Enio said.

"You have," Vex mumbled.

The Umbriarch spoke to Enio. "You say you two have practiced together?"

"Lots. Nothing ever worked."

"Still, your obvious nearness of spirit suggests you'd have a more intuitive sense of Par's mental landscape. His bestowing instead on you may allow me to use less numena."

"My mental landscape?" Par glanced at Enio.

His friend's eyebrows waggled.

"Very well," she said. "Sit together."

Enio replaced Vex on the floor. Par leaned his forehead against Enio's. He hated going through this again; the previous attempt had almost burnt out his brain and cracked his skull. But their plans were nothing without that sigil.

The Umbriarch's hands rested again on his head, and the foreign light reappeared in his mind, pulsing, hammering. The heat increased. Par fought against a rising panic. But just before crossing the threshold into pain, the intensity eased. Over and over this continued, no longer a blasting furnace but driving waves of splashing silver light. His confidence grew that he would not be overwhelmed. He was able to summon the complex sigil from his memory into his mind's eye.

An aura, a glowing sea of numena, swirled around the sigil. The sigil drank it in. Its edges brightened and sharpened until at last only the sigil remained, a dim celestial object in the night, an intricate silver design alive in the darkness.

The Umbriarch spoke in his thoughts. *Now, Par.*

As he'd practiced long ago, Par willed the sigil forward, pushing it out, out, to the limit of his perception—and his strength.

Then something reached in.

The intrusion broke Par's concentration. The sigil spit and sparked, throwing off licks of flame. The heat grew, threatening to overwhelm him once more.

Yet the new presence was familiar, friendly.

It was Enio.

Par's worry and distress ebbed away, replaced by a calm trust in his friend, made stronger by having cleared the air about Lani. The numena retreated once more within the bounds of the sigil.

Then the sigil gave a sudden bounce or jiggle. Par smiled. It was, as Enio had said, like a fishing cork. Par had never accomplished a bestowal, yet he recognized something in the sensation. His soul was being touched—as his friend had done in other ways, many times.

Like a boat catching a current, the bright sigil sailed away. Par's mind darkened into a peaceful night.

He opened his damp eyes. This time, he wasn't sick. In fact, he hadn't felt this good in quite a while. "Did it work?"

Everyone looked at Enio.

Enio tapped his own head with his knuckles. "Holy sticks, that's a tangled one."

"Indeed it did work," the Umbriarch said and helped Par stand. "You both performed admirably."

Par filled his lungs, as happy that it had worked as he was at not having to do it again. He helped Enio off the floor. "Couldn't have done it without you."

"Damn right." Enio grinned.

"When Enio has had time to better learn the sigil," Vex said, "he can bestow it on me, and I will pass it to Kaj and Agatha."

"And then you go to the Immortus?" Par asked. It sounded like their plans were at last coming together.

"That depends," the Umbriarch answered, "on whether the Aubade demands use of the Threshold first."

"I don't understand," Par said.

Vex laid a hand on Par's shoulder. "He plans a secret attack through the Threshold, and to destroy your capital."

Chapter Forty

D URING THE CHARIOT ride to the palace, Vex had mentioned war. That was bad enough. But a secret attack through the Threshold? Par could barely believe what he was hearing. "Destroy Argent?"

"Vex has explained," the Umbriarch continued, "that we cannot use the Threshold to breach the Argent outpost that protects Cronus and Legate. However, with a regiment of our strongest wizards, and the element of surprise, the Aubade intends to bring down the cliffs of Argent on top of them."

"But they've still got the Abbot." Par glanced at Vex for help. None came. "The High Temple, our entire government, is on those cliffs. That's murder, not war."

The Umbriarch raised her regal chin. "Arcana is a just and moral society. We do not murder innocents. The leadership of Argent and of Ortu threaten war. The Aubade's strategy will remove them from power and save thousands of lives."

"But Cronus *isn't* our leader." Why couldn't she see that?

"He wears the mantel of your Eminence. There is no higher authority in Eloria."

Par searched for another argument, but she was right. Cronus controlled the body of the Eminence. The people, and the navy, would follow his commands.

Vex said, "We don't know if killing Cronus will stop the Ortu, Majesty. If the Aubade allows us to try our plan at the Immortus, we may avoid untold bloodshed."

"By your own admittance, Alexander, disabling only half the Sentinels, especially outside the Ortu's ritual of rising, promises far from certain success. Those odds do not sway the Aubade. He will attack once he can again open the Threshold."

Par tried a last, weak point. "But don't you run half the country? Why can't you order the Aubade—"

"No one orders the Aubade, Par." Her expression softened. "I and the Aubade rule Arcana together, for half each daily cycle. Sometimes we hold contrasting opinions, yet understand that we both wish first the safety of our people."

"Majesty," Vex said, "Legate will stop at nothing to attain Par and so perform their ritual. Yes, that moment would be our best opportunity to stop the Ortu. But it is the most risky. The chances with our alternate plan, though slim, are real. Even if we fail, we may still weaken the Ortu and discourage Legate and Cronus from proceeding until it recovers. Would they not then withdraw their navy and try by other means to acquire Par? That would give the Aubade more time to formulate his attack. And we could use that delay to search the tomes for more guidance."

"And if you fail," she said, "Legate and Cronus will not next time be taken unawares. Their ritual will be all the more carefully executed."

Vex frowned. "Maybe."

"You give me many maybes, Alexander. And while I have grown to trust you, I must still deliver the keystone back to the Aubade." She held out her palm.

"Yes, Majesty." The wizard handed it over. "But it's late. The

Threshold won't open for another day. These boys should get some sleep. Perhaps tomorrow will bring new solutions."

"Let us hope." She dismissed them.

Back at Vex's chamber, they bid goodnight to Agatha and Kaj, who shared a separate room.

"Par," Vex said before they settled in for the night, "I must tell you, everything considered, the Aubade's intent to destroy Argent may be the least worst option."

Par turned on him, astounded. "You can't mean it."

Vex was silent.

"But," Par added, "The Abbot… I thought you were on our side. At least, not on Arcana's."

"I gave up sides when I joined the Vigil, whose mission has always been to promote what's best for all. But we must make a terrible choice, made worse by the Abbot's imprisonment. What do you think he'd say?"

The Abbot would certainly put his own welfare last. Was that it, then? Did they have one day left to stop a slaughter? The gears in Par's mind began to spin. There had to be a way. He had to find it.

He curled up in a chair, his thoughts grinding through the rest of the night, sleeping, not sleeping, he didn't know.

Until the harsh glow of morning seeped through the balcony curtains. Enio and Vex sat at the table, peering over parchments.

Par joined them. "What're you doing?"

Fresh drawings of the sigil, in pieces and in full, lay across the table.

Enio said, "We're working this thing out. It's pretty weird: lots of roots and channels, but"—he pointed—"this way looks best for numena, this way for lumina, and this for the élan."

"So what's the plan?" Par asked.

"Get your breakfast." Vex gestured to a plate of boiled eggs and fruit. "Then we will speak to the Aubade."

After eating, Par left Vex and Enio tracing the sigil and slipped out. He was about to knock on Kaj and Agatha's door when he heard voices.

"He speaks through the Ortu, as do we all." That was Kaj.

Par paused and listened.

Agatha replied, "We must be careful."

"Yes."

Par knocked. "It's me."

A moment later, Agatha opened the door. She smiled. "Good morning, Par."

"Good morning. We're going to see the Aubade."

"We'll be right there." The door closed.

Unsure of what he'd heard, Par headed back to his room. He already had enough occupying his mind.

Shortly after he'd joined Vex and Enio, Agatha and Kaj arrived. Vex summoned the guard, who led them to the throne room.

The Aubade sat in his pomp and finery on the throne. The Prograde chairs were empty.

Vex bowed. "Thank you for meeting us so early, Majesty."

"I have much to do today, Alexander."

"So said the Umbriarch. You make plans to attack Argent?"

The Aubade nodded. "The Threshold can be opened for passage at next dawn?"

"Even this midnight, if you desire. But... I am hoping we might first try our proposal with the Sentinels."

"Yes, the Umbriarch has informed me of that." The Aubade frowned. "There are many unknowns in war, Alexander. We must assume Eloria's navy is in motion and will pass the Boundary Islands in one to three days, depending on their haste. Once I am sure their fleet is far enough across the sea, I will destroy their capital, leaving the ships leaderless and demoralized as they learn of their loss."

Vex sighed and made no objection.

Par worried the wizard was about to give in. In desperation, he decided to suggest an idea of his own.

"Majesty." Par stepped forward and bowed. "I know how to find more about the progress of Eloria's navy."

"Indeed?" the Aubade said, along with Vex.

"I've been to the Boundary Islands, so I can open the Threshold to its high lookout. That gives a full view of the seas two days from here. And if we don't step through when it allows, you can still use it to attack Argent."

"That," the Aubade said with less steel, "would be most helpful."

Par pushed the point. "Does this remove enough unknowns to let us travel to the Sentinels?"

The Aubade pursed his lips and seemed to consider.

"Majesty," Vex said, "Par's idea has merit. If we are successful in weakening the Ortu, Legate and Cronus may withdraw their ships. You will have more time to plan your attack."

The Aubade rocked slowly, back and forth. "Yes, I see. Very well. If their fleet remains remote, I will permit you to visit your Sentinels."

Par breathed again.

"Yet I will continue my preparations," the Aubade added. "If events warrant, I may still attack Eloria as early as tomorrow."

Vex bowed. "Of course, Majesty."

The Aubade stood. "I order it so. The guards will take Par, and Par alone, to the Threshold upon the Astrologer's Aerie where he will watch the seas."

"I am not to accompany him?" asked Vex.

The Aubade gave a wry smile. "I do not entirely trust you, Alexander, and will not allow you near the Threshold at this time." He offered Par the keystone.

As Par received it, the man continued. "My guards will report of any change on the seas to me. If at dawn tomorrow I decide we can afford the delay, you may attempt your scheme with the Sentinels." He dismissed them.

Par and his companions were escorted out. Before the guards split them up, Vex said, "Fine thinking, Par. For now, I will continue helping Enio navigate the sigil. He will bestow it on me, and I on the others. If everything goes well, we will see you at next dawn."

"When you go to the Sentinels," Par asked, but guessing the answer, "will I come too?"

"No. We can't risk your presence. Everything depends on keeping you away from Cronus and Legate."

"But they'd still be in Argent, right?"

"Nevertheless, I won't allow you anywhere near either location. And if worst comes to worst, we may even hide you again in the Citadel."

Par nodded. "We—" He swallowed a catch in his throat.

Vex eyed him. "What's wrong, Par?"

"It's just, I wish we could've finished this together. That I could have helped more."

"Thanks to you, we have everything we need. Remember: they will not attempt to release the Ortu while you're safe. That at least gives us this chance."

Par turned to Enio and forced a smile. "Just be careful. And no showing off. Don't take any chances."

Enio gave his broken grin. "Me, gamble?"

Appreciating the humor, Par chuckled. After hopes for success all around, he was escorted away from his friends and out to a chariot. Again, they flew him to the Aerie. More guards waited there.

Par grasped the keystone and opened the Threshold to the high lookout where he and Agatha had once been shipwrecked.

The captain with the long blond hair stood by his side. "Amazing," she said.

"See a fleet?" Par asked.

She peered through. "I do not." She turned to one of her

guards. "Inform the Aubade. The rest of you get comfortable. We're going to be here awhile."

As the day's shadows crawled across the city below, Par opened and closed the Threshold, each time fearing a line of Elorian ships setting the Aubade's plans in motion. But the horizon remained flat and undisturbed. The guards shared their lunches with him, and he napped in fits and pieces throughout the afternoon to make up for the long night. They even let him explore the tunnel, which he figured must lead to the rest of the Vigil's Aurix outpost, like the one in Argent. But it ended in an empty cave. If there was anything more in there, it was well hidden.

Late in the day, a messenger brought a note from Vex. It read: *Enio has mastered the sigil enough to bestow it upon me, and I upon Agatha and Kaj. He is quite talented—don't tell him I said so.*

Par smiled a little. Things just might work out.

Eventually, the sun set, and finally the moon and stars marked the passage to midnight. He opened the Threshold several more times, the moon still bright enough to show the seas. There remained no change. If this kept up, Vex would get his chance at dawn.

But on the next opening, to Par's horror, little lights dotted the horizon.

"Guard!" yelled the captain. "Tell the Majesty that we've sighted the Elorian fleet."

"Yes, Captain!" A guard leapt from the Aerie on his shield.

Par's spirits crashed. Then this was it. Their plans had been for nothing. The Aubade would attack Argent at dawn. Hundreds would die.

Unless Par did something, and did it now.

An awful possibility that had been festering deep in his mind, one that he'd refused to consider, broke loose. There was nothing left to stop it.

As Vex had said, they could disable only half the Sentinels.

The chances of preventing the rise of the Ortu were slim. But if they disabled those Sentinels while Legate performed his ritual, it would increase the odds.

And the odds of saving Argent, along with the Abbot.

The problem was that Legate wouldn't attempt his ritual without Par, Vex wouldn't turn Par over, and the Umbriarch didn't have the leverage to persuade the Aubade to hold off his attack. The door to save the Abbot, and the lands from the Ortu, seemed shut. Par was the hinge. And he realized that, while it betrayed everyone's trust, he had a way to swing the door open.

He let the Threshold close. "It has to rest," he lied. "I'll open it again soon."

"Notify me when you do." The guard stepped away.

Par waited a moment. With his heart pounding and a last glance around, he reopened the portal to the cliff ledge of the Argent outpost. He tensed every muscle, hardened every resolve, and with a burst of energy, leapt through.

"Stop!" yelled the guard.

Par tossed the keystone back through the portal. It closed.

His chest still heaving, he scanned the dark, barred tunnel before him. Now Cronus would have everything he needed to call forth the Ortu: he had Par. And when he used Par in the ritual, Vex would have his best chance to stop it forever. Par had forced the Majesties to send Vex to the Sentinels instead of attacking Argent.

At least, he prayed so. And though he'd told Enio to take no chances, Par was making the biggest gamble of his life.

The sea below crashed against the rocks, like the terror crashing in his chest.

After one last breath of freedom, he shouted, "Cronus, I'm here!"

Par squeezed his eyes shut as he realized another irony.

I'm home.

CHAPTER FORTY-ONE

THE THRONE ROOM glowed with pre-dawn light. Progrades filed in, bowed to the already speaking Umbriarch, and took their seats. Enio stood next to Vex and fidgeted. He could barely focus on the Majesty's words, given how pissed he was at Par. His *friend* went to face Cronus without him? Par knew how much Enio wanted to kill that bastard. The man needed to die and stay dead. This was Enio's fight more than anyone's.

"We did not put Par up to this," Vex said.

She turned the keystone in her pale, slender fingers. "I see the truth in your words, Alexander. Agatha and Kaj have said the same. But the Aubade will be furious. Once the Threshold recovers, he will send our sorcerers through and destroy the capital of Eloria."

Enio perked up. "But Par's there."

The Umbriarch was silent.

"Majesty," Vex said, "Cronus and Legate will take Par to the Sentinels as soon as possible, perform their ritual and usher the Ortu into our world. From what I've learned in the Vigil's tomes, this will happen at the coming midnight."

She nodded. "As the saying goes, small hours for large magics."

"And sometimes for dark ones. But after witnessing the Ortu's power, the Aubade must understand that attacking Argent at that point will be useless."

"What do you suggest?"

"When midnight arrives and our Threshold is again available for passage, allow us to travel to the Immortus. Because of its distance, midnight there occurs some hours after it does here. That gives us time to prepare for Legate's arrival. We will also need to determine how to safely subdue Cronus, since I expect he will arrive in the body of Par rather than that of the Eminence."

"He'll possess Par?" Enio said, and wondered if Par had thought of that.

"I suspect so, Enio, and he'll do it before he leaves Argent. The Fondiscate is the closest to the gods of anyone in Eloria. Cronus knows that man's powers, and won't risk a fight if the Eminence recovers during the ritual. No, he will leave the Eminence before he travels to the Immortus with—I mean inside—Par."

"Now that they have Par," the Umbriarch said, "why does their navy still approach?"

"Perhaps Legate and Cronus have lost interest in its progress now that they've gotten what they wanted." The wizard rubbed his chin. "In any case, if the Eminence survives once he is free of Cronus, he will pull back Argent's fleet. The Eminence has always promoted peace with Arcana. Tell the Aubade this. It may delay hostilities."

"And if your plan fails?"

"If we do not stop the Ortu, at least there's the chance of Eloria and Arcana uniting to fight it together."

The gong that signaled dawn rang through the tower.

"I shall present your wishes to the Aubade," she said. "But do not be too hopeful."

Vex bowed. "Hope is often our best weapon, Majesty."

Servants doused the wall sconces, already unneeded with the early morning light.

The Aubade entered alone. All stood aside as he strode through the room. He stopped before the thrones. "My Umbriarch."

She stepped forward. "My Aubade."

As before, they held their hands palm to palm. Their glories reached out and mingled. When they'd finished, the Aubade flared his robes and took his seat. The Umbriarch stood aside.

The man gripped the arms of his throne. His face nearly turned purple. His glory grew, reaching out in spear-like spikes. The floor began to tremble, then the entire throne room shook. Dust fell from the pillars. A window near the domed ceiling shattered, the glass falling upon scattering guards.

Enio fell to his knees. "He's crazy!"

Vex huddled near him.

But the tremors lessened and stopped. Peace returned to the room.

Enio brushed dust from his shoulders and marveled. If one man could shake this place to its foundations, a group of his sorcerers could, without doubt, bring down the cliffs of Argent.

The Progrades peeked from behind their chairs. The Umbriarch had laid her hand upon the Aubade's, and the color in his face faded to a mottled pink. He gave a brief nod to the Umbriarch. She returned it and proceeded out of the chamber.

When her footsteps had echoed into the distance, the Aubade spoke. "With Par's passage through the Threshold, it seems I must wait another day. We attack Argent at next dawn."

"Aubade," Vex began, "I—"

"I realize Par's defiance of my orders was not your doing, Alexander." His voice was empty of emotion.

"Still," Vex said, "I feel responsible."

"You are. Guards—get them out of my sight. Put them in the dungeons."

Chapter Forty-Two

"Majesty," Vex said. "I beg you. Listen—"

"I have listened. The Umbriarch has told me the rest." His expression was granite.

Enio dodged a guard that reached for his elbow, then darted toward the door. Before he'd taken two steps, his muscles went limp. Whatever magic had hit him made him collapse like a rag doll, still awake yet numb all over.

Vex moved to Enio's side. "We'll cooperate, Majesty. There's no need to harm—"

"He's not harmed," the Aubade said. "But that can change."

The guard bent to scoop Enio up. Vex interceded. "I'll carry him."

Unable even to speak, Enio spent most of his curses in his head as he lay helpless in Vex's arms. They proceeded from the throne room down through the palace. Enio's limbs began to tingle again. He cleared his throat to get the words out. "I can walk."

Vex set him on his feet. Enio found his balance and stumbled along.

They continued down. At length they passed the cells. The walls changed from smooth to rough. Then somewhere deep within the palace hill, they came to a dank cavern lit by torchlight. Chains hung from the walls, and chairs with leather straps stood at tables bearing iron bowls and tools. Guarded passages ran into darkness. An occasional groan echoed in the distance.

They were led into a tunnel. Primitive cells lined the shadowed walls.

"Enio!" Kaj called. She and Agatha pressed their faces through black bars.

The guard locked Enio and the wizard into the cell opposite and departed.

"Lady Agatha," Vex said through his bars. "Are you unharmed?"

"We're as well as can be expected. What's going on?"

"The Aubade plans to attack Argent through the Threshold first thing tomorrow."

"And Par's there," Enio said, anger at his friend still present but now mixed with worry. He turned to the sorcerer. "You can get us out, right?"

"Past the bars, perhaps. Out of the dungeon, no. There are countermeasures to prevent that, as you can imagine."

Enio found they had forgotten to take his knife. "Would this help?"

Vex snorted. "Are you joking?"

Enio tucked it away again. "So what do we do?"

"What *can* we do? Except hope the Aubade comes to his senses."

"That's not much of a plan," said Lady Agatha.

Vex settled on a straw-topped slab. "No, it isn't. However, while we wait, let's learn the sigil inside and out. We may need it quickly, if the opportunity arises."

Though Enio grunted, he agreed. He sat in a corner, closed

his eyes, and brought the strange, convoluted sigil to mind. He practiced sending the emerald light of the élan through its channels. Because of the many twists and turns, it took longer than any sigil he'd ever worked.

"Drat," Lady Agatha said sometime later.

"What is it?" Vex asked.

"I can't get around a curve."

Enio looked up. "Which curve?"

"Near the bottom."

"Let me check." He found the Elorian route and followed it, using lumina this time. "Take the other wiggle, before the dip."

Agatha was silent for a moment. "That did it. Thank you, Enio."

"Well done, son," Vex said. "But be careful. I have no experience in switching magics as you do. I expect it can be draining."

Enio shrugged. This time, out of curiosity, he used his numena on the route Vex would handle. He couldn't try the path Kaj would use—he didn't know how to gather Ortu magic—but he thought he sensed something of its direction.

At midday, a guard brought them bread and water. Then they returned to their practice, tracing through the sigil all afternoon, helping each other as they might. But Vex had been correct about switching magics, and Enio had become exhausted. At some point, he lay back to rest.

After what seemed a long, dreamless journey, someone called his name. He blinked open his eyes. Sunlight flooded the cell. Yet they were too deep in the dungeon for windows.

The cell bars were open. The Umbriarch stood outside. An aura shone from her body with such brilliance Enio had to shield his eyes.

"Hurry," Vex said. "The Umbriarch is releasing us."

Enio lurched to his feet.

The Umbriarch's light filled the tunnel. The guards at its entrance didn't seem to notice. They stood still, their faces blank, their eyes far away. She led Enio and his companions out of the dungeons, up the stairs, and finally to a terrace open to the night. Shieldriders waited beside a chariot. Only then did she cease her aura.

"The Aubade has changed his mind?" Vex asked.

"No," she said. "But I believe your plan must be given a chance before we rain death upon Argent."

"And you rule the night, right?" Enio smiled.

She didn't smile back. "There will be consequences for what I am doing. I accept them."

They mounted the chariot and were soon flying over the lights of the slumbering city.

Agatha gripped Enio's hand like a vise.

Enio gasped. She'd probably never flown before. He tried to pull away. "You'll get used to it."

She squeezed harder.

They arrived at the Aerie. The guards there helped the Umbriarch from the chariot. Agatha let go of Enio. Vex pried her other hand off the railing and helped her out.

The Umbriarch handed Vex the keystone. "May the stars speed your way."

"May they speed us all, Majesty." Vex turned to the Threshold. With a wave of the keystone, the space shimmered. The sands of the Devastation opened beyond. In the distance, a black circle of monoliths reached toward the moon. A shadowy violet glow moved among them like an evil fog.

"The Sentinels," Vex whispered. "The shadows herald the Ortu, but it should not be dangerous until it rises. And remember: the Sentinels still suppress most other magic."

That seemed an important point to have mentioned earlier. "Then how can we invoke our sigil?" Enio asked.

"It would make no sense if the Sentinels were controlled by a sigil no one could use."

Enio couldn't argue with that. But he had his knife, just in case. He slipped through the Threshold first. A brief burst of gritty sand on a stale wind scratched at his face. He grimaced and shielded his eyes. Other than the shifting sands and shadows among the monoliths, nothing moved, even to the horizons.

Agatha and Kaj stepped beside him.

Vex joined them. "Well, that's that. The rest is up to us." He pushed his way to the front. "Follow me."

They strode on. Enio ducked sudden sand bursts between calms, and he ground his teeth at the foul memories of Cronus squirming around inside his head. This was Enio's last chance to kill him. He wouldn't waste it, regardless of Vex's plans.

The Sentinels loomed ahead, rising into the night. A ramp led between two of them. Vex approached cautiously, but there was no sign of Legate or Cronus.

Inside the circle, where once scaffolding and a cage had hung above the flashing rift to the Higher Realms, nothing remained, not even the pit. But strange sigils still glowed on the faces of the Sentinels, and ghostly purple shadows drifted and sometimes leapt. The wind didn't reach through the gaps between the monoliths—or dare to.

Vex halted them just inside the entrance. "Three above. Three below. Two the balance, then and fro."

"Then and fro?" That had always bothered Enio. "What's that supposed to mean?"

"I don't know. I didn't write it." Vex gestured to the two monoliths where they'd entered. "But those are the Balances. I've found no other reference to them and they don't concern us. The three Sentinels running left deal with the Higher Realms: first lumina for Lady Agatha, then the élan for Enio, and numena for me."

"Which one is for Ortu magic?" Kaj asked.

"After numena, they continue with three Sentinels for the

Lower Realms. The final one of those is Ortu, completing the circle."

Enio moved to the one for the élan. He rubbed his hand on his stone's surface. "Where's our sigil on this thing?"

"Near the base of each. But wait for Legate and Cronus, and for the Ortu to begin its rise, before invoking." He crossed the circle to the numena monolith. "We'll wait behind the Sentinels, but the winds there can be hazardous. The wooden structures that once filled the circle, the Abbot and I cast into the sands. I suggest we find a few boards and use them to help shelter and hide ourselves in case Legate arrives from an unexpected direction. When he enters the circle, be ready, but wait for my signal."

At least it was a simple plan. Enio also had simple plans for Cronus. He stroked the knife in his shirt.

Vex seemed to notice. "Enio, I think you should give me that."

"Like hells."

The wizard frowned. "Cronus will most likely come in the body of Par. Will you stab your friend to take your revenge?"

Enio started at the question. He hadn't considered that. But he had to kill Cronus! Could he force Cronus out of Par into someone else? Legate maybe? And if not… Would Par want to live with that bastard inside him? Enio knew the answer for himself.

"I'm serious, son," Vex said. "Do not approach Par. If you go after him, or Legate, before the Ortu rises, you will give us away. Our plans will be for nothing."

When Enio failed to answer, Vex held out his hand.

"No," Enio said flatly.

"Vex is right," Agatha said, coming closer.

Enio took a half step back.

Kaj joined Agatha. "Enio—"

"No!" Enio shouted. He drew the knife. His mind flashed on Cronus, with a knife in his chest, or in Par's chest…

No, Enio mouthed.

The three before him stopped their approach. Enio squeezed the dagger and held his ground.

"If you act on your anger," Vex said, "you doom us all. I will go see about my shelter."

Kaj took Agatha's arm. Something seemed to pass between them.

Agatha nodded.

Before Enio asked, Kaj said, "We're going to help Vex. Take some time to think things over." They followed the wizard out.

Enio turned away and stood for several minutes, looking past the Sentinels to the dead, dry sands. It was ugly, but peaceful. He tried to slow his breathing. Why did people think he couldn't control himself? But he'd make sure Cronus never controlled anyone again. Hurt no one again. That Cronus paid for—

"Enio," It was Kaj's voice.

He turned.

Kaj stood in the center of the circle. Lady Agatha was at her side. Vex was nowhere to be seen.

Then black and purple light bloomed from Kaj's head.

Enio stumbled back. Dark clouds formed before his eyes and within his mind. His strength left him. The dagger slipped from his hand.

As Kaj came forward, she gave a small smile. "I'm sorry, Enio. Change of plan."

Chapter Forty-Three

Par knelt in his cage before a half-eaten meat pie. Cronus and Legate had been delighted at his surrender. They'd even given him a meal. He'd insisted they also feed the Abbot, still blind and chained against the cell wall. They had. Beyond that, they'd left their prisoners alone.

"I'm not sorry," Par mumbled, poking through his food. "You sent me to find Vex, and I did, and he thinks he can stop the Ortu like you'd hoped." He raised his eyes. "I had to force the Aubade—"

"You're too young to appreciate the stubbornness of monarchs," interrupted the Abbot, though not harshly. "The Aubade will allow no one to disrupt his plans. From all you've told me, he will send his sorcerers to attack Argent at next dawn."

Par pushed aside his meal. He couldn't taste it anyway. Surrendering might have been the worst decision of his life. Still, the Abbot had once told him that wisdom is knowing on which side of the bars we do the most good. Par had to trust he'd picked the right one.

Footsteps in the hall sent his heart racing. Shadows approached.

"Listen," the Abbot's words came hushed. "Cronus will exit the body of the Eminence and possess you instead."

"I know," Par said sullenly.

"There's nothing I can do to stop it. Yet I'm convinced that neither Cronus nor Legate truly understands the Ortu, or perhaps each other. Exploit this if you can."

Though he had no idea how, Par nodded.

Legate arrived outside the cell. Cronus followed with Juris.

"I hate to gloat," Legate said, "but who would have imagined a single boy would spoil the Aubade's secret attack? And the very boy we'd spent so much effort to capture. We now have everything we need, and exactly when we need it. See, brothers? Not only the stars and the gods favor the faithful. Such things come from trusting the Ortu."

Par's jaw tightened. What about those who had trusted *him*? But betraying the Aubade's plans had forced Legate and Cronus to prepare their ritual without delay. Vex would understand this and get to the Sentinels first.

He had to.

"Do not blame yourself, young Par," Legate continued. "The Ortu's rise, whether by tonight's moon, or the next, or the next, was inevitable."

"Well, then," the Abbot said, "I suppose I must congratulate Master Cronus. His long ambitions seem at last within reach."

Cronus stepped beside Legate. "They should be your ambitions as well, Cornelius. History has proven that peace is achievable only with the lands under one rule. And from peace will paradise arise."

The Abbot asked the same question Par was thinking. "But under whose rule? Yours, Cronus? Legate's? The Ortu's?"

Legate answered. "The Ortu cares not how we rule. It desires only freedom. Those who make possible that freedom will be most blessed."

"We, and our followers," Juris added.

"Quite right," Legate said. "And the Ortu will not forget your role, my boy. You will take part in those blessings, as will your family, your friends—if you so wish."

Par kicked his plate from his cage. Gravy splattered across the floor. "To hells with your blessings. "

"You may change your mind," Legate replied coolly, "once the Ortu has risen."

"Never," Par said, and glanced at Juris, who bowed at Legate's last statement. Kaj had said Juris was her father. Did the man still have feelings for her?

"What about *your* family?" Par asked him. "Or your daughter? Kaj hates the Ortu."

Juris frowned. "You lie. She delivered you to me."

"To make amends. She wants you back in her life. She wants a father."

"Enough of this," Legate said. "Prepare for travel, brothers."

Cronus approached Par's cage. Par shrank back.

"No more games." Cronus unlocked it. "Or the Abbot will suffer."

The Abbot rattled his chains. "Considering the Aubade will likely crush me and this entire outpost under a mountain of rock, your threats carry little comparative weight."

But Par couldn't abide the thought. "You promised to release him, Cronus!"

Before Cronus replied, Legate answered again. "I proposed such a trade to the Umbriarch. But you surrendered on your own."

It didn't seem possible, but Par's spirits slumped another notch. There had been no opportunity to renegotiate before he leapt through the portal. "Then at least cure the Abbot's blindness. Please."

Legate chuckled. "Worry not. Before the Aubade can attack,

the Ortu will have risen. When you meet it, the Abbot's welfare can be your first request."

There seemed nothing left to bargain with. Nothing left to do. With his heart as heavy as a brick, Par slid from his cage.

Cronus led him from the cell. The Abbot called from behind, "No matter what happens, Par, trust yourself and your friends. Don't give up."

At the end of the hall, they passed through the thick door carved with an eight-pointed star. A large ghostly sphere filled most of the room beyond: the monitor. Par hadn't seen it since last year. Each sparkling point on the globe showed a sigil being invoked somewhere in the city outside. But none of those invocations could help him now.

In the room's far wall waited the outpost's Threshold, a dead-end indentation with a single black step. Legate stopped there and faced Cronus. "It is here we part ways, dear Fondiscate of the gods." He smiled with the last word. "Bring the boy forward."

Cronus ushered Par before the Threshold's step. Legate and Juris seized Par's arms.

Despite the hopelessness of the situation, Par made a final struggle. But his resistance lasted only an instant. Cronus gripped his head from behind and the air chilled, as if winter had broken its summer chains. The stone wall beyond the Threshold vanished into a black void, a night without stars. Around its edges swirled the bruised light of the Ortu.

With a sudden jolt, Par plunged into that night. The sensation was the same as when Cronus tried to enter his body once before—when the Eminence got in the way. Par felt untethered from the world. Darkness wrapped him, squeezed him, seemed to fold him inside out. He screamed and fought as he fell.

Then, as quickly as his plummet began, it ended.

Par lay on a smooth, white floor, not sandy like the Devastation, not cold like stone. He rose to his knees in a corridor so long he couldn't see either end. Portraits lined the walls. For a moment, he thought he'd arrived back at the Citadel. But that notion disappeared when he looked for the ceiling. There wasn't any. The walls rose to infinity, into an endless, swirling violet night.

He stood. And the pictures weren't portraits at all. They were mirrors. His reflection stared back from each.

Where was he?

At that thought, the nearest image dissolved into a murky landscape. He touched the glassy surface. It gave no warmth, no chill.

"Par."

He spun.

Within a frame on the opposite wall loomed a tall, imposing man. Dark, intense eyes glowered under a thick brow. His face was long and ashen. Black hair flowed over white robes. The purple darkness of the Ortu surrounded him.

It was Cronus, the real Cronus, no longer hidden behind the face of the Eminence. Not only did he watch from that single mirror, but from each frame along that wall.

"Cronus!" Par said. "What's happened? Where are we?"

"We're in you."

"In me?" Par glanced up and down the hall.

"This is Possession." The man gave an oily grin. "Not so bad, right?"

Possession. Then it was done. Yet, despite his imprisonment in this strange corridor, Par still felt in control, at least of his mind. "And the Eminence? Did you kill him?"

"His body remains in Argent—dead or alive, I don't know. As to your next question..." Cronus pointed behind Par.

Par turned again to his closest mirror, or window. The view followed two silhouettes—Legate and Juris—as they strode across the moonlit sands of the Devastation. Ahead towered a circle of black monoliths: the Sentinels. While Par's mind seemed intact, he had no control over where the mirror pointed. Where his outside eyes turned.

The sound of boots crunched over the dry sands.

And he had no power to choose where his physical body went.

"I must say," Cronus added, "this is much more pleasant than it was with the Eminence. After some rude words, he locked himself deep away."

Par clenched his fists. "So now you're stealing my memories, like you did to Enio?"

"I never possessed Enio, only searched his rebellious, twisted little mind. And I am not in your thoughts. I only see the things you allow."

As Par's mind reflexively turned to his memories, his other mirrors changed to new images. In one, Agatha, Enio and Kaj chatted on the road from Wishbone. In another, a basket of pastries rose to Alba's window at the Mercy House. The images continued: Enio sailing the *Sea Dog*, Leo and his family, and Lani healing a wounded chameleon spider.

Yet the view directly before him followed Legate and Juris up a stone incline between the Sentinels. Shadows darted there like wraiths. Lady Agatha and Kaj stood together in the very center of the stone circle. Their faces showed no alarm.

What was going on? If Par's strategy had been successful, if he'd forced the Aubade to support Vex's plan, and forced it to be enacted during the Ortu's rising, where was Vex? Where was Enio?

Kaj bowed. "All is prepared."

"And the others?" Legate asked.

"Buried in the sands," she said. "They never suspected."

CHAPTER FORTY-FOUR

BURIED IN THE sands!

As if struck down himself, Par couldn't talk or move or think.

Legate spoke to Agatha and Kaj. "Well done, blessed of Ortu."

"Well done, daughter," Juris added. "There is hope for you yet."

"Thank you, father."

Par barely heard them. Fury burned away his shock. "No!" he screamed. With all his might, he threw himself against his window to the outside world. "No! No!" He pounded it with his fists. His shouts echoed down the lonely corridor of his mind.

"Unfortunate," Cronus said behind him.

With another desperate shout, Par spun and slammed into the man's image. The wall, the corridor itself, shivered. Cronus flinched in the mirror and stepped backwards.

Par crashed into it again. And again. And again. But Cronus had regained his composure. Par's rage had no further effect. At last, he sank to the floor, tears burning his eyes.

"I…" Cronus began. "This wasn't my doing, Par. I'm sorry."

"You're not sorry." Par wiped his face and forced his gaze up. "You hated them."

"Hate is a strong word. For all of Enio's stubbornness, I admired his strength. And Alexander's only failing was that he lacked vision, like the rest of the Vigil. In fact, he and I were friends, long ago."

A mirror next to Cronus changed. There, a younger Vex yelled and flailed over a table spread with books. The wizard pushed closer to the mirror, to the Cronus before him. Then they broke into laughter and slapped each other's backs.

"Maybe, once, he was your friend," Par said, "if you even know what that means. But you betrayed him."

"You think Vex an innocent? He, with the Vigil, betrayed us all."

"And you murdered *them* too."

Another mirror came alive with an image of Cronus peering through a Threshold, a tall jar of bugs—skarix—in his hands. Beyond was the Council Chamber, and the Vigil leadership, as yet alive.

"Killing the entire Vigil," he said, "was not my intent. Just the council. But they drove me to desperation. I over-prepared the skarix and—"

"You murdered them," Par repeated, pulling himself to his feet. "You, the High Sigil Master of Eloria, Quantificate Supreme, Keeper of the Hearths, Compass of the Realms. A true High Sigil Master guides the people and their families in the knowledge of the gods. He doesn't deal out war and death."

"As I've said, war is a last resort." Cronus straightened his robes, which, though just an image, had ruffled. "Try to under-stand, son. The Vigil, from its founding, has been at war with Eloria and Arcana. But a secret war of spies and manipulation. They fueled the people's prejudices, kept the countries always at odds, the magics always separate in a foolish hope to prevent another rift. The Vigil was the true enemy. I was the only justice possible. The only guide to lasting peace."

"You're mad." Par didn't see how this was helping. He turned again to his outside view, to where Kaj and Agatha stood in the circle of monoliths. He simply could not accept Enio was lost. Or Vex. And right then, he refused to believe that Agatha, or Kaj, had betrayed him. He'd hold on to that, trust himself and his friends, as the Abbot had said. If he didn't, that's when he'd be lost himself.

He steadied his trembling hands. He still believed his surrender was their best chance for victory over the Ortu. But what could he do? What did he have?

Par glanced up and down his wall of memories. He still had those.

And the ear of Cronus.

"Master Legate," Agatha said, "I was promised the blessings of Ortu."

"Soon, sister." Legate waved them aside and stood near the circle's center. The ghostly shadows flew with new frenzy.

"Will the Ortu now take me?" Par murmured.

"No," Cronus answered. "Your presence is enough for the ritual of rising."

Then Cronus spoke outside, to Legate, in Par's own voice. "We are ready."

Legate gave a horrible grin. He didn't really see *Par*, locked deep in this corridor. That, Par understood. Only a facade, a mask worn by Cronus. But if eyes were the windows of the soul, whose did Par's show?

The dark light of the Ortu surrounded Legate's head. He lifted his arms. "Rise, Ortu. Rise!"

The leaping shadows paused in their paths. They dove together, collecting in a single spot on the ground before Legate.

Cronus, both inside to Par and outside, said, "The Ortu comes."

The shadows swirled into a digging vortex. It was the same spot where Par had helped close yesteryear's rift to the Higher Realms. But today's pit did not shine bright. The dismal glow of the purple hells bubbled from its depths.

Then, from that abyss, emerged a featureless human head, but of shadow, like a puncture in the very air. As Legate conjured, and Cronus's words came from Par's own mouth, and the Ortu began to rise, Par fought not to flee deeper into his mind.

"My children," Legate said, and laughed, "you have done well. Your blessings are near."

"Please," Agatha called from near a monolith, "let me receive my Dark Reckoning before the Ortu arrives."

"Yes, yes! Blessed of Ortu, kneel. Cronus, guide her."

Par's outside voice spoke. "I cannot conjure from this body, Legate. The boy's soul—"

"Of course. Juris, help her along her path."

"Very well." Juris stepped before Lady Agatha.

I know you, Par said somewhere in his soul, deeper than Cronus would ever touch. He brushed his fingers across her image in the glass. *I trust you.*

Then, past Legate and across the circle, something moved. Near the base of the farthest Sentinel, just visible in the gloom, the hem of a robe fluttered.

Vex?

Par almost cried out but caught himself. Cronus didn't seem to notice. At least one thing Cronus had said was true: Par's thoughts were still his own.

The ominous shadow figure continued to rise, appearing to its chest. Even from Par's prison, he sensed the creature's emptiness. Its hunger.

"Soon!" cried Legate. "Soon, my friends, we'll no longer hide in shadow. Soon, we'll walk among the mighty, and they shall bow before us."

Juris stood before Agatha. "Kneel, sister, and praise the Ortu as you are Dark Reckoned."

Par held his breath, or what passed for breath in this corridor.

Kneeling now before Juris, Agatha spoke with her head bowed. "I've spent many years in the glare of riches, my lord. They enticed me, I pursued them, I married for them. Of the lessons I learned among the rich and the poor, the good and the bad, one now stands clear."

As Juris laid his hands on her head, the sickly aura of Ortu glowed around his own. "What is that, sister?"

She straightened her back and raised her chin. Even before she answered, Par saw the ferocity in her eyes—and the Lady Agatha he trusted.

"I learned," she said, "that more than anything, I *hate* being used." She hauled back, and with the force of an angry mule, punched Juris in the groin. He gasped and crumpled.

Hope flared hot from its last embers—though Par couldn't help but wince.

"Now!" Vex cried from across the circle.

The foul creature of the lower realms had emerged to its waist. While indistinct, it was clothed in a robe of shadows woven from the fabric of nightmare.

Agatha invoked her golden glory and spun toward her Sentinel.

"Stop!" Legate raised a finger in her direction.

"Hey, curly!" Kaj yelled and sent a volley of knives at the man.

Legate snapped toward her and gestured. In an eye blink, the Ortu's shadowy robes flared out. The knives disappeared into their depths.

"Apostates!" Legate shouted.

Vex's glory blinked brightly. He thrust his hand on the face of his Sentinel. A sigil carved into its base flashed silver.

With the sound of a furious beast, the shadow creature roared. It ceased to rise.

Enio jumped from behind another Sentinel. Par couldn't contain himself any longer. His friend lived! "Yes!" he shouted. "Yes!"

An emerald glow surrounded Enio's head as he touched a monolith. The Ortu howled again, half out of the black vortex. Par's surrender had not been futile. His friends were invoking their sigils as the Ortu entered our world, their best chance of sending it back.

Then Legate thrust out a hand. "Ortu!"

The figure of shadow copied the movement. Bolts of black lightning shot from the creature. One caught Lady Agatha in her side. She groaned and slumped against her stone. Others struck Enio and Vex. They dropped to their knees.

Par's hope turned to horror.

But Kaj dodged and herself conjured with Ortu magic. Something like knives, but daggers of shadow, shot from her hands.

Legate swept an arm. "No!"

Again the shadow man's evil wrappings reached, absorbing the missiles from Kaj—then enfolding her as well.

"Kaj!" Par shouted.

As she thrashed, the creature drew her closer, finally into its body, embracing her in shadow.

She struggled, screamed, and was silent. When the monster released her, she fell motionless to the ground.

"Kaj!" Par yelled once more. Enio called her name too, but his voice was weak and he still couldn't stand. Vex was bent in obvious pain. Agatha leaned against her Sentinel, holding her head. Sigils at the bases of their three monoliths now glowed the color of their magics: green, silver, and gold. The monolith near

Kaj remained as it was. She had not reached it. But her attacks had distracted Legate, allowing the others to get to theirs.

Juris recovered from Agatha's punch and stumbled toward Kaj, who lay unmoving beside the Ortu. "Daughter?" The man knelt beside her and raised her limp head.

The creature of shadow resumed its rise. A deep purple—the color of festering wounds—shone around and within it. Another roar came from its depths. But Juris remained focused only on Kaj.

Legate's smile was awful. "The Ortu has had its first taste of freedom."

Juris looked up, his face twisted. "You've *killed* her. My Kaj."

Par's heart nearly stopped. *Gods, no.*

"She betrayed the Ortu." Legate's tone was flat.

Brushing his hand over Kaj's hair one last time, Juris laid her down; her face was white and withered.

He stood. His voice trembled. "We were promised—"

"The Ortu promised freedom," Legate said.

"My daughter—"

"Received only the freedom she deserved."

"This is not the freedom of Ortu!" Juris spit his words with anger and grief. "You betray us!"

"Mind your place, brother."

"I shall not! You are not worthy—"

"Silence!" Legate swept an arm, and the shadow man enveloped Juris as it had Kaj. When it withdrew, Juris slumped to the ground, shriveled and lifeless.

"And there," Legate said, "is your own freedom."

Though there was nowhere to run, Par stepped back in terror and despair,

"That was unnecessary," Cronus suddenly said to Legate.

Legate laughed. "Who are we, the humble servants of Ortu, to question its judgment?"

Par stood halfway in the corridor of his mind, between the outside world and Cronus. Was there nothing he could do? Some of Par's mirrors were changing: Kaj and her father, alive one moment, dead the next; Enio and Vex and Agatha attacked by the creature of shadow. The Father Abbot chained in a cell.

At his last memory of the Abbot, Par paused. The man had said Legate and Cronus didn't understand the Ortu.

Or each other.

Rallying the last of his wits, Par spoke over his shoulder. "I thought *you* were in charge, Cronus."

"We serve together," Cronus answered.

"Then why does the Ortu look more like you than Legate?" Par had just realized this. It was featureless, but tall and brooding. Even the ripple of shadows around its form resembled Cronus in his robe.

Cronus hesitated. "Yes… interesting. But it makes sense. I met the Ortu soul to soul. It knows me better than any."

One of Par's mirrors changed to his memory of the Higher Realms, when he'd floated between this life and the next, and where he'd met the mage Ridiax. Cronus had been there too, his soul dark and loathsome, falling toward the purple hells.

"When you fell," Par said, "what did it promise you?"

"It does not speak as we do. It is ancient and makes its will known in other ways."

"Vex said the Ortu is a mindless beast."

"How can Alexander know the Ortu better than I?"

"From the Vigil histories."

Cronus's chuckle seemed forced. "Perhaps the Ortu has grown since their time. It now has greater ambitions."

"Since it met you?"

"It… is beyond our understanding."

The creature continued to rise. Par's friends remained helpless in their pain.

He spoke faster. "Legate seems to understand it. He says it wants freedom."

"Yes, and—"

"But isn't freedom what *Legate* wants? What *you* want?"

Again, Cronus paused. "Everyone wants freedom, in some form. I, to bring paradise, as in the days of the Gardens of Gê. That is freedom from—"

"Don't you see?" Par said as something else snapped together. "The Ortu wants only to feed. That's the only *ambition* it's ever had."

Cronus said nothing.

Par went on. "After you fell into the purple hells, when you used the Ortu to return, you led it closer to our world—fresh grounds to feed. It followed you. Now it follows Legate, jumps at his commands like a dog to its master. It's *will*, as you call it, is a reflection, like all these mirrors. And Legate twists the word *freedom* to his own purpose. If he controls the Ortu, he'll use its power for *his* ambition: to rule. And once he has that power, he'll rule you too."

"Legate is not my superior," Cronus said. "Or even my equal."

"He calls you brother."

"His cult uses such quaint family terms. The meanings are empty."

"They weren't always empty—not to you."

"To me?"

"You lost a family."

Cronus didn't reply.

But his mirrors did.

CHAPTER FORTY-FIVE

A TALL, FAIR woman stood before a glowing fireplace. She wore a brown robe with the hood thrown back, like a nun. Ebony hair spilled down her shoulders. A toddler sat before the hearth, playing with a doll.

The next mirror was lit by the glow of a single candle. A trembling hand gripped a stained yellow parchment. Par leaned closer to read the words.

My dearest Cronus,
I leave with our daughter.
She deserves a life outside your absences,
Outside the ambitions that demand the fulness of your love.
In truth, you will always be in my heart.
But do not follow.
— Julia

Agatha said she'd heard that Cronus cast off his family for his career. But now Par saw they were the ones who'd left.

Cronus spoke, his voice subdued. "These things are private, Par."

"So are mine. Leave, if you want."

Cronus fell silent.

The hand crumpled the parchment. Another rested beside it.

Candidate Reckoner Cronus Ikliam Horphesus,
With great sorrow, we report a passenger barge carrying your wife
and daughter was lost…

Legate's voice brought Par's attention back to the outside.

"We shall keep these traitors alive. The Ortu will appreciate a good meal upon its arrival."

As the shadow man continued to rise, now beyond its knees, it loomed larger—and the inky pit shrank. When that pit disappeared, Par realized, the Ortu would be fully in this world. They had little time left.

He spoke again to Cronus. "The paradise you're after, how many more lives is it worth? How many more families?"

Cronus had closed his eyes. "This grows tiresome. With the power of the Ortu, we can avoid the losses of war and—"

"That power is Legate's now, not yours."

"No, Par. Legate—"

"—killed Kaj," Par snapped, the pain still ripping through him. "Legate will have his freedom from all who oppose him. You can't be so blind not to know that includes you."

Cronus's eyes opened. "The Ortu comes in *my* form. It will obey *me*."

Par went on. "Like you said, the Ortu formed as you because you met it, soul to soul. But Legate summoned it, body to body. It's done nothing but answer to *him*. Legate brings the Ortu as his own. He feeds it. He holds its chain."

All of Cronus's mirrors showed Legate before the Ortu. The creature now stood as a giant in the night, the pit almost gone.

"It obeys Legate," Par added desperately. "And Legate brings it to feed. Peace and paradise may be your ambition, High Sigil Master Cronus, but it's not his."

Another silence. Then, "We shall see."

Par's outside view moved forward.

"Stay," Legate said.

"Why?" came Par's voice. "I am as much—"

"The Ortu must complete its rising. See to the others. Ensure they do not interfere until the Ortu deals with them itself."

The last of the vortex was absorbed into the shadow man.

"Ortu," Cronus commanded, "come here."

It towered over them now, seeming to study its new world.

"Ortu—" Cronus tried again.

"Do not interrupt," Legate barked out. "I must guide the Ortu."

"We will guide it together."

"Mind your place, Cronus, or join Juris in his." Legate focused again on the shadow man. "Now come to me, Ortu. Come, and we shall be masters of this realm."

"No!" Cronus cried out.

"To me!" Legate repeated.

With a sudden lurch of Par's mirror, Cronus dove toward Legate.

Legate swiped an arm. A sheet of shadow, slicing like a blade, shot from the Ortu.

Cronus dodged it by a hair. "To you, then!" He barreled forward. As he did, Par threw himself at the mirror, adding anything and everything he might to the attack.

They slammed into Legate. Par actually felt the chill of the impact and fell back.

Legate toppled into the shadow man. "No!" he screamed, and

invoked. His dark, evil aura spewed forth. But the Ortu drank it in and enveloped the man. Legate thrashed in its embrace. His screams weakened as his flesh shriveled. When at last he fell away, nothing was left except naked bone.

Cronus panted before him. "No man shall ever be my master."

But before Par could breathe in relief, the Ortu threw back its head and gave a soul-rending howl, like a starving beast rejoicing in a kill. Its sinister inner light intensified.

Par's friends had disabled three of the Sentinels. But the Ortu had still come.

And with Legate dead, none held its chain.

CHAPTER FORTY-SIX

"OBEY ME!" CRONUS shouted.

The creature had grown even larger with its killing of Legate. Unrestrained, it bent back like a half man, half beast, and howled once more.

"It's loose!" Vex called, trying to stand. Enio had recovered enough to help him up. They hurried toward Agatha.

Enio turned as they reached her. "Par! Over here!"

"That's still Cronus," Vex said.

"I'm inside!" Par shouted at his mirror.

Enio's eyes widened. "Cronus!" He started forward.

Vex and Agatha grabbed him. "And Par!"

At least *they* remembered.

But Enio struggled, his eyes wild. "Where's my knife? Give me back my knife."

Par couldn't believe what he was hearing. Did Enio hate Cronus so much he'd kill *anyone* to get rid of him? Even Par? And with the shadow creature now threatening them all?

"We've no time for this," Vex said. "Agatha, hold Enio."

She clutched and, with a heave, sat on him. He splayed on

the ground like a flattened spider, his eyes nearly popping from his head.

Vex faced the Ortu, raising his arms, trying to invoke. But as he'd warned, within the circle of stones, the attempt was useless. Only Ortu magic now worked here.

The Ortu bent down to Juris's body.

"What's it doing?" Agatha asked, atop Enio.

Vex shook his head. "With no master, it follows the only purpose it knows."

"What purpose?"

"To feed. In this case, on the last traces of energy in that lifeless body. When it tires of the dead, we'll be next, and then the lands beyond."

Vex had long ago told Par that the spaces between the Sentinels were Thresholds. Since Vex had the keystone, he and the others could escape. But the wizard did not try.

Par guessed why: this was their last chance to stop the Ortu.

Aloud, Cronus said, "I've been a fool."

Vex ignored the comment. "Our only hope is to disable the fourth Sentinel. Cronus, you must do it. I will give you the sigil and—"

"No, Alexander. I can't cast it from this body, or from any that cannot use Ortu magic."

"You must find a way," Vex said, "or we're all lost."

Cronus gestured toward Enio. "That one can cast sigils of multiple realms. If I were to possess him—"

"No!" Par said inside his corridor.

"No!" Enio gasped beneath Agatha.

But Vex slowly nodded. "That may work. It's risky, yet I see no other option."

Enio spit and writhed. Agatha shifted her weight and kept him from doing gods knew what.

"I cannot force him," Cronus added. "I am weakened, and for such a conjuration, he must cooperate."

The shadow creature rose from the ghastly grey body of Juris and turned toward Kaj.

Par realized Vex was right: Enio was the only one left who might channel the magic for that sigil. But Vex could never persuade Enio to allow Cronus back inside his mind. Still, while the Abbot said Cronus and Legate didn't understand each other, Par knew Enio, inside and out.

"Cronus," Par said, "can I talk to him?"

"Yes, that is possible."

The glass before Par shimmered, then seemed to melt. While still not free from his prison, he again breathed the stale air of the Devastation. He could move his physical hands.

"Enio," Par said through his real mouth. "It's me."

"You bastard! I'll kill—"

"No, it's Par."

"Liar!" Enio thrashed beneath Agatha.

Par came closer.

Enio froze and narrowed his eyes.

Par leaned in. "Holy sticks, Enio, you *still* smell like a dead mud-maggot's armpit."

Uncertainty flashed across Enio's face. But his grimace returned. "You've got Par trapped. You're Cronus."

"Cronus is in here too."

Enio made another futile lurch. "Give me my knife, dammit!"

The Ortu moved toward Kaj's body.

Par spun to Vex. "Do you have his knife?"

"I do. We had Kaj take it after we arrived, lest he lose control and expose us."

"Give it to me."

Vex raised his dark brows. "Are you sure?"

"I'm sure," Par said, staring down the hate in Enio's eyes.

Mostly sure.

"I hope you know what you're doing." Vex handed Par the knife.

Enio's eyes followed the blade.

Par held it in a sweaty palm. The metal reflected the ugly, black light of the Ortu towering over Kaj.

"Now," Par said, "let him up."

The wizard turned to Lady Agatha. "Release him."

She shifted off Enio, who groaned and stood. He stared at Par with a strange mix of rage and something Par couldn't quite make out.

Par offered him the handle of the knife.

A grin, a sneer, spread across Enio's face, his broken side teeth gleaming like the blade. Before Vex or Agatha reacted, he sprang at Par and snatched the knife. Par didn't resist. Then Enio was on him, grappling him from behind, the sharp steel at his throat.

Vex and Agatha moved forward.

Par raised a hand. "Don't."

They stopped.

Cronus murmured in Par's head, "That boy is unhinged."

"What else is new," Par whispered back.

Enio's grip tightened. "The *real* Par knows what Cronus did to me. He'd *never* ask me to let him back inside."

"Yeah," Par said, not daring to move a muscle.

"And Par wouldn't want to live with *Cronus*—" Enio choked up a moment, then shouted, "Par wouldn't want to live that way!"

"You're right." Par took a breath. "Maybe it's the end for us, and you should kill me."

The sharp blade pressed harder. Out of the corner of his eye, Par saw the Ortu sniffing Kaj's body. He swallowed and couldn't watch further. "The thing is, Enio, I know you, cap to keel. You've never killed anyone."

"Lies can't save you this time, Cronus." Enio's words came as a growl—yet with a stammer that probably only Par heard.

He kept his voice calm. "Of course, if you kill me, whoever I am, you won't be Enio anymore. The Enio who was my friend."

"Shut up!" The knife remained where it was.

"But how do I convince you *Cronus* isn't saying that, right? Or whether I'm just speaking out of my butt."

Enio said nothing.

Par tried again. "I don't think possession works that way. It's one or the other in charge. Right now, it's me. Par. But I'm not sure how to prove it. So I'm trusting you, and you have to trust me."

"I—I can't!"

"Don't be thick, Enio. There's nothing a traveling mage can't do. When we traded, you said you owed me, remember?"

"Owe you?" Enio gave a rough laugh. "You're stealing Par's memories, Cronus. The same as you stole mine. Here's what I owe you."

The blade scratched Par's throat. He gasped, but the cut wasn't deep.

Not yet.

The shadow man let out another howl. It drew back from Kaj, leaving her ashen and drained as it had left Juris. Its featureless face turned toward Par and his group.

"Hurry," Vex urged.

There wasn't time to explain Par's mirror-world. "Listen, Enio. Killing Cronus won't help; you said he's already spoiled your memories. If you kill him, he'll be in them forever. But he can fix them. After this, he'll get out."

Cronus spoke in Par's ear. "I never said I could do that."

But you will, Par shot back.

Enio seemed to be thinking it over.

"And Enio, even if Cronus *can* mess with our memories, he can't think like us. Right?"

Enio hesitated. "Maybe."

"Then think about this. All this time, I'd been searching for a place to call home. A place that would have me. But you always wanted to run. I thought you were running from your old life. Then I realized you were chasing something too. Cronus, it turned out. That seemed crazy, and I got kind of scared. But in the end, it didn't matter."

Par lifted a hand to his neck, and touched Enio's wrist. The blade shifted but didn't cut. "Because whatever we were doing, we were doing it together. We'll do this together."

The Ortu now loomed nearly as tall as the monoliths. Its empty form blocked the moon and stars.

"Besides," Par continued, "we were looking for the same thing. Not a place, or a person. We were looking for a family." He squeezed the wrist. "But we've never been without one."

Enio's breathing had slowed.

Par's own breath matched it. "So kill me, or trust me. But make it quick. You really need that bath." That was everything he had. He hoped it was enough.

"Well, do *something*," Vex cut in.

Almost imperceptibly, the knife slackened. "I lost track," Enio murmured, "whether I'm angry, convinced, or crazy."

"Why choose?" Par lowered Enio's hand from his throat and faced him. And though Par was still trapped inside his own mind, his friend's expression confirmed that the most important parts of them were present, and together, outside this mirror.

"Want a hug?" Par asked.

"Don't push it." Enio glanced at Vex. "There's no other way?"

"None," Vex said.

"This is all very sweet," Cronus uttered in Par's ear. "But if you'd like your friendship to last beyond the next few minutes—"

"Enio," Par said, "even if Cronus possesses you, he'll never get closer than I'll always be."

Enio squeezed his eyes shut, filled his lungs, tilted his head back and shouted into the night. The sound was strange and bitter, the echo as loud as the Ortu's roars. Then he steadied himself and faced Par. "All right." He snatched his feathered cap off his head. "Keep this safe."

"What's so special about this thing, anyway?" Par took it.

"Nothing. It's ugly. And it's weird. So am I. But nobody ever tries to take it. Nobody else wants it."

"Like us?"

Enio grinned his wide, broken smile. "And it's the *style*."

"Cronus!" Vex shouted. "Hurry!"

The Ortu loomed closer. A violet gloom burned around its edges.

"One other thing," Enio said quickly. "Take care of the *Sea Dog*."

"Me? But—"

Par was yanked back into his corridor. Cronus again took over Par's hands and grasped Enio's head.

Then Par's corridor collapsed. He fell into darkness, and an instant later hit hard ground. It took a moment to get his bearings and pull himself to his knees.

He was free of Cronus.

Enio was already at the Sentinel, the one Kaj had tried to reach. A black-purple glory burst around his hair. He touched the sigil.

The creature spun. It stepped in Enio's direction, but a puddle of shadow now bled from its feet. The Ortu shrieked and stumbled.

As Enio slumped to the ground, Par hurried beside him. "Enio?"

"It is still I, Cronus." The words seemed strained.

Par peered into his eyes, into the window where his friend must be watching—or going insane attacking Cronus's image. "I know you can see me, Enio. Hang on. It won't be much longer."

Vex and Agatha joined them.

The shadow man clawed and gripped the ground but was sinking.

Then it stopped and sank no further.

"Cronus," Vex said. "Did you complete the invocation?"

"I did," Cronus gasped.

"Blue blazes." Vex's voice swelled with alarm. "Were four Sentinels not enough?"

Yet something was happening to those four monoliths. The edges wavered and blurred, like steaming ice.

The Ortu roared again, stuck between its world and this one.

"Vex!" Par shouted. "What's happening?"

The wizard shook his head. "I read nothing in the tomes about *this*!"

PART FOUR

SENTINELS

CHAPTER FORTY-SEVEN

CRONUS, STILL IN the body of Enio, struggled to stand. Par helped him up. Four of the eight monoliths continued to boil and steam.

"Get away from those stones!" Vex shouted.

As Par ushered Enio back, a flash of light and a blast of air sent them stumbling to the ground.

Par checked Enio. "Are you all right?"

His friend, or Cronus, nodded weakly. The shadow man twisted and clawed, still half-caught in the pit.

Agatha pointed. "Look at the Sentinels!"

The four monoliths on which they'd used their sigils were gone. Instead, four robed figures—two men and two women—now stood in their places. Glories surrounded their heads: one each of emerald, silver, gold, and black-purple.

"Who are they?" Par yelled over the Ortu's fury.

"I don't know!" Vex called back.

The Ortu roared again. And again. The glories of the robed figures increased. Their rays reached out, two focusing on one of the remaining four Sentinels, two on another. The sigils at the base of those monoliths flashed. The stones steamed and wavered, as had the others. And with another explosion of light, two more robed figures appeared in their stead; one's glory was a dirty red, the other's bronze. Where six of the eight Sentinels had been, now six robed figures stood. Only the two monoliths flanking the entrance ramp hadn't transformed.

The shadowy creature could no longer resist the vortex beneath. It howled and flailed as it sank from view. The abyss closed and melted away, leaving behind only smooth, undisturbed ground.

The glories from the six figures drew back, lingering on each like the separate roots of a rainbow. The night became still and silent beneath the pale moon.

Vex was the first to speak. "Who are you?"

A voice shook the circle: a single voice or a chorus, Par wasn't sure. "We are mages of Gê," boomed the words. "For millennia, we have contained the rift created by Ridiax."

"Sentinels," Vex said with awe. "I never realized."

Par watched from the ground beside Enio. The mages must have given their lives for the long task of containing the rift. And with the Vigil dead, no one remained to release them once the rift had been closed—assuming the Vigil, through their own centuries of secrets, had even remembered the origin of the Sentinels.

Vex had begun to ramble. "Yes, I see now! You must forgive me: interpreting thousand-year-old tomes was no simple task. But my calculation that we needed four—of course, two must have been needed to release a third and shift—"

"Vex," Par hissed.

"What? Oh. Pardon me." The wizard faced the figures with a solemn dignity. "Thank you, great mages of Gê, for all you've done to protect the lands, through the centuries to this very day."

They said nothing in response.

Vex cleared his throat. "There's much I would ask. That you might teach us."

Their glories faded. As the monoliths before, the outlines of the mages wavered and blurred.

Par found his voice again. "Can you heal Kaj?"

The shapes faded further. "Our task is complete, our power spent. She has journeyed on. So must we."

"What about the last two Sentinels?" Vex asked.

"Their work is not yet done." The words echoed into the night. "And neither, we suspect, is yours."

The figures surged once more with light, their colors merging into a brilliant white dawn. Par flinched at its sudden glory. Then the light was gone, along with the six monoliths they had embodied. The two untouched Sentinels now stood alone. All around, the Devastation spread grey and silent.

"You'd have thought," Par said, gazing sadly toward Kaj's crumpled body, "with their power, they could have done something."

"Other than saving the world?" Vex said.

There was that. Par sighed.

"They said the work of the last two stones wasn't finished," Vex added. "Since those Sentinels are still intact, we can use the Threshold between them to return home. Perhaps that's what they meant."

Par turned to Enio. He could tell from the eyes that Cronus still possessed his friend.

"You need to leave him," Par said.

Cronus's voice was oddly subdued. "You realize, in this body I might live a new lifetime."

"Then return to me. I won't resist. But you can't stay there."

"Can't I?"

"No! You—"

"I know." Cronus gave a thin smile. "As much as I might admire Enio's talents, together we would not long remain sane. And I think you'd agree, it's past time I moved on as well."

Relief flooded Par, even mixed with a little pity.

It must have told in his expression, because Cronus's smile widened, enough that Enio's broken teeth showed along the side. "Do not think your arguments alone swayed me, boy. Even if I forever possessed new bodies, I'd be kept from the other Realms—perhaps even from Julia."

"Your wife," Par said. "Or from your daughter."

"Yes, my Olivia. I'd only ever allowed one child to tell me what I must do. You are the second."

Par eyed him in a way he never had: with gratitude.

But Cronus laughed. "I do this for myself, of course. Selfish to the end, eh, Parynius?"

With no warning, Enio's mouth snapped wide and every muscle in his body convulsed. Then he went limp.

Before Par could react, Vex pushed in, laid his hands on Enio's head and invoked. This time, the final two Sentinels didn't prevent his magic. When he'd finished, his expression was grave.

Fear grew in Par's chest. "What's wrong?"

"He lives," Vex said. "But…"

"But what?" Par leaned closer. His friend's eyes were open, yet dull and distant. He shook him. "Enio?"

A glint of focus returned. Enio gave a slight grin, until a wince drove it away. When he spoke, his words came rough and slow. "Cronus is gone, Par. From my mind. From my mother's memories."

Par began to relax. But Enio grimaced and groaned.

"What is it?" Par asked.

Enio's hand clawed at Par's side and gripped his shirt.

"What does he want?" Vex said.

"This," Par said, and wrapped his arms around his friend.

Then Enio's entire body slumped. He seemed to have stopped breathing.

"Enio!" Par again shook his friend.

No response.

"Help him!"

Vex lifted Enio's hand and examined his face. He turned to Agatha. "Assist me."

Agatha bent beside him. They invoked together, the lustrous gold of one nation's magic mixing with the starry silver of another.

At last, they sat back. Vex sighed. "We almost lost him."

Par studied his friend. The stomach moved in shallow rises and falls. "Will he be all right?"

The pause from Vex lasted an instant, but long enough to betray his worry. "We must hurry him to your healers. And we still need to stop a war."

Agatha nudged Par aside and lifted Enio into her arms. They followed Vex to the two unchanged Sentinels. He held out his keystone.

They passed through the Threshold onto the stony lip of the Argent outpost. With Enio limp in Agatha's arms, they approached the cliff-side tunnel. A locked iron gate blocked the way. Vex waved his hand, and the gate flew open. Around the next corner, the guard Lucius sat slumped in a chair. As he turned, another invocation from Vex sent him flying down the hall, followed by a heavy thud.

The Abbot, still hooded and chained, sat alone in his cell.

"Father Abbot?" Par called.

The Abbot raised his head. "Par, is that you?"

The wizard sent the cell door clanging open.

"Help him," Par said to Vex. "I'm bringing Enio to the Eminence." That seemed Enio's best chance.

Par led Lady Agatha down the hall to the monitor room. The Eminence lay before the Threshold. A faint golden glow circled the man's head: the ever-present glory of the Fondiscate.

"Eminence?" Par rushed to his side.

The man roused, met Par's eyes and said, "Cronus? The Ortu?"

"Both gone." Par helped him sit up. "Cronus possessed Enio to invoke an Ortu sigil. Then Enio collapsed."

"I see. Set him down."

Agatha laid Enio on the floor.

Vex, with the Abbot hanging onto his arm, arrived in the monitor room. They stood silently by. The Eminence studied Enio's face, then laid his hands on his head. As he did, the Eminence's glory expanded until it filled the room with golden splendor.

Par watched, and prayed.

When the Eminence withdrew his hands, his expression was grim. "Physically, he is unharmed. Yet…"

"What?" Par asked.

The man's kind eyes spoke more than his words. "Perhaps he's stunned from his ordeal. We will use Eloria's every resource to aid his recovery."

Par's insides twisted at the vagueness of the answer, but he nodded.

"Eminence," Vex said, "your navy and that of Arcana speed toward battle."

"Yes." The man rose to his feet. "While Cronus possessed me, I stayed hidden in my mind, yet echoes from the outside reached my consciousness. Fill me in on the rest."

The Abbot stood on his own now. He joined Agatha and Par at Enio's side while Vex detailed the looming battle. But Par heard little. Enio seemed merely to slumber, yet there was a blankness, an emptiness, that Par couldn't match to any expression he'd ever seen on his friend's face, awake or asleep.

At last, the Eminence said, "We must stop this war before it begins."

"Can we send a navigaunt?" asked the Abbot.

"A navigaunt must know its precise destination. We cannot

determine that for any specific navy vessel. Even if we could, the bird wouldn't reach it in time."

Par looked up from Enio. "I last saw the ships approaching the Boundary Islands. What about the Threshold? I've been to those islands, so I can open it to there."

Vex shook his head. "Cronus and Legate already used this Threshold to get to the Immortus. It will take another day to—"

"But Ortu magic opened it," Par added, "not the keystone. Does that make a difference?"

"Good blazes, it might. It's worth a try." Vex gave the keystone to Par.

Par took a last look at his unmoving friend, the breath still shallow. Then he focused on the Threshold. It flickered and opened into the night atop the tall hill of the island.

Vex examined the portal. He pushed his hand in. It passed. He kept it there, as if holding open a door. "Go, Eminence."

The Eminence stepped through. As he stood high above the moonlit sea, his glory expanded, becoming so bright that Par had to turn away. When he could again bear the sight, the visage of the Eminence filled the skies, horizon to horizon, the eyes shining like twin suns.

"I see them," the man said.

Then his voice thundered across the waters.

"I, Pompeius Maxima Arcalus, Fondiscate of the Divine, High Eminence and ruler of Eloria, hereby end this war. My navy shall return without delay to Argent."

Par covered his ears. He had no doubt everyone out there got the message.

The Eminence spoke once more. *"I command this in the name of Oä, Glory of the Gods. Thank you, and have a nice day."*

The Abbot leaned to Par. "When they say the Fondiscate is closer to the gods than any, they aren't kidding."

Chapter Forty-Eight

THREE LONG DAYS had passed since the Ortu's defeat and the stopping of a war. Par sat on a thin, uncomfortable bench in an empty hallway. Late morning sun slanted through barred windows, and muffled chanting drifted from behind a thick wooden door. Lofty things like wars, ancient mages and the Outer Realms seemed far away compared to Par's focus now.

Enio remained unresponsive. The Eminence promised to assist with any treatments as needed and sent Enio straight to the High Temple. The Confessors and Reckoners examined him, but despite all their invocations, furrowing of brows and curling of lips, they couldn't reach his mind. Finally, they proclaimed he required rest, observation and longer-term care.

Yet no one would tell Par exactly what was wrong with his friend.

After the High Temple, they brought Enio here, to the Mercy House. Par stayed close—most of the time, outside that door. A small stack of books rested at Par's side. He held one that contained the Histories. This chapter was a tale about the Gardens of Gê:

So it is told, in the days before men, that the gods proposed a contest. They planted each a garden, and once tended and grown, would judge whose was best…

He read the lines several times over but couldn't concentrate. Still, to hold the book, turn the pages, helped with the waiting.

"Par."

He looked down the hall to see Lady Agatha approaching.

Par put his book aside and began to stand.

"No formalities," she said and sat beside him. "What progress?"

"Nothing yet."

"Well, we have to give him time."

That's what everyone said. He changed the topic. "How was it?"

"Beautiful. They buried Kaj and her father together on a lovely rise near Aurix. Alexander didn't retrieve Legate's bones; they'd blown into the Devastation. Good riddance, right?"

"Yeah," Par said absently. Enio would have wanted to attend the funeral. Par had too. But as things were…

"The Umbriarch was there," she added. "So was the Aubade."

"Really?" Earlier, when Lady Agatha had explained what happened after Par surrendered to Cronus, she'd mentioned the Aubade condemned her and the others to the dungeons, and that the Umbriarch later defied that order.

Lady Agatha noticed his surprise and shrugged. "He's forgiven everything. In fact, he's offered Alexander a position as a Prograde."

"That's great, but—the Aubade didn't seem like the forgiving type."

"The Umbriarch had a role in softening him up."

"What did she do?"

"She married him."

Par's jaw dropped.

Lady Agatha laughed. "I understand it's been a while in the works." Her mirth faded. "Speaking of marriages, I have other news. I'm leaving Blandus."

"Your husband? The Ambassador?"

"Yes. We never had much of a marriage. He tried to talk me out of separating—said it would hurt appearances. Guess what I told him?"

"What?"

She brushed back her frazzled hair. "Neither of our *appearances* are worth worrying about. Know what else?"

Par shook his head.

"I told him I was tired of being the convenient society wife of a politician—that I hate being used."

That's what she'd said to Juris before she... Par grimaced.

Lady Agatha raised a hand. "No, I didn't punch him. We'll go our own ways. He keeps the manor. I get the jewelry shops. I realized there are the families we get, but also the families we make. We're, every one of us, responsible for the boundaries of both. You taught me that."

A truth Par had been learning as well.

She leaned in. "So now I consider you part of mine. If you or Enio need anything—food, money, a roof—my door is open. Always."

"Thanks," Par said, though at this point he had no thoughts for the future. The present held worries enough.

The chanting ceased. It did that now and then before resuming.

But the door clicked.

Par jumped to his feet.

Dressed in plain white robes, the Father Abbot stepped out. "Hello, Par. Lady Agatha."

She smiled. "You're looking well."

"Thank you, I—"

Par tried to peek into the room.

The Abbot ushered him back. "Wait until they've... tidied him. Let's have a seat."

"I was just leaving," Agatha said. "Keep me informed, Par. I'll be back tomorrow."

They hugged.

"Don't lose hope," she whispered.

"I won't," Par said as she left. He sat back down.

The Abbot gathered the hem of his robes and settled beside him. "The Eminence made another visit while you slept."

"How is he?" Par had seen very little of the man since their return.

"Busy. He's got a country to run, you know. But he spent his time here helping to examine Enio."

"Did he find anything?"

"Nothing new, I'm afraid."

"It's been days. Can't the Fondiscate ask the gods to help?"

"I'm sure he has. But the gods don't appear to work quite like that. Our lumina comes from them, yes. The Fondiscate's soul is more elevated than others, and so collects more of it. But, admittedly, divine personages don't pop in at every invitation."

With a sigh, Par nodded. "Years ago, when I realized I was different, that I couldn't invoke, I wondered why the gods didn't listen to me." A strange chuckle, a more mature one, escaped his throat. "Maybe they don't listen to anyone."

"Oh, I don't know about that," the Abbot said. "But speaking of your long days of waiting, you've spent most of them on this bench."

Par had, though sometimes he wanted to run, scream,

through the streets. "I just wish someone would tell me what's wrong with Enio."

"There's no denying the situation is most unusual. As is your friend."

Par pictured Enio in his feathered cap. "That's for sure."

"Well, he is certainly his own person. But he's unusual in another sense. We each grow toward one source of magic or another, not unlike the trunk of a tree that grows toward the sun. But a few, rare individuals turn their faces, like flowers, to follow the light. Enio is one of those few. It's how he learned to use Arcanan sigils and those of the nymphs."

"And the Ortu."

"I doubt he'd have managed such an extreme feat without Cronus's intervention. And as a consequence, Enio experienced an almost unimaginable trauma. The anchor of his soul, so to speak, was strained beyond limit."

The Abbot paused. "You wanted an answer, Par. And I believe it is this. His body's connection to his soul is all but severed. He is not dead, but… he drifts."

At least that made some sense. Last year, when Par fell through the rift, he'd drifted between this world and the next. The mage Ridiax had been there and helped him return.

But Enio traveled alone.

Par recalled his friend's plea to take care of his beloved boat. Had Enio guessed what using an Ortu sigil—or being possessed by Cronus—might do to him?

The door creaked. Three hooded figures emerged, robed in checkered white and black. One carried a basin and towels. They mumbled prayers as they ambled away.

"They've never seen a case like his," the Abbot said. "Some minds are harder to access than others, yet there's always a presence. But they've detected nothing, not even a whisper. They're not sure what to try next. Except…"

Par turned to the Abbot. "A Reckoning?"

The Abbot stayed silent, which said enough.

"And after that," Par added, "they can't say how much Enio will be left."

"It may be his only chance."

Again, Par looked toward the door. "I want to see him."

The Abbot nodded and led him inside.

Enio sat robed and motionless in the single chair of the small private chapel. Before him rested a bare stone table. Racks of candles burned in tiers along the walls, among small statues of the saints and symbols of the gods. An odor of over-sweet flowers hung in the air. On Par's first visits, the incense had turned his stomach. But he'd gotten used to it. The smell hid worse ones, and there were no windows in here to freshen the air.

He stepped closer. His friend's face still hung empty, like a blank canvas.

"He's well cared for," the Abbot said, "and will continue to be while the next steps are decided."

Enio's eyelids were half open, like his lips, as if he might speak—but no words had yet come. His hands lay unmoving in his lap.

"Who decides the next steps?" Par asked.

"We can discuss that later."

Par looked into Enio's eyes. They were clear, glassy, like winter ponds. "I need to know."

The Abbot sighed. "When a Reckoning is proposed for the health of the candidate rather than for a criminal sentence, the candidate's family makes the decision. We have thought to track down Enio's father—"

"No," Par said flatly. Enio and his father didn't have any kind of relationship.

"Well, where there's no family, the Hierarchy intercedes."

"I'm his family."

"Of course," the Abbot said gently. "What might be your decision?"

Par rested his hand on Enio's. "No Reckoning. Ever."

"But if he doesn't improve—"

"I'll take care of him."

The Abbot squeezed Par's shoulder. "Have your visit. I'll stall the others if they return."

"Thank you, Father Abbot."

The man left.

Par hauled himself up to sit on the table and faced his friend. "Hey, Enio, look who's back."

Enio's breathing remained steady, the rise and fall of his chest his only sign of life.

"Before I forget—" Par dug the feathered cap from his shirt. "See? I kept it safe, like you asked."

Nothing.

"Yeah, you're right, it needs cleaning." Par tucked it away. "Oh, listen to this. Lady Agatha said she'd take care of us if we needed anything. If you want my opinion, I think she wants to adopt you." Par forced a laugh. "Better run while you have the chance."

Still nothing.

Par gripped the table's edge and squeezed. "I bet you could hide in Wishbone. They liked you there. Remember Happy the Table?" Par took a breath and sang a few notes. "*Happy the Table where...*"

He choked off.

Enio continued to gaze with all the awareness of the statuettes in their shadowy nooks.

"When you're well again," Par managed, "let's visit St. Livius. Not through the Threshold—we'll take the *Sea Dog* up the Greening. Like old times, right? See my family, the abbey, Buckets and everyone. It'll be fun."

Enio stared quietly.

Par looked at a rack of candles. He chewed his lip as he watched their lively flickering. "I was thinking about it some more. How when we left St. Livius, we both wanted different things." He waited, giving the proper pause for a response. "Sure, we both needed to find out what happened to Lani. But I also wanted a place to live, and you dreamed of sailing away..."

Par turned back. "I know now I was looking for a family. I just forgot I had you the entire time. But even though you've... sailed farther away than ever, we're still together. See? We both got what we wanted there too."

As suddenly as an ember might engulf a forest, an unexpected rage flared in Par's chest. He didn't have the strength to examine or fight it. He trembled, and it burst out, a shout echoing through the room.

Then he surged off the table. "Dammit, Enio. Don't leave me!"

He slapped his friend.

Enio's cheek reddened, but he didn't even blink.

For a moment, Par watched him—then crumpled beside the chair, his forehead pressed against his friend's arm. "Dammit, Enio. It should have been me."

A rap sounded at the door.

Par wiped his face and stood. "That'll be the Confessors," he whispered. "No one's giving up on you. Ever."

He moved to the door, paused with his hand on the latch. "They'll take care of you—until I come back. Not only am I where I belong, I found a job. From now on, I'm your Sentinel."

Chapter Forty-Nine

A CHILL DRIZZLE had fallen all morning. Par sat on a rock along a barren shoreline, his hooded cloak tight and his knees drawn close. The Father Abbot had insisted Par take breaks from his Sentinel duties, so yesterday he'd visited the Mercy House's children's wing. One small ray of sunshine was that Alba and Felix hadn't yet been Reckoned. A final order required the Eminence's approval, and with everything that had happened, he'd put those decisions off.

In truth, Par didn't want to be around people right now. Today's stroll outside the city solved that problem. No one seemed to care for this stony stretch below the eastern walls, so he could spend his time alone.

A dim white disc behind the clouds brought midday. Par needed to return; they let him help feed Enio. But as he lingered, something sparkled far out in the choppy grey water. A green glow drew a line across the sea—straight toward him.

He lurched to his feet.

When the light reached the shoals, the antlers of a sea stag broke the surface. A figure rode on its back.

"Lani!" He rushed to the water's edge.

She dismounted, and with a wide smile, splashed through the shallows. "Hi, Par!"

He met her at the shoreline and they embraced. Par held on for several moments—as if he'd found a grip in a storm—until embarrassment at the long hug made him withdraw. "I, um, wondered when I'd see you again. How did you find me?"

"I still feel a strong connection to Argent's waters. I sense its life, at least at some level. But yours stood out."

Though the drizzle continued, Par warmed on the inside.

"I've been worried," she added, her brow pinching. "Enio never used the Sea Call I gave him."

A sheen of water collected on Par's face. He sniffled and wiped it off. "Let's get out of the rain."

They stepped closer to the towering walls. Lani laid her hand on a mound of rocks and invoked, or enchanted, as she'd said the nymphs called it. The stones bloomed red with heat. Par pushed back his hood, and as they huddled in the warm glow, he told Lani all that had happened since they'd parted on the shores of Arcana. When he got to Enio's possession by Cronus, she turned pale, gazing at the sea during the rest of the story.

At last, she said, "Can I see him?"

"He's up in the city." Par paused. "Enio told me about the Deep World, and why you can't go much on land."

She gave a brief laugh. "They asked him to keep the Deep World to himself. But I figured he'd tell you."

"Why the secret?"

"They want nothing to do with humanity, its greed and intolerance and violence."

"No, I mean, about the decision *you* have to make. Between living on the land or in the sea." Par was no longer jealous or suspicious of these secrets. But, depending on her decision, he might never see her again. He didn't think he could stand another loss right now, especially one so unthinkable.

"We're not sure," she said, "if that's how it will work after all. I didn't want to worry you until I knew more."

"Then you don't have to decide—" Par began, his hopes rising.

"I may still. Half-nymphs are rare enough, but the Asrai said it's even more unusual that I haven't had to decide already."

"The Asrai?"

"Sort of their sea queen. She's ancient—been around a long, long time."

Par nodded. Enio had mentioned someone like that.

Lani went on. "In any case, I don't need to decide right away. Or I might have more choices than anyone thinks. Or one morning I'll just wake up as a codfish."

"Did you just say—"

She laughed. "I'm kidding. At least about the codfish. In the meantime, I've learned there once was a kinship between the Deep World and the lands of men, destroyed millennia ago with the Devastation. Perhaps it's time to rebuild those bridges, and maybe I can help. I'm not sure how, but I'm keeping my options open."

In that instant, Par wanted, more than anything, to ask her to choose life on the land. But it seemed wrong to put his wants above such grand designs as reuniting kingdoms.

Wrong, but difficult.

Instead, he said, "If… if there's any chance the Asrai can help Enio, take him with you, all right?" It took Par's full willpower to suggest it. Enio had explained only those of the élan were permitted in there. Par would not be allowed to follow.

"I will indeed ask the nymphs." Her words were soft, cushioned further by a sigh. "But each realm of magic, like each person, has its special strengths. The Arcanans are masters of the elements. The nymphs, of life's ebb and flow. And those in Eloria understand the ways of the spirit better than any. From what you've told me, Enio's condition is not an injury of flesh, but of spirit. We should first allow your healers to do everything they can."

The Abbot had speculated the same. Par nodded and dropped his head. He suppressed another wave of helplessness.

Lani took his hand. "Enio's strong. He's going to surprise us, you watch. But whatever happens, you're not alone. I'll be close." She leaned in and kissed his cheek.

For a moment, Par froze.

Then he kissed her back.

It happened so fast, he didn't think. He caught the corner of her mouth, the edges of her rough, salty lips, though he'd been aiming for her cheek.

Hadn't he?

His brain fogged over. How old was Lani, anyway? He'd never given it much thought, and had assumed not much older than him. But she was half nymph. Was she ancient, like the Asrai? And was it normal to feel whatever he was feeling about someone who might be older than his mother?

Or might become a codfish?

"Don't worry, I'll see you again soon." The voice came from the shallows. While Par had been lost in his own little world, Lani had backed into the water.

"Wait!" he yelled over the surf.

But she splashed away through the shoals. He waved as she mounted the stag and disappeared into the sea.

Then he whispered, "It's a date."

The rain and mist had thinned, and the sun now speckled the waves like bright coins. He turned, remembering they'd be feeding Enio soon.

Par retraced his path outside the city wall, hopping from one rock to another, then dancing a little as he leapt. For the first time since he'd returned to Argent, he felt light, buoyant.

And the world seemed less lonely.

CHAPTER FIFTY

AFTER LUNCH, THE Reckoners and Confessors returned to examine Enio while Par waited on the bench or wandered the halls. At sundown, they let him back into the chapel to again feed his friend. Enio had always been on the skinny side, and as his chewing had become weak and automatic, it was important he eat as much as possible. Par spooned in the porridge. A cotton bib caught the dribbles.

When as much food came out as went in, Par gave up and sat back. Enio's eyelids seemed heavy. Maybe he needed to sleep. Par had already told him about Lani's visit—except for the kiss. Next time he saw her, he'd ask if the stags could bring back the *Sea Dog*. Enio would like that.

A knock sounded at the chapel door.

"Come in," Par said.

The Father Abbot entered. "How's our wandering magician this evening?"

"Traveling mage. But no more travels today. He's ready for bed."

"I'll inform the others. Let's take him to his room."

Par nodded. He pushed a lever on the side of Enio's chair, unlocking the wooden wheels. He and the Abbot rolled him into the hallway.

"Are you limping?" the Abbot asked.

"Slipped on a rock."

"Want me to—"

"It's nothing," Par said, skipping the details of his dancing mishap.

They followed a winding ramp up a level. Par was allowed to sleep at the Mercy House, though not in his friend's room. The Father Abbot had said Enio needed complete, solitary rest. Probably the Abbot just wanted Par to get some peaceful rest of his own.

They arrived at Enio's private room and laid him on the cot. A table and chair sat near a barred window. A rack of candles, like those in the chapel, stood dark and cold on the table.

While Par tucked Enio in, the Abbot invoked, bringing a few wicks to life.

"Do we need those?" Par said. "Enio's going to sleep."

"Technically, candles aren't even allowed in the candidate's rooms. But I've gotten the odd feeling he likes the flickering."

Enio's gaze, though dull, reflected their cheery glow.

Par sat on the edge of the bed, his mind weary and wandering. "We use candles a lot in Elorian ceremonies. Arcanans have a thing for crystals. Why? Do they help with magic?"

The Abbot shrugged. "In a way. And the merchants who sell them are happy to agree. But candles and such just set a mood. Only people with sigils can invoke magic."

"The Thresholds are magic," Par countered, "and the charm on the rock below the cliffs. And the Vigil's blue light orbs. And Augle and—"

"Yes." The Abbot chuckled. "Well, apparently there's more to the world than we are taught." He brushed Enio's messy black hair from his forehead. "Let's let him sleep. Walk me out, would you?"

Par slid off the bed. "I almost forgot." He reached into his shirt and pulled out Enio's feathered cap. "I had it cleaned." He left it on the table, glanced at his friend once more, and followed the Abbot to the door.

As he was leaving, he noticed a shadow flutter across the wall. He turned. The feather was on fire.

"Crap!" He rushed to the hat and slapped it out.

"That's one reason candles aren't permitted," the Abbot said. "Little accidents like that—"

"The feather wasn't near the flames." Par eyed his friend. "Do you think—?"

"A breeze through the window bent the feather, Par."

Enio's face hadn't changed, though the candlelight still danced in his eyes. And his mouth, was it open slightly farther, a wider crack on the side near his broken teeth? But no, it was also a passing shadow.

The Abbot laid a hand on Par's shoulder and ushered him out. They eased the door closed and walked back to the hallway near the chapel.

When they reached Par's bench, the Abbot stopped. He lifted the book Par had been reading. "The Histories?"

"To pass the time."

"You left it open to a tale about the Gardens. It's one I haven't read in a while." He settled on the bench.

Par waited a moment, then sat beside the old man.

With a deep rumble, the Abbot cleared his throat and began to read...

So it is told, in the days before men, that the gods proposed a contest. They planted each a garden, and once tended and grown, would judge whose was best.

They labored long and their gardens grew. Silver-boughed trees reached into the skies, their leaves unfurling above the clouds, their lofty crowns brushing the very stars. Vines of sweet-perfumed flowers wove through the cosmos, and their fruits, when ripened, became worlds of their own. Mountains rose from the fathomless voids, their roots sometimes atremble with deep, mysterious violence.

All the gardens were alike fantastic, except for one: the garden of Gê. Hers did not touch the stars nor spin new worlds. Hers did not tremble with hidden fury nor fill the empty voids. While verdant and fair, it lay quiet, humble, and small.

Since the power of the gods is exceeded only by their wisdom, they knew it would be difficult to agree on a winner. But they saw it could not be Gê. So they asked her to judge, since she was as honest as any, and would not chose her own.

Gê accepted but reminded them of the rules. The judging must wait until each garden was tended and grown. Hers remained yet unfinished. Thus, the gods left their gardens and turned to other things.

The pastimes of immortals, however, can pass time immemorial. While the gods tarried elsewhere, their gardens changed. The trees that brushed the stars caught fire and burned. The vines, weary of their spinning, left their flowers, and their worlds, to dry and wither and blow away. Even the mountains crumbled and sank into the voids without echo or trace.

Then one day, the gods remembered their contest. They summoned Gê to ask if she had yet judged.

"Come and see," she said.

Her garden lay as it had been, plain and green. But it had spread, beyond the horizons, over the dust of the others.

As the gods beheld the result of their neglect, they were humbled, and they named Gê the winner.

But she declined the victory.

"For," she said, "I have not yet finished."

✳

"It's not one of the Hierarchy's favorites." The Abbot thumbed through the pages. "These days, they consider Oä the primary creator, not Gê."

Par's mind still wandered through the story's gardens. "Does the goddess Gê represent the élan?"

"The Histories don't mention the élan, and many of the accounts are more fable than fact. Perhaps it's meant to convey a vigilant labor ethic. A childhood teacher once used it to admonish me to do my homework."

Par chuckled.

The Abbot put the book aside. "But after everything I've learned this past year, I'm not hasty to dismiss the reality of the Gardens themselves."

"Or of the Devastation that wiped them out." At the memory of that lifeless landscape, Par's thoughts returned to Enio.

"Indeed," the Abbot said. "Frankly, I've always felt the tale reminds us to nurture what we value, in the soil, or in the heart."

They were silent for a few moments.

The Abbot seemed to read Par's own heart. "Enio will come back, Par. But he's a long way off. Such a journey takes time."

"He really is a traveling mage." Par forced a smile, fighting to believe it. "In far-off waters, like the *Sea Dog*."

"Waters that no other mage has traveled. But like Gê's garden, his story is not over. We must have patience."

The Abbot stood. "Get some sleep. Tomorrow's a big day."

Par rose too. "It is?"

"Don't tell me you've forgotten the Summer Festival?" The words came as feigned shock.

In fact, Par had lost track. "Well, I'm not sure I should leave Enio right now."

"Nonsense. Bring him along. It will do you both good. Promise me."

"All right, I promise." Getting Enio outside wasn't a bad idea.

The Abbot strolled away. "The ceremony begins at dawn. So come early. Goodnight."

Par remained near the chapel a little longer, gazing out the hallway windows. People passed the Mercy House without a glance. Whatever happened inside wasn't their problem. He couldn't deny the irony. This place of Reckonings, the last place Par had ever wanted to find himself, he now had to be coaxed to leave.

But yes, he would go to the festival. Cronus and the Ortu were gone. Enio was eating. And Lani…

Par took a deep swallow of the cool evening air. The weather had cleared, and the stars shone like jewels. Tomorrow was shaping up as a fine day for a celebration.

CHAPTER FIFTY-ONE

IT WAS NEARING the dawn of Oä's Day, the first official day of summer. When the sun rose, every village and town in Eloria would celebrate, nowhere more splendidly than in Argent.

Par was dressing Enio. He finished lacing the shirt and slipped on one of his boots. "The Eminence himself is kicking off the holiday. If he sees us, we might get good spots."

As expected, Enio didn't respond. Par still wondered about the burning feather. Maybe the Abbot was right: a breeze had moved it. Besides, Enio hadn't exhibited the faintest glory, Elorian or otherwise. But Par was determined to believe Enio was in there, someplace. Every candle flicker, every time the dozens that lit the chapel had one more burning than he'd noticed when he'd arrived...

He slipped on Enio's other boot. "We're not in Arcana anymore, in case you forgot. So if you ever feel like invoking an Elorian sigil, you can."

Enio stared blankly.

Par helped him into his rolling chair. He set the feathered cap on Enio's head and made it neat. "If you do, just don't go showing off, all right?"

He pushed Enio out of the Mercy House. Their pace was slow; Par was in no hurry. They travelled the gloomy lanes of the eastern quarter as the approaching dawn stole one star after another. Then, with no warning, a wagon of revelers barreled around a corner.

"Hey!" Par yelled and pulled his friend into an alley. The horse and riders roared past.

The alley was the same one where he and Enio had shared a meager breakfast before the whole Ortu mess began. Next to a crate still lay the broken mirror. Par toed it over and peeked at his reflection. No strange shadow appeared. Back then, Par's shadow, and his lack of means to make a living, had filled most of his daily thoughts and worries. With Cronus gone and Agatha's offers of help, those things were no longer problems.

So he should relax. He tried to smile, but his reflection only winced. The mirror showed the truth. He'd trade everything to have Enio healthy again, begging for coins, eating stale pastries, hiding his drinking and gambling, complaining of their woes.

Par eyed his friend. Good gods, he even missed the weird, broken smile.

He continued with Enio deeper into the city.

The Court of Saints lay at the very heart of Argent, where the road from the main gates ended and the four quarters met. The solemn statues and cozy little temples were today surrounded by festival food stalls alive with smoking fish and sizzling sausages. On a normal day, this was the most active public space in Argent.

Today it was packed like pickles.

"Excuse me," Par said, trying to edge in closer. But the jostling crowds made it too difficult.

He stopped. "Well, let's back out and find us some breakfast."

A hand landed on his shoulder.

It was a guard.

Par's old instinct was to run. But he didn't. He'd done nothing wrong. What would they do, lock him in the Mercy House?

"Come with me," said the guard. A second one stood behind him.

"Why?" Par asked, holding his ground.

The guard answered. With the mob's chatter, Par didn't catch the words. "What?" he said.

"Make way," shouted the guards, and pushed through the crowds. They didn't grab Par or Enio but instead made a path for them.

Curious now, Par took his friend forward.

To his surprise, the guards led them to the center of the court, where a round marble stage, topped with columns and arches, rose before them like a grand stone garden. Fountains leapt from floral designs carved into the outer sides and emptied into a surrounding pool.

Standing on the stage were the noble Lady Melora, who held the office of Lord of the House, and the thunderous Lord Simeon, Judge of the Doors. They were second in the Hierarchy only to the Eminence and comprised two of his three supreme councils.

The third, High Sigil Master Cronus, was of course absent from the trio.

Two opposing bridges arched up to the stage. A man sat below, on a low wall beside the pool. It was the Father Abbot. He waved. "Over here!"

Par headed there with Enio. The guards didn't stop them.

"Excellent," the Abbot said, standing. "I was about to get a Location sigil done on you."

Before Par could thank the Abbot for the formal escort—if the Abbot had sent it—a horn blast cut through the morning air.

The crowd hushed and turned. Par raised on his toes to see.

A dozen city guards in striped white and purple appeared along the main road. The vanguard held banners arrayed with the three-pointed crown of the city. The horn blowers followed. Pikes came after, leading a shining black carriage, trailed by more noble horses and pomp.

The crowds before the parade parted and cheered.

"Is that the Eminence?" Par looked at the Abbot.

He only smiled.

The carriage halted not far away. A fancy-dressed man with a frilly collar bounded onto the stage. He faced the crowds and unfurled a scroll.

The people fell quiet.

"His Eminence," shouted the man, "the Most High Pompeius Maxima Arcalus. Fondiscate of the Divine. Ruler of all Eloria."

The crowds cheered again. The carriage door opened and the Eminence, in flowing golden robes, stepped out. A bright glory, like a herald of the coming dawn, shone around his head. Par grinned at seeing him well again. The congregation bowed as their Fondiscate passed. Par bowed too, but raised his eyes to watch.

As he did, the Eminence seemed to catch his gaze. Par couldn't be sure.

The regal man strode onto the stage. His councils stood back. He faced the crowds.

Everyone hushed.

"My friends," the Eminence began, his voice echoing as clear as the horns, "we shall soon begin the festivities of Oä's Day. I have much to tell you over the coming weeks. Newly discovered things in our Histories, and in our world. Some we will celebrate. Others may be hard to accept."

Murmurs of uncertainty bubbled through the crowd. Par figured what this must mean. He whispered to Enio, "I guess the Vigil and Cronus and everything else won't be our secret anymore."

The Eminence continued. "Traditionally, such revelations are given under the auspices of the High Sigil Master. But I tell you now: the rumors of Master Cronus's death are true."

Gasps came from the throng, mixed with a few grunts. The nearest citizens to Par didn't appear too disappointed.

The Eminence raised a hand, and the murmurs quieted. "Cronus is part of the story you will be hearing. But first, I want you to meet your *new* High Sigil Master, Father Abbot Cornelius Ianarius."

Par snapped his head toward the Abbot.

The Abbot waved to the Eminence and spoke to Par from the corner of his mouth. "Just found out myself. So much for retirement." He left Par's side and, to light applause, crossed the nearest bridge to the stage.

The Eminence motioned the Abbot beside him, patted his shoulder, and spoke again to the crowd. "You'll get to know Cornelius better, and, I hope, admire him as much as I."

The Abbot gave a deep bow.

"Now," said the Eminence, "one more thing before we open the taverns." He dropped his gaze straight onto Par. "Come up here, Parynius. You and Enius."

More used to hiding from attention than stepping into it, Par frowned. Was the Eminence going to begin his revelations by recognizing Par and Enio's roles in them? They'd both been through a lot, but if anyone deserved praise for what they'd done, it was Enio. And Par would make sure he got it. He rolled Enio onto the stage. The Abbot ushered them to the front.

The Eminence turned and lowered his voice. "How's he doing?"

"About the same," Par said.

"Never lose hope."

Par nodded.

"What about you?"

"Me? All right, I guess."

"Very well." The Eminence straightened and faced the crowds. His voice thundered out once more. "This young man's name is Parynius Ignatius. Next to him with the, um, feather, is his friend, Enius Marius."

Par felt himself blush a little. Should he smile? Wave? Raise his chin to look more dignified?

But he just stood there like a shrub.

"You might be interested to learn," the Eminence went on, "that Par has lived a great deception. He has lied to you all to hide that he can't invoke the gods."

Par almost choked.

Once again, the crowd began to murmur:

"Poor, poor boy."

"See, Porcius, dear. That's what comes from disobeying your parents."

"It's the Mercy House for him."

"Outcast!"

Par started to sweat. In any other situation, he might run for the hills. But there was no escape. And he wouldn't abandon Enio.

"Silence!" boomed the Fondiscate. His voice rang with absolute authority.

The crowd rumbled to stillness like the air after a thunder clap.

"Yes," the Fondiscate continued, "we have taught that such deception is wrong. Yet we deceive ourselves. Par represents something we all know—or should—but sometimes forget. The length of our robes, the volume of our chants, the height of our candles, the power of our sigils—these are not the measure of a soul. Look instead to a person's acts of kindness, and what they sacrifice for others. And I'll tell you, you couldn't ask for any better examples than these two young men. You will learn more of their exploits in the days to come."

The Abbot leaned closer to Par. "I don't know about you, but I was tiring of you saving the world and no one finding out."

Par fully blushed now. But in truth, he was tired of his secrets too.

"Therefore," the Eminence said, "let word go out to every province. Reckonings are no longer the unavoidable fate of those who cannot invoke the gods. Such individuals will enjoy the full blessings of our lands. They will eat beside us, work beside us, serve in the Hierarchy or in the guard or in any way they find to put their hands. Our Mercy Houses will live up to their names, providing healing to those who need it, yet always with mercy and kindness."

He stopped speaking. All was silent except for a distant seagull.

Then someone called out, "Praise the Fondiscate!"

Another. "Thank you, Eminence!"

Others joined in with more hails and tribute.

"Thank you, Parynius!" "Thank you Enius!"

Par gripped Enio's arm. Goosebumps ran along his own. "Hear that?"

Enio's expression suggested he'd heard nothing.

The Eminence raised a hand. The people quieted. "And now, let us begin our celebration of Oä, Glory of the Gods. Present your candles."

Everyone in the spreading crowd dug into the folds of their robe or their hats or their baskets and held up candles they'd brought for the occasion. Par had forgotten to bring any, but was content to watch.

Then the Abbot tapped his shoulder. He held out a few short, skinny ones. "I always bring extras to these things."

Since Enio's arms remained limp, Par took only one. "Thanks. We'll share."

The Eminence held up a candle too. The new day's sunlight seeped into the city, brushing the buildings and steeples. "And as we—" he began.

The man's candle lit. Immediately, motes of fire leapt from

the flame and lit the candles held by those closest to the stage. Those, too, sent more flames leaping and lighting others.

Par gasped. He'd never seen the candle ceremony done on such a large scale, and it was dazzling. From wick to wick, person to person, family to family, the lustrous flames swept through the crowds as if guided by some invisible hand. Waves of good cheer followed as the people's very spirits seemed to take flight. Par's spirit joined them.

City bells tolled. The Fondiscate lowered his arms. The crowd erupted into cheers.

Par's candle had also lit. He whispered to Enio, "Ever seen anything like this?"

The clear light of dawn sparkled in his friend's eyes.

The Abbot spoke to the Fondiscate, his words just loud enough for Par to hear. "I'm happy to see you've recovered, Eminence. That was an exceptional invocation."

"Yes," the Eminence said, keeping a smile and waving to the crowds. "I am quite well, Cornelius, thank you. However, I had not finished my speech, nor had I even begun the invocation."

Now Par glanced at Enio. The tip of his cap's feather burned like its own little candle, and the hint of a grin twinkled across his broken teeth. Par knew then that Enio had just performed his most amazing fire-fly yet. Enio had found his way home.

And Par had, too.

With his heart nearly bursting, and blinking away something in his eye, he leaned toward his friend. His brother.

"Welcome back," Par said. He reached up and snuffed the feather.

"Showoff."

The End

Dear reader,

I hope you enjoyed the story of *The Sigil Masters:
Dark Reckoning* as much as I enjoyed telling it.

You can continue the journey with Book Three, *The Last Nowen*

Sweet sailin's and fair landin's

Rick

ABOUT THE AUTHOR

Rick Duffy writes to discover new worlds and wander from the familiar. He grew up on the boundary of street-lit suburb and shadowed forest, reading second-hand fantasy and science fiction books often out of order. He now writes them himself (in order) and is best know for his award winning *The Sigil Masters*.

Rick lives in Colorado, is never far from a biking trail or a cup of tea, and hopes we all find time everyday to explore.

Connect with him at *rickduffy.com*